THE STRAINS OF MALICE

BOOK ONE of The Nessemiah

Andrew Beardmore

For my Mum, who sadly passed away just before this book was published, but who is undoubtedly smiling down on me now. Miss you much.

This novel is entirely a work of fiction. The characters and incidents portrayed in it are the work of the author's imagination. However, a number of character names are anagrams of real, historic people, long-since deceased. Examples include the 7th century monk Ebde (based on the Venerable Bede), Jake Oscom (based on the 18th century explorer and naval captain, James Cook), and one of the most recent, David Grey-Doogell (based on the early 20th century British Prime Minister, David Lloyd-George), while the 18th century ruling dynasty in Glennad are the Havreno family (an anagram of Hanover, the monarchical dynasty of Great Britain and Ireland in the 18th century). Other character names can be portmanteaus – a blending of two names such as Calidius (Caligula + Claudius), or combinations, such as the corpse smugglers Williams and Hauberker (based on William Burke and William Hare). Occasionally (as with Grey-Doogell), I have loosely aligned the character's past career to be similar to their historical alter ego as well. Elsewhere, real (but deceased) horses are referenced, too, such as Horsed Credit (Desert Orchid), Rum Dearg (Red Rum), Broriece (Corbiere) and The Snail (L'Escargot).

First published in Great Britain in 2025
Copyright © Andrew Beardmore

All rights reserved. No part of this publication may be reproduced, stored in a retrieval system, or transmitted in any form or by any means without the prior permission of the copyright holder.

British Library Cataloguing-in-Publication Data
A CIP record for this title is available from the British Library

ISBN 978 1 906551 55 1

Ryelands
Halsgrove House,
Ryelands Business Park,
Bagley Road, Wellington, Somerset TA21 9PZ
Tel: 01823 653777 Fax: 01823 216796
email: sales@halsgrove.com

 Part of the Halsgrove group of companies
Information on all Halsgrove titles is available at: www.halsgrove.com
Printed and bound in India by Nutech Print Services

The Strains of Malice is a major departure for Andrew Beardmore. A professional copywriter in the IT industry, Andrew is also the author of many non-fiction books, including the nationally popular "Unusual & Quirky" series of county history books, also published by Halsgrove Publishing. However, another of Andrew's literary loves is epic fantasy and he has finally joined the fray with this four-book historical fantasy series, known as *The Nessemiah*. It was David Eddings who first captured his fantasy heart in the early 1980s – the same time that a seventeen-year-old Andrew was playing guitar in his father's dance band, supporting bandleader giants like Victor Silvester and Joe Loss!

Praise for Andrew Beardmore:

The Strains of Malice: This is an authentic and well developed epic fantasy world with lots of heroes to root for and villains to dislike. It reminds me of 'A Song of Ice and Fire' in terms of format and genre, and Prince Magnus certainly gives Joffrey a run for his money! *LoveReading*

The Strains of Malice: Andrew Beardmore is a fantastic storyteller with a penchant for meticulous details. He crafts a world so humanistically flawed and tremendously intriguing. I am bouncing in anticipation of the second book, and would give an arm and a leg to have this book directed into a movie series. *onlinebookclub.org*

Up The Ramblings: "This is an incredibly clever story...and which also showed a huge amount of wit on the part of the author." *Stephen Booth*

Back From The Dead: "This was an extraordinarily well-told and economically written tale about a gangland killing with a real twist at the end." *Don Shaw*

Derbyshire Unusual & Quirky is delivered in a lateral and humorous format that promises to engage readers. If you think you know Derbyshire – think again! *The Buxton Advertiser*

Nottinghamshire Unusual & Quirky is a real gem. With beautiful photographs, maps and well-researched information, this book is written in a charmingly conversational style. If you buy it as a gift, I promise you will find yourself reading it before you hand it over! *The Bookcase*

Quirky facts abound, but there is much more to *Leicestershire and Rutland Unusual & Quirky*, as the entire history of both counties is covered in detail from the Stone Age to the 21st century. *The Stamford Mercury*.

Theran Maps: Western Thera: 1789

Theran Features

- The super-continent known as Epanaga circumnavigates the Theran globe. Boats cannot therefore sail from the Northern to the Southern ocean and vice-versa.

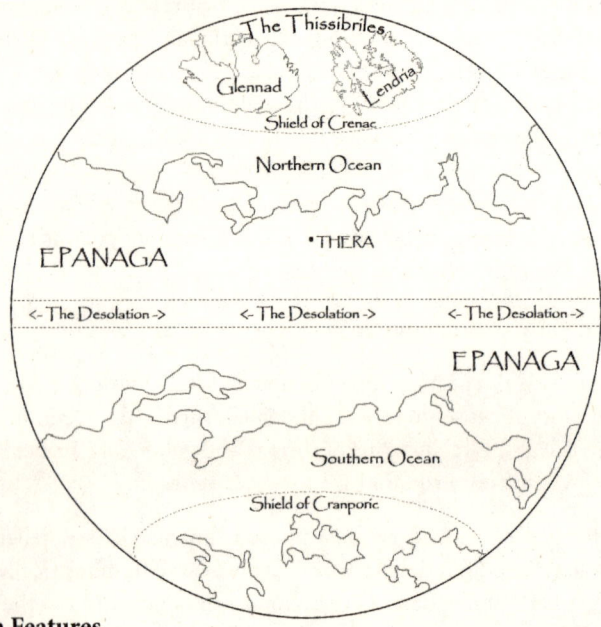

- The arid central Epanagan area known as The Desolation also circumnavigates the Theran globe, and is uncrossable, due to day-time temperatures of up to 165 degrees above zero.

- In 1789, with the power of flight yet to be invented, folk cannot by any means get from one hemisphere to the other.

- Indeed, no one in the northern hemisphere has ever been to the southern hemisphere in post-prehistoric times, or knows what it looks like – and vice-versa.

- Hence northern hemisphere globes look like that shown above, while globes in the southern hemisphere only map the south, with the north an uncharted empty space.

Theran Maps: The Thissibriles: 1789

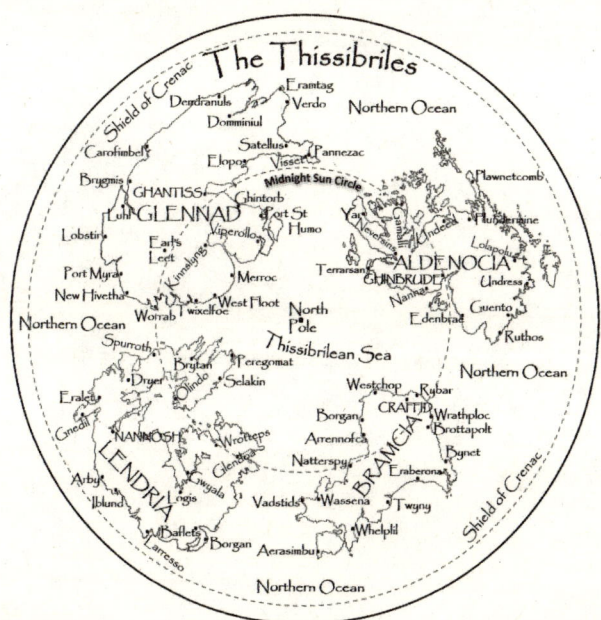

Theran Features

- The Thissibriles are comprised of four major islands ranged around the North Pole. They are heavily populated as the polar regions on Thera are temperate.

- The "Shields" appeared in the year 410 AT.

- They are enormous magnetic fields that form two lethal, unbroken belts around Thera at c.55 degrees north and south.

- The sea eddies around them, forming chains of whirlpools, and the air above fizzes with an electro-magnetic current.

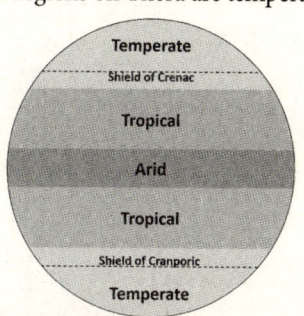

- Crossing them is fatal:
  - It scrambles the brain on approach.
  - Those who cross suffer "The Madness", before their bodies begin to shut down.
  - Death follows within three days.

- The Shields thus become a punishment for criminals, and are also used as a dangerous sport by others.

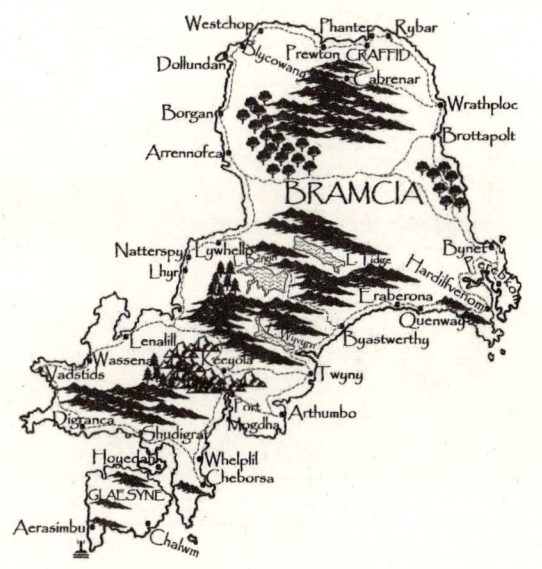

Theran Maps: Western Epanaga (North)

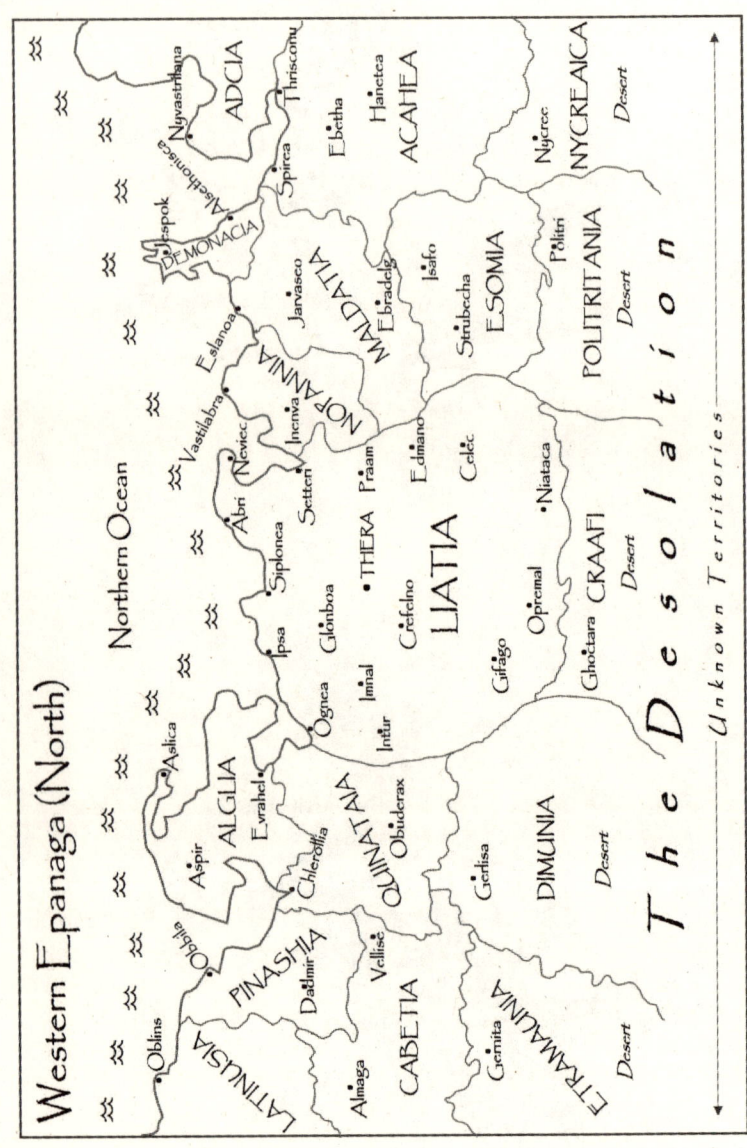

Theran Daily and Monthly Cycles

The following table lists daylight hours in Ghantiss at each equinox and solstice:

Vernal Equinox		Summer Solstice		Autumn Equinox		Winter Solstice	
Theran Hour	Light/Dark	Theran Hour	Light/Dark	Theran Hour	Light/Dark	Theran Hour	Light/Dark
01:00	Dark	01:00	Twilight	01:00	Dark	01:00	Dark
02:00	Dark	02:00	Twilight	02:00	Dark	02:00	Dark
03:00	Dark	03:00	Light	03:00	Dark	03:00	Dark
04:00	Dark	04:00	Light	04:00	Dark	04:00	Dark
05:00	Dark	05:00	Light	05:00	Dark	05:00	Dark
06:00	Twilight	06:00	Light	06:00	Twilight	06:00	Dark
07:00	Twilight	07:00	Light	07:00	Twilight	07:00	Dark
08:00	Light	08:00	Light	08:00	Light	08:00	Dark
09:00	Light	09:00	Light	09:00	Light	09:00	Dark
10:00	Light	10:00	Light	10:00	Light	10:00	Dark
11:00	Light	11:00	Light	11:00	Light	11:00	Dark
12:00	Light	12:00	Light	12:00	Light	12:00	Twilight
13:00	Light	13:00	Light	13:00	Light	13:00	Twilight
14:00	Light	14:00	Light	14:00	Light	14:00	Twilight
15:00	Light	15:00	Light	15:00	Light	15:00	Twilight
16:00	Light	16:00	Light	16:00	Light	16:00	Dark
17:00	Light	17:00	Light	17:00	Light	17:00	Dark
18:00	Light	18:00	Light	18:00	Light	18:00	Dark
19:00	Twilight	19:00	Light	19:00	Twilight	19:00	Dark
20:00	Twilight	20:00	Light	20:00	Twilight	20:00	Dark
21:00	Dark	21:00	Light	21:00	Dark	21:00	Dark
22:00	Dark	22:00	Light	22:00	Dark	22:00	Dark
23:00	Dark	23:00	Light	23:00	Dark	23:00	Dark
24:00	Dark	24:00	Light	24:00	Dark	24:00	Dark
25:00	Dark	25:00	Twilight	25:00	Dark	25:00	Dark
26:00	Dark	26:00	Twilight	26:00	Dark	26:00	Dark

- The Theran year lasts for 365.256 days – the time it takes Thera to orbit the sun.
- Every 4 years, Primar has 46 days to make up for the surplus .256 of a day it takes to orbit the sun. This re-synchronises the Theran calendar with Thera's orbit.
- The Theran year is also subdivided into 52 weeks of 7 days apiece.
- Day numbers are also accumulated throughout the year – hence the last day of the year is Day 365 (every fourth year accumulates up to Day 366).
- The two equinoxes and two solstices occur on the 1st day of the 2nd month of the season: Winter Solstice: (1st Primar); Vernal Equinox (1st Tertiar); Summer Solstice (1st Quinar); Autumnal Equinox (1st Septenar).

Theran Month	Season	No. Days
Primar	Winter	45
Secondar	Spring	46
Tertiar	Spring	45
Quarternar	Summer	46
Quinar	Summer	46
Senar	Autumn	46
Septenar	Autumn	45
Octonar	Winter	46

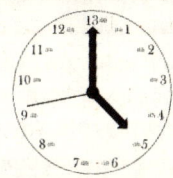

Thera and the Inner Solar System

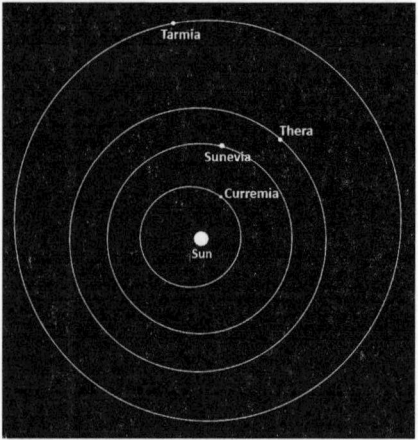

Thera and the inner solar system (not to scale).

Planet	Tilt (degrees)	Diameter (miles)	Circum. (miles)	RotSpeed at Equator (m/hr)	Rotation (hours)	Length of Day (hrs)	Rotation Direction
Curremia	0.03	3,032	9,525	6.7	1,407.60	4,222.6	AntiClock
Sunevia	177.36	7,521	23,628	4.1	5,831.50	2,802.0	Clock
Thera	22.74[1]	3,963	12,451	498.2	25.98	26.0	AntiClock
Tarmia	25.19	4,220	13,263	539.4	24.62	24.7	AntiClock

Planet	Mass (% Thera)	Orbital Speed (m/sec)	Orbit (days)	Density (kg/m³)	Mag Field (x Thera)	Gravity (% Thera)	Mean Temp (C)
Curremia	11.0	29.5	87.97	5,427	0.0006	37.8	332
Sunevia	163.0	21.7	224.70	5,243	0.00	90.5	867
Thera	100.0	18.5	365.26	2,757	1.00[2]	100.0	85[3]
Tarmia	21.4	14.9	686.98	3,340	0.00	37.9	-149

Key Points

[1] Thera's tilt brings about the four seasons of winter, spring, summer and autumn.

[2] Thera has an unusually strong magnetic field for such a relatively small planet. The other inner planets either don't have a magnetic field at all (Sunevia and Tarmia) or the magnetic field is negligible (Curremia). NOTE: That the outer gas giants have much larger magnetic fields than Thera.

[3] Thera has a high mean temperature as it doesn't have any icy polar temperatures which would counter-balance the hot equatorial and the blistering desert temperatures.

PROLOGUE PROLOGUE

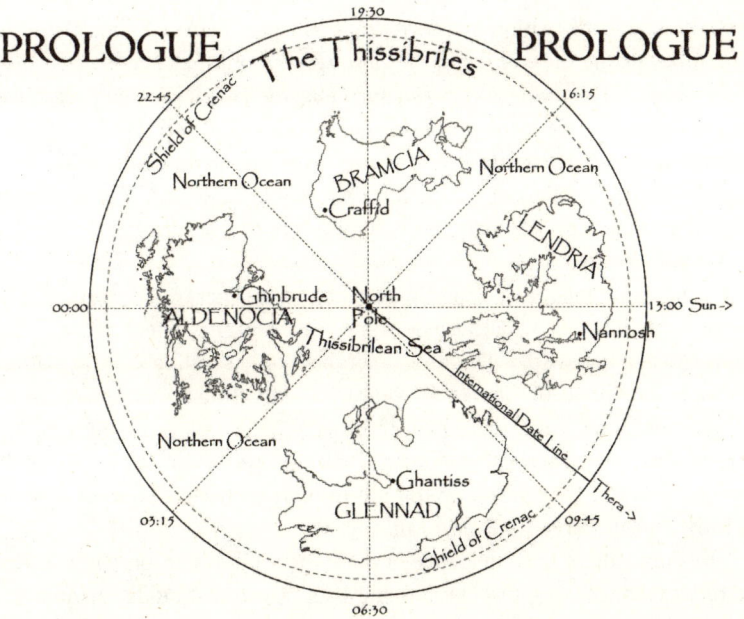

Extract from *Thera: Our World, Not an Empire*, by Andrew Dobbig, published 1781, summarising Thera's early history until the year 410.

No one knows where it came from or how it came into being. According to the 5th century *Theraeon Cosmography*, the Shield of Crenac just appeared one day in the year of 410 AT. There is no reason to doubt this – particularly as earlier works mention nothing of shields, magnetic or otherwise, and Therans were clearly free to visit and enslave the Thissibriles unhindered before the year 410. Furthermore, thousands of Thissibrileans were being sent in the opposite direction, also unhindered, to live out miserable lives as slaves in Northern Epanaga. Or at least they were before the year 410.

The earliest pre-410 literature to have survived and been translated was, of course, penned by our Father of History, Theodorus, after whom our periods of ancient and modern history are divided. He was aged thirty-five when he first dipped a quill in ink and began recording history on a roll of papyrus. Ten years later, in the now-official year of 10 AT, he began work on his great atlas, *Orbis Theraeum* – a work which, significantly, did *not* contain any references to magnetic shields in the Northern Ocean, or anywhere else for that matter.

What *Orbis Theraeum* did showcase, though, was a talented team of ancient cartographers. Not only were those first maps in Theran history a reasonable approximation to northern Epanagan maps of today, but in circumnavigating the continent, they also worked out that Thera was orb or globe-shaped. Then, when they went on to map the Thissibriles, they reasoned that our islands were at the northern apex of our globe, and posted the first-ever theories as to what might be at the opposite end of our world, too.

But, as the 8th century Thissibrilean monk Ebde said, some seven hundred years later: "One day, we will rejoice in this knowledge."

Yet still, we wait.

I must now backtrack slightly, to satisfy the Theran Conspiracists, a movement which is gathering some momentum, these days. The Conspiracists believe that Theran scholars have been sending disinformation through the Shield of Crenac for centuries. Anything to disadvantage us should the Shield ever disappear, and part of an alleged centuries-old masterplan to enslave us once again, taking our fairest ladies for their harems, and our strongest men to fight in their barbaric gladiatorial pits – as they once did over 1,300 years ago!

Of course, there is no evidence of these institutions and practises in our literary exchanges with the Therans, but I suppose one should keep an open mind. So, humouring the Conspiracists, one of the main vehicles of this disinformation, they say, is that today's maps of Northern Epanaga resemble very closely those of the 1st century. Since we can't pass through the Shield to disprove that theory, the Conspiracists retain their voice. Personally, I have no problem believing the Therans – as the *Neo*-Therans of the 18th century have had almost a millennium and a half to develop the more enlightened culture that they portray in their literary updates. How, after all that time, could a modern-thinking and forward society, whose contemporary inventions are parallel with, and sometimes exceed our own – how could such a society remain underpinned by foundations based on brutality, slavery and conquest? That equation just does not add up.

What I can say with absolute certainty, though – thanks to serving for twenty-seven years on the United Thissibrilean Universities Committee for Knowledge Exchange – is that we Thissibrileans return a perfectly accurate account of *our* culture to the Neo-Therans, keeping them up-to-date with our scientific, medical and engineering advancements. There have also been some remarkable examples of collaboration between we Thissibrileans and the Neo-Therans, with plans for modern inventions being passed back and forth over the Shield of Crenac. Recent examples include the development of the miners' safety lamp, the creation of the steam engine and the introduction of the stethoscope. There certainly doesn't appear to be any element of disinformation from my viewpoint, which leads me to believe the Neo-Therans on another major social issue – when they tell us that they ceased producing weaponry three centuries ago, and as a result, their multiple nations live in permanent peace. Naturally, the Conspiracists dispute that claim, always pointing out the occasional messages in bottles that reach our shores painting a very different picture of constant war and bloody conquest – which, in turn, the Neo-Therans dismiss as the work of cranks and troublemakers.

But back to cartography, and let's assume that modern Neo-Theran maps are indeed accurate. This places Liatia at the heart of Western Epanaga along with its capital, the city of Thera – this being located a hundred leagues south of the Liatian port of Siplonea on the Northern Ocean. What is remarkable about those early 1st century cartographers, though, is that they also mapped two hundred leagues of terrain *south* of Thera, as well. And despite the passage of over 1,350 years, today's maps reveal little more than those of the Ancient Therans – fading away at the bottom into the unknown vacuum of *The Desolation*, an area still blistering and arid, bereft of shelter and therefore still uncrossable. Again, the Conspiracists dispute this. But what would the Neo-Therans gain from withholding southern geographical evidence? It is of zero use to us, penned in as we are at the North Pole.

It *is* fair to say, though, that later Theran maps from the 2nd and 3rd centuries deliver a less-accurate outline of the Thissibriles, but surely this was down to the infancy of cartography back then, combined with the difficulty of mapping the rugged, complex and island nature of our polar homelands. They could certainly be forgiven for missing off some of our nine hundred-plus islands, particularly the multitude which surround Aldenocia, and they do at least place our islands in the correct positions, suitably ranged about the North Pole. By contrast, mapping their own continent must have been comparatively straightforward, given only one mappable (albeit vast) coastline. And let's not forget that it still took we Thissibrileans another one thousand years to improve on those ancient Theran maps of our islands, plus another three hundred and fifty to perfect them!

But we digress. My inbound point on this debate about ancient cartography, is that the Shield of Crenac is conspicuous by its absence from those 2nd and 3rd century maps; it clearly didn't exist, back then.

Moving away from maps, it is also thanks to Theodorus and his Theran successors, that we know some of the basic detail of our own cultural development, here in the Thissibriles. Clearly, during Theodorus' lifetime, these islands were home only to barbarians, whilst the 'enlightened world' lay to the south of Glennad and Lendria, in north-western Epanaga. At this time, northern Epanaga was dominated by the First Theran Empire, which ran from roughly 200 BT to 425 AT, and the centre of this empire was, of course, the ancient city of Thera – also the name of our world – but in terms of name alone, the city came first. Theodorus, himself, explains when writing in 11 AT: "*It was around two hundred years ago that we Therans decided to name our world after our First City – thus ensuring that should the empire ever fall, its name will live on forever.*"

Back to the Thissibriles, though, and it was in the year 43 AT that the First Theran Empire conquered our polar homelands. And although we only have the Therans' word for how that panned out, and how they then ruled here for nearly four hundred years, our extensive modern archaeological evidence suggests that their accounts are accurate. It is certainly clear that at the time of the Theran invasion, the islands of the Thissibriles were still locked in the Iron Age, which began here in around 700 BT – the point at which the local Iron Age tribes began constructing vast hillforts. Many of the ditches and ramparts of these hillforts survive across our islands, demonstrating how elaborate those defences were, whilst within, there were closely packed round huts, some used for accommodation and some for storage. Some of the larger Iron Age hillforts supported over a thousand people.

Alas, these hillforts were rapidly overrun in 43 AT, by the organised and sophisticated Ancient Theran legions. The nearest of our main islands to Liatia, Glennad and Lendria, were taken first but, suitably forewarned, Bramcia and Aldenocia proved far more difficult to conquer, having organised a fierce resistance. They were led by the legendary Accrataus, and it was he who led his famous 'last stand' against the Therans in 51 AT, having successfully resisted the invaders for eight years. That said, it is thought that Accrataus unwittingly brought on the invasion in the first place. He was a chieftain of the *Levitucalutan* tribe in central Glennad, and prior to the Theran invasion, he had begun to expand into neighbouring *Trebastea* territory. The ousted *Trebastean* queen, Revica, fled to Thera and appealed to the emperor, Dacu Lius, for help. This was allegedly the excuse Dacu Lius had been looking for to invade the Thissibriles, which he promptly did in the summer of 43 AT.

According to Theran records, Accrataus' 'last stand' of AT 51 was smashed by the Therans in a battle somewhere in Bramcia. Accrataus was captured and surprisingly spared execution – albeit to be sent in chains to the city of

Thera, where he would see out his remaining days as a gladiatorial slave. Accrataus is said to have fought bravely in the Theran amphitheatre known as the Mesocluso (which allegedly still survives today) for over three years, but accounts state that he was killed in a bout where the odds were 'stacked absurdly against him', much to the anger of his growing army of fans – an event that was said to have sparked the riots which brought down the rule of Emperor Dacu Lius (41 AT to 54 AT).

Back in the Thissibriles, though, the capture of Accrataus in 51 AT brought about the total subjugation of the islands, and the ancient Thissibrileans would not know freedom again for another 359 years. Despite this, Theran rule in the Thissibriles brought unprecedented technical and social progress to the islands, and although the Therans mined Thissibrilean ore and farmed Thissibrilean lands to help service their vast war machine back in Epanaga, their advanced civilisation slowly began to bring the natives out of the backwardly-oriented Iron Age. Parts of some of those ancient Theran cities still survive on our islands, offering us an insight into the structure of their settlements, with forum, basilica and public baths, and clever water systems supplied by enormous networks of aqueducts, while their sumptuous villas were equipped with tessellated mosaic flooring, sophisticated thermal underfloor heating systems, and even had plaster and wallpaper on the walls.

It all came at a cost to Thissibrileans, though. Indigenous males aged fourteen to forty were packed off in their droves as chained galley slaves, pulling the oars on Theran warships off conquering Eastern Epanaga, and feeling the lash on their backs every day of their lives. Others, like Accrataus, were conveyed to Liatia where they were forced to kill friend and foe in fighting pits and varying-sized arenas. It wasn't always against other men armed with steel, either. Their reward for defeating endless other slaves from across Northern Epanaga and the Thissibriles, was occasionally to pit their wits against pre-enraged and half-starved lions, tigers, boars and even bears. Such was ancient Theran sport.

Alongside this, girls and woman aged from eleven to thirty, deemed to be of fair appearance, would also be packed off to Northern Epanaga – mostly to the towns and cities of Liatia, to serve out their lives in the harems of ruling officials. And of course, back in our homelands, very few Thissibrilean men or women achieved positions of status – a situation which lasted until 410 AT.

What happened next isn't entirely clear – but it is almost certain that the Shield of Crenac appeared in 410 AT. Alas, the largely illiterate Thissibrileans couldn't record events north of the Shield. Thankfully, our southern neighbours continued to communicate with their stranded compatriots by sending messages back and forth across the Shield by unmanned boat. Some of those accounts have survived the interim 1,371 years, and they talk of mass death – of ships with over one hundred souls on board – whole legions, in fact – all reduced to what soon became known as 'The Madness'. This applied whether heading south-to-north or north-to-south. Thereafter, victims' bodies were said to gradually shut down, and every single person who crossed the Shield of Crenac was dead within three days.

As they still are today.

Of course, we know it is still lethal today because of the regular executions coming across from the south. The Neo-Therans distance themselves from these deaths, stating they are nothing to do with the Theran state, but merely ruthless individuals carrying out executions which are impossible for them to police. That doesn't help us, though, as we nurse too many of these poor unfortunates through their final hours and then bury them – assuming we actually come across these floating coffins first. Alas, most of them die a lonely and terrible death at sea and their tiny boats either succumb to storms or wash up on the shores of Glennad or Lendria along with their grisly cargo. All of which provides more ammunition for the Conspiracists, of course, and their fixation on this brutal, linear, millennia-old Theran civilisation.

Naturally, we Thissibrileans aren't completely innocent of exploiting the Shield of Crenac, and there have been a number of disappearances over the years for which the Shield is a likely explanation. And then there are those occasional drunken imbeciles who play the insane game of Shield Shooting for dangerous kicks, running their boats right up close to the Shield, sometimes with northerly winds at their backs. Inevitably, some lose either their bearings or control of their boat…shortly followed by their faculties and then their lives.

As for the genesis of the Shield of Crenac, the latest scientific research suggests that a dramatic shift of the North Epanagan tectonic plate occurred in 410 AT, resulting in the release of a vast magnetic phenomena from Thera's iron core which, in turn, is surrounded by churning, molten metal. It is this combination at the heart of our planet that also maintains the vital magnetosphere, the magnetic barrier surrounding the planet which shields us from solar radiation. However, on this occasion, in 410 AT, the released magnetic properties struck out as a lethal magnetic field line in both directions to form a continuous belt around Thera at a latitude of around fifty-five degrees north.

Of course, attempts have been made during the intervening thirteen centuries to cross the Shield, with all sorts of increasingly protective clothing and headgear, and at all points around the belt. All have failed, and all have resulted in the death of those crossing over.

Recently there has been increased activity, thanks to developments in hot air ballooning, but none of the animals sent up in the balloons has survived. However, as those balloons become capable of flying ever-higher, we can-but hope that, one day soon, this will provide our route back into the other five sixths of planet Thera. Inevitably, the Conspiracists disagree with that viewpoint, and remain happy with our isolation, determined to keep it that way.

We now return to 410 AT for one last time – for at a stroke, the playing field in the north had changed forever. Unable to cross the Shield of Crenac, the Therans of northern Epanaga were no longer able to send legionary reinforcements to the conquered lands of the Thissibriles, and their supply lines were now also cut. Inevitably, the Thissibrileans revolted, and overthrew the ruling, but vastly outnumbered Theran hierarchy and claimed the islands back for themselves. To our eternal shame, we then rounded up every single Theran – whether man, woman or child, whether legionnaire, official or even tourist – and sent them back over the Shield of Crenac. And although more than 1,370 years have passed since then, many Thissibrileans fear that should the Shield ever disappear, we may still be held to account for that ancient crime – by a regime that the Conspiracists argue is every bit as brutal today as it was back then…

CHAPTER I — EMILYA

1st Tertiar, 1789 — Day 92, 06:55

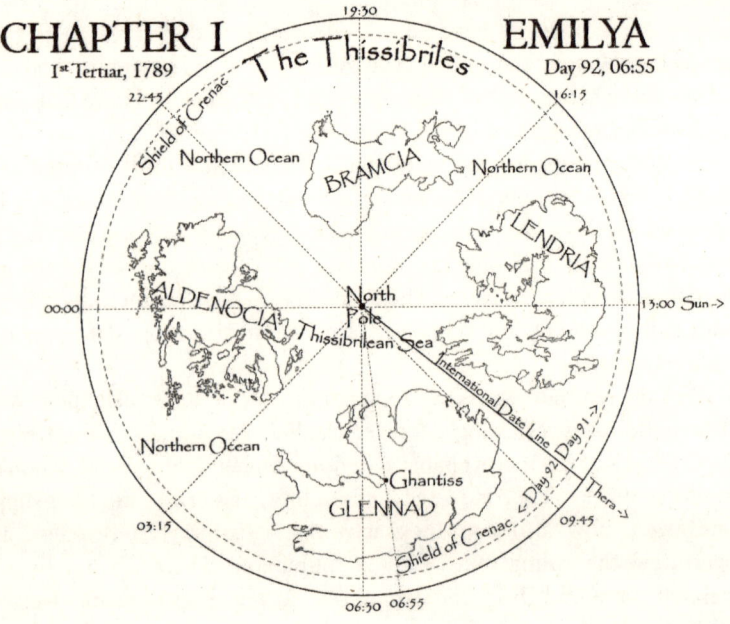

Emilya Luca loved architecture. Her grandfather had once told her that ninety-five per cent of people who walked around Ghantiss, missed ninety-five per cent of the best architecture. When she'd asked him what he meant, he'd said: "They don't look up, Em."

She was doing that now – looking up Irongate at the upper reaches of buildings on both sides of the street, taking in the extraordinary diversity. There were barely two buildings the same. Modern red-brick three-storey houses, with brick-stacked chimneys, sash windows, and pedimented door hoods, rubbed shoulders with older two and three-storey timber-framed houses, one of which had a startlingly yellow plaster infill. These older houses sported mullion and transom-style windows, while the example directly opposite included two long, horizontal timber beams which separated storeys one from two, and two from three – and which ran in wonky, warped lines that didn't remotely run in parallel with each other.

In her mind's eye, Emilya was visualising uneven internal floors and ceilings when her attention was caught by an officious-looking gentleman striding up Irongate with purpose. He had a leather document holder tucked under one arm, his long open coat fanned out around his legs, and his knee-length boots clicked loudly on the cobbles. He whisked past Emilya without acknowledging her existence and entered her father's bakery – just another early-rising official, accountant or solicitor anticipating hot sausage roll for breakfast.

Emilya sighed with impatience. Where was Drasner? The miller was never late with his deliveries. 'Drasner the Reliable,' or so her father had christened him. Emilya glanced at the parts of the glass-fronted counter which were visible between the seven or eight people queuing, and which was looking ominously under-populated. With Irongate still clear of either horse, carriage or wagon, she made a snap-decision. Drasner usually stuck to the same routine, and the bakery owned by her father, Danny Luca, was always third in his delivery schedule. If Drasner hadn't visited either the Thomas or the Colin bakeries, there was likely a significant delivery problem.

Emilya waited until her apron-clad father glanced up, and when their eyes met, she made a quick thumb-jabbing gesture down the road. Danny Luca nodded his approval, his mouth set in an unusually grim straight line. Business was business, and his early-morning queue of officials and professionals were unlikely to sympathise with supplier issues. With this in mind, Emilya ran for the alley five doors down Irongate, and then began weaving in and out of frowning folk walking in both directions. One balding man dressed in a curate's outfit turned around and shouted after her: "Heavens above! Slow down, boy!"

Emilya smirked. A common mistake, but she didn't care. Her unfeminine roughspun brown breeches gave her the comfort she preferred, and her flat cap hid her curly, shoulder-length, dark-auburn hair which was tied up and concealed within; her baggy smock-top and matching brown jacket hid the other tell-tale signs.

Seconds later, Emilya burst out of the alley, turning left into Sadler Gate. Fit as a fiddle, she then hared up this new set of cobbles, her flat sandals making '*slap, slap*' sounds, before she arrived outside Colins Bakery, still breathing relatively normally. Unfortunately, Drasner's horses and wagon were nowhere to be seen, and the look on Rex Colin's gaunt face, coupled with a remonstrating customer and a largely bare counter told her that she didn't need an update from Rex.

Instead, Emilya raced on up Sadler Gate, past the noisy tanneries and blacksmiths with their unique leathery-cum-horsey-cum-forgey smells that she loved, and then turned right into Ghantiss' enormous and spectacular Market Square. Surrounded on all four sides by magnificent buildings, the huge square within was graced by many permanent stalls with gaily-striped awnings, which competed for space with myriad flower-beds and two-dozen tinkling fountains of varying sizes. Despite the early hour, the place was already busy and there were several carriages and wagons around the periphery of what was the trading heart of Glennad – although none of them bore the legend 'Markus Drasner: Miller to the Masses'. Stranger still, Thomas' Bakery – which was obscurely wedged in between two grand, portico-fronted houses to the north – was all shuttered up and clearly closed.

Emilya paused to take stock – just as the Gothic town hall clock began to chime seven o'clock. She briefly flicked her eyes to take in the striking tower and multi-crocketed spire, and noted that just beneath the ornate clock-face, the garish merry-go-round of carnival figures, mostly playing instruments or riding horses, was working again. She then headed for an alley on the opposite side of the Market Square, just as the porcelain dancers under the town hall clock began their twirling around to more discordant bells. Emilya's hope, now, was that Drasner was delivering in reverse order today – which meant that Richards Bakery on the harbour frontage was worth a visit, as it was usually delivered to last.

The alley which connected the Market Place with the harbour was long and was also dark in the filtered early-morning daylight, so Emilya slowed her pace whilst keeping her eyes drilled to the floor – as the alley was also notorious for not being the cleanest. She had moved around three-quarters of the way down the alley when she heard the first whimper. Emilya stopped, stock still, all thoughts of missing millers immediately forgotten. The sound seemed to have come from behind a wooden gate a few paces further on to the left. That awful sound had conveyed the most desperate need. And if there was one thing that Emilya Luca would never turn her back on, it was an animal in need.

She held her breath, waiting for another sound to enable her to hone her bearings. Then she heard the anguished cry again – which was followed by a harsh laugh. "Hard lines, Dolly!" exclaimed a very posh voice. "It's still alive! Time for Reaper to finish the job."

"Aw come on Mags! My Scrapper's done all the hard work," whined a second voice.

Emilya felt her hackles rising. She knew exactly what this was. The posh students from Ghantiss University were notorious for it. It was called 'Let us Prey'. Two competitors, two dogs – usually large and savage – and the Prey. Held in a confined space, with nowhere to escape, the two dog-owners took it in timed, thirty-second bouts to unleash their slavering dogs on the Prey – usually a small animal, typically a stray puppy or kitten – although they weren't averse to kidnapping family pets either; you allegedly received greater winnings for that due to the risk factors in acquiring the Prey. Other small animals like rabbits, piglets and rodents were also considered fair game. The winner was the owner of the dog who eventually kills the Prey in their thirty-second bout. It was hideously brutal and entirely unworthy of enlightened Ghantiss, but the authorities did little or less to stamp it out as the perpetrators were usually rich and systematically defended or protected by their wealthy families.

"Sorry, Dolly, old boy," came back the cultured reply from the first man, the one called Mags. "You're out of time. Rules are rules, and this one's mine, old chap. You can pay me my winnings back at the palace."

"Aw, spoilsport!"

"Just get Scrapper back on his leash, Dolly. I'm not having him spoil Reaper's fun."

As Emilya's brain processed this new information, her heart began to bounce off her ribs. Mention of the palace, along with Mags' plummy accent could only mean that he was that lousy idler, Prince Magnus – despised by the folk of Ghantiss as a work-shy bully, philanderer, drunkard and several-times rapist, but totally untouchable thanks to his birthright. He'd probably been out on an all-night Prey-fest, gambling huge amounts of money, and had decided to pick on a stray dog on his way home as a bonus. What was she to do?

Emilya then heard the victim whine again, followed by another callous laugh from one of the men – almost certainly Mags. Emilya's blood began to boil. Unable to stop herself, she sprinted towards the gate, gathering pace, and dropping her left shoulder on approach, her mind momentarily considering before impact that there was a good chance that she might dislocate it.

She didn't. The wood was a good deal rottener than it looked in the dawn light, and she smashed through it, sending wood splinters flying in all directions.

Absolute pandemonium erupted in the courtyard beyond. Both young men reacted initially with squeals of terror – which set both of their dogs barking with maniacal frenzy. Fortunately, one of the dogs – a vicious-looking rottweiler – was tied to a post, but the other – a doberman of some sort – slipped its leash and launched itself at Emilya. Luckily, it went for her arm first, which she'd put up to protect herself – although Emilya cried out in pain as it sank its teeth in and shook its head from side to side. As she fell backwards, though, instinct took over, and she picked up a shard of wooden door and battered the dog once over the head. It immediately yelped and then flopped to the floor, making dreadful screeching noises. For a second,

Emilya was unsure what had happened, but then realised that she couldn't pull the shard free of the dog. A three-inch nail in the back had embedded itself into the doberman's left eye.

By this stage, the two young men had recovered their poise, but the still-tethered rottweiler continued to bark its brain out. One of the men went straight down on his knees to the stricken doberman and started sobbing when he saw the damage. The other man showed little compassion. "Oh, for pity's sake, Dolly – pull yourself together man. It's only a dog." He then turned his attention to the barking rottweiler: "Reaper! Quiet!" he commanded. Remarkably, the rottweiler ceased its aural assault immediately.

Alongside this, Dolly was still trying to soothe his dog – clearly Scrapper, given the overheard conversation – stroking his flank as the screeching subsided to whimpering. He then slowly stood up and turned to face Emilya – who had remained half-paralysed with remorse at what she had accidentally done. "You bitch!" cried Dolly, through his tears, his address making Emilya realise that she'd lost her cap in the door assault and that her hair was now draped wildly across her face. She swept it back and glared at the man she now knew was called Dolly. He stopped, two paces in front of her, and pointed. "You'll pay dearly for this, you urchin."

Emilya tried her best to control her pounding heart and reviewed her predicament. Dolly's face was distorted in anger, but instinct told her that he was of weak character. Slightly below medium height, he had a pasty face, curly hair somewhere between blonde and ginger, and no discernible chin – even though he wasn't particularly overweight. Meanwhile, his companion – who was dressed in the finest clothes she'd ever seen at such close quarters, and whom she had now visually confirmed was indeed the hated Prince Magnus – was very different. Tall, dark and handsome, for starters, and also very laid back. She briefly noted that his chiselled features were framed by thick and wavy, collar-length dark hair, and two stylish, manly sideburns – just like his portrait in the town hall – while the jacket of his dark blue, three-piece suit was exquisitely piped in gold around the cuffs and collar along with two panels of gold buttons running up the centre. In stark contrast to his pasty and very angry friend, Magnus was also smirking and seemed to be enjoying the whole situation. "Well, Dolly," Prince Magnus said. "Make her pay, then. Make her pay *now*."

The man called Dolly hesitated, looked at his dark-haired friend, then back at Emilya. "No," he said, turning to Magnus again, now apparently back under control. "I've a better idea," he added, nodding towards the tethered rottweiler. "To the victor the spoils, methinks."

"Ah," said Magnus. "I see what you mean. Poor Reaper is indeed in need of his breakfast, after all," he added, turning towards his tethered but slavering pet.

"Release that dog, and I'll run you through right here," announced a new and gruff voice.

Emilya looked up to see a middle-aged, dark-haired man in a white nightshirt, holding a cutlass to Magnus's throat. "Cos that aint no way to treat a little girl, matey," he added.

Magnus stood stock still, his stance still somehow mocking, despite the obvious danger to him. "You do know who I am?" he asked.

"Oh, I know who you are, matey," replied the man. "And everyone in this town knows *what* you are, too."

Magnus's eyes flashed dangerously at that, but he wasn't stupid enough to provoke the man. Instead, he appraised his foe. He should have been a comical sight dressed in only a white linen nightshirt that ended just below the knee, but he was as tall as Magnus, and his thick arms, barrel chest and upright stance spoke of a dangerous and physical adversary. This wasn't a man to back down from a fight, and he clearly cared little for Magnus' status. Magnus therefore changed his tack. "We appear to be at an impasse," he said.

"Keep still!" barked the night-shirted man, his order directed at Dolly, who was moving to his right.

"I need to tend my dog," said Dolly, frightened that Scrapper's whimpering had now ceased. "The urchin you're defending has grievously wounded him."

"Aye, and clearly in self-defence! If it's any consolation, boy, your dog will live if you care for him right. It'll obviously be blind in that eye, mind."

"Can we, erm, negotiate, please?" asked Prince Magnus, his hands still half-raised in surrender.

"Gladly. Girl," barked the night-shirted man. "Make yourself scarce."

Emilya slowly stood, now very aware that her bloodied left arm was hurting badly. She looked at the man, for the first time noticing that his nose wasn't straight, running slightly off-centre from top left to bottom right. She briefly imagined the likely brawl that had caused that. Then she heard that pathetic whining sound again – the sound that had brought her crashing through the gate in the first place. Her eyes flicked towards a dark corner of the courtyard where she spotted a small terrier for the first time. He or she was desperately trying to stand up, failed, and then flopped back down, whimpering again.

Emilya moved quickly over to the terrier, her bottom lip trembling at the sight. Its thick grey fur was matted with blood, while half of one ear was missing, and at least one leg was broken. Gently, Emilya crouched down and tenderly picked the animal up, briefly noting it was as heavy as a bag of beans. It squealed and panicked, but Emilya held firm, shushing the poor creature and gently stroking its matted fur – just as the first of her tears began to run down her grimy cheeks. "Shush, my darling," she said. "You're safe now." Then, despite her predicament, and good fortune, Emilya turned to face Magnus. "One day," she said, her eyes narrowing to squints, "you *will* pay for this."

Magnus's response was a standard smirk. "And one day," he responded, "you will pay, too, my dear," he leered, parting his lips and flickering his moistened, royal tongue at her.

The cutlass was pressed harder against his throat, and a tiny rivulet of blood slid down the inside of his pristine white silk shirt. "Go," said the night-shirted man.

"What will you do?" asked Emilya, as it began to dawn on her how perilous the man's situation now was.

"I can look after myself, girly," he replied gruffly.

Emilya delayed a second longer, before looking the man right in the eye. "Thank you," she mouthed. Then she turned around, and with the bloodied terrier cradled gently in her arms, she passed through the shattered gate and hurried back to her father's bakery.

CHAPTER 2   ALICYA
1st Tertiar, 1789   Day 92, 07:55

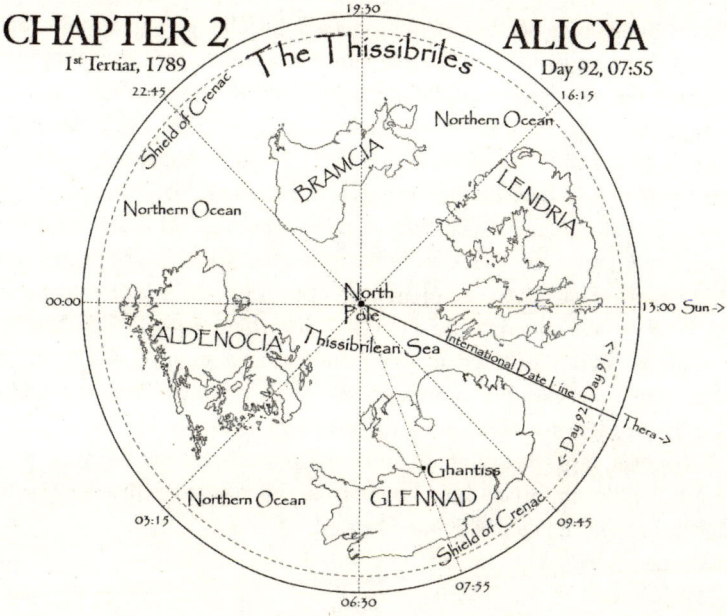

Princess Alicya swept her soft body brush one last time across the shining coat of her chestnut colt and stood back to admire her handywork. "There you go, Sebastian," she cooed. "You shall go to the ball, my dear."

"Not with a tail like that, he won't," announced a gruff voice.

Alicya turned around, a half-smile already playing across her aristocratic features. "Very funny, Maddox," she said, moving aside one of the long strands of lustrous dark hair that had fallen across her pretty face. "And for just how long have you been spying on me?"

"Saw the lot," he said, before issuing a huge double sniff. He then turned and hobbled towards the stable door. "Five out of ten," he threw back over his shoulder.

Alicya's face immediately went into pout mode. "Oh, Maddox! You're such a cruel stablemaster." But Maddox didn't respond, he just kept on hobbling out of the stables. Alicya's face fell, disappointed that Maddox hadn't engaged in their normal banter. "You could at least check his hooves for me," she shouted.

Still nothing. Disappointed, Alicya turned her attention back to Sebastian. Standing to one side, she began by separating the worst of Sebastian's tail-tangles with her fingers before grabbing the tail brush and gently working her way up from the bottom of the tail, taking extra care over the bony upper section. As she finished the job, two sounds coincided. Firstly, she heard the distant clopping of horses' hooves, but then they were drowned out by the palace clock tower striking eight o'clock. She was therefore taken by surprise when Maddox re-entered the stables leading a chestnut filly. The old stablemaster's face broke out into a crooked-toothed grin. "Told you I'd have her by the end of the week, didn't I?"

"Oh Maddox!" she exclaimed, moving smoothly across to the new arrival, and then gently placing the flat of her hand against the horse's face. "She's beautiful." Tears welled up in both eyes. "Can you imagine the babies they'll have?" she added, glancing back at Sebastian.

Maddox merely grunted at that, while Alicya stepped across to the stablemaster and gave him a peck on one of his stubbled cheeks. "Maddox from the Paddocks strikes again," she joked.

"Give over, lass," he said, both awkward and delighted at the same time. He hid his discomfort by hobbling across to Sebastian, where he ran his fingers through the tail. "Not bad," he said.

Alicya immediately beamed.

"Six, I'd say."

Alicya's face fell.

"I'm only joking," replied Maddox. "It's a grand job."

Alicya was about to comment when a commotion from outside diverted their attention. It sounded as if the courtyard door had just been smashed off its hinges, and that explosive sound was immediately followed by her brother's ranting diatribe.

"I swear to God, Dolly, I will rip that bastard's heart out with my own bare hands and eat it for breakfast myself. And as for that little bitch of an urchin who caused all of this…"

Alicya trotted out into the courtyard, Maddox hobbling behind. She suddenly stopped dead in her tracks, put her hand to her mouth to stop herself from laughing, and then put her hand over her eyes to stop herself from seeing. In the meantime, Dolly had taken shelter behind Magnus.

"What?" demanded Magnus, absolute fury written across his face.

Despite his evident wrath, Alicya couldn't help herself. "Well, brother dear," she began. "What *have* you been doing, this time?"

"This isn't funny, Alicya."

"All right, so please tell me why Dolly is missing his breeches…" Alicya tailed off, as she took in the half-mast white breeches that Magnus was wearing, and which weren't the splendid dark blue ones he had gone out in the previous night. Furthermore, the bottom of the breeches rested just above his knees, revealing white knee-flesh above his boots, while the rest of the material was far too tight around his thighs and crotch area. She began to laugh hysterically.

Magnus's response was to stride towards her aggressively, whilst the luckless Dolly attempted to keep pace to protect his modesty. "I'm warning you, little sister. You may find this funny now, and I might even laugh with you about it in – oh, I don't know – in about *fifty* years-time! But if word of this gets out," he said, his eyes narrowing, "I will know exactly where it has come from, and you *will* be sorry."

"All right Mags," said Alicya, her laughter now subsiding. "So, you've got caught again with your breeches down by some vengeful husband, and poor Dolly here had to donate his to cover your own modesty!"

For a second, Magnus's chin jutted, while his fists were bunched, and Maddox took an instinctive step forward. "You what?" sneered Magnus, eyeing Maddox with disdain.

"Oh, leave him alone Magnus and go get yourself and Dolly dressed."

Magnus looked as though he was going to escalate the confrontation, but then he uncharacteristically backed down.

"No offence meant, Your Highness," said Maddox, briefly catching Magnus' eye. "Here," he said, shrugging off his coat. He hobbled forward and passed the coat to Dolly. "Put this around your waist, son."

Without a word, Dolly took Maddox's roughspun coat and draped it around his waist, holding it very tight at the front – thus enabling him to step out from behind Magnus.

"Thank you, Maddox," said Magnus. "I'm glad you're here, actually. I'd like you to cut along to the kennels. There's a dog in there that needs your care and attention."

"What's wrong with it?" asked Maddox.

"I don't pay you to ask questions, Maddox. Just do as you're told. Please," he added, with a toothy but ice-cold smile.

As Maddox moved away, he couldn't help firing back a parting shot. "You don't pay me anyway. Your father does."

Despite his perpetual smirk, Alicya could tell that her brother was rattled with that statement, not to mention a tad undermined. Nevertheless, she decided to pull their conversation back into line

"All right, so, *not* a vengeful husband then?" probed Alicya. Magnus maintained his silence on the matter. "Oh, come on!" exclaimed Alicya. "What happened?"

"We were -," began Dolly, only to be cut off by a light, backhand cuff to his left cheek from Magnus, that forced Dolly to stagger...and drop Maddox's coat, too.

This time, though, Alicya didn't laugh. Thanks to this latest exchange, and the previous reference to an injured dog, Alicya suddenly saw through them. She rounded on her brother. It was now her turn to be angry. "You promised me you'd never do that again."

Magnus rolled his eyes. "They're only dogs."

"Only!" screeched Alicya. This time it was Magnus who got a slap across the face. "There are times when I swear that you're not of the same blood as me," she snapped, but as she turned to stalk away, Magnus grabbed her wrist and pulled her back, savagely.

"I've told you before, Lissy," he said, through gritted teeth. "You can't rule and be weak." He then deliberately squeezed her wrist as hard as he could, feeling bones begin to shift.

Alicya wrenched herself free. "I don't ever *want* to rule," she said, rubbing her numbed wrist. "I'd rather stay *human*, thanks very much." Despite her brother's typical bullishness, Alicya stood her ground as curiosity caught up with her again. They both regarded each other for several seconds. "You might as well tell me everything, though."

"What's the point," replied Magnus, calmer now. "You'll only come down on her side."

"Whose side?"

Magnus kept his mouth shut, so Alicya turned again to Dolly. "Whose side?"

Dolly paused for a second, caught between loyalty to either prince or princess. Finally, he found his voice. "The urchin."

"What urchin?"

"Don't forget the old sailor, as well, Dolly," said Magnus, spikily.

"What sailor?" asked Alicya.

"The one who had the nerve to do this," said Magnus, pointing to the sore-looking nick on his neck, "and then decided to slash my breeches with his cutlass, to stop me tracking him back to his hovel."

"Wow, brave man!" Alicya was genuinely shocked. "Was he drunk? I mean, there isn't a man in Ghantiss who doesn't know *your* face."

"No, he wasn't drunk. But he'll be wishing he was *blind* drunk when I catch up with him."

"What are you going to do?"

"Anything I please, little sister. And as for that urchin -"

Magnus immediately regretted his words, as his sister knew him too well. "Whoever she is, you will leave her alone," demanded Alicya. "I think I've got the measure of this now. The old sailor was defending the urchin, after the urchin defended the Prey, am I right?"

Silence confirmed her theory. "Well, good on 'em both, then. In fact," she added, "I might try and search for them myself – to congratulate them and give them a reward!"

And with that, Alicya turned and flounced back towards the stables.

CHAPTER 3
1st Tertiar, 1789

MAGNUS
Day 92, 08:15

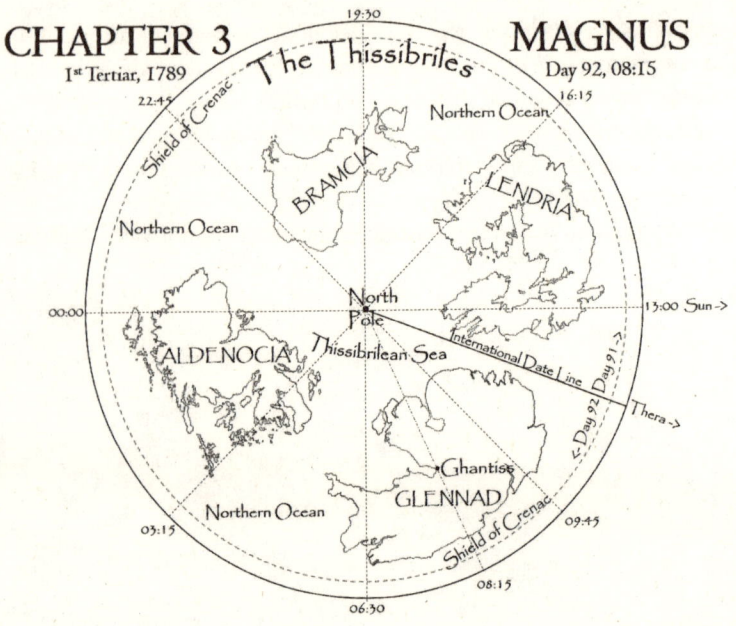

Magnus watched Alicya's lithe form with a spreading smirk, as she flounced back to the stables. Half of his mirth came from the pleasure of upsetting his younger 'perfect' sister, but the other half was due to the dawning realisation that there was wider game afoot. Despite the demeaning nature of this morning's events, it had turned out rather well – as the prospective hunt for the sailor and the urchin promised some fine sport.

"Well, Dolly," he said, turning to his erstwhile friend. "There's no time like the present, is there, old boy?" Observing his vacant friend's expression, he put his arm around Dolly's shoulder and steered him towards the rear of the palace. "I am suggesting that we go and have a little chat with Mr Nash."

"Ah," responded Dolly, realisation dawning.

"Although first," he said, looking down, "we clearly need to resolve our little wardrobe mishaps."

That said, the two friends turned for the palace and walked quickly past the marquees that were laid out on the still-dewy grass alongside the rear terraces, Dolly steadfastly clutching Maddox's coat around his lower regions. At the top end of the sculpted terraces with their riot of springtime yellow and red blooms, they ascended two dozen steps that swept around in a semi-circle opposite an identical set on the other side, eventually giving access to the Council Room via a pair of enormous open glass doors.

Magnus and Dolly breezed past the rich red velvet drapes and across plush carpets before entering a network of flagstone-floored corridors. As they arrived at the foot of a set of plain stairs, Magnus looked at Dolly. "Servant stairs. Let's take a short-cut. I'm not in the mood for a lecture from my mother."

Ten minutes later, they clattered back down the same set of service stairs, Magnus clad in a pair of splendid dark blue breeches, and Dolly back in his less-than splendid and now-slightly stretched white breeches. "It's this way," said Magnus, turning left and striding up the corridor. Eventually, he found the office he was looking for, briefly rapped on the door, and then entered before being bidden. He pulled up short at what he saw.

Nash, the unflappable Head of Royal Security was sat at his desk, as Magnus was expecting. What took him by surprise was the presence of the Lord Chamberlain and the Lord High Constable, seated in chairs facing the desk. And whereas he and the thirty-something Nash had a cautious understanding, there was no love lost between Magnus and the other two tight-faced, late-middle-aged officials. As next in line to the Glennadian throne, though, Magnus outranked them all – hence his natural cockiness was soon reasserted as he flopped down into an armchair to one side of Nash and planted his black leather boots firmly on the Head of Royal Security's desk. "Please," he said to the three officials. "Don't let me interrupt your discussion."

As the most senior officer of the Royal Household, the Lord Chamberlain wasn't used to insubordination – Prince Magnus aside, of course – and this was indeed standard Magnus behaviour. Similarly, the Lord High Constable, as Commander of the Royal Army and Master of Horse, was used to having his orders obeyed unquestioningly. A quick look passed between them, before the Lord Chamberlain spoke. "Your Royal Highness," he acknowledged, with a slight incline of the head. "As a matter of fact, we were just leaving."

"Didn't look like it to me, Cecil," replied Magnus, somehow making usage of the Lord Chamberlain's surname sound like an insult. "What were you discussing?"

"A delicate matter of state, Your Royal Highness," answered the Lord High Constable.

"Would you care to enlarge, Mr Russell?"

The solemn Lord High Constable didn't rise to the bait. Instead, he turned back to face Mr Nash. "We'll re-visit this issue tomorrow, when we know more," he said. With that, both royal officials got to their feet, swished past the nervous-looking Dolly, and exited the office.

When the door closed behind them, Magnus – without looking up – pointed at the closed door. "That was very rude. Don't you think, Mr Nash?" he asked, now looking up.

Nash's eyes remained steady and neutral. "I think it would be better if we were all singing from the same hymn sheet, Your Royal Highness."

"And what do you mean by that, Nash?" asked Magnus, now sounding slightly irritated.

"That we all have the royal interest as our number one priority. Now," he began, cleverly brushing any further questioning aside. "What can I do for you, Sir?"

Magnus realised that he'd been gently stood down and that any further probing would demerit his superiority. Nash was a clever man. Hence his elevated post for one so relatively young. Besides, Magnus was also keen to set the appropriate wheels in motion, so he began his tale of the early morning's events. He did nothing to play down his own villainy in the episode – Nash was being paid well, and knew better than to offer counsel to Magnus, anyway. Furthermore, as he'd just said, Nash had royal interest as his number one priority, too. Instead, Nash listened intently, showing no sign of mirth at the fate of Magnus's breeches and their impact upon poor Dolly. On the contrary, his face showed the vaguest flicker of annoyance – presumably with Magnus for putting himself at such risk in the first place.

When Magnus had finished, Nash cut straight to the chase. "And you want the old sailor dead, naturally. But what of the urchin? She will likely be missed. Fourteen or fifteen years old, you say?"

"I don't care if she's missed, Nash. Fifteen or not, that wildcat somehow got the better of me, and that story," he said, leaning forward, his index finger jabbing Nash's desk, "cannot be told. And anyway," he said, shrugging his shoulders. "Girls and boys run away from their parents all the time in Ghantiss. Who will give a flying fig over one scruffy urchin?"

"Very well," agreed Nash. "I'll put my best men onto it. But obviously, I'll need some descriptions first."

"All right," said Magnus. "The sailor was mid-forties, I'd say, with dark hair, slightly greying at the temples. He had a salt-and-pepper stubble, his nose wasn't straight – the likely result of a brawl – and he was also tall; about my height, I'd say, and pretty well-built, too."

"And he had a faded tattoo," piped up Dolly. "Looked like a scorpion. On his right forearm. The arm holding the cutlass."

"Well, that narrows it down quite nicely," said Nash. "We shouldn't have any trouble turning *him* up."

"If he's still in Ghantiss," said Magnus. "He knew he was signing his death warrant." Magnus's lip curled in a sneer as he remembered the sailor's insult. *And everyone in this town knows* what *you are, too!* If Magnus had been weak, he might have admitted that saving the girl from a vicious dog didn't deserve the death penalty. Unfortunately for the sailor, Magnus was not weak – and the further insults of the nick on his neck and the shredded breeches, along with that one-line slur, might even have persuaded his pacifist father to hunt the sailor down.

"We'll need to move fast then," Nash was saying. "But don't worry. I've soldiers and spies in every port in northern Glennad. He won't get far, even if he has already cut and run."

"Excellent, Nash," said Magnus.

"And the girl?"

"Yes, more difficult, that one," said Magnus. "Other than she had dark reddish-brown hair – and curly, too. Fairly wild, in fact."

"And she'll have some nasty teeth marks on her left arm," piped up Dolly. "So, you could make inquiries at the infirmary, for starters."

"Good shout again Dolly," said Magnus, approvingly. "My, you really aren't as stupid as you look, are you?"

Dolly positively beamed at that.

"What was she wearing?" asked Nash. "As in, what *type* of clothes was she wearing? What was her class?"

"No class whatsoever, Nash. The girl was an urchin."

"I'm not so sure she was," responded Dolly.

Magnus and Nash turned to look at him in unison, a new level of respect accorded. "Go on, Dolly," encouraged Magnus.

"I think she might have looked like an urchin because she'd just crashed through a wooden door. And she'd had a doberman tearing at her sleeve, too! Furthermore," said Dolly, his index finger raised, and his eyes narrowed, "I remember noticing her sandals."

"What about them?" asked Nash.

"They were well-made," said Dolly.

"She could have stolen them," responded Magnus.

"Yes, true," said Dolly. "But what about her vocabulary? No, the more I think about it, the more I think she was educated."

"In what way?" questioned Nash."

"When she went to the terrier, she said: 'Shush, my darling, you're safe now.' Like a well-bred mother talking to a child. And then when she challenged you at the end, Magnus, what did she say?"

Magnus snorted. "I believe she told me that 'one day I would pay' – the insolent brat!"

"Excellent," said Nash, "this is all very useful information, gentlemen. I think," he began, whilst rubbing his prominent and clefted chin, "we *will* check the infirmary – although I doubt an urchin would venture there, and neither would an educated girl who had just threatened the heir to the throne. So, I think – based on Dolly's observations – we should also look at tradesmen's daughters."

"But there must be hundreds of them in Ghantiss," protested Magnus.

"Yes, but how many up so early?" asked Dolly, now feeling quite the professional detective.

"All of them!" stated Nash, instantly deflating Dolly's bubble. "Tradespeople are all up with the lark – for obvious reasons. But anyway," he said, rising to his feet. "I've got plenty to work with and I assume you're keen for me to get started straight away, yes?"

Magnus also stood and held out his hand to Nash. "Yes indeed," he agreed, as Nash returned a firm handshake. "You'll keep me informed?"

"Of course, Your Royal Highness."

"Thank you, Nash. And please – keep the girl in one piece. I have special plans for her. The sailor – do whatever is necessary – but do keep him alive. I have very different plans for him."

CHAPTER 4 — JAKE
2nd Tertiar, 1789 — Day 93, 17:30

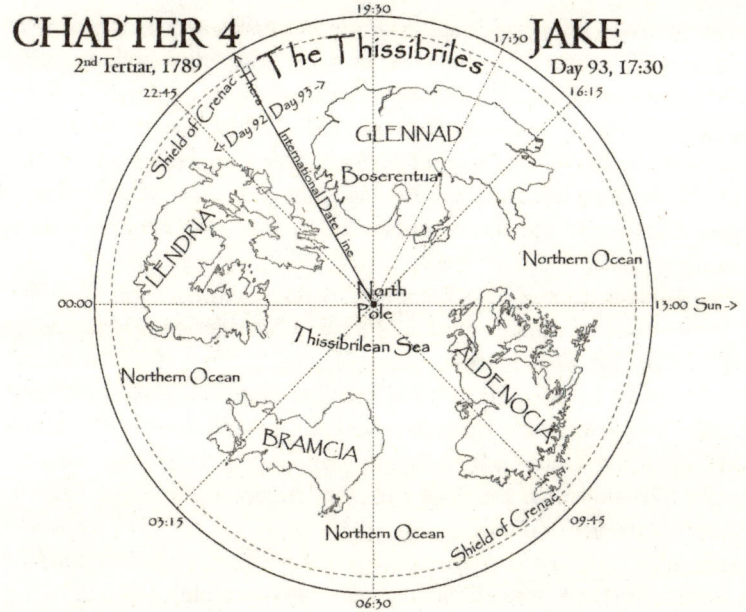

Jake Oscom spotted them at the very last second – and ducked back around the corner, immediately re-tracing his steps. He knew Nash's men when he saw them; seems they knew him now, too!

He kept walking, away from the sea-front and the jetty from where he'd been hoping to take a boat up the coast to Port St Humo. His pace up Boserentua's High Street was brisk but not fast enough to draw attention. After about fifteen seconds, he risked a quick look back. No one was following him, so he stopped outside a fruit and vegetable wheelbarrow, and made a play of eyeing the displays, but all the time looking for movement from the sea-front direction. Still nothing.

Jake gradually relaxed. He smiled at the middle-aged woman behind the display. She smiled back – with not a single tooth in her mouth. Feeling both guilty and conspicuous, Jake bought a couple of apples and then lost himself in the backstreets of Boserentua, before reaching the woods which stretched down to half a mile-or-so from the coast. He walked for a further two minutes away from the main path until, happy he wasn't being followed, he sat down with his back to a large oak tree and bit into one of his apples. Time to take stock.

Most men would be nervous in his position, but this wasn't the first time he'd rescued a party in distress. Three years ago, he'd rescued one of his crew from a couple of Bramcian thugs in an inn in Byastwerthy. He'd hit one of them so hard, he was out cold before he fell, cracking his skull on a table corner as he went down. He later learned that the impact of skull on table had killed the thug – who also happened to be the son of a nasty local crime lord. With a hefty price on his head, Jake had been forced to leave his native Bramcia, giving up his naval commission in the process, and had settled in Ghantiss on the opposite side of the North Pole, over three hundred leagues from Byastwerthy.

Lost in his memories, Jake ran an index finger down the profile of his off-centre nose, the memento of another punch-up in another Bramcian port. That hadn't been his fault either. He'd often thought that men and alcohol should be an outlawed combination. Not that alcohol had had anything to do with this latest intervention, though, and Jake certainly didn't regret his actions either. Prince Magnus, was an odious oaf who thought that enormous privilege gave him licence to do as he pleased, without conscience or mercy.

Jake shook his head and contemplated his position. The coast north of Boserentua was now out of bounds, and that was a blow. As one of the largest ports in the Thissibriles, Port St Humo would have got him to anywhere he cared to go. He had been favouring Lendria, home to the dark stuff – which never tasted the same in Glennad as it did in Gwyala, Nannosh or Iblund. Worse still, the presence of Nash's men on the hunt suggested that the girl was probably in danger, too. Jake had hoped that Magnus would be too lazy to do anything about it, or too embarrassed to mention their encounter to Nash. Seems he'd hoped for too much.

Then again, he had made a mess of those navy breeches!

Jake smirked at the memory. The look on Prince Magnus' face: outrage, shock…and then blue murder! Nevertheless, he'd had to do something to stop the Prince from following him, and at least he hadn't injured the Royal Oaf – much though he'd deserved it.

Jake let out a long sigh. In a way, this setback was good. He'd had a nagging guilt about the girl all the way from Ghantiss to Boserentua.

And one day, you will pay, too, my dear, the smug Prince had said. The same way many other girls had paid, no doubt.

Anyway, now he knew that Magnus was serious, he needed to return to the lion's den to rescue her. Indeed, returning to Ghantiss might actually play to his advantage – as Nash's men were clearly looking elsewhere. They could then make their escape over land to the *south* coast. Nash hopefully wouldn't be expecting that – not from an old sea dog like him, anyway!

Still, first things first. He had no idea where the girl lived in Ghantiss. But he knew some men who probably did.

Jake did a quick arms check, and all was present and correct. His trusty cutlass was strapped just behind his left side under his grey greatcoat, his serrated gutting knife holstered in a sheath to his right-hand side, and two wickedly pointed dirks strapped and hidden inside a boot apiece. Reassured, Jake closed his eyes, giving himself an hour or so to nod before darkness fell.

When he opened his eyes an hour and a half later, daylight was starting to fade. Immediately wide awake, Jake stood up and did a few stretches of his leg, torso and back muscles, enticing several comforting cracks and clicks. *Plenty of life in the old dog yet.*

Resolved on his course of action, Jake re-traced his steps through the woods and back streets, and onto High Street, and then headed for the seafront, the seagull concerto increasing with each stride. As he approached the end of the road, he took the last side street on the left, took a right at the end of that street and then quickly crossed the promenade, dropping down onto the pebbly beach with a light crunch. Not that there would be an issue with sound at this distance, as the tide was coming in a few yards to his left and obliterating most other noises as it crashed against the rounded pebbles and then slid back with a mournful hissing sound, only to repeat the action seconds later.

Satisfied that no one had seen him, Jake edged along underneath the promenade until he was close enough to view the jetty. Shadowy boats bobbed back and forth on the incoming surf on both sides, while a couple of figures were in the process of securing another. At the point where the jetty met the promenade were Nash's three men. Given the last boat must have sailed half an hour ago, Jake was relieved they'd stayed put; they'd obviously given it until dusk in case their quarry turned up to book late passage on a dawn departure, or tried to steal a boat and do a solo run at night. They'd almost hit the jackpot, too!

Jake settled himself into the blind side of one of the breakers, where it met the promenade at its highest point. It was a waiting game now, so he busied himself by studying his targets.

Two of them were facing the sea, the other – a younger man – facing the promenade. All three were dressed like gentlemen – fine tricorn hats, embroidered knee-length coats, waistcoats, fancy neck-stocks, pristine breeches, long socks and buckled shoes. Even from this distance, Jake could see that the younger man was tall and fair-haired, while one of the older men was as thin as a rake with angular features. The other man was easily in his forties, relatively small, rotund, and sporting a beetroot-coloured face and a bulbous, drink-soaked nose. Hardly the sort for tracking a wanted man, but Jake was certain he was an associate of Nash's as he'd seen them together before.

After five minutes, the two figures who had secured the last boat walked back up the jetty towards the promenade and disappeared off up High Street. The three men had a look around, quickly conferred, and then ambled off in the opposite direction to Jake.

It was easy for Jake to trail them. They soon took a right turn that must have run adjacent to High Street – this road being populated on both sides with houses, shops and inns of all shapes and sizes, made of various combinations of brick, stone, timber and tile; there was even one cruck-framed thatch. His quarries eventually turned left into the black and white timber-framed Jolly Admiral – leaving Jake musing whether he now had a major problem, because if all three were staying at the inn, how was he going to catch one of them in isolation?

Jake walked on past the inn, crossing his fingers that the men would be stopping elsewhere, preferably at different digs, enabling him to take one of them out, later. He just needed to wait and take any opportunity offered. Jake immediately found a useful hiding place – a shop on the opposite side, a few doors up from the inn, and which had a large awning that cast a total shadow onto the pavement.

Jake was busy planning for alternative scenarios when the inn door was suddenly flung open, and the noise of the hubbub inside became much more audible. A young man staggered out leading a woman who was wearing a tight-fitting, very low-cut dress. A series of raucous cheers and lewd suggestions were issued by unseen drinkers inside. Jake eased back into the shadows and watched the young man attempt to kiss and grope the woman at the same time. He then observed the likely landlord shaking his head in disapproval before pulling the inn door shut. The young man didn't seem to notice. Eventually, the woman pushed him gently away. "Now then, Master Sam," she began, giggling lasciviously. "We need to save our strength, don't we?" She then took his hand and led him towards where Jake was concealed. "I'll make it worth your while, though."

Jake pulled right back into the shadows. As they walked past down the middle of the road, Jake got a nose-full of overpowering cheap perfume, and also realised that he'd underjudged the woman's age by at least a decade. Once they'd moved out of sight, though, Jake eased back out again onto the pavement.

There were various other comings and goings – including another lady of the night and a punter heading in the same direction as the previous pair. Around two hours must have passed, before Jake finally got his reward. The door to the inn had opened to reveal another couple – except this time, the significantly inebriated gentleman was one of Nash's men – the middle-aged portly one with the bulbous nose.

He staggered towards Jake, leaning on a girl who was a good twenty years younger than him, whilst constantly trying to place his hand up her skirts. "Stop that, Mister Horrocks," she said. "Ooh, you never change, do you?"

"And you wouldn't want it any other way, would you, my sweet?"

Jake saw the look of disgust that passed across the girl's face before she turned to Horrocks with a sweet little smile, put her forefinger on his nose and said teasingly: "Of course I wouldn't, Humphrey."

"That's my girl," he replied, patting her rear again – at which point, Jake noticed Horrocks' large gold wedding ring – before Horrocks playfully chased the girl up the street towards what was clearly the local brothel. As Jake watched them turn down a narrow street on the left, he felt a wave of sympathy for Mrs Horrocks. He then left his cover and followed, observing them enter a timber-framed, three-storey house on the left-hand side. Perfect. Horrocks was unlikely to be spending the night there and would almost certainly be coming out on his own before making back to the Jolly Admiral or to wherever his digs were.

Jake had a quick look up and down the street. It looked like the top end gave out onto a mixture of scrubland and long grass, with a birchwood a little further back. The moon was a problem though – very full and casting far too much light for Jake's liking.

For another hour, Jake staked out the brothel, observing lots of comings and goings. Eventually, the door to the property opened, and Horrocks staggered out, looking even drunker than he had when he'd gone in. His young companion gave him a peck on the cheek and then pushed him in the direction of the road before hurrying back inside.

Totally sozzled, Horrocks staggered and wobbled out into the street – at which point, Jake came running up to him, grabbed his arm and effected a high-pitched whining tone. "'scuse me Mister, can you 'elp me please? Me dogs got his leg caught in a trap in the woods."

"What? No! Go away you horrible man!"

Seeing the street was clear, Jake whipped out his serrated gutting knife and held it between two of Horrocks' quivering chins. "I'm afraid I insist," he growled, in a totally different tone. "Now move, otherwise I'll slice you open from ear to ear."

"Wh-, wh-, what do you want?" stammered Horrocks, his eyes now as wide as saucers.

"I want you to help rescue my dog."

"No, you don't, you -." Horrocks turned around wild-eyed and opened his mouth to cry for help. He never got the chance. Jake slammed the hilt of his knife into Horrocks open mouth, dislodging at least three teeth. Horrocks was lucky enough to gag instinctively and eject the tooth that had been threatening to disappear down his gullet.

"You make another sound, fancy-pants, and I'll carve your face up." Jake then hauled the whimpering Horrocks towards the scrubland and birchwood beyond, his captive dragging his feet through the long, damp grass and spitting out the occasional tooth. Eventually, Jake pushed the bloody-gummed Horrocks up against a tree and put his knife to his throat again. "Now then, you work for John Nash, yes?"

Horrocks went all wide-eyed again, as the penny dropped. His gaze dropped to Jake's exposed right forearm where the scorpion was just about visible in the moonlight, and he began to babble in panic.

Jake pressed the knife a little harder and drew blood. "You need to keep calm, mate, and just answer my questions. Now, who do you work for?"

"Yes, you're right, I work for Mr Nash."

"And what are you doing here in Boserentua?"

"I think you know -".

"Just answer the question."

"We're looking for a man called Jake Oscom." Horrocks looked Jake in the eye. "You."

"Thank you, that wasn't too hard, was it? And?"

"And what?"

"What were you going to do with me?"

Horrocks appeared to have lost his ability to communicate – and so the knife bit a little deeper.

"Stop, stop, stop!" panicked Horrocks. "We were to hand you over to Prince Magnus."

"Oh, really. Is he inviting me up to the palace for tea?"

The wide-eyed Horrocks didn't know what to say to that, so Jake pressed on. "What did *His Royal Highness* plan to do with me?"

"I don't know, I don't know," whittled Horrocks. "Our job was just to… to…to apprehend you."

"Well, I'm quite insulted that he sent a man like you. I can only hope that he suspected he wouldn't find me in Boserentua."

"I'm not the muscle, sir," said Horrocks in a vaguely haughty tone. "I'm a magistrate."

"Well of course you are," said Jake, everything now much clearer. "And you were presumably going to try me, and sentence me to death, no doubt? Or sentence me and hand me over to Magnus?"

Horrocks kept his mouth shut. Meanwhile, Jake was beginning to tire of the game. So far, he'd learned little more than he already knew, other than the fact that Horrocks was a magistrate – which he really should have guessed, anyway. Time to do what he came for. "Well, I would very much like to be a fly on the wall when you try to explain this little episode to your employer."

Hope flared in Horrocks' eyes. "You mean…you're not going to…"

"Not if you answer my questions, no. You obviously know why the Prince wants me. So, my first question is: who is the girl?"

"The girl?"

"You know which girl."

"We don't know her name yet."

Jake increased the knife-pressure.

"We don't know it! I swear it!"

"What *do* you know then?"

"We think she's a tradesman's daughter."

"Ha!" exclaimed Jake, with satisfaction. "And there must be – what – three or four thousand tradesmen in Ghantiss?"

Again, Horrocks remained silent.

"And what does His Royal Highness plan to do with her – assuming he eventually finds her?"

Horrocks went all wild-eyed and tongue-tied again, so the knife-pressure increased. "He plans to…to…to teach her a lesson."

"What kind of a lesson?"

Jake saw the terror flare in Horrocks' eyes, and he almost felt sorry for him. "Ah, *that* kind of a lesson. What a pleasant little monster your prince is. Why ever do you work for him? No, don't bother answering that. It really doesn't matter."

And with that, Jake crashed the hilt of his knife against Humphrey Horrocks' temple, knocking him clean out.

CHAPTER 5   ALICYA
3rd Tertiar, 1789   Day 94, 11:55

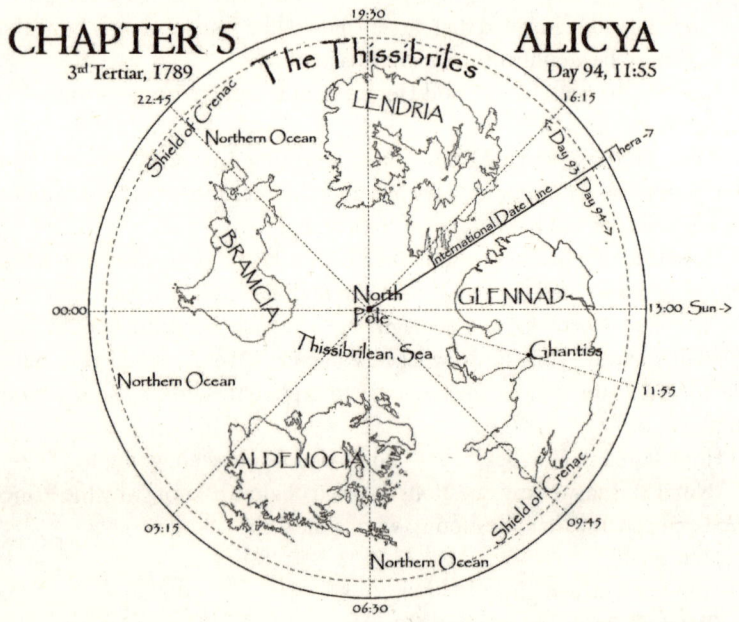

Alicya circled three hundred and sixty degrees to take in the vast Ghantiss Docklands. She had never been here before, although you could see part of the docklands from the top floor of the palace. That view only revealed the tops of the six-storey buildings that enclosed this enormous complex of man-made inlets, though; being here, in person, was a very different matter. The docklands were a little claustrophobic, for starters. The offices that surrounded the deep-water docks cast long shadows over much of the relatively still water, while the docks themselves were cluttered with every kind of ship imaginable: cutters, clippers, galleons, cruisers, merchant shipping, and even two warships – neither of which had ever been deployed in anger. And everywhere, there were masts – even on the smaller cogs and tugs and fishing boats. No sails, of course; they would only be unfurled once the vessels had left the docks and begun their next journey, some on central masts which rose to around one-hundred-and-fifty feet.

The crowds were also claustrophobic. Boisterous, cheerful and colourful, many waving red and white Glennadian flags, but hemming them in on all sides as they crowded the gangways and walkways that snaked around these inner docks, craning their necks to get a good look at the royal family. Men, women and children from all walks of life, from upper to working class; some dressed in finery, some in near to rags; a multitude of different professions, too, and many who had travelled from afar to see the launch of the twin merchant ships, the King George and the Queen Maud – soon to be launched by her parents after whom they had been named. The place was vibrant and alive.

Moved by the pulsating diversity, Alicya looked quizzically at her brother – who was resplendent in his official uniform of blue and gold, with its lavish piping, gold-tasseled epaulettes, red sash of office and ceremonial sword. No doubt he was feeling a little extra-superior today, as he reminded everyone that he was the Commander-in-Chief of the Glennadian Navy, despite being only twenty-two years of age. Not that he'd ever served in anger, of course – although he did enjoy travelling to the three other islands on official business, soaking up every second of his elevated rank. Nevertheless, Magnus did acknowledge his sister and even raised one eyebrow, whilst a vague smirk played about his handsome features.

Alicya's attention was suddenly interrupted by a very loud ringing bell to her left. She turned to observe the town crier, who was standing on a raised wooden platform. The crier was a stout, grey, balding man of around sixty-five, who wore a splendid jacket of red trimmed with gold: double golden rings around the end of the voluminous sleeves, and piped with gold at the shoulders all the way down the lapels and along the hem. He also wore a fine gold and blue waistcoat, dark blue breeches, white stockings and black-buckled shoes, while a white shirt, heavily laced at the throat and cuffs and his black tricorne hat completed the grand ensemble. The town crier's voice, however, proved to be even louder than his infernal bell. Alicya put her fingers in her ears as he bellowed out the usual commencement of a proclamation. "Oyez, oyez, oyez!"

The hubbub from the crowd gradually diminished, such that the next set of oyez's was even more cavernous. Her father had told Alicya earlier that the crier, John Martin, held the Thissibrilean record for the loudest cry – at 119.8 decibels! Apparently, he also held another record for vocal endurance – this after he issued a one-hundred-word proclamation every fifteen minutes for a period of fifty-two hours. Alicya found herself wondering if there was a Mrs Martin! Did the man perhaps order his supper in this manner, she wondered. The thought made her lips twitch slightly, and she nearly burst out laughing as she visualised a slightly naughtier image. Alicya managed to compose herself. And on second thoughts, she reflected, perhaps John Martin was a mouse at home, dominated by a small and slight woman with an acid tongue – and this was how he let off steam!

As the crowd noise subsided, John Martin began his proclamation. "We are gathered here today," bellowed Ghantiss' town crier, "to witness the launch ... of the two finest merchant ships that the Thissibriles has ever seen." Martin paused to draw in more oxygen. "It is only right and proper ... that they be named ... after our beloved King and Queen of Glennad."

A big cheer went up, with many waving hats and flags. Alicya briefly noticed the variety of male headwear being waved – everything from various expensive tricornes and the new, fashionable top hat, down to grubby little felt hats and cloth caps. Alicya felt a pang of guilt and sorrow for the poor before she returned her attention to John Martin.

After a further five minutes of bellowing, Martin finally turned to invite Alicya's mother and father onto the wooden platform. He then directed King George to the jetty on his left and Queen Maud to that on the right – each of which led to a long pole aligned to the stern of their eponymous vessels in the docks, with both poles having bottles of champagne attached to them via a long rope. As ever, her parents were a total contrast; her father, large in every way, sweating and red-faced in his heavy ermine cloak; her mother, small and slim, but certainly not frail – despite being drowned by her own ermine.

Her father went first, sensibly removing his crown and placing it on the jetty. He then grabbed the champagne bottle firmly before making his proclamation. "I hereby declare the *King George* officially launched." And with that, he flung the bottle with all his strength, which smashed, satisfyingly, into a thousand pieces on the stern of the *King George*. Deafening cheers and applause greeted the act.

Alicya's mother didn't fare quite so well, though. After three failed attempts to smash the bottle, which bounced harmlessly off the ship's hull before an official retrieved it and returned it to her, Magnus rather heroically began to walk up the jetty to assist. Initially, Alicya smirked at her brother's apparent gallantry, but she was then shocked to hear what sounded like unrest from the crowd, and even booing – as well as a few forthright and flagrantly slanderous barbs as well.

Alicya glared at the crowd. She knew that Magnus was no angel, and she was still sore at him for re-indulging in *Let Us Prey* two days ago. But the rumours about him being a monster who forced himself on women of all ages were clearly untrue. Why couldn't they see that?

As Magnus reached her mother, Alicya could tell from his body language that he was furious – and even though he was trying to ignore it, he would be feeling hurt and humiliated, too. Despite his waywardness and arrogance, he was a proud man and he was still her brother. Thankfully, there were still plenty among the crowd who were cheering him on as well, and so Magnus helped his mother to hurl the champagne bottle at the ship one more time – this time successfully.

Again, though, Alicya heard a few boos intermingled with the cheers. The next thing she saw was a disturbance on the gangway to her right, and then an attractive young blonde woman forced her way through the line of officials. She was carrying something which, as she got nearer, Alicya realised was a baby in swaddling clothing. "Your baby!" she was shouting. "Your baby, Prince Magnus!"

Several officials had now caught up with her and were attempting to haul her back, but Alicya's eye was then drawn to a further disturbance behind the woman. Fists were clearly flying, and then a burly man with wild, brown curly hair and his shirt ripped open, forced his way through the struggling throng and pointed his finger at Magnus. "Rapist!" he accused.

The accusation was greeted with uproar. The crowd to the right of the disturbance surged forward to get a better look, and the low-lying barrier of chains linked to periodic wooden posts at the waterfront was never going to be enough to hold them back. Within seconds, officials and public alike were being forced over them and found themselves tumbling into the murky still waters, causing a multitude of tumultuous splashes. Those up top were now frantically trying to curtail their forward momentum, whilst screams and shouts of consternation went up all around them. An instant later, John Nash was at her elbow, shepherding her away from the advancing mob, while his men quickly gathered in the King, Queen and Prince. Those in the water were either swimming for the nearest dockside ladders or were helping those who couldn't swim to safety.

For the royal party, that should have been the end of it: steered to safety and leaving law, order and rescue to the officials and the platoons of soldiers that were now forcing their way towards the dock frontage. However, Magnus was incandescent with rage. He shrugged off the soldier attempting to lead him to safety and, despite the chaos all around them, he advanced towards the man with the torn shirt, drawing his ceremonial sword in the process. "I am no rapist, sir!" he snarled, his words barely audible above the general bedlam. "And I'll have your tongue for suggesting it." For a second, Alicya was terrified that her brother was going to commit murder in public, but thankfully, he stopped three paces short of the accuser and held his sword-tip to the man's chin. "Retract your words, dog. Or die like one."

The man just looked back at Magnus impassively. He then held up a gauntlet which he had wrenched from one of the officials in the earlier struggle and threw it flat into Magnus' face.

An exclamation of shock went up from the crowd, nearby. Magnus just stared back at his adversary, appearing unmoved. "Very well," he said. "If that's the way you want it." He lowered his sword and without turning around he raised his voice by several decibels. "Mr Nash."

"Yes, Your Royal Highness?" responded the unflappable Nash. The Head of Royal Security had already moved silently to within three paces of the duo.

"Relieve two of our men of their pistols, please."

A whoosh of emotion went up from the assembled crowd, who had all now retreated to a safe distance from the edge of the docks: emotions of shock, consternation, excitement and anticipation. At the same time, Queen Maud was whittling incoherently until her husband calmed her down with a few unheard words in her ear. Meanwhile, Alicya observed the briefest of doubts cross John Nash's face, but then it was gone. Nash wasn't a man for displaying emotions, and certainly not in public. He also knew better than to question his prince in public. Instead, Nash turned without a word, approached two of his men, and walked back towards the pending duellists with two identical-looking, single-shot flintlock pistols, both roughly twelve inches long, with wooden handles and shiny metal barrels. He handed one to Magnus, who firmly sheathed his sword before taking it. Nash then handed the other to the man with the torn shirt.

"Might I know your name, sir?" asked Magnus.

The man with the torn shirt ignored him, instead studying his pistol. "I demand a switch," he said.

Magnus' top lip tightened at yet another slur, but he held his hand up before Nash could intervene. "It's all right, Nash. By all means – swap them over."

Once the swap was done, Nash saw no point in drawing this out. He immediately started barking out orders to his officials, commanding them to get the public and those being rescued from the dock-waters to positions of safety. With the public moving backwards, they had now left behind a long unoccupied stretch of dockside as well as clearing the access point to the two jetties which stood between the dockside frontage and the two recently christened merchant ships. The jetty to the *Queen Maud* was now going to double up as part of a duelling track. Nash then called in the duellists to the dockside end of the *Queen Maud* jetty, and a relative silence fell over the docks.

"You will stand back-to-back," announced Nash. "Both pistols are primed and loaded. I will count to ten, and at each count, you will take a step away from your opponent. After the tenth step, I will shout 'turn'. You will level your pistols, but you will not fire until I announce the word 'fire'.

Do you understand."

"I understand," agreed Magnus.

"Rapist!" responded the other man.

Alicya saw the veins pulsating on Magnus' neck and forehead. She doubted he had ever been this full of rage before – and yet, somehow, he managed to control himself. "You have uttered your last," he hissed.

"The Lord will protect me," the man responded, grimly. "But he won't protect the likes of you."

Alicya could scarcely take it in. This man was convinced of Magnus' guilt. And it was all happening so quickly. There had been a carnival atmosphere only five minutes ago. Now, her brother might be seconds from death. "Magnus, please," she shouted from the safety of the dockside.

"Be quiet, Alicya," he ordered.

"Turn gentlemen, please," requested Nash, who had now retired to a safe distance on the dockside himself.

Both men turned, now back-to-back, pistols raised. Alicya was mortified to note that Magnus would be walking out down the jetty while his opponent would have the benefit of firmer dockland ground. It seemed not to be worrying Magnus, though.

"Release your safety catches."

Both men complied.

"On my count. One, two, three…"

Alicya found that she was holding her breath, her entire body tense. She briefly wondered if there was any way she could intervene, but immediately put that thought to one side; that would dishonour Magnus even more. He would *never* forgive her.

"Four, five, six…"

Alicya quickly looked to her parents. Her father had a stoic look on his face and eyes drilled on the unfolding tableau before him. Her mother could not look, and had her head buried in her father's ermine cloak.

"Seven, eight, nine…"

The crowd's reaction was a kaleidoscope of emotion. Most were tense and open-mouthed, some were horrified, while others were actually grinning in anticipation. The last thing Alicya noticed was the woman holding the baby. Her look sent a chill down Alicya's spine. It was hatred, revenge, justice. She clearly had no doubt as to the outcome.

"Ten," announced Nash. "Turn."

Both men turned and levelled their pistols. You could now hear a pin drop.

"F-".

There wasn't time for Nash to complete the word. Magnus' pistol had already been discharged. His opponent fired a split-second later but had clearly been affected by Magnus' astonishing speed. The man's bullet ripped past Magnus' head to his left and buried itself in the stern of the *Queen Maud*. Before that impacted, though, Magnus' bullet had taken the man between the eyes.

"Noooooo!" cried the woman. "Noooooo, Samuel!" she shrieked, as she ran towards her fallen husband. "My Samuel," she sobbed, reaching him and cradling his ruined head with one hand, her baby still cradled in the other arm.

Magnus, meanwhile, had barely stirred on the jetty, although Alicya could read triumph beneath his implacable mask. She half-expected him to blow the end of his pistol, but he did not. He eventually lowered his shooting arm as Nash joined him, and silently handed the pistol to the Head of Royal Security. One of Nash's men went to retrieve the other pistol from the dead man's hand.

The inconsolable woman then looked up at Magnus – to find her anguish met without pity. Magnus leaned in towards Nash. "Make sure you charge her for the damage to the *Queen Maud*."

CHAPTER 6 — DAVY

3rd Tertiar, 1789 — Day 94, 10:00

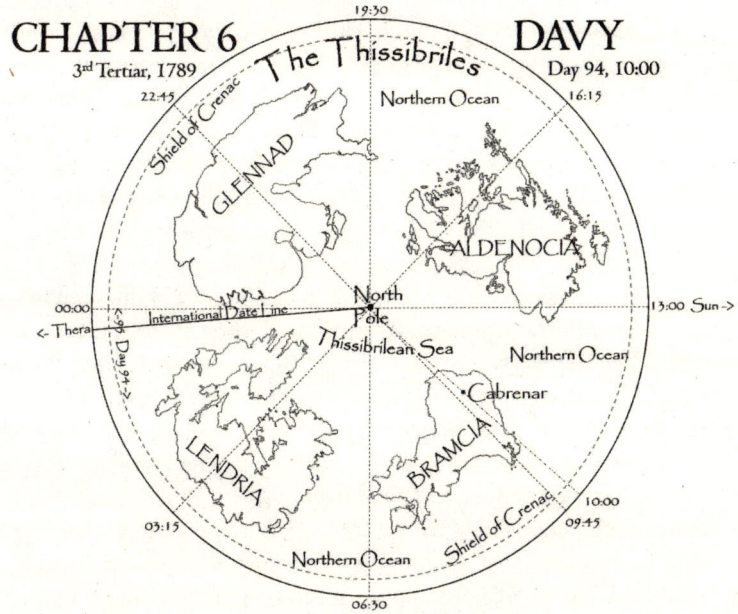

Davy Sheerin hacked one last time at the coal face with his pickaxe, and felt the whole section loosen and drop to the floor. "All right, lad," he said, turning away from the plumes of coal dust. He pushed his miner's cap back and wiped sweat and grime from his forehead. "I reckon that's enough for now. Let's have us some lunch."

His apprentice, young Will Lowe beamed back at him, then sat down on the floor, reached into his pocket and pulled out his lunch which was wrapped up in a grubby old cloth. Davy settled down beside him and arranged both safety lamps on the floor so that they had plenty of light. Despite the air still being full of coal-dust, and both having filthy hands, Will took a bite out of his first sandwich that his Mam had packed for him last night. "Cheese," he said, through food-muffled lips.

Davy took a bite out his. "Same," he said.

For the next five minutes, they ate their lunch in companionable silence, both listening to the familiar noises coming from up and down the length of the roadway; the crunch of pickaxes and the *chink, chink, chink* of hammer and chisel; the heavy rumbling of coal wagons – or corfs as they were also known – ferrying their bounty back up the roadway towards the main shaft, and the lighter rumbling as empty wagons returned; and above all of that, the chatter and banter of their brotherhood below ground.

Will had been with Davy for four weeks now and was proving to be a real asset, despite only being twelve years old. Only nine years older, but already a veteran, Davy was a hewer, one of many coal-cutters working this particular seam, and he'd been teaching Will the ropes and educating him on the different configurations of coal galleries and of the dangers that each held. Will also helped Davy shovel up the loosened coal into their waiting wagon. Once they'd filled the wagon, it was Will's job to move it from the coal face to the base of the lift shaft; a role known as a hurrier. Previously, Will had been a trapper – a role nearly always fulfilled by a child, sometimes as young as four or five, who opened and closed wooden trap doors inside mines to allow the wagons to pass through – an act which also allowed fresh, cooler air to flow into the mine. For that job, Will had often sat in total darkness for up to thirteen hours at a time, waiting to let the coal wagons through the door. Davy smiled to himself. There was no wonder Will was enthusiastic about his current role!

"Right, young man," said Davy, shaking out the crumbs and then screwing up his lunch cloth before putting it back into his jacket pocket. "Let's see you work that safety lamp again before we fill the wagon up."

"Easy-peasy," responded Will with another of his beams. He then blew out the flame on his lamp, shook the lamp gently to ensure the wick was immersed with oil and then hit the thin metal striker bar at the base of the lamp with the heel of his hand. The flint struck first time, ignited the wick, and the lamp flared into life. He then adjusted the screw underneath the safety lamp to expose more of the wick, and the flame grew to fill the gauze container inside which it was housed. Naturally, this success prompted yet another beam from Will.

Davy couldn't help but smile back. "All right, clever clogs," he said. "Why don't you tell me why we need safety lamps."

"Because of the fire-gases," responded Will, the whites of his big blue eyes widening amid a blackened face.

"Which are?"

"Gases found in mines – like methane – and which are most likely released from the goaves when we hack the coal away."

"And what can happen then?"

"The gases can react to naked flames. An exposed candle can ignite them. Especially methane. And methane is lethal because we can't smell it, so we get no warning. The first you know about it, is when the flame turns blue – but by then, you're already toast!"

"Very eloquently put, young man," said Davy, approvingly, recognising one of his own phrases.

"Got a good 'un there, Davy," shouted a voice from the next bay.

"He's got the best teacher, Robbie," replied Davy.

"Give over, man. Give the lad some credit."

"Oh, he's good, mate, I agree." Davy turned to Will. "In fact – why don't you explain to Uncle Robbie next door, why the flames in the safety lamp *don't* trigger gas-related explosions – seeing as how Robbie's never understood it himself," he added, with a smirk.

"Piss off, Sheerin!" came his best friend's jocular reply.

Will was happy to oblige. "So, when the fire-gas meets a naked flame, it ignites the gas and it explodes outwards," he said, flinging his hands out in opposite directions. "So, if you're in a tunnel like ours, it shoots all the way along the fire-gas, igniting it as it goes, burning anything in its path; men, wooden pit-props and even the coal itself."

Will looked up at Davy, who just nodded his head and gave him the thumbs up. "So," continued Will, "to stay safe, we have to shield the naked flame. In the safety lamp, this is done by putting the wick inside a gauze shield. Then, when gas is released in the mine, it still comes into contact with the flame, and the gas still passes through the gauze…but the flame doesn't escape. They get trapped inside. They can't," Will screwed up his face in concentration, "what's the word?" His face then lit up. "Flames can't *propagate* through small holes."

Robbie had crossed into Davy and Will's bay and was looking at the boy in wonder. Will hadn't noticed. He hadn't quite finished yet. "The way it was explained to me," he continued, frowning as he tried to remember the right words, "was that the metal wires that form the gauze, absorb most of the heat from the flame, cooling it so it isn't hot enough to ignite the fire-gases." He looked up and saw Robbie's open-mouthed face next to the safety lamp he was holding up.

"You are totally wasted down here, son," said Robbie. "You need to get yourself to school and then university. Propper boffin, you'll make."

"Nah, that's not me," replied Will. "And in any case, me Mam'd never let me. Needs the money too much."

"What does your old man do?"

"He hasn't got an old man, Robbie," said Davy gently. "He was down here in '79."

"Oh God, Will. I'm sorry, mate. I didn't know."

"That's OK, Robbie," responded Will, affably. "I was only two."

That made it worse for Robbie; he was now truly mortified.

"So, it's just me Mam, me and me twin brother, Dylan," finished Will, inadvertently twisting the knife a little more.

All Robbie could do was lean forward and pat Will on the shoulder, while Davy wondered again how Will and Dylan's Mam had kept her family out of the workhouse. "Aye, it was a bad one," said Davy eventually, if only to just say something and break the awkwardness.

Will looked at Davy. "Would you mind explaining to me what happened please, Davy? People shy away from telling me because of, well…" he tailed off. "I have a right to know," he finished.

Davy had a quick look up and down the runway for any sign of the foreman, well aware that his latest hewings needed shovelling up into their wagon. However, the innocent appeal on Will's face was impossible to ignore. "All right" he said, sitting back down on the floor, cross-legged. Will and Robbie joined him, three safety lamps on the floor now forming a warm arc of yellowish light around them. Further afield, the comforting noises of the mine and the men continued.

"So," began Davy, his eyes fixed downward on the mine's floor. "This all took place the year before the safety lamp was invented. Basically, ninety-three men and boys," he said, flicking a glance at his two listeners, "would still be here today if they'd invented it a year earlier. But they hadn't. And we weren't the first. My Da reckons that over sixteen thousand miners were killed by explosions before 1780 in Bramcia alone – but the government always keeps those kinds of numbers under wraps.

"Anyway, in late '79, I'd have been your age," said Davy, in a moment of realisation. "And I was doing the same as you – working as apprentice to old Russ Evans. Old Russ was a fireman – someone who tested the mine for fire-gas prior to every shift. I can see him now, shuffling forwards on his hands and knees, holding a candle out before him."

"Why was he on his hands and knees?" asked Will.

"For protection," answered Davy. "Although I use the term loosely. I mean, he did have protective clothing with a thick hood – which was made of leather and pre-dampened. That's why they were nicknamed 'penitents' or 'monks' as well – you know, because of the hooded garb and the kneeling. And obviously, they were down low to the ground hoping that any ignited gas would pass over the top of them.

"Anyway, as he went, the candle was held at arm's length in one hand, with the other shielding everything but the tip of the flame. Every now and then, he raises the candle, and if the tip stays the same, it means that part of the mine is free from fire-gas. But if the tip turns bluish-grey, and starts to increase in height, then your fire-gas is present. Now the fireman – he can't panic. He has to slowly lower the candle, shuffle backwards – keeping the flame covered with his other hand at all times – and then the foreman will consult with the mine owner about how best to ventilate the area. Sometimes, if there wasn't a lot of the gas, they used to deliberately fire it before the next shift commenced – you know – just to burn it out."

"What happened to the fireman if the fire-gas ignited?" asked Will.

"He prayed hard, kept his head down and as soon as the explosion passed over, he had to stand up – well, as much as he could, depending on the gallery – you know, to avoid the worst of the after-gas."

Noticing Will's frown, Robbie joined in. "The after-gas is what's left after the explosion or firing. It's toxic. And the worst one is carbon-monoxide – that's lethal – because we can't breathe it."

"And hence it kills you, very quickly," finished Davy.

"Is that how my Da died?"

Davy and Robbie looked at each other. "Probably," admitted Davy.

"So, it was quick then?"

"Almost certainly."

"Good, I'm pleased," said Will, his eyes briefly distant, perhaps trying to picture his Da's face. He then refocused. "So, what exactly happened then? And were you down here when it happened, Davy?"

"Me and Robbie had just gone off shift. Your Da and a hundred others had just started. But for some reason that no one knew at the time, and we still don't know why today, five of the men on our shift had stayed down the mine. They never clocked out. We should have been counted out, you see, but the Counter Man had already bunked off home and no one else knew about the five men – until after the disaster, of course – when none of them returned home."

"So, what happened to the five men?"

"We don't know. They were never found – although it wasn't just them who were never found. As for the explosions, they started just after six in the morning. There were seven of them, and the final one was so violent, it blew the lift right back up the shaft and into the headstocks – killed another seven workers in the immediate vicinity. Sorry to say, Will, mate, but your Da and all of those below ground never stood a chance. The only consolation is that no one suffered for long. See, usually, when we have these types of disasters, miners can survive for up to three days below ground, but often, they're horribly burned and later die from their injuries. Others survive for long enough for a rescue party to get them out, but they also die within twenty-six hours due to carbon monoxide poisoning. That's no way to go either."

"Oi! What's going on here, Sheerin?" demanded an approaching voice, unusually high-pitched for a miner. It was unmistakably the voice of Stan Eckersley, the foreman. All three miners jumped rapidly to their feet, but the bulging-eyed Eckersley wasn't finished with them. "What do think we're paying you for, eh lads? Not sitting around on your arses and gossiping like fishwives, that's for sure. Get that bloody wagon filled pronto, otherwise I'll be docking you half your wages."

"Sorry Mister Eckersley," responded Davy, his voice shaking. "We were just educating young Will here on the safety lamp, and how -."

"Educating my arse!" interrupted the sharp-featured Eckersley. "All he's here for," he said, nodding at Will, "is to get that coal shipped along to the foot of the shaft. Except there's little point when the wagon's bloody empty, is there?"

"I'm on it now, Mr E," said Davy, shovel already in action and loading up the wagon.

"If I catch you on your arse again, Sheerin, I might just fire you there and then – never mind half-wages."

A cacophony of coughing was suddenly emitted from the adjoining bay, in the middle of which was a word which sounded remarkably like "tosser". There was no way Stan Eckersley was going to let that go. He took five paces further up the roadway and lifted his lamp. "Robbie Russell! I might have guessed. Well, you can definitely go on half-wages this week for that." He directed a weak smile at Robbie, revealing his decaying teeth. "Now who's the tosser? Eh?"

"Aw, Stan!" whined Robbie.

"Don't you 'Aw Stan' me, you cheeky bugger. It's Mister Eckersley to you. Now get back to work, the bloody lot of you."

As Eckersley moved on down the line, there were rumblings of discontent that followed him all the way – from miners both old and young – and there was a lot stronger language than "tosser" used, too…

CHAPTER 7   JAKE
4th Tertiar, 1789   Day 95, 12:45

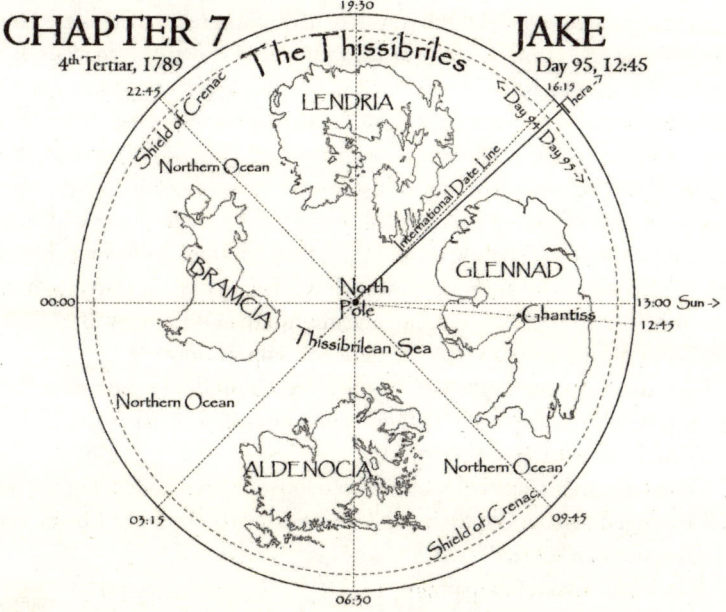

Jake Oscom had arrived back in Ghantiss the previous day – although he didn't look like Jake Oscom any more – off-centre nose apart. The wealthy three-storey house he'd gained entry to on the outskirts of the city had provided him with the beautifully-cut dark brown three-pieced merchant's suit that he now wore, along with very un-Jake-like white stockings and buckled shoes. The owners wouldn't even know they'd been broken into, courtesy of the entrance to the wine cellar having been left unlocked, and which had provided entry into the main house via a flight of internal steps. His disguise had then allowed him to move freely around the city, from one tradesman's premises to another, using his new persona's natural conversational skills to find out what he needed without raising suspicion – albeit without success, so far.

Today was also proving unfruitful: butchers, grocers, milliners, tailors. Hence as he turned into Sadler Gate, Jake knew he was relying on outrageous luck to get to the girl first, given the number of agents Nash would have on the case. Indeed, Nash had perhaps already found her – in which case Jake would need to leave Ghantiss alone, but at least knowing he had tried to help. That would feel bad, though.

Jake was about to enter the first shop on his left – a tanners – when he noticed three gentlemen entering a bakery further down Sadler Gate on the other side. Something about the way they had swaggered in had alerted him. Abandoning the tanners, Jake casually sauntered down the road until he reached the haberdashers next door to the bakery. He stopped, apparently interested in the window-dressings, although his eyes were diagonally riveted to the shop to his left – where there were now clear sounds of an altercation. Seconds later, a couple of outraged customers were pushed out into the street, empty-handed of pastry, by a brutish-faced thug, heavily moustached and heavily eyebrowed. The thug looked right then left, took in the well-dressed but startled merchant in front of next-door's haberdashers, glared at him – and then shut the bakery door, turning around the OPEN sign to CLOSED. He then drew the curtains over the door and shop window.

Jake turned to one of the ejected customers, a middle-aged professional dressed much like himself. "Is there some kind of a problem, sir?" asked Jake, in his best cultured accent.

The man and his lady companion both looked quite shaken, but the man still managed to sound indignant. "Not in all my years have I been man-handled out of a bakery!"

"But why?" asked Jake, simply.

"Peasants, sir," replied the man, haughtily, whilst dusting down his coat. "Something to do with the baker's daughter, I believe." And with that, he steered his female companion away and up Sadler Gate.

Inside, Jake was exulting. His instincts had been right, and these likely were Nash's men. His mind was now turning over how to play the situation. Should he go in, claiming to be a customer? He soon shut that action down; not really an option, given the bakery was now 'closed'. And loitering up and down outside the bakery would look far too suspicious. Making his mind up, Jake went into the haberdashers, the welcome bell jingling as he entered.

"Can I help you sir?" asked the haberdasher from behind his counter.

Jake looked at him, noting his dapper attire, olive complexion and slicked-back black hair that emphasised his widow's peak. "Yes, I'm looking for gold buttons that match these on my waistcoat," said Jake. "I have another the same but lost one of the buttons last week."

"One moment, sir," said the haberdasher, as he lifted the counter bar and walked towards the back of the shop, where shelving covered the entire rear wall. He pulled out a wooden stepladder and ascended a couple of steps to give him access to the top shelf. Jake, meanwhile, was watching the street outside. Just as the haberdasher found what he was looking for and descended the stepladder, the door to the bakery opened and the three men stepped out into the street, two of them holding a young girl firmly between them – who Jake was relieved to see *wasn't* the girl who had interrupted Magnus' sport; too tall, for starters. Inevitably, the girl was distressed, as was the baker and his wife who followed them out, both imploring the men to leave the girl alone; the baker and his wife made an odd-looking couple, too: he tall and thin, she small and round. During the action, Jake also noticed that one of Nash's men was missing his left eye, which he had presumably lost when he'd acquired the vivid scar that ran from his forehead down to the bottom of his cheek. Not a face to meet on a dark night – or on any other night, for that matter.

"I think you'll find these to be a close match," the haberdasher was saying, until Jake shushed him. A flicker of annoyance crossed the shopkeepers face until he saw what Jake was focusing on. "What the deuce…"

Jake raised his hand again to quieten the man. The girl, who Jake noticed did at least have shoulder-length and dark reddish-brown hair, was protesting. "Get your stinking hands off of me, you ugly oaf!"

At that, the man with the heavy eyebrows promptly backhanded her across the face. The reaction from the baker and his wife was instant, the wife still holding a useful-looking bread knife. However, it looked significantly less lethal when Mr Eyebrows whipped out his rapier and pointed it at the baker's throat. "Get back inside, baker," he spat, spittle flying everywhere, "otherwise I'll run you through right here."

"Good Lord!" exclaimed the haberdasher.

Jake turned to him. "You've no idea what this is all about then?"

"Not a clue. They're good, honest people, Mr and Mrs Colin. They don't associate with ruffians like that."

"I suggest we go and offer our help then, Mr erm…"

"Oh, Mr Crowle. My family have been haberdashers in Ghantiss for three hundred years."

"Jack Morse," said Jake, using one of his aliases. "Furniture merchant."

The two men briefly shook hands before exiting the shop. The three villains and their guest had already disappeared up Sadler Gate, while a great wailing was now coming from within the bakery. A crowd had also gathered – daily shoppers and tradespeople who had witnessed the out-of-place altercation. Jake and Mr Crowle entered the bakery, with the baker and his wife relieved to see a familiar face. "Oh, Mr Crowle," sobbed the baker's plump wife, "they say they were Prince Magnus' men. They've got it into their heads that our Freya has had something to do with an assault on His Royal Highness."

"An assault on the Prince! Well, that's…that's…*preposterous*!" exclaimed Crowle.

"Not as preposterous as you might think," said Mr Colin, fingers massaging his forehead and thumbs massaging his temples.

"What! What do you mean, Rex?" asked Mrs Colin, craning her neck to look up at her husband.

"I…I shouldn't have been listening. But I overheard Freya and Emilya discussing something yesterday in whispers. I kept hearing Magnus' name mentioned. And something about a dog."

"Magnus! A dog! Our Freya!" Poor Mrs Colin was now even more confused.

Jake, however, had greeted the news with grim satisfaction. Forcing himself to keep his voice calm he asked: "Who is Emilya?"

"She's Danny Luca's daughter," explained Rex Colin. "The Luca's are friends of ours. They run a bakery on Irongate. Freya and Emilya are the same age, friends since they were little. They're still in the same class at school now -." Rex suddenly broke off with worry. "Do you think Emilya is in danger, too?"

"I think we should get up there right now," responded Jake.

"But what about our Freya?" wailed Mrs Colin.

"We know where she is," said Rex. "We've got witnesses. They'll soon realise this is a mistake and she'll be returned to us."

"We *don't* know where she is at all, you old fool!" responded Mrs Colin. "Those men could have been anyone. They hit her! We may never see her again!"

"Mrs Colin," said Jake, taking the baker's wife's pudgy hands in his. He looked earnestly into her confused eyes and gave her hands a reassuring squeeze. "I promise you, those men *were* from the palace. They work for a man called John Nash, who is Head of Royal Security."

Jake watched Mrs Colin's face flush first with relief and then confusion again. "But how do you *know* that?" she asked, frowning.

"Please, Mrs Colin. Trust me. Your daughter will be returned to you soon – as she had nothing to do with the assault."

"So, there *was* an assault?"

"The only crime committed was by Prince Magnus himself. Emilya got caught up in it by accident. And she is in much greater danger than your Freya. I need to go to Emilya now. I'll take your husband and explain everything along the way. Mr Crowle?" he said.

"Yes, Mr Morse."

"Please look after Mrs Colin. Mr Colin will be back soon and will explain everything." And with that, Jake took Rex Colin by the arm and steered him out of the bakery – leaving Mrs Colin and Mr Crowle looking at each other with their mouths wide open.

Eventually, Crowle found his voice. "Well, I can probably tell you one thing, Mrs Colin."

"You can?"

"Yes. I don't think our Mr Morse is a furniture merchant!"

CHAPTER 8   MAGNUS
4th Tertiar, 1789   Day 95, 13:15

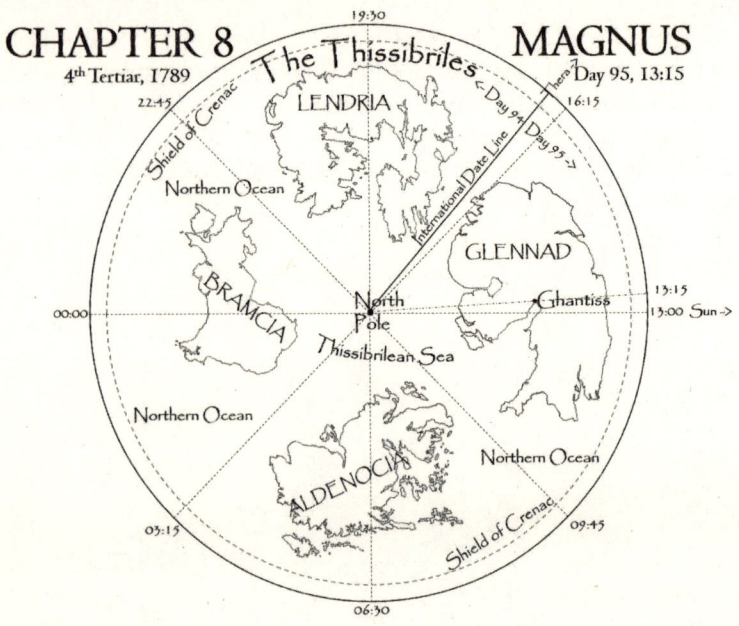

The two thugs escorted a still-protesting Freya Colin into the palace billiard room. "Do you mind," said Prince Magnus, briefly looking up from the billiard table with irritation. He then proceeded to play his shot, and only then did he turn around and look at the girl held between two of Nash's men. "It's not her."

The man with the heavy eyebrows stepped forward. "But Sir. She's fifteen, a tradesman's daughter, shoulder-length hair -."

"Her hair is too red, and it's straight, not curly. And have you checked her arm?"

"Her arm?"

"Yes, Hoskyns. Her arm. Must I do everything myself?"

Magnus stalked up to Freya and wrenched up the sleeve of her left arm to reveal smooth and unblemished skin. Freya then yanked her arm free, pulled the sleeve back down again and glared at the Prince.

"Another feisty one, mind," said Magnus, his expression mocking. "Is this a Ghantiss baker's daughter trait, perhaps?" he asked, eyebrows raised. He then took a step back and looked hard at Freya, his pupils assessing up and down, clearly making her uncomfortable. "And quite tall for one so young." He raised his fingers to her cheek – the opposite cheek from that bruised by Hoskyns earlier on Sadler Gate. "What secrets, I wonder…lie beneath here," he added, now looking her plain brown dress up and down again, this time with a more feral look in his eye.

Freya physically shuddered.

Magnus noticed, and was not impressed. He was, after all, the most handsome man in the kingdom. He briefly checked his reflection in the billiard room's large mirror. Not a hair out of place, stylish sideburns, chiselled chin. He turned back to Freya. "I really don't need your approval, my dear. You know that don't you?"

Freya maintained her silence.

"What is your name?"

Freya remained tight-lipped. It was Marler, the man with the long facial scar and missing eye, who responded. "She's the daughter of Rex and Peggy Colin, Sir. Both bakers. Most likely Freya Colin, aged fifteen."

Magnus turned to look at Freya again. "I don't suppose you know of any other fifteen-year-old tradesman's daughters, with..." he gently intertwined his fingers into her hair, "such lustrous dark red hair, and..." he moved his lips close to her ear and then gently took the top of her ear between his teeth, "nasty-looking dog-bites on her left arm." He pulled back slightly to look at her. "Do you?"

Freya was now ramrod straight, barely breathing. That, and something in her eyes gave her away. Magnus took a full step backwards in surprise. "You do, don't you?"

The fear in Freya's eyes sealed it for Magnus.

"Oh, Mr Hoskyns," he began. "You really do have the Luck of the Lendrian, don't you?"

Hoskyns just looked confused. Meanwhile, Freya had recovered. "I don't know what you're talking about."

"Oh yes you do," said Magnus, now walking right up to her again, nose-to-nose. "But you haven't thought this through, have you?"

Freya shrank away from Magnus' sherry-laden breath and took a stuttering step backwards. "What do you mean?"

"What I mean, my dear, is that I hold all the aces. You, your mother, and your father."

Freya's will finally broke. "You leave my parents alone!" she cried.

"And do you have any brothers and sisters?"

Freya's eyes darted left and right.

"Ah, you do. Younger, I suspect."

Freya's shoulders slumped slightly, before she looked back at Magnus defiantly. "What she said about you was all true."

"Well, very probably," agreed Magnus. "But that doesn't help you, does it? So, choose."

"Between my family and my friend, you mean?"

"Hoskyns," said Magnus, cocking his head. "Observe and digest."

"I'm sorry, Your Royal Highness?" Hoskyns was confused.

"He means, pug-face," responded Freya, glaring at Hoskyns, "that you're as thick as pig-shit!"

Magnus clapped his hands together, once, and then pointed at her. "Oh, I do like you, Freya Colin. In fact, I like you so much, I will return you untouched to your mother and father...*if* you tell me the name and address of the girl I'm looking for."

Freya's face creased in anguish. "I can't!"

Magnus issued a big sigh, and then put his hands together underneath his nose as if praying. He closed his eyes for two seconds, opened them and then dropped his hands. "I'll tell you what," he began. "I am so impressed with both you and your friend – honestly, I am – that I will leave you both alone – if you just tell me who she is."

Freya's response was a sardonic snort.

"All right, so you don't accept my kind offer then. That's fine Freya. I shall therefore instruct Mr Hoskyns here to re-visit your shop."

"Don't. Please don't."

"Oh, it's 'please' now, is it?" exclaimed Magnus, eyebrows shooting up a whole inch. "Look," he began, now attempting to sound reasonable. "I know I must seem very intimidating to you. Royal, impossibly rich, and no doubt lazy and indolent, too. And, yes, very low morals because I can do as I please. Etcetera, etcetera. But do you know what? I *will* make an exception with you and your friend. I pledge, here and now, that I won't hurt either of you. And neither will I hurt either of your families. I will just expect a little...something, in return. Do you understand what I'm saying?"

Freya remained silent, but Magnus could tell she was considering her predicament. He was also confident she would eventually assent – as she was clearly a clever girl, and all other options ended in bad things happening to her family. Sure enough, she eventually looked up at him. "You'll bring her here, she'll be with me, and you won't harm her?"

"I give you my word."

"We stay together at all times – me and her?"

"If that's what you want. I must say, the thought isn't...unappealing," he said, his top lip twitching. He briefly remembered the wild look in the urchin's eyes.

Meanwhile, Freya's head had dropped once again. "Oh God!" she exclaimed. "This is so hard!"

"Just relax Freya, and tell me who she is," coaxed Magnus. "You know it's your only sensible choice."

Freya issued another big sigh, but then straightened up. "She's called Emilya Luca. Daughter of Danny Luca who runs the bakery on Irongate. My family and hers have been friends for many years."

Magnus' face was triumphant. "Mr Hoskyns?"

"Yes, Sir."

"This time, I shall accompany the three of you. But before we go, please lock up Freya here in my bedroom and post a guard outside."

A brief sob escaped Freya's lips before she pulled herself together and glared at Magnus defiantly. Magnus responded with coldness. "We'll be back shortly, and all three of us can talk about this like adults. Are we agreed?"

Magnus saw hope enter Freya's face for the first time since she'd entered the room, although her tone remained sullen. "Agreed."

Oh dear, thought Magnus. You foolish child…

CHAPTER 9   JAKE
4th Tertiar, 1789   Day 95, 13:15

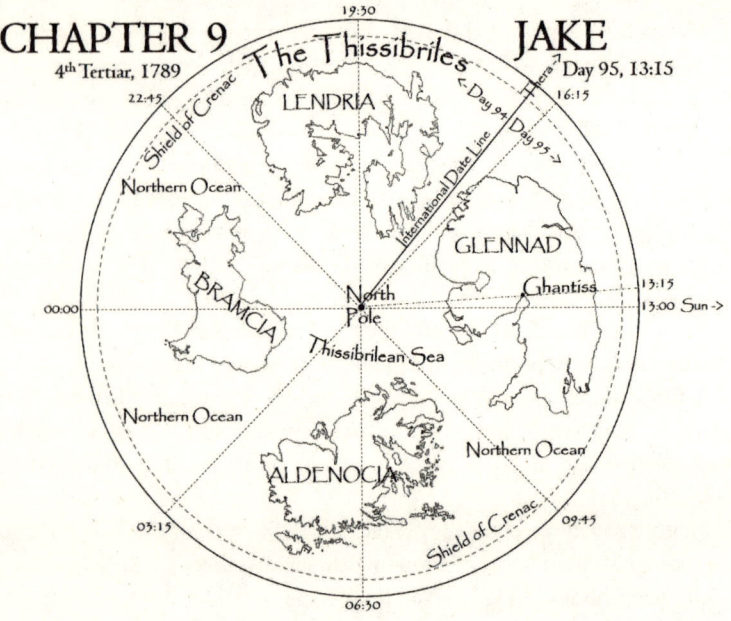

Jake and Rex walked briskly up Irongate and entered Luca's Bakery. Mimicking the action of Hoskyns earlier, Jake flipped the OPEN sign around to CLOSED. As Danny Luca took his money from the latest customer, he looked up and saw the two men. His face creased into a half-smile, half-frown at seeing his friend, Rex – who just waved back, giving Danny a tight smile. They waited until Danny had served the last two customers in the shop and then walked up to the counter.

"I'm sorry Danny, we've had to close your shop," said Rex, nodding at the sign over the door – which currently read OPEN from the inside. "We have some bad news."

"Emilya!" he cried. "I've only just sent her to get some coal. She's not…"

"We need to find her immediately, Danny. She's in great danger."

"This is about Prince Magnus and that dog, isn't it?"

"She's told you then?" asked Rex.

"She's told me everything. She was petrified that something would happen to Magnus after the incident. The last Emilya saw, Magnus had some brave man's cutlass at his throat –." Danny broke off, looking at the smartly-dressed merchant alongside Rex. "You're the man, aren't you? The man in the night shirt?"

"I am," said Jake. "My name is Jake Oscom. And it was my pleasure to assist. Your daughter is a remarkable and very brave young lady."

Danny stepped forward and shook Jake warmly by the hand, putting his other hand on top as well. "She's too brave for her own good," said Danny. "I don't know any other fifteen-year-old girl who'd go barrelling in on a group of men running a dog-fight." He paused, looking up and down at Jake's pristine brown and gold three-piece suit. "You don't particularly match her dress description, though."

"Listen, Danny," interrupted Rex. "We need to find Emilya. Now." Rex quickly recounted events of the last half hour.

Danny was horrified. "But what about Freya?"

"We're pinning our hopes on Nash's men returning her unharmed when Prince Magnus confirms she's not Emilya," said Rex.

"In the meantime, we need to intercept Emilya before she comes back here and take her somewhere safe," added Jake.

"But where?" asked Danny. "Wait! She can go to her cousins in Dominniul. My sister runs a guest house there with her husband."

"Not a great idea, Danny," said Jake. "Depending upon how badly they want her, friends and relations of yours will be the first places they'll look when they realise that she's no longer in Ghantiss."

Danny Luca closed his eyes and let out a trembling breath. "But why is he going to these lengths?"

"Because the stories are true, Danny," said Jake. "He's a bored psychopath with a licence to do whatever he pleases. And at the moment, *this* is what he pleases."

CHAPTER 10   EMILYA
4th Tertiar, 1789   Day 95, 13:30

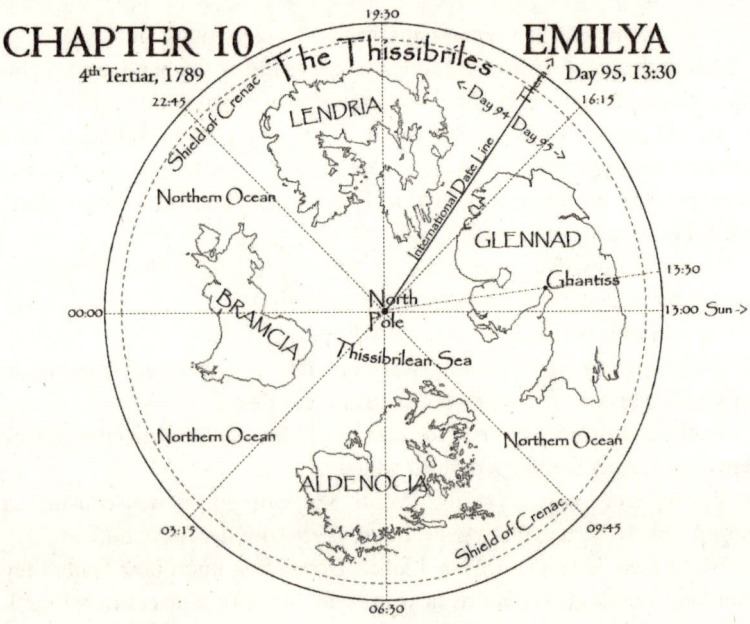

Emilya was pushing a wheelbarrow containing two large bags of coal up Fullers Gate, as ever, dressed in her brown tomboy outfit. She was halfway up, when her father came rushing around the corner accompanied by Rex Colin and -.

Emilya's heart missed a beat. It was the sailor in the night shirt – although considerably better dressed; more handsome in the daylight, too – in a rugged kind of a way. Unfortunately, his presence couldn't possibly mean anything good. She set down her wheelbarrow as the three men hurried towards her. "Father?" she asked, cautiously.

"Magnus has got Freya!" he said, breathlessly.

"What! Oh no! Oh, Rex, I'm so sorry."

"You've done nothing wrong, Emilya. Everyone knows he's a bully and a psychopath and...worse."

"The problem is, Emilya," added her father, "it's *you* that he wants."

"And he *will* get your address out of Rex's daughter, I'm afraid," said the well-dressed 'sailor', concern etched deep into his worldly brown eyes. "He may already have it. He may be on his way over, right now."

"Oh..." was all Emilya could manage, her mouth wide open. She looked at her father. "What are we going to do?"

As her father considered that question, Emilya turned back to Jake. "Thank you so much for what you did for me the other night. They *were* going to set that dog on me."

"Aye, I know they were, lass. Which is why they can't be allowed to get their hands on you again."

"I liked your sailor's accent, back then," said Emilya. "You certainly had me fooled."

"Release that dog, and I'll run you through right here," said Jake in his gruff sailor's voice.

Emilya laughed at that. "Prince Magnus' face was an absolute picture."

"I seem to remember it still being too cocky."

"You were very brave, erm?"

"Jake," he responded. "Jake Oscom."

"Emilya Luca...but I guess you've already worked that out."

"Yes, and actually, you're not far wrong. I was once a captain in the Bramcian Navy."

"But not now?"

"No. A long story."

Throughout the exchange, Danny watched them, agonising over the momentous decisions that had to be made without any time to consider them appropriately. Alarmingly, his only option appeared to involve entrusting his eldest, yet very young and vulnerable daughter, to a man he had only met for the first time, ten minutes ago. It was totally absurd that he was even *considering* such a thing – but did he have a choice? If the rumours about Prince Magnus were only half-true, he couldn't let his daughter fall into his hands, and he was silently praying that Freya Colin would come out of this unscathed, too. Danny eventually turned to Jake, his eyes beginning to glisten. He was struggling to come up with a way of asking.

Jake just took his hand between both of his, knowing what it was that Danny was unable to vocalise. "I'll take good care of her, Danny. I know enough tricks to get us to the south coast without being intercepted." Jake then gave Emilya's father a brief smile. It was a kindly smile, decided Emilya. "I'll take her to Lendria for a few months," he was saying. "Long enough for this to blow over. And you never know. Some vengeful father or husband might stick a dagger in Magnus' heart whilst we're away."

"Someone nearly did that down at Ghantiss docks, yesterday," said Rex, dryly.

"Lendria!" exclaimed Emilya, ignoring Rex's intervention, a look of stupefaction on her face. She then quickly re-focused. "But I've got no clothes other than these," she protested, holding both arms out. "And I'm not going anywhere without Theo."

"Who is Theo?" asked Rex.

"The little terrier, no doubt," answered Jake, with a smile.

"He was in such a bad way," said Emilya. "I can't leave him after giving him so much love and hope over the last three days."

"Saints preserve us, Emilya!" moaned her father. "The rest of the family will look after him. And in any case, he needs Elyse."

"Listen, I'll check ahead," said Rex, still on tenterhooks. "Make sure the coast is clear." His long legs then propelled him rapidly towards the top end of Fullers Gate.

"Elyse?" queried Jake, turning to Danny.

"She's a healer – of animals as well as people. She set and splinted Theo's broken leg, and treated his other wounds. It would be wonderful if Elyse could…" Danny tailed off, looking at Jake rather bashfully.

"No offence taken, Danny," responded Jake. "I would be full of disquiet, too, if I'd just entrusted my daughter to a stranger. Maybe Elyse will make that decision for herself, anyway. And I would welcome her assistance… and her presence as a chaperone!"

Danny Luca's features relaxed with relief and so Jake patted him on the arm. "Rest assured, Danny, that I will do everything to keep Emilya safe, whether Elyse joins us or not. But right now, we need to act. Let's get the dog, grab some clothes and then go and see Elyse."

"I'll write to you father," said Emilya as she picked up the wheelbarrow again.

"Best not, Emilya. Your letters may get intercepted."

Emilya looked to Jake for confirmation. "I wouldn't put it past him," agreed Jake.

"Oh, that man!" said Emilya through gritted teeth. She was about to push off with the wheelbarrow when she saw Rex, hurrying back from the corner where Fullers Gate met Irongate. He was as white as a sheet.

"Bad news!" he gasped. "We're too late. The royal carriage has just pulled up outside your shop!"

CHAPTER 11   MAGNUS
4th Tertiar, 1789   Day 95, 13:50

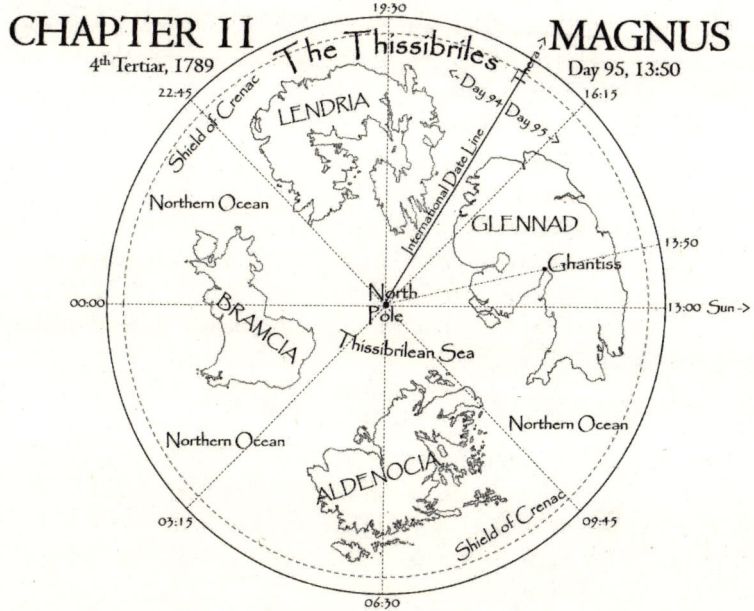

"Odd, don't you think," said Magnus, looking the empty shop up and down. "To be shut at lunchtime. I think we may be too late, Hoskyns."

"Your Royal Highness, gentlemen, my apologies."

Magnus turned around to see a breathless middle-aged, balding man in a baker's apron hurrying down Irongate towards them.

"An urgent matter of business. If I'd have known that I was going to have such an illustrious customer…"

"No matter, my friend," said the Prince, sweetly. "But I was told this morning that your steak pies are to die for, and hence I decided that there's no time like the present."

"I will be honoured to serve you, Your Royal Highness," said Danny, fumbling with his key in the lock. The door opened and Danny ushered them in, surreptitiously switching the sign from CLOSED to OPEN. As soon as his back was turned, Hoskyns switched it back again, whilst also giving a nod of the head to the one-eyed Marler – who promptly exited the shop and took a right turn.

"Are you going to have to cook them?" asked Magnus.

"Not at all, Your Royal Highness. I only popped out five minutes ago. Robert, my apprentice, will have some ready right now. Will you be wanting anything else with the pie?"

"Just the pie, for now, thank you. Times three if you please." And with that, Magnus and his two henchmen took a seat at one of the tables that was furthest from the bakery frontage, not wanting to attract undue attention.

"Just the three?" asked Danny.

"Yes, Mr Marler has business elsewhere."

"Right you are, Your Royal Highness."

All the time that Danny served them, Magnus was watching him like a hawk. The man was sweating profusely, and his eyes were all over the place. Danny Luca knew exactly why they were here, which meant that his daughter had explained to him what had happened three days ago. Nevertheless, even though the bakery was closed, it wouldn't do to make any unpleasant scenes, so the Prince was quite happy to play out the charade.

When the pies arrived, they were truly delicious. "My goodness me, Mr Luca," purred the Prince. "These pies really are fit for a prince!"

"Thank you, Your Royal Highness. You're most kind."

"Please," began Magnus. "Come and take a seat with us, and I'll explain my other business with you."

The look on Danny Luca's face was priceless, and Magnus could almost hear the baker's knees knocking together. To Luca's credit, though, he managed to keep his face straight and took a pew opposite the Prince. "Oth-, other business, Your Royal Highness?"

"Yes, I'm afraid so," said Magnus, taking another large bite out of his pie. He continued to chew for several seconds, apparently deep in thought. "You have a daughter, I believe."

Luca looked like he was about to pass out. "I do indeed, Your Royal Highness," he managed to croak, eventually, licking his dry lips in the process. "In fact, it's Tammy's eleventh birthday next month."

"Is that so? How nice. However, I was referring to your other daughter, Mr Luca."

"I...I...I don't have another daughter, Your Royal Highness. Just my son, Sammy – he's nearly ten."

"Hmm," responded the Prince, still apparently deep in thought. He took another bite out of his pie, chewed and swallowed before continuing. "So, we have some interesting things at the palace, Mr Luca – one of which is an enormous volume of information which goes by the name of 'The Ten-Year Census'. This reliably informs me that you had a seven-year-old daughter called Emilya in 1781 – which means that she should be, oh, round about fifteen right now."

Danny Luca was briefly paralysed, but then recovered, attempting to keep up the pretence. "She died, Your Royal Highness. Five years ago. Cholera. It was heart-breaking."

"Yes, I'm sure that it was," responded Magnus, with zero sincerity. "Ah," he began, looking over Danny's shoulder. "Good man, Marler. And what do we have there?"

Danny turned around to see the fourth man, the one-eyed Marler – who'd had apparent 'business elsewhere' – sidle into the parlour from behind the counter...holding a tiny dog in one hand. "It's just as you described it, Sir. At least one broken leg, half an ear missing, gashes all over. Someone's done a good job at patching it up though."

The tiny terrier mewled in fright, although it appeared as though Marler hadn't inflicted any further damage on it – yet.

As for poor Danny Luca, he now had little doubt that the game was up. His head went straight into his hands. "Your Royal Highness, please, she's my little girl...".

Magnus finished eating his pie before responding, also pausing to mop his lips with a serviette. "Now I really don't want to make a scene, Mr Luca. But are you aware of the penalty for lying to your prince?"

"What are you going to do with her?" asked Danny, boldly ignoring the Prince's question.

"I'm under no obligation to explain anything to you, Luca. But for what it's worth, I genuinely do admire her."

Danny looked at Magnus, the tiniest ray of hope dawning in his eyes.

"I do, I do," continued Magnus. "*And* her friend, Freya Colin. They are two extraordinary fifteen-year-olds. But we now have a situation, you see. Young Emilya, well, it's stretching the imagination to say that she *assaulted* me – I'll admit that much to you; 'defied me' is a better way of putting it. 'Humiliated me' is probably better still – although she is likely unaware of what happened after she departed the scene."

Magnus noted that Danny Luca was listening intently to every syllable, even though his follically-challenged head was still lowered. The fool was still hoping this episode might turn out all right for his family.

"My problem is, Luca," continued the Prince, "that a small number of people know what happened. And I cannot allow that knowledge to go public. Neither the humiliation nor the initial dog-baiting – as I do have a reputation to preserve." He paused for several seconds. "So, I'm prepared to buy your silence with an offer."

At that hardening of the Prince's voice, Danny looked up and met

Magnus' eyes.

"And my offer to you is very simple. You come to no harm. Your daughter comes to no harm. Even that ridiculous creature that Mr Marler is holding… will come to no further harm."

Danny was now looking confused.

"Oh yes," said Magnus with a wide, but ice-cold smile that didn't come anywhere near to reaching his eyes. "You weren't expecting that, were you?"

Danny could only manage to shake his head.

"There is a price, of course. Although it will be a very profitable one for you and young Emilya."

"Your Royal Highness!" said Danny, finally finding his voice. "If there is anything that I or my family can do to ensure that this whole episode remains buried, we will do it, I swear it."

"Excellent. Well, you will be surprised to hear, that the price for this being kept secret…is for both Emilya Luca and Freya Colin…to become apprentices at the palace. They will be taught how to become ladies in waiting to my sister, the Princess Alicya, and will be offered the opportunity to study at Ghantiss University when they turn eighteen years of age. For this, I expect everyone's silence."

Magnus broke off temporarily, annoyed by the terriers' continuous frightened mewling. "Oh, for heaven's sake, Marler. Put it back where you found it."

Marler promptly disappeared into the back-office and kitchen areas.

"So," said Magnus, turning to Danny. "What do you say?"

"I say," said Danny, with a new respect audible, "that you are very much misunderstood, Your Royal Highness. Your offer is extraordinary, and of course, I accept. With gratitude. And Emilya will also accept, I will ensure it."

"Excellent. So, all's well that ends well, then. May we speak with Emilya, now?"

"Well, that's a little tricky," said Danny, still clearly on tenterhooks. "You see, of course, she told me everything. And, of course, I feared the worst. Your reputation amongst the working class is unfairly misaligned, Your Royal Highness."

Magnus inclined his head in agreement.

"I therefore made arrangements two days ago for her to go and stay with my sister at her guest house in Dominniul."

Magnus looked hard at Danny Luca. Surely the man had bought his tale – hadn't he? "Well, that is a shame," he said, keeping his voice neutral. "But now that we have our little understanding, will you not arrange for Emilya to return to Ghantiss right away?"

"I will, Your Royal Highness. I will send a messenger."

"I have a better idea," said Magnus. "We will send your letter by the Royal Post – and we will bring her back direct to the palace via one of our royal coach teams. Is that fair?"

Luca didn't dare dodge that one. "Perfectly fair, Your Royal Highness."

"Excellent," said Magnus, rising to his feet. "Someone will return for your letter later this afternoon, a letter in which you will explain everything to Emilya – leaving her in no doubt as to how fortunate she has been. In the meantime, we will keep Freya Colin at the palace, and pander to her every whim!"

In other words, we have a hostage pending good behaviour.

"Your Royal Highness is most generous," said Danny, with a weak smile.

"Indeed. We will now leave you to re-open your bakery. And thank you once again for your most delicious meat pies," he added, drawing out three crowns from his money bag and handing them to Danny.

"Oh, I couldn't possibly, Your Royal Highness," declined Danny, holding up both hands.

"I insist," responded Magnus, posting the coins into one of the pockets on Danny' apron. "So long, Danny Luca," he said, before turning and swaggering towards the door which was now being held open by Marler. "Oh, and Mr Luca?" said the Prince, turning around on the threshold.

Danny looked up.

"Please, do look after your nearly-eleven-year-old daughter and your nine-year-old son."

Magnus' eyes bored into Danny's for several more seconds. His point made, he then exited the bakery and boarded the royal carriage, exceptionally pleased with his well-crafted little drama.

CHAPTER 12   EMILYA
4th Tertiar, 1789   Day 95, 13:55

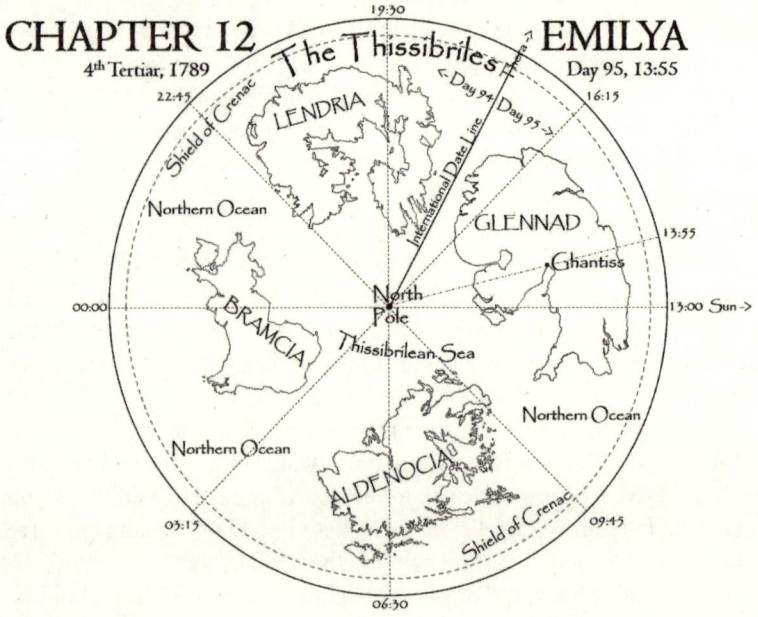

Emilya and Jake were watching the rear of her father's bakery from behind some beaded curtains. Albert, the white-haired, hunch-backed clockmaker, hadn't asked any questions when they'd asked to be admitted. Instead, he'd walked them upstairs to a rear bedroom. 'Dear Albert' as Emilya thought of him, had been an ever-present in her life, occupying the clock-making premises that backed onto their own since long before her father had taken over the bakery on Irongate.

The window from Albert's bedroom offered the perfect vantage point, and their vigil was soon rewarded when the head of a man with an evil-looking scar and missing eye appeared above the fence to their right. Emilya and Jake both moved back a step but could still see the adjoining back yards from the shadows behind the beads.

"One of Nash's men," whispered Jake. "He was one of the three who took Freya, earlier."

The man cast his single eye about from left to right and then seemed to look straight at them. Emilya issued a sharp intake of breath. Jake put his hand on her arm to calm her. "He can't see us," he whispered. "It's too shadowy in here, and the sun is behind us, too."

Sure enough, satisfied the coast was clear the one-eyed man hauled himself over the fence before entering the rear of the bakery. Emilya had already taken to biting her nails. *What was happening in there?*

Jake sensed her disquiet. "Your father will be fine, Emilya. There's no way Magnus will do anything in public in broad daylight. He'll just be trying to intimidate."

"So, what's that...*thing* doing in our back yard then?"

"Nothing good, admittedly. But there's nothing we can do until Rex comes back with the all-clear."

Hearing a noise, Jake turned to see Albert shuffling into the bedroom, carrying a tray of tea and oatcakes. "I thought you might be in need of refreshment," he said, setting the tray down on a small bedside table.

"My thanks again, sir," said Jake respectfully, before turning his eyes back on the rear of the bakery.

"Oh, it's nothing," said Albert, beginning to pour the tea into three blue and white china cups on blue and white china saucers. "I just hope that everything turns out all right for you – whatever it is that is so wrong." He then passed a cup and saucer each to Emilya and Jake.

Emilya immediately put hers down on a sideboard and took Albert's bony, vein-strewn hand in both of hers. "Dear Albert," she began. "My father will explain everything to you. I'm afraid I'll have to go away for some time, and…"

"Oh, there, there, my dear," began Albert, as Emilya's tears began to fall.

"Oh Albert," she cried, gently putting her forehead on the old man's shoulder. Albert put his hand to the back of her head and patted it but was only able to console her with a few more 'there, there's'. Emilya then took a step back and wiped her tears away. "But I will be back," she stated, her mind briefly pondering the awful thought that Albert might not still be around in a year's time.

"Yes, of course you will, my dear," agreed Albert

Another ten minutes passed before they heard a knock at the door, downstairs. Jake held up his hands to calm Emilya. "It'll be Rex. I'll go."

Sixty seconds later, Jake ushered Rex Colin into the rear bedroom. "They're gone, Emilya, and your father is unharmed – although he is a little shaken. You need to go in the back way, grab whatever you need, come back here…and I guess it's then over to Mr Oscom."

"Right," said Emilya, straightening her spine and lifting her chin.

"I'll come with you – just in case," said Jake.

"Me too," agreed Rex.

"I'll come too if you want," added Albert. "I've got a hefty stick somewhere around here," he said, looking behind the door. He came out holding a sturdy chestnut walking stick.

Despite their situation, both Emilya and Jake had to smile. "That won't be necessary, sir," said Jake.

Emilya just threw her arms around Albert and kissed him on the cheek. "I'll not put you in danger, Albert." She then paused. "Thank you for taking us in. And for all the lovely memories. I promise I'll come and see you as soon as I return."

"Godspeed, my dear."

Emilya then plunged out of the bedroom without looking back, her body racked with sobs. Jake shook Albert's hand, solemnly, and then followed her, with Rex trailing Jake. They quickly gained entry to the rear of the bakery where Emilya was overjoyed to see little Theo on his dog bed, although he was still looking very sorry for himself. She picked him up gently and kissed his face; Theo responded with several loving licks. Emilya then walked into the parlour to find the bakery still closed and her father sitting at a guest's table looking shell-shocked. "Father?"

Danny Luca stood up immediately and walked over to her. "Emilya," he said, putting a hand behind her head and pulling her towards him, taking care not to hurt Theo. He kissed her on her forehead.

"So, what happened?" asked Emilya, once they had parted.

Danny recounted his encounter with Prince Magnus, although he omitted the veiled threats about Emilya's brother and sister; she had enough worry on her plate already. At the mention of the palace apprentice offer, Emilya had just shuddered and confirmed that she didn't believe Magnus for one minute. *And one day, you will pay, too, my dear.* The Prince's flickering tongue had suggested the rest.

Emilya re-focused on the present, where Jake had just approved of Danny's strategy of mis-directing the Prince's search to Dominniul.

"There's no way I would put Emilya under the care of that man," Danny was saying. "He sat there," he said, nodding at the now vacant table, "eating my steak pie, revelling in his game, knowing damn well he was putting the fear of God into me. It was clear to me that people count for nothing in his eyes; we're all pawns in his game. I dread to think what he would do with my daughter if left to his own devices."

"It doesn't help *my* daughter much, though, does it?" said a pale and drawn-looking Rex.

Emilya watched as her father's mouth dropped open. He'd been so ravelled up in trying to extricate his own daughter from this mess that he'd forgotten about Freya's predicament: at the mercy of a man with an alleged reputation of doing as he pleased with young girls.

Danny was still at a loss for words, so Rex spoke his mind. "Will you come with me to the palace and help me bring her home, Danny? Later today? We can even agree to the apprentice and university thing. Anything to get my Freya away from there, then we take stock later."

"Danny patted Rex on the shoulder. "Of course, I'll go to the palace with you Rex. But please, let's get Emilya on her way first."

Emilya handed Theo over to Jake, and then embraced her father properly, clinging on until Danny pulled back. "Emilya," he said, cupping her tormented face in his hands. "You must go and pack your things, now. Take the large carpet bag in my room. But please be quick."

Without a word, Emilya ran into the back room and then up the stairs, grabbed her father's carpet bag, and then went into her bedroom. Despite the urgency, she couldn't help but stop and look around, taking everything in; who knew how long it would be until the next time. Every object in this room was of the utmost importance to her. Her eyes fell on Jemima, her wooden doll, remembering the Christmas Day when she had found her sitting under the Christmas tree. She picked Jemima up and ran her hand over the velvet skirts, training herself to remember how it felt – as Jemima could not possibly travel with them. Neither could Neddy, the hobby horse, all chipped and battered now, courtesy of many-a-ride and many-a-tussle with her siblings and cousins – front-ways, backwards, kneeling, upside-down. Emilya couldn't help but smile at the memories, the tumbles and the jumbled-up bodies. Then there were her other possessions – kites, puzzles, board games, stick horses, and so many books. This room had been her sanctuary for all of her fifteen years. But now…

Emilya gritted her teeth and then dived into her wardrobe and chest of drawers, cramming as much clothing as she could into the carpet bag. She then hurried downstairs, where she found Jake still holding a docile Theo. Emilya's heart swelled to see him. Theo was worth a thousand Jemima's and Neddy's; he was even worth her banishment, because had she not intervened, Theo would be dead now. And he needed her. He also needed Elyse before they left Ghantiss. She needed Elyse, too: at the very least to show how to treat Theo and to provide them with a supply of her magic salve.

Emilya went first to Rex. "I'm so sorry, Mr Colin," she began. "Please tell Freya that I'm sorry. I had no idea…" she tailed off. Then, for the first time in her life, she embraced her best friend's father.

Rex Colin was deeply touched. When they parted, he echoed old Albert. "There, there, my dear," he said, placing his hand gently on her cheek.

"You're a lovely girl, Emilya. And you've done nothing wrong."

"Oh Rex! It doesn't feel as if I've done nothing wrong," she cried. "It feels as if I am devastating lives."

"There's only one person doing that, and it's not you. Safe travels, Emilya."

"Please tell Freya that I love her."

"I will. Now, as your father says, you must hurry. We could get picked off any time standing here." Rex then turned back to Danny. "And I need to get back to my Peggy. She'll be worried sick."

As soon as Rex left the shop, Emilya turned to her father for one last time and voiced one of her many fears. "What do you think Magnus will do when he finds out I'm not at Auntie Prue's?"

"I shall tell him you must have decided it was too risky to go there and that I have no idea where you are."

"He won't believe you."

"Perhaps," agreed Danny. "Nevertheless, I will play the desolate father, frantic with worry for his missing daughter. It shouldn't be too difficult," he added wistfully. "Maybe I could lead him on a wild goose chase all over his wretched kingdom, until he loses interest!"

"Or until he finds another target and forgets all about Emilya," suggested Jake.

Emilya wanted to believe them both, but she feared that Prince Magnus enjoyed his sport too much, and didn't back down at any cost – as he had proven only yesterday, by all accounts, following some altercation in the docks and a subsequent duel.

Her father then took her face in his hands again. "We *will* see each other again, my darling, and soon. There *will* be happier times." He kissed her once on the forehead, and then gently ushered Jake and Emilya out into the back yard and across to Albert's yard.

Emilya held on to her father's hand until the last moment. Then she turned and followed Jake back into Albert's house, and to goodness knows where beyond there.

CHAPTER 13   DAVY
4th Tertiar, 1789   Day 95, 24:10

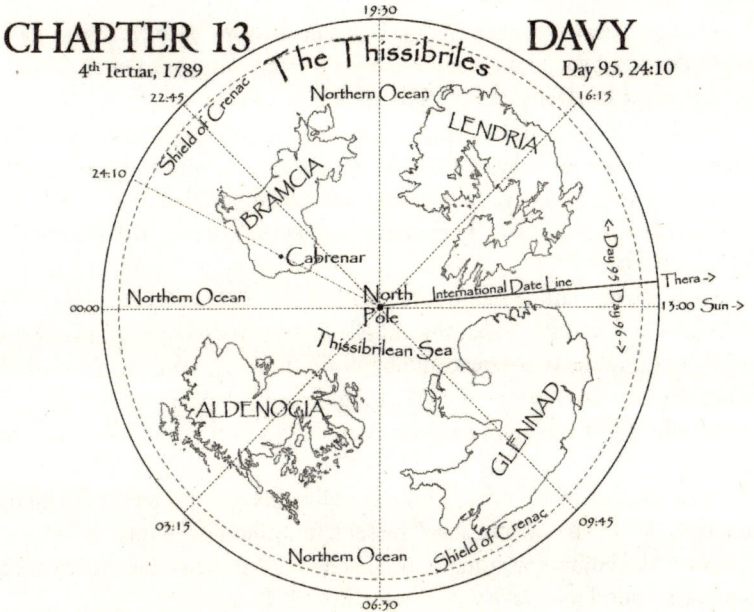

"What am I going to do, Davy?" slurred Robbie. He was sat across a table from Davy in the Red Dragon, a tankard of ale held fast in one hand, his other propping up his dark, stubbled chin. Davy noticed that he hadn't cleared all of the grime off his face, although to be fair, he'd not long since completed a double shift, and at least he'd changed out of his filthy pit clothes into a brown sleeveless woollen waistcoat with a white linen shirt underneath. "What am I going to do?" he repeated.

"Well, keep your stupid mouth shut for starters," Carys was saying, casually tucking a strand of fair hair behind her ear. "And for seconds, do double shifts for another four days to make up for your own idiocy."

"You see, Davy," said Robbie, holding his hand out, his grey-green eyes twinkling. "This is what happens when you make an honest woman out of 'em."

Davy couldn't help but smirk at Robbie's comment, for which his friend got the desired result from both wife and sister-in-law.

"You cheeky sod, Russell!" came Carys' sharp retort.

"Yeah, give over, Robbie. You'll put Davy right off," complained Daisy.

"Yes, we'll be having words, later, Robert," added Carys, eyeballing her husband.

Davy just laughed and took hold of his fiancée's hand. "You wouldn't scold me in public like that, would you, Daisy?"

"I'm sorry, boys," replied Daisy. "But I'm with my sister on this one. I might not scold you, but I wouldn't be very happy with you, either."

"Oh, come on, Daisy!" cried Robbie. "I only called him a tosser."

"Yes, but he's your supervisor, you dimwit!" objected Carys, back on the attack, her blue eyes bulging. "You know. The person who you're supposed to respect – *and* who pays your wages," she added pointedly.

"Old Eckersley doesn't pay my wages," objected Robbie. "Jed Morris, the mine owner does."

"Now you're splitting hairs."

"And why should I respect the old git, anyway. We were teaching Davy's apprentice, young Will Lowe, all about safety lamps. And then he asked about '79. Eckersley just read it all wrong."

"So what? Just apologise next time, go back to work…and *don't* call him a tosser."

"All right, girl, all right," said Robbie rolling his eyes. "I can see I'm going to have to sort you out later, love," he said, his mouth twitching.

Carys looked back at him, quite unable to keep the smirk off her face. "Ooh, it's a good job I love you, Robbie Russell!"

"That's a 'yes' then, is it?"

"I'm surprised you've got the energy after a double shift."

"There you go, Davy," he said with a wink. "She never turns me down. Ouch! That hurt!"

"Good!" responded Carys, flexing the palm that had just stung her husband's shoulder.

Robbie issued a sheepish grin before taking several long swigs of ale, whilst Carys looked across the table at Davy and Daisy and rolled her eyes. Davy smiled again and squeezed Daisy's hand – at which point, she lay her fair head affectionately on his shoulder. Her hair smelled of honey and lemon. *How lucky am I?*

"Oi, you two," said Eric, the landlord, who was passing the table with four foaming tankards in his massive paws. "No canoodling in here," he added, winking at the two of them, a huge grin on his face.

"Right you are, Eric," said Davy.

"Is Will Lowe one of Edyth Lowe's lads?" asked Carys, changing the subject.

"Aye," confirmed Davy. "Will and Dylan are twins. His brother works in another seam apprenticed to Jack Musson."

"They're ever-so polite whenever we see them in the street, those boys. And them without a father, too."

"Oh, Will Lowe's an absolute diamond, Carys," said Davy. "Real clever, too."

"He's a right boffin, that's what Will Lowe is, Carys," said Robbie, joining in. "He blinded me with science earlier today, telling me exactly how a safety lamp works. In the deepest mumbo-jumbo detail, too."

"I often wonder how poor Edyth kept those lads out of the workhouse, though," said Davy, a frown creasing his brow. He then noticed the knowing look that passed between Carys and Daisy. "Oh, you're joking!" he exclaimed. "Please tell me it didn't come to that?"

"Well, what's the poor woman supposed to do, Davy?" said Carys. "It's either that or -."

"- the workhouse," finished Davy, shaking his head in dismay. "What a rubbish world we live in."

Daisy put a long arm around him and kissed his cheek. "Hey, you," she said, patting his rust-coloured woollen waistcoat. "Things aren't that bad, are they?"

Davy smiled at her and kissed her back on the cheek. "Not for me they aren't, love. I couldn't be happier. But not everyone is so fortunate."

"Thank God for safety lamps, that's all I can say," said Carys.

"Aye," agreed Robbie, now somewhat less morose. "We ought to count our blessings, really."

Davy raised his tankard. "I'll drink to that." Four tankards clashed together, after which Robbie drained his. "Time for another, I think."

Carys put her hand over the top of Robbie's tankard. "I think not, Rob. You two need to be up at five, sharp."

Davy and Robbie looked at each other and the smiles drained from their faces. "You had to go and ruin it, didn't you?" said Robbie. "You see, mate, this is what it's going to be like."

Despite his reticence at having to get up so early, Davy put both arms around Daisy and hugged her tight. "Bring it on, mate."

He then noticed the ape-like duo of Bryn Gascoigne and Rhod Brush staring at him from the next table, both of their mouths wide open, tankards held in mid-air. "Sheerin!" said Gascoigne, eventually. "Do you want me and Rhod to barf all over Eric's nice clean floor, or what?"

CHAPTER 14 — ALICYA

5th Tertiar, 1789
Day 96, 15:20

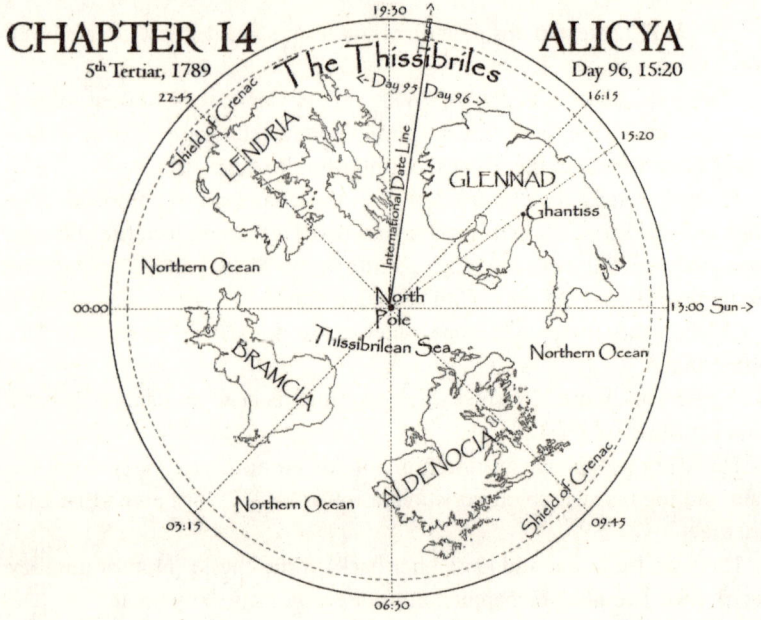

Alicya laughed delightedly as she rode her graceful new filly, Tabetha, across the palace meadows, with Maddox keeping pace on Sebastian. Her riding attire was strikingly smart, comprising a white chemisette, and a maroon cutaway coat and waistcoat trimmed with gold and matching gold buttons. Her black leather riding gloves emerged from large turned cuffs on the jacket, and her long maroon skirt was split up the back to enable astride riding while the cutaway coat preserved her modesty as it draped around Tabetha's rear. The ensemble was topped and tailed by a stylish black top hat and low-heeled black boots. Needless to say, Maddox was in his usual practical stable-wear.

"Right Maddox," Alicya said, as she pulled the reins around and faced Tabetha towards the palace, a quarter of a league away. "I want you to drive Sebastian hard," she commanded, as she took off her hat and threw it to the floor where it landed amid a mosaic of yellow, pale blue and pink wildflowers. "Let's see how far Tabetha has to go."

"Right you are, Your Highness," responded Maddox, dutifully.

"On my command, three, two, one, go!"

Both of them touched their heels to the flanks of their horses and were into full gallops within seconds. The wind whipped at Alicya's thick, dark brown hair, pulling hairpins out so that it flowed out behind her just like the mane on the chestnut mare she was riding. Very gradually, Sebastian began to edge ahead and then pull away, but the winning margin was only around eight lengths. Tabetha was from very good stock indeed.

They were soon trotting towards the stables, both riders delighted and excited, both horses slightly lathered and steaming. When they reached the yard, Alicya jumped off Tabetha and handed the reins to Maddox. "Stable them both for me please, Maddox," she commanded. "I'm slightly late for an appointment," she added, taking out her pocket watch. It was twenty-seven minutes past two in the afternoon, and she was unlikely to make it for the appointed time. "Oh, and would you be a darling please Maddox and send one of the stable-boys to retrieve my hat. My mother will only reprimand me if she thinks I've lost it."

"Right you are, Your Highness," agreed Maddox.

With that, Alicya strode off towards the rear of the palace, wound her way through the marquees on the palace lawns, across the terrace and then trotted up the curved left-hand staircase. She walked straight through the enormous rear doors, past the rich red velvet drapes and into the Council Room, then headed out the other side into the network of palace corridors. She briefly checked her pocket watch again, which showed the time as thirty-one-minutes past two: 15:31. She gave a brief nod of satisfaction, deciding that turning up slightly late was likely to play into her hands, as she was less likely to be spotted.

Turning into her target corridor, she was pleased to find it deserted. She chose a door on her right-hand side, rapped twice on it with confidence, and then entered. As she had hoped, the Lord Chamberlain's office was empty. Having familiarised herself with all of the palace officials' itineraries, Alicya knew that James Cecil was having his weekly meeting with the House of Lords between 14:00 and 17:00, and he generally took his direct reports with him. So far, so good. But was her brother having his daily 15:30 update with Nash, next door?

She stopped, stock still – and was delighted to hear the murmur of voices next door, one of which bore the careless but haughty tones of her brother. Taking Cecil's empty drinking glass off his desk, Alicya placed it against the partition wall between Cecil's and Nash's offices.

"So, you found him and lost him, then," her brother was saying. "No wonder you kept this from me. My, my, Nash – we're not quite the super-spy we thought we were, are we?"

"It's only a matter of time, Sir. He can't leave Glennad without me knowing. We've got every port covered from Visset in the north-west on the Wrenko peninsula, to Twixelfoe on the east coast."

"That's only half the coast of Glennad, Nash. The northern half."

"Yes, Sir. But we don't have endless resource. And he's a professional sailor. A captain for the last six years of his career. He'll make for a port, but he's unlikely to travel over land to the south coast."

"Well maybe he's thinking that's what *you're* thinking, Nash. This really won't do. I want that bastard here. I want him *here*, Nash."

Alicya frowned. Her brother's voice was fluctuating in volume and pitch, clearly rattled, but she failed to understand why. She was certain they were talking about the sailor who had interrupted their fun with the so-called urchin and the dogfighting; the urchin who had disabled Dolly's doberman that was now missing an eye. But why was this so important to Magnus? Sure, the sailor had humiliated him in front of Dolly with the shredded breeches, but Dolly wouldn't dare say anything to upset Magnus, and the event hadn't happened in public. No one else knew. And if the sailor bragged about it, Magnus could just deny it.

Alicya's frown deepened. This didn't make sense. And to go to the enormous lengths of watching all ports in northern Glennad? *What a ridiculous waste of the public's money!* Was Magnus really that insecure that he couldn't allow *anyone* to get one up on him? Or was this just some cruel sport for a bored royal? And what would he actually *do* with the sailor if he *was* apprehended and brought to the palace?

Anything I please, little sister. Anything I please," echoed Magnus' words from a previous conversation.

Alicya's shook her head. She was beginning to re-assess her brother's propensity for cruelty. Maybe some of the rumours were more than just rumours after all. Alicya shuddered at the thought.

The conversation about the sailor had ended. They had now moved on to an interesting new development. "They'll likely be coming to the palace later today. I will not be available. I expect you and your men to fob them off. You are to assure them that I am being true to my word, and that I am taking both of their daughters into the palace to become apprentice ladies-in-waiting to my sister."

Alicya's heart jumped. She hadn't expected to hear her own name mentioned; she was usually way beneath Magnus' machinations.

"And their names, Sir?"

One of them is Emilya Luca's father – Danny Luca. The other is Freya Colin's father – I don't know his first name."

"And they're both bakers?"

"Yes, Nash, they're both bakers. Found by *my* men, not yours."

Alicya had heard this line about tradesmen before. They had obviously struck lucky and found the supposed urchin – although whether that person was Emilya or Freya she didn't yet know.

"My men whom I lent to you, actually, Sir," Nash was pointing out.

"Don't split hairs with me, Nash. They were acting under *my* orders."

Nash didn't bother to respond to that and changed the subject. "So, what, exactly, are you doing with Miss Colin?" asked Nash.

Alicya instantly tensed up. *Oh my God! He's got one of them here! Here, at the palace!*

"That's no business of yours, Nash!" she heard Magnus snap back.

"My apologies, Sir, but it most certainly *is* my business. I need to know what I need to protect you from. Especially given her father is turning up, later."

"I've told you, Nash. I expect you to fob him off with the apprentice story."

"And what if he demands to see her? Can I grant him that wish?"

"No, you most certainly cannot," snapped Magnus.

"Why?" came the direct reply.

"Why! You can't ask me why, Nash. Do you want to keep your job?"

Nash stuck to his guns. "As I said, I need to know what I need to protect you from. So, have you hurt her?"

A silence ensued, presumably sullen. Then Nash's voice again. "I'll take your silence to be bad news, then."

Another long pause. "Is she still alive?"

Alicya's heart missed a beat. This was a thousand times darker than she'd ever suspected.

"Yes, of course she's alive, Nash," responded Magnus, tetchily. "Unfortunately, it would not be…prudent to allow her to see her father. Not for a few days, anyway."

"I see," came Nash's response, followed by a long pause. "Well, thank you, Sir. That's probably enough to know for now in terms of dealing with the two bakers. For now. But reading between the lines, I take it that Freya Colin won't be going back home at all?"

"Not very likely."

"So, how do you propose to get out of this mess, long-term, then?"

"How do *I* propose!" cried Magnus. "*I'm* not the Head of Royal Security, Nash. That's your job!"

"Well, can we honour the apprentice promise – and keep her here, alive and well?"

"That is possible, I suppose. Although we'll need leverage."

"Leverage?"

"To buy her silence, Nash – I'd have thought that was obvious. The same applies to Emilya Luca when you bring her here from Dominniul. If she *is* in Dominniul! I still think Danny Luca was lying to me."

"Well, we'll soon know on that front, Sir. I've got officers heading for that address as we speak."

"If she's not at that address, Nash, I will personally gut her father for lying to me."

"You will do no such thing," stated Nash.

"I beg your pardon."

"You heard me, Sir."

"*I pay you to do as you're told!*" Alicya could well imagine Magnus' gritted teeth.

"No, Sir. You pay me to keep you out of trouble. And that's what I'm doing by advising you to leave Danny Luca alone. It's more-than enough that you're kidnapping his daughter. We cannot afford to have anything more to cover than your dalliances with two fifteen-year-old girls."

"How *dare* you -."

"What you do behind closed doors is your business," cut in Nash. "So long as you steer clear of murder. Because so long as we've got two faces to show to Papas Luca and Colin – ideally two un*blemished* faces – we can keep *your* head above water. True, we may need to scare them into submission by threatening their families. I doubt we'll have much trouble after that. Especially if we treat them *nicely!*"

Magnus didn't reply, perhaps uncharacteristically digesting what Nash had just told him. Meanwhile, Alicya hadn't exhaled for a while, making her rather light-headed, and so she slowly released her breath.

"I'm sorry for having to speak to you in this way, Sir," said Nash, eventually. "But you're straying too close to the boundaries – and I'm doing you a huge favour by telling you so."

Alicya heard a sardonic laugh. Then her brothers' voice. "You're a brave man, Nash."

"Not really, Sir. Being frank, if you were foolish enough to harm those girls' families, I would no longer be willing to bail you out."

"You what!" spluttered Magnus. Alicya could hear various other incoherent sound-effects and could well imagine her brothers' face contorted in rage. She could also picture the cool, dark-haired Nash remaining perfectly unflappable in the face of her brother's fury. "What did you just say?" repeated Magnus.

"I'm willing to quietly take out a former naval captain, down on his luck, who happened to assault a member of the royal family. That could be construed as duty. Just about. But killing innocent bakers? No! I am not prepared to defend the indefensible, Sir."

"Now you listen to me, Nash," began her brother, dangerously, positively spitting out the Head of Royal Security's surname. "I can have you fired – or worse – on a whim."

"Then do it, Sir. Fire me. And then go and find someone else to confront the bakers."

"I won't forget this, Nash."

"You need to grow up, Magnus." A pause. "And perhaps keep off the sherries, too."

Silence for a few more seconds. Alicya was holding her breath again. Finally, Magnus spoke, in a quieter, more menacing tone. "I can have *all of this*," he began, "pinned on you, Nash. On you! If I want."

"You overstep yourself, Sir," came the calm response. "And I rest my case about growing up. I suggest you leave now and come back when you've had a re-think. You need me on your side more than any other man in the kingdom – because of *what* I know."

"This can't be *happening*!" retorted Magnus, the last word shouted.

Nash continued as if Magnus had said nothing. "So, I need you to not go around killing innocent people, Sir. Abducting, beating and confining to the palace, I can just about deal with. Your dalliances, too. Just about. Killing innocent people, I cannot."

"Are you dismissing me?" demanded Magnus.

"I'm merely suggesting that we re-convene when you've had a chance to think things through. Like an adult, please, Sir. By tomorrow, we should have Emilya Luca, I will have placated both her father and Mr Colin, and we can start putting the façade in place in terms of apprenticing the two girls to Princess Alicya."

And that was that. Seconds later, Alicya heard Nash's office door open – after which it was positively *slammed* closed, followed by Magnus' stalking footsteps disappearing down the corridor.

In the sudden silence, Alicya became aware that her heart was beating rapidly in time to the rhythmic pounding in her ears, making her feel slightly faint again. With a concerted effort, she began to breathe deeply to slow down her heart rate. As she regained her composure, Alicya began to count the revelations.

Number One: she already knew her brother could be unpleasant. But she would never have believed him capable of grievous bodily harm on innocent fifteen-year-old girls, much-less casually threatening to kill bakers. The rumours about him were starting to look rather less wild.

Number Two: a young girl called Freya Colin was being held here at the palace against her will and had almost certainly been physically assaulted by her brother. She had to face the fact that poor Freya had probably been sexually assaulted as well. At present, shock – and to some extent, shame – was holding back white-hot anger on that one.

And Number Three: she already knew that Nash was a cold fish, but even she had been shocked at how he had just talked to her brother. Icy, efficient and unintimidated – and he obviously had leverage over Magnus, as well. Likely damning evidence by the sound of it. She really didn't want to think what that might be.

Alicya was about to creep out of the Lord Chamberlain's office when she heard Nash's bell ring. Sixty seconds later, she heard one of Nash's clerks enter his office. "Ah, Kethnen. Three things. Firstly, please go and tell Mrs Alsnow to prepare afternoon tea for three people – to be served at four thirty this afternoon, precisely. Secondly, please arrange to have the Havreno Summer House appropriately furnished for serving afternoon tea. And finally, please inform Mr Terry that I'll be expecting two visitors later this afternoon – a Mr Luca and a Mr Colin. They are to be escorted to the summer house as soon as it is ready, and then tell Terry to come and fetch me. That's all, Kethnen."

Alicya pursed her lips. That didn't take much working out. Nash was going to deal with the bakers personally, and buy more time – time to enable poor Freya Colin's bruises to heal.

Alicya considered her options. She couldn't betray her brother – the scandal might bring down her family. But she could give Freya some moral support, take her under her wing, and make sure that Magnus left her alone in future. After all, it sounded as if Freya – along with Emilya Luca – was to become a lady-in-waiting. Alicya found herself looking forward to that. It would make a nice change to have friends who hadn't been born into the gentry. And despite what had already happened to them, there were worse fates for young girls than being groomed to attend a princess. So, yes, she would do her damnedest to make amends for Freya's appalling treatment at the hands of her brother.

Alicya stood up with purpose. Starting immediately…

CHAPTER 15   MAGNUS

5th Tertiar, 1789   Day 96, 15:45

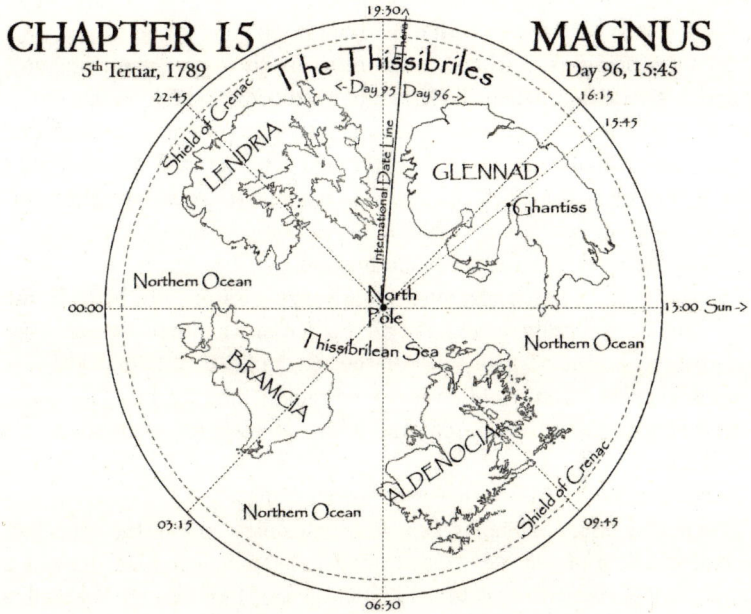

"You are causing me a lot of problems, my dear."

Freya Colin glared back at Prince Magnus, with the bed sheet pulled up to her neck. "Oh, boo-hoo," she said, twisting her face in disgust. It was a face sporting two black eyes, one of them completely closed.

"The question is," continued Magnus, completely ignoring Freya's response, and then taking a large sip of red wine, "how are we all going to come out of this without any more…unpleasantness?"

"You could let me go?" suggested Freya, her face now emotionless, her one open eye looking unseeing into the distance. She then refocused and looked at Magnus. "You told me we'd be safe here."

"Well," began Magnus, before taking another large swig of wine, "that was before your stupid little friend decided to run away from Ghantiss."

"Good for her," said Freya, defiantly. "I wish I had."

"And what else do you wish for, my dear?" asked Magnus, his eyes falling lazily on her slender, exposed left arm. He set down his wine.

Freya immediately tucked her left arm back under the sheet. "A quick death," was her sullen response, before lying back down. A single tear spilled out of her 'good' eye and ran down her swollen cheek.

"Oh, come, come," said Magnus, beginning to unbutton his shirt. "Am I really that much of a toad?"

Freya glared back at him with fire. "Toad is too good for you."

"Ah, you see, this is what I...admire so much in you," said Magnus, pulling his shirt over his head. He caught his toned reflection in one of the bedroom mirrors, shook his hair back and pursed his lips at his double. The double smouldered back. "Now," he continued, unconcerned by his captive's misery. "Before I left, I asked you to consider something different. Have you been considering something different, Freya Colin?"

"It's not natural. You were only kidding me."

"Ah, but was I?" teased Magnus, now advancing towards the bed. He saw Freya look at his taut breeches, and he revelled in what they revealed. She said nothing, and so Magnus knelt on the bed, and then straddled her, still kneeling. "I think you're old enough," he said, licking his lips, "for some further education," he whispered. And with that, he grabbed the sheet and pulled it back.

Freya launched at him with a small, serrated meat knife.

Despite the drink, Magnus' reflexes were still quick, and the knife that had been destined for his left eye, scraped along his left temple instead, drawing a straight red line back through his hair. Blood gushed immediately. For a split-second, Magnus felt relief, as this was nowhere near as bad as it could have been. However, Freya had already raised her right hand for a second stab, but Magnus was lightning quick and seized her slender right forearm in his large left hand. The knife was still perilously close to his face, but Magnus held on, eventually forcing the arm and Freya back onto the bed, all the time dripping his blood over her and the pristine white bedsheets. Her other hand tried to punch him, but he grabbed that too. With Freya now pinned to the bed, Magnus squeezed as hard as he could with his left hand, forcing Freya to open her hand and drop the knife.

Now back in control, Magnus let his anger flow. "You stupid little *bitch*!" he cried. He then released her left arm and punched her full on the nose with his right fist. They both heard Freya's nose break. The struggle immediately left her, but Magnus was now in a frenzy. He lifted both of his hands to Freya's neck and began to squeeze.

Freya's one good eye opened in panic, and she immediately began to choke. "No," she managed to gasp. But Magnus was beyond reason. Any assault on him was punishable by death. An assault from a fifteen-year-old girl, though. No one could know of this. And she had marked him. Probably for life. Even as he squeezed the life out of Freya, half of his mind was wailing at his own potential disfigurement. Thank God it had gone backwards from the temple, and not forwards.

In something of a stupor, Magnus didn't know how many minutes had passed before his senses returned. He still had his hands firmly wrapped around Freya's throat, but warmth was already leaving her body. Her one open eye stared unseeing at the ceiling, whilst her dark-red hair fanned out against the white pillow.

Feeling the killing frenzy retreat, Magnus eased his hands from Freya's throat, and sat back on his haunches. His hand went to his left temple and came back thick with his own blood. "Bitch!" he said, directly to Freya's lifeless face.

Still holding his left hand to his left temple, Magnus walked into his en suite bathroom and grabbed a pristine white towel. He held it to his head, now looking at his reflection in the bathroom mirror. His mind was already working overtime – but he soon decided that this new development was not so much more of a problem than it had been before. The solution was still the same. Get Marler and Hoskyns to dispose of the body. The only difference was, he'd saved them the bother of killing Freya Colin as well.

As for an explanation, that remained unchanged. They'd allowed Freya to go home just as dusk was falling, so that she could share the great news of her forthcoming apprenticeship with her parents.

"Oh, Mr Colin, I'm so sorry," hammed up a sincere, doe-eyed Magnus into the bathroom mirror, confident that the resourceful Nash was, right now, doing his job of fobbing off the concerned baker. "I will personally take charge of the hunt for Freya's abductors; you have my *sincerest* promise on that."

He then laughed at his impression of himself. "Cheers," he said to his reflection, holding up an imaginary glass and winking once.

The action made Magnus crave a real drink, so he headed back into the bedroom to find his wine, still holding the now red and white towel to his temple. He spotted the glass where he'd left it on top of a chest of drawers, picked it up and drained it in one go. He then turned to face the body of Freya Colin and raised a real glass this time. "Cheers," he repeated, perfectly comfortable with the way things were turning out.

Then his sister burst into the bedroom.

CHAPTER 16 — ALICYA

5th Tertiar, 1789 — Day 96, 16:00

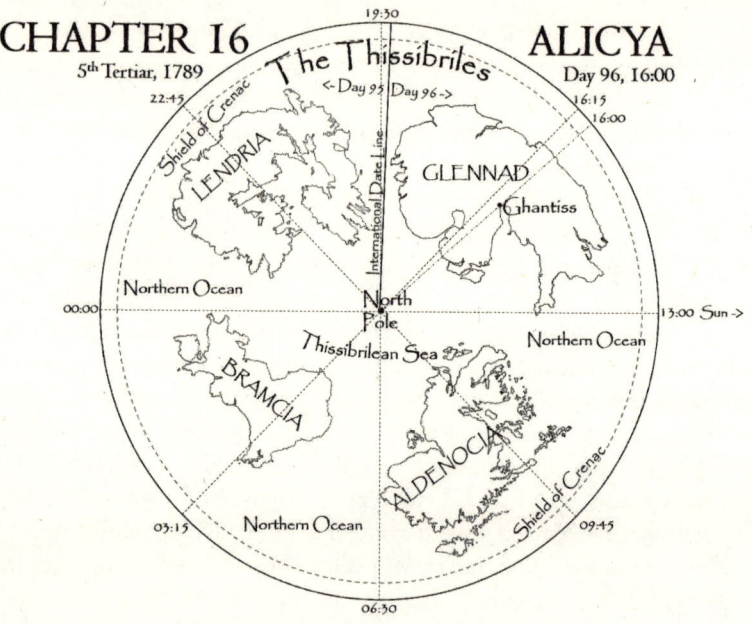

Alicya just couldn't take it in. The first thing she saw was her brother, half-naked, holding a blood-stained towel to the side of his head, and holding an empty wine glass in his other hand. For a nanosecond, she was concerned for him. Then she saw Freya Colin.

Alicya's shocked face whipped back to look at her brother. Her mouth was open, but no words would come out. It took several more seconds to overcome her shock and then she rushed to the bedside and knelt, grabbing one of Freya's hands. It was limp.

She then looked to the face for signs of life – and recoiled at Freya's death-scream – formed in a face already deformed by two black eyes and a broken nose. Alicya kept looking at the poor girl's face, but all the time, a white-hot anger was slowly boiling up within. Eventually, she turned slowly on her brother. "You *monster!*" she spat.

But Magnus was already busy – locking the door to his bedroom and pocketing the key. "She was only a peasant!" he said, dismissively.

Alicya was no fool. Brother or not, she instinctively knew she was in grave danger, but anger still won out over fear. "Peasant!" she spat. "She was a girl! A human being! A baker's daughter!" She turned to look at her. "A beautiful baker's daughter," she added more softly, before taking hold of the bedsheet and covering Freya's distorted face.

Alicya stood, vaguely aware she was still in her maroon riding gear, whilst Magnus was regarding her with narrowed eyes. "How do you know she's a baker's daughter? Have you been eavesdropping on me, Alicya?"

Alicya ignored him, anger still overriding fear. "You have no right!"

"I have every right! I'm Prince Magnus. In less than ten years, I'll be King Magnus. How many times have I told you not to be weak, Lissy?"

"What, and you think that killing young girls makes you 'not weak'? You think that," she said, pointing at Freya's corpse, "makes you strong?"

Alicya's scorn struck a nerve, and Magnus advanced on her. Alicya backed off and stumbled as she felt the solid bed behind her legs. "Father will kill you!" she spat, defensively.

"What? You think I'm going to hurt you?" said Magnus, reading Alicya's fear.

Alicya answered with silence, her mind working overtime trying to read the situation.

"I wouldn't hurt you, Alicya. You're my baby sister."

"I'm no different from Freya Colin, Magnus."

Magnus just laughed at that. Alicya's eyes flashed to see such callous disregard, but again, she kept silent.

Magnus regarded her again through narrowed eyes. "You need to make your mind up whose side you're on, little sister."

"What do you mean by that?"

"Are you a Havreno? Or are you a traitor?"

"A traitor!"

"We have to look out for each other, Alicya. If this gets out, our royal line is finished."

"Well, you should have thought of the royal line before you did that," retorted Alicya, gesturing with her head towards the bed again.

"Alicya," began Magnus, walking over to the dressing table and picking up the bloodied towel again. He dabbed it at the side of his head, pleased to note that the blood-flow was reducing, whilst adrenaline continued to limit the pain. "You're not going to tell anyone about this. Are you?" It was a clear challenge.

"I'll be telling Mum and Dad, for sure."

"Now that would be very, very stupid, Alicya."

"Why? You think you can cover this up? You do this regularly do you -." Alicya cut herself off. "Oh my God! You *have* done this before."

Magnus said nothing.

"You, you, you -." Alicya was stammering in renewed shock. "You get

Marler and Hoskyns to…"

"Marler and Hoskyns are faithful servants of the Crown, Alicya."

"But, but -. When? I mean -. How many?"

"Not many. It doesn't matter."

"Doesn't matter!"

"Alicya," said Magnus, dangerously. "You're beginning to bore me with your over-sensitivity."

"Over-sensitivity! My God, you really don't have a soul, do you?"

"Souls are over-rated," responded Magnus, casually, now walking back to the dressing table. He put the towel down again and reached into the top drawer for something; did something with his hands.

Now terrified, Alicya craned her neck to see what Magnus had taken out of the drawer – but as he turned around, he kept whatever it was behind his back. "Now!" he began, walking slowly towards her. "Promise me, here and now, that you will *never* speak of this incident to anyone else. Not even to me."

"I can't promise you that, Magnus," responded Alicya, her voice now shaking with fear.

"That's the wrong answer, Alicya."

Alicya tried to back off but the bed with its grisly content was all that was behind her. "What are you…what are you going to do?" she babbled.

"Last chance, Alicya. Promise me – and everything will be all right."

"Not for her, it won't," Alicya heard herself saying. She knew it was a fatal response, but she stayed true to her heart.

"In that case, I'm really sorry," said Magnus, hollowly. "I genuinely did like you, you know."

"Oh my God!" gasped Alicya, who, despite her terror, recognised Magnus' use of the past tense. "You can't." Alicya tried to fend him off, but he just grabbed her arm in an iron grip before his other hand came out from behind his back. In a flash, Magnus grabbed Alicya with both hands and savagely twisted her around so that he was behind her, ripping her white chemisette in the process. He then held the chloroform pad hard to her mouth and nostrils.

Alicya immediately breathed in the sweet, cloying liquid and her head began to swim. She struggled, but her brother was strong, and she was already weakening.

Within seconds, she had lost consciousness.

CHAPTER 17 — MAGNUS

5th Tertiar, 1789 Day 96, 16:05

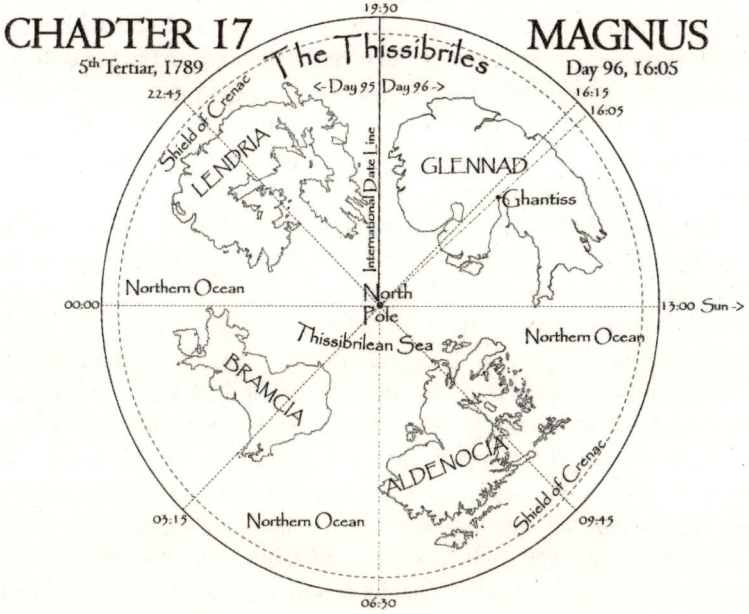

Magnus looked down at the unconscious form of his eighteen-year-old sister, whom he now held in his arms. He reasoned with himself that he genuinely hadn't wanted to do this. And yet…did he feel bad? He couldn't say why he suddenly smirked at that point. He really couldn't.

Magnus continued to look at Alicya, curiously. He touched a lock of long dark brown hair that had fallen across her pretty, unblemished face, and brushed it tenderly aside. His gaze then tracked downwards to the torn chemisette, and he stared, mesmerised by the rise and fall of her chest. *Oh, how tempting.*

But there were limits. Weren't there…

Shaking his head slightly, Magnus realised he had a more pressing need – which was to sort this new mess out. He remembered Nash's words from earlier. *And how do you propose to get us out of this mess?*

Magnus frowned – more from the look the Head of Royal Security had given him and his tone than what he had actually said. *You need to grow up, Prince Magnus,* Nash had said. Well, there was no way that Nash could find out about any of this. But what to do? He had reached a point of no return where Alicya was concerned. He didn't particularly want her dead, but there was no way this could now end well for him with Alicya still alive.

Sighing, Magnus removed himself from beneath Alicya and rested her head and shoulders gently on to the floor. He then walked back to the dressing table, and this time took out a vial of liquid from the top drawer. Crossing back to Alicya, he sat behind her again, and propped her head up into his lap. Without hesitating, he parted her lips with the fingers of one hand and, turning the vial upside down with his other, he let several drops splash into her open mouth.

He then counted to ten. Sure enough, as he reached ten, Alicya's body convulsed once, twice, thrice. And then she was still. This time, there was no rhythmic movement of her chest.

Magnus sighed again. "You were just too stubborn, my dear," he said, stroking her hair for one last time. He then stood up and began to put his salvage plan into action, surprising himself by how little he felt at what he had just done. His first port of call was the bathroom. He looked at his cut in the mirror. It was nasty, but it had stopped bleeding now. Picking up a cloth, he immersed it in his jug of clean water and began to wipe away the bloodstains from his face and hair, wincing every time the cloth caught his cut. Once that was as clean as he could get it, he stared hard at himself in the mirror. Yes, it was nasty. But it would heal. In fact, he mused, the scar might even add an extra dash of character. He narrowed his eyes and pursed his lips, enabling his reflection to prove the point.

As he stared in the mirror, Magnus sought to find an advantage from the conflict with Freya Colin. *You need to grow up, Prince Magnus.* Those words had enraged him at the time. But perhaps Nash had a point. He certainly needed to be more cautious in future. And certainly not careless enough to leave serrated meat knives lying around. Magnus gritted his teeth with annoyance at himself.

Still staring in the mirror, Magnus cleaned the rest of the blood away from his torso. He then put on a fresh outfit – a dark red tunic richly embroidered with gold, a white silk shirt and stock and black breeches before returning to his wardrobe for a suitable hat to hide his wound. He found the perfect article – a soft black felt affair with a plume of white feathers tucked into one side. When pulled down, hat and feathers covered all of the cut – although even the soft felt was abrasive against the wound.

Magnus looked at the result in his full-length bedroom mirror and nodded in satisfaction. No one would know. He then took the bedroom door key from the top of his dressing table and made for the door. He turned the key in the lock, but before exiting, he turned around to look at the two dead teenage girls. "Don't go away," he quipped, and then slipped through the door into the corridor, locking it behind him.

Magnus walked confidently through the palace corridors, nodding at anyone he saw in his normal, superior way, as he made his way towards the Games Room. As he approached, he could hear the drunken hubbub, which ceased the second he appeared in the doorway. Despite his men being largely a collection of lower-class thieves and murderers, they all sprang to attention at his appearance – the exception being Dolly, the only gentleman amongst them, but who was currently slumped over a chaise-longue in a garish mustard-coloured ensemble, his mouth catching flies whilst he snored like a pig. "At ease, men," said Magnus.

He scanned those standing. As ever, Hoskyns was quite the worse for wear. His heavy moustache and eyebrows emphasised rather than hid his brutish face, but his shock of wiry black hair was also a mess, and his white stock – a futile attempt to look like a gentleman – was all over the place and covered in blotchy stains. "I see you've been losing again, Hoskyns," said Magnus, nodding at the billiard table.

"How do you know that, Sir?" he slurred.

"Because you aren't sober," responded Magnus. "And unfortunately, I need you to sober up pretty rapidly. Are we going to have to dunk your head in a barrel of icy water again, Hoskyns?"

"No, Sir," he responded, attempting to stand up straight and flatten down his hair.

"Excellent. Mr Marler?" commanded Magnus.

"Yes, Sir," responded the one-eyed thug, his scarred cheek twitching with anticipation.

"Can we trust these two men?" he asked, nodding at his two twenty-something colleagues.

"I would trust Williams and Hauberker with my life, Sir," responded Marler.

"Well," began Magnus, a mirthless smirk on his face. "You or they may live to regret those words, Mr Marler." He now had all four men's attention. "I require a huge favour – from all four of you. You will all be handsomely rewarded if you carry out my plan to the letter. Meaning, under no circumstances do you let *anyone* see what you are doing."

He still had their undivided attention – despite the continued snoring from Dolly.

"There are two parts to this plan," he began, walking over to the Games Room door and closing it. "I'm afraid, Mr Marler, that I've had another accident in my bedroom!"

Magnus eyeballed Marler, daring him to show any emotion. Marler didn't. "I understand, Your Royal Highness. Will the same plan that we used for the last one work for you again?"

"Yes, it will," agreed Magnus. "Although this time…there are two of them."

"Two of them, Sir"?

"Yes, two of them, Marler. One likes to…experiment." Magnus didn't even bother to come up with an excuse as to why the 'two of them' were dead, and Marler and Hoskyns knew better than to ask.

"I have one very specific request for you this time, though, Marler."

"Yes, Sir?"

"Before you instruct your two friends here how to get them off the palace premises, I want you to provide me with two empty grain sacks."

The faces of Marler and Hoskyns remained impassive, but Magnus noticed a quick look pass between the two younger men, Williams and Hauberker. Magnus whipped out his sword, and both men's eyes flashed with fear. "I am a generous master, gentlemen," said Magnus, levelling his sword at them. "But if you fail me, or worse, betray me, I will personally cut you both up into a thousand pieces and feed them to my dog, Reaper. Do you understand?"

Both men mumbled their terrified assent.

Magnus turned to Marler again, sheathing his sword. "Seeing as Hoskyns here is a bit worse for wear, I suggest you cut along to Maddox' stable and acquire the two sacks. Bring them back here where I will await your return. I will then need your men to give me half an hour before they turn up at my apartment masquerading as laundry men. Is that clear?"

"Yes, Sir. Rough grain sacks, you say?"

"Yes, Marler. Large enough to go over a human head."

Again, Marler's face remained impassive. This time, so too did the faces of the two younger men.

"You mentioned two parts to the plan, Sir?" stated Marler.

"Yes, Mr Marler. And you're going to love the second part."

Marler raised the eyebrow above his one good eye, questioningly.

"Oh, yes," confirmed Magnus. "I want you to kill Mr Nash!"

CHAPTER 18 — EMILYA

6th Tertiar, 1789   Day 97, 10:30

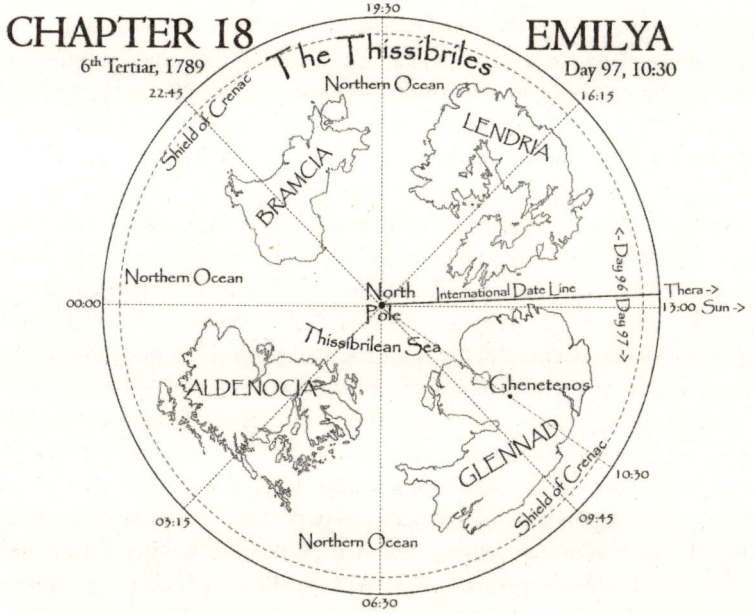

Emilya was starting to enjoy the feel of a horse beneath her. She'd been hapless two days ago, when Jake had returned to Elyse Dolmen's cottage with two horses that he had 'just acquired'. The healer had laughed as Emilya had tried to mount her horse for the first time – but not in an unkind way. There was nothing remotely unkind about Elyse. Although Emilya did wonder if she cared more for animals than people. "Animals are much better than people," she'd said on numerous occasions over the last two days. Emilya couldn't argue with that.

The thought prompted her to look down at the harness that Elyse had given her, which contained an impossibly cute young male terrier. Theo looked back at her with large and beautiful brown eyes, that always seemed so full of sorrow. He blinked once, highlighting his long and delicate eyelashes, making Emilya go all gushy. Meanwhile, his pointed ears – one with a piece missing out of it – were at least one size too big for his head, and his shaggy, dark and light grey fur along with his beautifully contrasting white bib, made him look even more adorable. Feeling brave, Emilya took one hand off her reins and stroked Theo's head. He continued to look at her sadly, but Emilya felt there was love in that look, too. He may only have a small brain, but she felt sure Theo knew that she had saved his life.

Of course, Theo also looked that way at Elyse. Even though it had hurt when she had splinted his leg and treated his raw wounds, he somehow knew that she was caring for him. No doubt the soothing effect of the salve helped, substituting Elyse for whoever his mother had been and his mother's gentle, healing tongue.

Emilya became aware that Elyse was looking at her and smiling. "He's so beautiful," was all Emilya could say.

"You always wanted a dog, right?" said Elyse.

Emilya looked at Elyse and smiled back. This woman was probably the cleverest person she'd ever known – and stunningly beautiful, too, with long, tousled dark blonde hair and azure eyes that looked right into your soul. It was difficult for Emilya to gauge her age, but she reckoned somewhere between thirty and forty. Elyse was a trend-setter, too – the first female horse-rider Emilya had ever seen wearing breeches instead of a riding skirt. Emilya herself didn't count – as she was no equestrian, and she wore baggy breeches for comfort, anyway. Of course, all the men noticed Elyse's white riding breeches. It was hard not to, with every contour of her long and slim legs accentuated.

Emilya's thoughts soon flicked back two days again. After she had said her painful goodbyes to her father, Elyse had been stood waiting outside her quaint little white cottage on the north-eastern outskirts of Ghantiss, with its thatched roof and gorgeous wisteria which rambled between the pale green shutters and door. Even before Emilya had introduced Jake, the healer had tuned in to their sombre mood. She had then listened to Emilya's story with great concern. Emilya had finished by explaining that they needed supplies for Theo for their long journey – at which point Elyse had told them that she would be joining them on the grounds that Theo needed her continued care. Emilya suspected there was more to it than that, recalling Jake's wry comment two days ago about Elyse playing chaperone. "At the very least," Elyse had said, "I will accompany you all the way to Earl's Leet." Jake had seemed very happy with that!

Of course, Emilya had been very grateful for Elyse's presence, too, and they had already had some warming heart-to-hearts. She was fairly sure the healer had already made her mind up about Jake Oscom as well. He had his rough edges, but he was clearly a good man, too. Elyse and Jake were certainly striking up a comfortable understanding, with Elyse teasing the former naval captain about a number of things. Jake just took it all in his stride, maintaining the briefest of smiles, and never uncomfortable. Emilya sensed that Elyse liked that about him.

These thoughts passed through her mind in milliseconds before she answered Elyse's question. "My father wouldn't allow it," she responded. "Because of the constant baking. Said his customers would end up with dog-hairs in their pies."

Elyse laughed, musically. Even her laughs were pretty, thought Emilya, wistfully. "What a pity Prince Magnus didn't choke on a dog-haired pie!"

Emilya had recounted the meat pie encounter to Elyse in as much detail as her father had explained it to herself, Jake and Rex Colin, and the healer's eyes had flashed more than once during the telling. Emilya briefly smiled at Elyse's jest, but they soon triggered another worry. Her eyes met Elyse's. "I hope my friend is safe."

Elyse moved her horse closer and reached out her right hand. Emilya took it with her left, managing to still safely steer with her right. "So many people to save," said Elyse, giving Emilya's hand a reassuring squeeze. She then looked at Theo. "And animals, too."

Emilya let go of Elyse's hand and ruffled the fur on Theo's head. "He's worth every hardship, though."

"Emilya Luca," said Elyse. "You remind me of a girl I once knew."

Emilya caught Elyse's eye, immediately knowing who she was talking about. "And is that girl happy?"

Elyse appeared to consider, then responded. "Most of the time," she said. "That girl made one terrible mistake, though," she added, her eyes now distant.

They were both quiet for a few seconds before Emilya responded. "And is this a story that the girl is likely to tell?"

More consideration from Elyse. "Perhaps," she said, a vague smile now playing about her sensual lips. She turned to look at Emilya. "Perhaps," she repeated.

Emilya felt strangely honoured. She sensed that this was not a story that had been told to many – if any. She decided to bide her time. The moment wasn't right, just now.

At that moment, Jake slowed his horse to allow his two companions to draw level with him. "I see Ghenetenos," he said, pointing to a plain in the distance before them. They were heading due east, and it was still mid-morning, so the sun was not far to the right of where he was pointing.

Shielding her eyes with one hand, the other now holding the reins more confidently, Emilya could see an array of dark objects arranged in a rough circle. The famed Ghenetenos. Two circles of stones – outer and inner – built four thousand years ago and thought to be an ancient temple, which had probably served some kind of ritualistic or ceremonial purpose which, in turn, may have been related to solar and lunar alignments. Ghenetenos was the most complete and famous of several of these spectacular edifices which were dotted about the Thissibriles. The area around Ghenetenos was also heavily populated with ancient burial sites or barrows which dated from around and after the time of the stone circle. The whole area was thick with an aura of the past.

"If we encounter any druids," said Jake, "just leave them to me."

"Well, you can always let me wish them '*dia duit*', if you like," suggested Elyse.

"Ah, I might have known," said Jake, with that ghost of a smile on his craggy face.

"You're a druid?" asked Emilya.

"I might be," replied Elyse, unwittingly mimicking Jake's ghost of a smile. She raised her eyebrows. "Then again, I might not."

Jake let out a soft laugh. "The lady likes to maintain her air of mystery."

"The gentleman is more intrigued than he likes to make out."

"Am I getting in the way here, guys?" asked Emilya, smirking.

"No!" both Jake and Elyse responded in unison. All three of them laughed, although Emilya didn't miss the split-second eye-contact between Jake and Elyse.

"Well," said Jake, breaking the awkward silence. "So long as you've not got any plans for me and the Wicker Man, I'll not pry any more."

"The *what* man?" asked Emilya.

"Wicker!" exclaimed both Elyse and Jake in unison again. They then both laughed in unison, as well – whilst Emilya looked even more confused.

Emilya looked from one of them to the other and then back again. "So," she prompted. "An explanation, please."

"Well," began Jake. "Why don't you come and ride between your Uncle Jake and Auntie Elyse and we will tell you all about the Wicker Man."

"All right," said Emilya, dragging out the syllables, unable to hide her smile. She ran a hand through her tangled, dark-auburn hair, well aware that Elyse and Jake already felt like a surrogate aunt and uncle. Their warmth and companionship had certainly helped soften her heartache at having to leave her real family behind.

"So," began Elyse, as the three horses began walking forwards again. "Firstly, the Wicker Man is a very old tradition."

"Although you wouldn't appreciate the oldest traditions very much, Emilya," said Jake.

Emilya's head began to swing left and right as the tale began to unfold. Amusingly, little Theo's head started doing the same, too.

"No, indeed," agreed Elyse. "It was originally a form of sacrifice practised by the ancient druids."

"But this wasn't a quick knife across the throat sacrifice," said Jake, taking over. "Oh no. This one took days-worth of preparation."

"Yes, it was an *event*, you see," said Elyse. "And it was hugely artistic, too. You see, the Wicker Man was a giant representation of a man – at least six times the height and width of an average man – its frame built out of wood and sticks all woven together with willow."

"But it was hollow in the middle – arms, legs, torso – all hollow."

"And that was where they used to put the sacrifices," continued Elyse. "Usually criminals, but sometimes slaves when they were short on cons."

"And even children, when the harvests had failed," added Jake. "As children were thought to appease the gods the most."

"Children!" exclaimed Emilya, interrupting for the first time. "Appeasing the gods!"

"A long time ago, Emilya," emphasised Elyse.

"And no doubt they set fire to the Wicker Man and burned them all to death?" asked Emilya.

"Ah!" exclaimed Jake. "Are you sure you know nothing about druidic ways, girl?"

Emilya turned to Jake and just gave him her best teenage look. Jake grinned back at her reaction.

"Anyway," said Elyse. "They sacrificed people to either appease the gods, or appeal to them – such as an appeal for a good harvest. Or perhaps as an appeal to prevent some incoming disaster."

"But why 'wicker'?" asked Emilya. "What does that mean?"

"Wickering is the art or technique of making products – such as a chair or a basket – using a variety of pliable plant materials," explained Elyse. "The Wicker Man is just another variant of that technique."

"They still make them, you know," said Jake. "The druids, I mean."

"But you said it was only in ancient times," protested Emilya.

"That was for *human* sacrifices," explained Jake. "They still make them now to maintain tradition – but they put flowers in there, or fruit, or other things. And hence the offering is still, well…offered."

"And when do they do this?" asked Emilya, guardedly.

"Midsummer's Day," answered Elyse. "That's when we hold a big annual ceremony – with the Wicker Man burned right in the centre of the stone circle at midnight."

Emilya didn't ask any more questions. She kept her eyes focused on the stones of Ghenetenos as they gradually began to grow larger, her imagination running wild in all sorts of directions.

Elyse looked briefly across at Jake – who just winked, once, back at her. Elyse bit her lower lip to stop herself from laughing out loud.

CHAPTER 19   MAGNUS
6th Tertiar, 1789   Day 97, 12:00

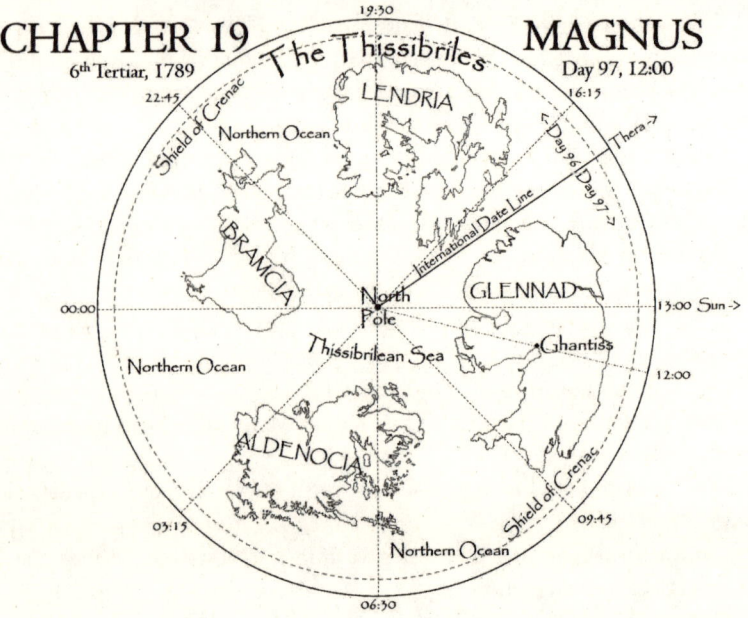

Prince Magnus was beside himself with grief as he strode up and down the throne room, dressed all in black save for his plain cream stock which was visible above his high-buttoned waistcoat. At some time yesterday afternoon, kidnappers had gained access to the palace, and taken his sister. It had been clear that John Nash, Head of Royal Security, had attempted to stop them, but he had been stabbed through the heart for his troubles, and was now lying-in-state in the palace chapel.

Nevertheless, despite his own personal grief, Magnus knew that he had to stay strong for his mother and father. They were going through hell right now, and they desperately needed his support.

Magnus knelt by his mother, took her vein-strewn hand and looked earnestly into her eyes. "I promise you, mother, Alicya is not dead. She's been kidnapped and we will shortly receive a ransom note. We are wealthy. The sum doesn't matter. We will pay the ransom, and Alicya will be returned to us, unharmed."

Queen Maud looked at her son with watery eyes beneath a grey fringe. "Do you really think so, Magnus?"

"I know so, mother," replied Magnus, vehemently. "This isn't the first time this has happened. It's less than fifty years since Princess Aurelia was taken. The kidnappers demanded two thousand guineas. A paltry sum. So, we wait. We pay. We get her back."

"Then why haven't we heard anything yet?" demanded his father.

Magnus looked at him. The crisis had turned his father's normally ruddy complexion an even darker shade of beetroot that ran all the way up and over his balding pate, and made the white of his bushy sideburns stand out even more starkly. King George of Glennad had been pacing the throne room since the alarm had been raised at 21:00 last night and hadn't had a wink of sleep. Sleep was unthinkable until his little girl was safely back with them. He'd ordered immediate searches of the entire palace. They'd started with the stables – the most likely location for Alicya – but Maddox, the stablemaster, had told them he hadn't seen her since the middle of the afternoon, at around 15:25 – which Magnus had suggested to his father was a suspiciously exact timing. Magnus had then casually mentioned how he had often caught Maddox looking at Alicya in an inappropriate way, but had quickly followed that up with: "But there's no way that Maddox would ever harm Alicya; the man is totally devoted to her."

Too grief-stricken to act rationally, King George had ignored his son's apparent reason and immediately had Maddox questioned and then thrown into the palace cells. Magnus smirked inwardly. It was that easy to load his father's gun.

"They're making us sweat, father," he said, noting that the worry and pacing had done nothing to lessen his father's girth. *I shall never grow so fat.* "It may be several more days before the ransom note arrives. In that time, we must remain strong."

"Well, why's Nash not organising a search of the city? Don't we pay that man enough money?"

Queen Maud got up from her throne and moved across to her husband. "George, dear," she began, gently, her hand on his arm. "John Nash is dead."

King George looked at her briefly before realisation dawned. He put his head into his hands. "Oh God! I can't think straight," he confessed.

"You should get some rest, father," suggested Magnus.

"Rest!" he remonstrated. "Rest! At a time like this?"

Magnus walked over to his mother and father. "I'm afraid you're no use to any of us, least of all Alicya, if you can't think straight, father," he said, earnestly. "You need to rest. Have Mr Terry prepare a sleeping draught for you. You can be sure that I will wake you, the moment there is news. The same goes for you, too, mother."

"Of course, you're right, dear," agreed Queen Maud, her pale face still markedly drawn.

"In the meantime, mother, father, *I* shall conduct enquiries, and the search of the city. I will use the palace guard, and Nash's own men, plus some of my own. The search will be discrete, as we don't want this news getting out yet. With a bit of luck, we'll receive the ransom, pay it and get Alicya back before anyone in Ghantiss is any-the-wiser."

"What about that girl who was going to apprentice to Alicya? Have you found her yet?"

"No, father, I haven't. I've an open mind about her. It's possible that Alicya somehow got to hear about the pending apprenticeship and therefore introduced herself to Freya Colin – and hence they've both been abducted together. A case of poor Freya being in the wrong place at the wrong time." Magnus paused to lick his dry lips. "However, there is also the distinct possibility, that Freya Colin is actually *involved* in Alicya's disappearance – on a more sinister level."

"Whatever do you mean by that, Magnus?" asked his mother, quite shocked.

"I'm not entirely sure, yet mother. Like I said: I'm keeping an open mind. After all, Freya Colin has disappeared. Whereas Mr Nash was killed on the palace premises and left where he fell."

"By God, you're right!" exclaimed King George, now seeing things from a different angle. "An open mind indeed. You're showing qualities fit for an heir to the throne, son," he added, with fatherly approval.

"Thank you, father. I do try my best, you know. Now," said Magnus, clapping his hands together once. "Off to bed with you both." He then rang the bell, and Terry the butler quickly appeared.

"Yes, Your Royal Highness," he asked, bowing.

"Ah yes, Mr Terry. Please could you organise a strong sleeping draught for both my mother and father and see that they are delivered to their chambers."

"At once, Sir," responded Terry, bowing and exiting.

"Now, come along mother, father," said Magnus, putting an arm around them both and steering them out of the throne room. "Rest. And when you awaken, I *will* have more news for you."

Magnus watched his two elderly parents walk off gingerly towards their chambers, one large, one small, one red, one pale, but holding hands despite both being in their sixties. Not that the sight elicited any emotion in Magnus. Instead, he fancied some more interesting sport.

It took him around two minutes to reach the flight of steps down to the palace cells. He jogged down them and as he turned the corner, the guards stood to attention. "At ease," he said, without even looking at them. He moved along to the third cell – where the shattered form of the stablemaster was sitting on a wooden block – the only item in his cell other than a foul-smelling bucket.

Magnus didn't say anything. He just looked at Maddox with grim satisfaction. It was Maddox who spoke first. "You know very well I'd never do anything to harm the Princess."

"Do I?" responded Magnus, condescendingly. Again, he didn't say any more. He was enjoying Maddox' misery too much.

"What's being done to find her?"

"That's for me to know. Of course, you could speed things up."

"What do you mean?"

Magnus raised his eyebrows, but again, said nothing.

"What do you mean, Your Royal Highness?" added Maddox, quite unable to bury his distaste.

"That's better, Maddox. What I mean is, if you tell me what you know, we'll be able to find her faster."

Maddox' whole body slumped at that. "Why are you here?"

"I really don't like the tone you are using, Maddox, or your repeated failure to use my correct form of address."

This time it was Maddox who chose to stay silent.

"Very well," said Magnus. "I am now going to organise a discrete search of Ghantiss. I have a few ideas where to look. I suggest that you start praying that we find Alicya – because if we don't, the next time you see me down here, I will be moving your interrogation up a notch."

Maddox just put his head in his hands. Magnus stared at the stablemaster's bald patch, a wicked grin spreading across his face. Poor Maddox. Accused of foul play against a person he would do *anything* to protect, and with the prospect of that going public! Well, he'd never liked the man – mainly because Maddox quite patently didn't like *him*. Magnus had always known he'd bring him down for that. He'd just had no idea the circumstances would be quite so perfect!

Nodding his head at his own cleverness, Magnus turned around and headed back up the stairs to commence his fake search.

CHAPTER 20 — ALICYA
6th Tertiar, 1789 — Day 97, 11:00

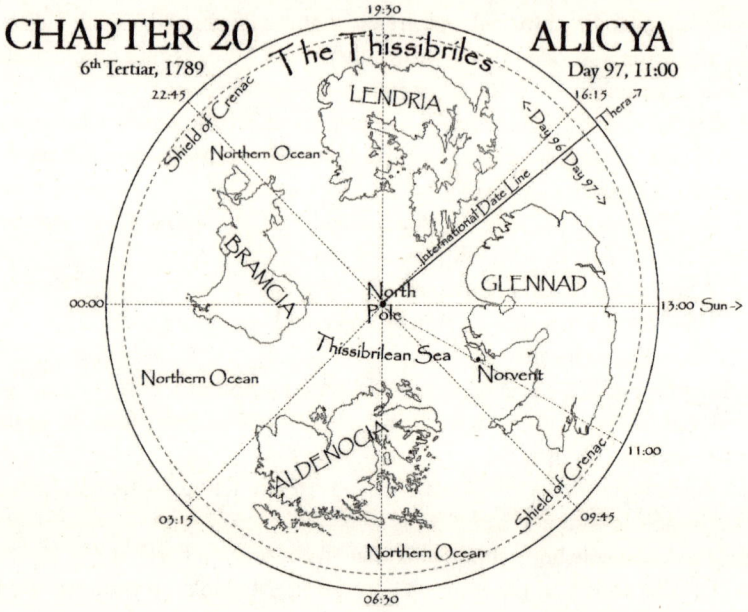

Alicya's head was swimming. As she eased back into consciousness, her first reaction was to gag at the unmistakeable smells of vomit and excrement. Next, she realised that she couldn't see a thing.

Both mysteries were answered as she moved her head. Firstly, her face was brushed by rough sacking that appeared to cover her entire head, while further movement revealed an abrasive constriction around her neck where the sack had been securely tied. Secondly, the vomit was clearly hers and had pooled within the sack, trapped, against the right-hand side of her face against which she was currently lying. It was thick in her hair, too.

With rising panic, Alicya tried to move her hands – only to discover they were bound behind her back with coarse rope. Her feet were tightly bound, too.

Desperately trying to quell her disquiet, Alicya focused on the fact that at least she was still alive. She was also lying on her side. Had she been lying on her back, she would likely have choked to death on her own vomit.

Next, Alicya forced herself to control her breathing and, gradually, the fug in her head receded. Only then did she collect her most recent of memories – and a mosaic of nightmares came flooding back: the single staring eye of Freya Colin; the way her brother had spoken of Freya as if she was nothing; the nasty gash on Magnus' scalp and the bloodied towel; the argument she'd had with him and his request of her to keep quiet; her fervent rebuttal and being called a traitor; and finally, the cloying sweet smell of the chloroform.

And, yet, she was still alive. So, what had Magnus done with her?

Alicya licked her lips. They tasted bitter and yet chloroform was sweet. Had her brother tried to poison her to death, post-chloroform? Given the murder of Freya Colin, and his admission that he had killed before, it was highly likely that he would attempt to murder his own sister to keep his secrets and to save his own neck. Poison would certainly explain the swimming head, stale vomit and bitter taste. It would also mean that the rumours about her brother were very true.

For a while, Alicya lay there, numb with shock. The miasma in her head gradually began to dissipate, though, and she soon found herself mourning for her parents, imagining their distress at what would appear to be an unexplained disappearance. It wasn't hard to imagine Magnus feeding them a pack of lies, either – accompanied by crocodile tears, whilst no doubt weaving a story about a kidnapping. She felt a raw anger welling up, but buried it immediately; she first had to work out where she was and how to make herself safe.

So, what did she know?

For starters, she didn't appear to be in any immediate danger – although the rope around her bound hands and feet was so tight, she could move them only a hair's-breadth apart. Why would Magnus bind her limbs, though, if he thought she was dead – particularly given he had left her un-gagged? That said, she wasn't yet ready to call out; she had no idea where she was or in whose company.

So, what else did she know?

The first thing she picked up was the gentle rise and fall of the world around her. Then she tuned in to the sound of a rushing surf and a vague salty smell that was largely held at bay by the other more unpleasant smells that were closer to home. Clearly on a boat, then, but not on deck. So, likely down below in a cargo hold. *And that smell!* Vomit and excrement, she had already identified – but there was something else, even stronger, more putrid.

Alicya concentrated again, this time picking up occasional voices from the crew, and although she couldn't make out the words, she was certain they were talking in Thissibrilean – there was a certain rhythm to it. Then again, that was pretty much a given since everyone north of the Shield of Crenac spoke Thiss-.

Alicya went into a wild panic. *The Shield of Crenac!* Suddenly she was certain that her evil brother would choose that as the perfect way to make her disappear forever. For all she knew, she may only have minutes left. The men up above would have been instructed to approach the Shield, drop anchor a few yards to the north, load her body into a small wooden boat, and then push it forward where it would cross the lethal Shield of Crenac.

Now certain there was little point in shouting for help, Alicya started straining desperately at her bonds, ignoring the rawness this caused – until she felt another sharp pain, this one in her right buttock which made her issue a sharp cry. She immediately pulled away from whatever it was that had caused the pain, albeit wary that she didn't plant herself somewhere else sharp.

Finding somewhere safe and pain-free, Alicya fumed, making a strange noise in the back of her throat. *As if her predicament wasn't already tough enough!*

Then the penny dropped.

Stock still for a few seconds, and still on her right side, Alicya knew she was now several inches away from where she'd been spiked. She therefore moved, very slowly backwards towards the object. After a few seconds, she felt the bottom of her right buttock come up against something sticking up from the floor. Adjusting her position slightly, and with her fingers still operational, Alicya eventually managed to touch the object with them. It was clearly an old nail sticking up out of the wooden floor of the hold. It was also a gift.

Slowly lowering her bound hands to the tip of the nail, Alicya gently moved them back and forth. Very gradually, threads began to break and the pressure loosened. Five minutes and three painful jabs in her wrists later, her bonds finally snapped free.

Remaining on her right side to avoid further nails, not to mention her own vomit, Alicya immediately rested her head against a sack of whatever the boat's cargo was, and used her freed hands to work at the knot that was holding her head-sack in place. It was tightly knotted, but she could feel it loosening bit-by-bit – which also meant that the action slowly released disgusting slops of vomit to slide down her neck and chest. It took another three minutes of work, but she eventually undid the knot and then ripped off the rough sack from her head. Alicya brushed her hideously-matted dark hair from her eyes, frantically wiped the vomit from her face – and then stopped, stone dead.

She gasped. There weren't any sacks. Just bodies. Everywhere. Lifeless, sightless bodies. That 'other' smell now made sense.

For a second or two, Alicya was rigid with fear – and then she jerked herself clear of the body her head had been lying on and gripped herself tightly, forcing down a rising scream. That was when she got another shock: she was totally naked. As were half of the bodies in the hold.

Despite the double shock, though, Alicya was now pretty certain where she was. *Not* close to the Shield of Crenac, thankfully, but probably not a lot better off – as she was almost certainly on the Body Boat heading for Cemetery Island, around sixty leagues north-west of Ghantiss. It was where all those bodies went for whom relatives couldn't pay for a decent burial. Or it was the final destination for those poor unfortunates who didn't *have* any relatives. Or, according to Glennadian rumours, it was also the final destination for those who had been secretly done over by someone, and subsequently went on to the Missing Persons register, never to be found again – as no one ever went to Cemetery Island other than the body porters – they almost certainly being the owners of the voices above, on deck.

Alicya briefly wondered if the porters on this boat had ever had one of their 'cargo' come back to life? In a civilised world, she ought to be able to climb the stairs to the deck, explain that a terrible mistake had been made and maybe even have a little chuckle about it with the porters. But Alicya had no idea who was up there. And whoever they were, they would probably laugh themselves silly if she announced herself as the Princess Alicya – particularly in this state! Alicya also knew enough about men to be afraid. One vulnerable and naked young girl, alive, and half a dozen men on a deserted island – that wasn't the most ideal of recipes.

Finally, Alicya knew that Magnus employed men like Hoskyns and Marler, as it amused him to observe the baser forms of life. What if they were up there now – making sure that Princess Alicya's body was never discovered? Once she'd been thrown into an unmarked grave like all of these other poor souls, with a convenient sack tied over her royal face, no one would ever know. Of course, the term 'grave' was a loose one; Alicya had heard they dug long communal channels which were populated and then filled in.

Alicya shook her head. Whatever the situation was up top, she couldn't afford to take the chance of announcing herself. Hopefully, once Hoskyns and Marler had done their dirty deed of throwing her into this hold, they had cleared off back to the palace, assuming the job had been done. And probably having had a good laugh at her naked royal body, too. And perhaps worse.

Alicya shuddered, but then focused on what she needed to do next, starting with using the nail in the hold floor to free her bound ankles. It took another five minutes of frenetic activity and left her with sore buttocks from the backwards and forwards motion and a couple of other piercings on her ankles from the nail. At last, unbound, she stretched her legs and massaged her cramped muscles. She then looked around for suitable 'clothing' – as not all the bodies were naked. Gritting her teeth, Alicya scanned the bodies nearest to her, seeking someone of a similar age -.

A gasp of shock caught in Alicya's throat. Despite her macabre setting, it was still a terrible jolt to see a familiar face. "Oh, Freya," she whispered, as she beheld the poor baker's daughter, with her face distorted by two black eyes and a broken nose. Freya was naked too. But then again, recalled Alicya, poor Freya had been naked when she had been murdered – by her monstrous brother.

Once again, Alicya closeted her white-hot anger. It would have to keep. Instead, she gently closed Freya's one staring eye, offering up a silent prayer for her soul. She was about to renew her search for appropriate clothing when she heard a creak from above, and a narrow shaft of light appeared around the hold trapdoor.

Alicya immediately threw herself to the 'floor' – very aware that she wasn't lying on wooden decking. Playing dead, she felt justified in leaving her eyes open to see behind her, upside down. She observed a young man dressed in little more than rags, walk down the first three steps and scan the sea of bodies. Alicya felt his eyes pass over her naked form but forced herself to remain totally still. After a few seconds, she heard the man say: "Nah, must have been the rats, Pete. They're all sleeping down here." And with that, he walked back up the steps and let the hold hatch slam down again.

Alicya's pent-up breath exploded. *Sweet Thera!* And now she knew she had rats to cope with as well! Rats that might have been nibbling at her bare toes while she was unconscious! At the same time, though, and despite all of the negatives that were starting to pile up, Alicya felt her body pumping with adrenaline at the joy of being alive against some pretty hefty odds. It was a surreal concoction of emotions.

Her eyes then fell on a middle-aged woman, with greying hair, of medium height and build. Someone had kindly closed her eyes, which made Alicya's grim task slightly easier. She was wearing the drab clothes of perhaps a farmer's wife – a full-length and plain grey dress with a maroon waistcoat and a white shift, while her white coif had been dislodged from her head. Alicya part-closed her eyes as she unbuttoned and removed the waistcoat, followed by the shift and dress. She was about to remove the lady's undergarments when she wrinkled up her nose in disgust – and then recalled someone telling her of a certain default bodily action, when all the muscles relax.

Pushing these dreadful thoughts aside, Alicya attired herself in just the dress, shift and waistcoat, and then grabbed the white coif. She applied it to her own head, tucking in her matted hair as best as she could. Finally, and somewhat bizarrely, the woman owned mismatching felt boots; one brown, one grey. Gently removing them from the dead woman and slipping them onto her own feet, Alicya mused once again that it was highly unlikely anyone would see *this* figure as a princess! And in any case, she might as well get used to being a peasant until she worked out exactly how she was going to take her life forward from here. Her first problem, of course, was getting out of this hold without being spotted. She had two choices. One: play dead, let the body porters take her and either try and escape before she was buried. Two: again, play dead, hope that she wasn't taken upstairs in the first batch of bodies, and whilst they were busy burying the first batch, climb up out of the hold and hide somewhere else.

The second option was the most appealing. But what then? Being realistic, there was little chance of remaining on board, undiscovered, for the return trip to Ghantiss, given an empty hold. And no one would believe she was the Princess Alicya. Which would mean that even if she *did* get back to Ghantiss undiscovered, she would still need to somehow make it into the palace dressed as a peasant. If she could just get to Maddox in the stables, Maddox would know what to do.

Alicya felt a wash of emotion when she recalled the gruff stablemaster. He would be missing her dreadfully. Was it really only yesterday afternoon that they had raced Tabetha and Sebastian? She then recalled the way Magnus had reacted aggressively several days ago, when Maddox had looked to support her in the palace courtyard. Maddox was less than a fleabite to Magnus, and turning to him for help would put his life in danger, too. And on top of that, there was still the overall dilemma: if she did return home, she would have to explain to her parents that their son had murdered at least one young girl in his palace bedroom and had also attempted to murder their daughter. Did her parents deserve that? It would destroy them, finish their family and probably their royal line, too. But then again, Magnus didn't deserve to continue that royal line, did he? And didn't she have a responsibility herself to the people of Glennad to make sure that he didn't?

Alicya sighed. There were so many unknowns in returning to Ghantiss. And who was to say that Magnus wouldn't find out about her return and have Hoskyns or Marler slit her throat before she'd gotten anywhere near to the palace stables? She'd end up back on this boat again. But this time, she really would be dead!

This left the other route, which was subtly calling her. To get off this boat and onto Cemetery Island unseen, and then somehow get back to the mainland and divest herself of her previous life; to no longer be a princess, but a commoner. To live a life which promised freedom and love; she could have a husband of her choice and not be married off to some ageing royal or member of the nobility. She could also stalk Magnus without suspicion, and then one day, take her revenge. If she so-desired. Because with her upbringing, her brains, her insights…she could be anyone she pleased.

Of course, if she chose this route, it would mean that her parents would believe her either kidnapped or dead. Tears welled up at that thought. Was she being cruel by not returning? Or would it be crueller if she did? There were so many potential ramifications.

Her thoughts were suddenly pulled back into the present by a flurry of shouting and activity up above. Alicya felt her heart lurch. She had expected more time to think, but it was too late for that. They had likely arrived at Cemetery Island.

CHAPTER 21   EMILYA
6th Tertiar, 1789   Day 97, 16:00

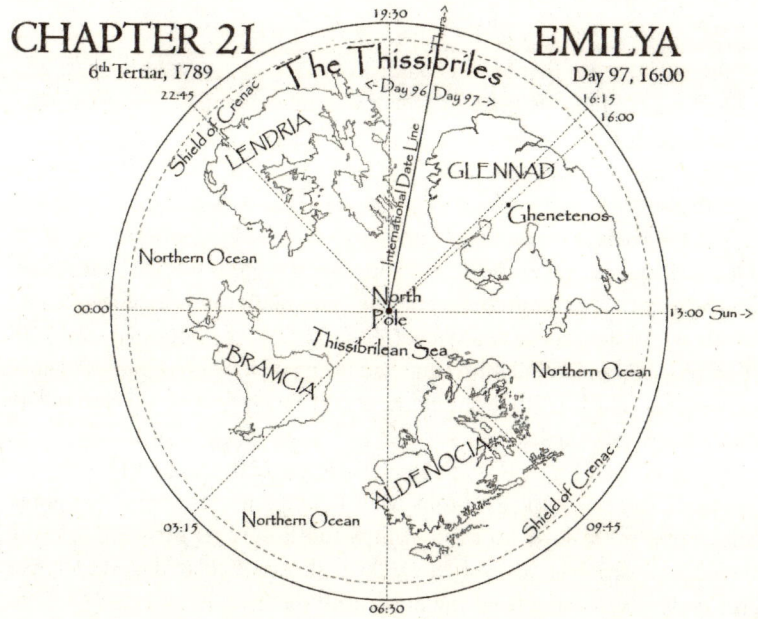

The stones of Ghenetenos were less than a quarter of a league away, and Emilya was beginning to understand just how impressive they were. To think that the stone temple had been erected over four thousand years ago was mind-boggling. In the age of small, brick-by-brick-built edifices, Emilya wasn't even sure how *today's* builders would manage such a feat, never mind folk from the New Stone Age. She certainly hadn't observed engines and pulley systems in Ghantiss that could erect on this scale.

Elyse noticed Emilya's intense scrutinisation of the stones. "Care to share?" she asked.

"What? Oh, sorry," said Emilya. "It's a bit of a pet vice," she admitted. "Architecture, that is. If that counts as architecture," she added, nodding at the stones.

Elyse pursed her lips, and then turned her penetrating, azure eyes on Emilya. "That's a fairly strange 'vice' for a fifteen-year-old baker's daughter, if you don't mind me saying."

"Very true," agreed Emilya. "It's my grandfather's fault. He was an architect, you see."

"That's a far cry from a baker," said Elyse, rather directly. "I'd have expected his son and granddaughter to have gone to private school and, well…"

"Better things?" suggested Emilya, with a half-smile.

"I could have put that better, couldn't I?"

"It's fine, I'm not offended. But there was an incident."

"An incident?"

"Well, more of a disaster, really."

"A disaster?"

"Yes, long before I was born. Grandfather was working on a six-hundred-foot canal aqueduct over the River Esou, twelve leagues south of Earl's Leet. He was only the junior architect, but he and another junior colleague had already questioned the lead architect, Professor Marx, about the depth and effectiveness of the foundations that had been laid for the six-hundred-foot brick pillars. They felt they should have run much deeper, and the pillars should have been thicker, too."

"Oh dear," said Elyse. "I think I can guess where this is going."

"Hmm," agreed Emilya. "From what Gramps told me, there's a gorge which runs from north to south which the Esou cuts through, and the aqueduct passes over it, west-to-east. On this particular day, there were force ten gales blowing from the north, and the Esou was a raging torrent courtesy of five days of constant rain. Cue a one-hundred-foot coal barge on the aqueduct, carrying around two hundred tons of coal."

Elyse was looking at Emilya in horror. "And it collapsed?"

"Yes," confirmed Emilya. "But incredibly, the barge crew escaped with their lives."

"From six-hundred feet up!" exclaimed Elyse, disbelievingly.

"The story goes that they had thirty seconds to wade back through the funnel in the direction they'd come from, as the collapse happened gradually, in stages. Eyewitnesses in the valley saw it all come hammering down – bridge, funnel, barge, coal, masonry – the lot."

"Must have been some event," said Jake, joining in. "My father was a young man himself when it happened. He often used to mention it."

"What happened to the architect?" asked Elyse. "This Marx fellow?"

"He tried to blame it on the junior architects. Said he'd delegated responsibility for the foundations to them. Thankfully, the inquiry didn't believe him, and stated that even if he *had* been telling the truth, he was still guilty of gross negligence, delegating such responsibility to juniors."

"Did he get his just rewards?" asked Elyse.

"Pretty much," confirmed Emilya. "He was sentenced to fifteen years in prison for gross negligence of a kind which could have resulted in a large loss of human life."

"Good for the inquiry," said Elyse. "What happened to your grandfather?"

"He and his colleague produced written, date-stamped evidence that they'd expressed concerns about the structure, and this was upheld; they were totally absolved. But Gramps never worked as an architect again. He decided he'd have less public responsibility, and less capacity for holding the key to life and death, if he opened a bakery!"

"Ah, and the rest is history," said Elyse.

"Yes. Of course, Gramps still loved architecture – and so he used to point out everything as we walked around Ghantiss together – a cruck-frame here, a post-and-beam there. As I got older, he used to draw plans for me. It became a game. I'd point out a building and when we got back home, he'd draw the plans for me. After a couple of years, he turned the tables on me. Of course, I got a lot wrong, initially, and he would always point out why my buildings would collapse – which is a good way of learning without casualties. It's amazing how you then remember and avoid mistakes the next time around. Gradually, I started to draw plans that weren't so dangerous. And last month he gave me my first nine out of ten – for a three-storey town-house."

Elyse's face was shining with approval. "Wow! And you work as a trainee baker?"

"I'm only fifteen, Elyse!" responded Emilya, quite hurt. "Who knows where I'll be in ten years' time."

"Back in Ghantiss, hopefully," said Jake, drily.

"Perhaps," said Emilya, having subconsciously picked up that line from Elyse. Elyse recognised this and just managed to hide her smile. "Perhaps not," completed Emilya.

This time, both Elyse and Jake smirked.

"What?" demanded Emilya.

"Nothing dear," replied Elyse, innocently.

Emilya looked from Elyse to Jake and then back to Elyse again. "You two are ganging up on me again," she accused.

Jake laughed gently at that and winked at her. Elyse moved in closer, issued her sparkling smile and then held out her hand to Emilya – her standard peace offering. Emilya took it begrudgingly. "Never," said Elyse, still smiling at her and squeezing her hand.

Emilya couldn't help but be disarmed and eventually smiled back. Meanwhile, the movement of Emilya's hand had woken up little Theo, who turned his head in Emilya's harness to look up at her. As ever, Emilya just melted. "Hello, little one," she said. "Have you had a nice sleepy?"

Theo just looked up at her with his big brown eyes and long eyelashes, so Emilya let go of Elyse's hand and gently stroked the fur on Theo's head. Theo nuzzled his nose deeper into Emilya's palm.

"Hello," said Jake, interrupting the moment. "We've got a reception committee."

Emilya looked up to see a posse of five riders trotting out towards them from Ghenetenos village. They were all dressed in cream-coloured cloaks and robes, tied at the waist with a brown cord, while each of them had their hoods up, which masked their faces in shadow. Emilya was immediately spooked.

Jake noticed her disquiet so was about to move ahead to greet them – but Elyse beat him to it. She tapped her heels to the flanks of her horse and cantered towards the five approaching druids. When she reached them, she swung herself fluidly out of her saddle and approached on foot. The rider in the middle of the posse did the same. Then they both stopped in front of each other.

"I honour your path," said Elyse.

"You may drink from our well," responded the druid, throwing back his cowl to reveal the face of a man in his thirties, with long black hair, and a long beard fashioned into dreadlocks intermingled with beads. He also had the image of a black sun painted onto his forehead; Emilya couldn't tell if it was permanent.

Elyse and the druid were now staring at each other, and Emilya felt the hairs raising on her arm. Then, all of a sudden, both Elyse and the druid burst out laughing and then embraced.

"I knew it," said Jake, quietly.

"You weren't sure, actually," responded Emilya, as the other druids threw back their hoods – revealing one of them to be a slender boy of around her age with shoulder-length, sandy-coloured hair. She caught him looking at her and immediately averted her eyes.

"Come, come," said Elyse to them, beckoning them forward. When they drew level, both Emilya and Jake dismounted. "This is my brother, Emrys," announced Elyse. "Emrys, may I introduce you to Emilya Luca, a talented young architect, and Jake Oscom – a erm, talented *young* naval captain."

"My word!" exclaimed Emrys, in a rich and cultured baritone voice. "You travel in such esteemed company, big sis."

"I'm retired, actually," said Jake, shaking Emrys' hand. "And I've not been young for, oh, twenty-five years," he added.

"Whereas I'll be at least twenty-five before I'm even a *novice* architect," added Emilya.

"Ah!" exclaimed Emrys. "Wherever she goes, my beautiful sister only befriends those with humility. As for those without…" he tailed off.

Emilya looked at Elyse and raised her eyebrows.

Emrys noticed. "My sister gives short shrift to braggarts," he clarified.

Emilya laughed at that. "She needs to meet Prince Magnus then."

"Ah, I fear it would not end well for the fair prince," came the mellifluous response.

"Well," responded Elyse, nodding at Jake. "Some of us have already humbled the fair prince."

Jake responded by looking at Emilya. "And some of us weren't the first to do so, either."

"Ah!" exclaimed Emrys again. "I am sensing an intriguing story here. Might I suggest that you regale us over dinner, this evening? You will join us, won't you?"

"Of course, Emrys," responded Elyse. "That would be lovely."

"And Edwyn," said Elyse, moving towards the boy who had also dismounted. She kissed him on his cheek. "So tall. You're catching your father up," she said, nodding at Emrys.

Edwyn laughed awkwardly and dropped his eyes, rather embarrassed at the affectionate exchange with his beautiful aunt, although Emilya did spot his eyes flicker briefly towards herself again. Strangely, she felt a rush of heat to her face and quickly grabbed her water bottle and drank from it, hoping it would hide any perception of interest.

Emrys then introduced the other three riders before Emilya, Elyse and Jake allowed themselves to be escorted in the direction of the village.

CHAPTER 22   ALICYA
6th Tertiar, 1789   Day 97, 14:00

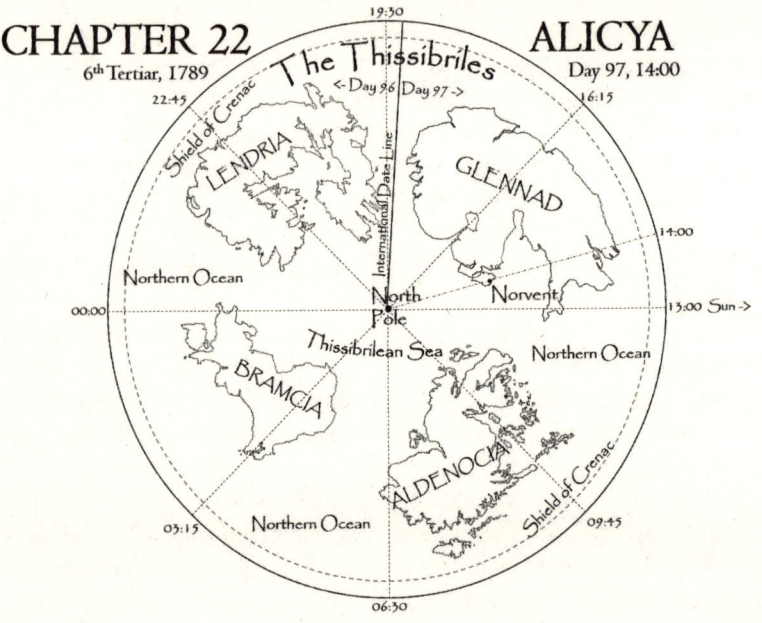

The body porters had emptied the hold of around a quarter of the bodies. Alicya, in her peasant's garb, had selected a place at the far end of the hold to play dead, figuring the porters would start with the bodies nearest the hatch. Thankfully, she was right. Through her staring 'dead' eyes, Alicya saw five different porters enter the hold, one after the other, and she counted each of them down four times apiece. So, twenty bodies had been taken, after which a visit for a twenty-first didn't happen.

A minute passed, then five minutes. During this time, Alicya could hear a great deal of activity on-deck. The boat was obviously moored to a jetty or a harbour wall, as she could feel it gently buffeting against a firm structure. She then felt the boat creak somewhere to the right, as if a weight had shifted over to that side. That had to be the porters disembarking with their grisly cargo.

Alicya racked her brains for what she knew about Cemetery Island. It had first been used as a location for mass graves after the Black Death had raged across the Thissibriles in the 14th century. The unfortunate islanders had been forced to leave their homes and re-start their lives on the Glennadian mainland – although some had emigrated to Lendria and some to Aldenocia. Unsurprisingly, very few people had ever ventured back to make Cemetery Island their home in the following two hundred years. Then, in the 17th century, the government passed a bill which ordered all unclaimed bodies to be buried in mass graves on the island – later extended to those families who couldn't afford a burial back in Glennad. Alicya also knew that there was only one port on Cemetery Island. Norvent, on its west coast, had been the island's capital back in the 14th century, and had remained the main docking point for body porters ever since. The first mass graves in the 14th century had been dug on the inland outskirts of Norvent, and new graves had been extended further and further inland ever since.

Due to the likely distance to the new graves, Alicya was expecting the men to use a horse and cart to transport the bodies, as she was fairly certain she'd heard equine noises above. Given the initial batch of twenty bodies, it was likely that they had two carts, as a single horse could probably pull a cart of ten bodies. The question was, how many men would go with the carts and how many would stay on-board?

After another five minutes of listing and creaking, Alicya heard the unmistakable sound of horses' hooves clopping down a wooden ramp to the dock. The voices then receded a little further – probably to the hitching point of cart to horse. Another ten minutes passed, and then Alicya heard horses' hooves again along with a new creaking sound – surely the laden carts. Thereafter, the only noises were the sound of the sea washing against the harbour walls, the creaking of the boat and the occasional seabird. Alicya briefly wondered what the seabirds fed on without humans to scrounge from as they did back in Ghantiss. Well, not living humans, anyway. She shuddered at that thought.

Alicya stayed put for five minutes before braving a foray up the exit ladder. She carefully picked a path through the remaining sixty-or-so bodies, before placing her foot on the first wooden step. It creaked, loudly. Alicya winced and froze. She remained in that pose for several seconds before gradually relaxing. Steps two and three only made the slightest of creaks. Step four let her down, though, Alicya glaring at it as if it had sentience. She then glared a warning, at the next six-or-so steps, before quickly completing the assent, relatively soundlessly. Carefully, Alicya placed the palm of her right hand on the underside of the hatch and pushed up gently. A thin crack of light appeared, very bright, causing her to shut her eyes. She was going to have to do this slowly.

Bravely, she left her hand in place and the crack remained. Nothing happened. Once she became accustomed to the new light, Alicya pushed a little harder. This time she could see the wooden deck of the ship. Another push and she could see the cabin and the forward mast, and then beyond that, the ruined port of Norvent. It looked desolate.

Alicya remained in this position for another thirty seconds. When nothing happened, she slowly pushed the hatch up to ninety degrees and climbed out onto the deck. Crouching, she looked around, pirouetting through three-hundred-and-sixty degrees on the balls of her feet that were now clad in those mismatched felt boots. She couldn't believe her luck -.

She had heard a noise. It sounded like the cough of an old man, and it was coming from the other side of the cabin. Alicya dropped back down into the hold and lowered the hatch, but left it open a crack. Then she saw him. Short, white hair, deep tan, a weathered face…and wearing a blue uniform. He was walking slowly around the bow, hands clasped behind his back, and was about to come around to the right-hand side, facing the hold. Reluctantly, Alicya let the hatch close, quietly. Just to be safe, she descended the steps again, ready to play dead in an instant.

Alicya shook her head. *The ship's captain!* How naïve of her to overlook the most important occupant of a boat! Nevertheless, it looked as though the porters had all gone, and at twenty bodies per trip, there would be three more trips – meaning they were likely to be here all day. The chances were, they wouldn't be back for another hour or so before collecting the next twenty bodies – although that would leave the hold half empty, and less places to hide. This meant her best chance for escape was now.

Her mind made up, Alicya re-mounted the hold steps, taking care to avoid steps one, four and eight. When she pushed open the hatch again, she was in luck. The captain had his back to her, hands still clasped behind his back, standing to her right at the top of the ramp, looking out at the ruined port. Then Alicya spotted some objects resting on a wooden chest, a few inches to the right of the captain: five tankards, one water flask and six plates – on which were the remains of some basic meal. Alicya suddenly realised how ravenous she was, not to mention thirsty. Two of the plates had hunks of bread left on them, and princess or not, leftover bread looked like a veritable feast.

Eventually, the captain turned and walked to Alicya's right towards the stern. Unfortunately, Alicya couldn't see what was behind her, so she was unable to gauge if she could make a dash for it without the captain seeing her. Instead, she decided to play it safe and wait until the captain was heading back towards the front of the boat. At the pace he was moving, she'd have time to get down the ramp and hide before he came back around the front right again.

It took the captain another five long minutes to appear to Alicya's left. He then sauntered towards the cabin, leaving Alicya worrying that the body porters would be back for their second consignment before she got her one and only chance to escape. However, the second the captain's right arm disappeared behind the cabin, Alicya pushed the hatch open and silently got out onto the deck – but this time she quietly closed the hatch, too. By this stage, the captain was fully obscured by the cabin. Grateful for her flat, soft boots – one brown, the other grey – Alicya moved quickly across to the ramp, opportunistically grabbing the two hunks of bread and the water bottle, and tucking them into her apron pockets. She then looked out at the ruined port, left and right, but saw no movement. She checked back on the captain. He hadn't yet appeared this side of the cabin. It was now or never.

The twenty-foot ramp led down onto a ramshackle wooden jetty which, in turn, ran for around twenty yards to the right to the crumbling harbour walls. To the left was a dead end – only open water. Alicya immediately saw her only option and went for it. She walked as lightly down the ramp as she could, constantly checking over her left shoulder for the captain's return. Then, when she got to the jetty, she braced herself, and then lowered herself over the far side into the harbour waters. She felt an immediate shock from the cold water, but forced herself to remain silent, whilst her borrowed farmer's dress floated up to surround her. She quickly gathered it in, lest the captain spot the dash of dull colour in the water behind the jetty.

Looking through the slats of the jetty, Alicya could see the captain continuing his slow circuit, currently down the starboard side of the ship. His pace wasn't doing anything for her body temperature. Already her teeth were starting to chatter, and mists of cold breath were gathered in front of her face. But as the captain approached the stern, Alicya used the jetty to help slowly propel herself through the water in the direction of the harbour, using a hand over hand technique above her. The motion created very little sound, and once the captain disappeared up the port side, Alicya threw herself face first into the water and began to swim hard, all the time making sure that the jetty kept her out of view from the boat. By the time she reached the foot of the harbour wall, the captain hadn't even got to the bow of the boat – which meant more waiting. She used the opportunity to remove her coif, and began to repeatedly soak her hair with seawater and follow this up by squeezing it and working out the hideous globs of vomit. By the time she had finished, the captain had begun his walk back up the port side, so Alicya hauled herself up onto the jetty, seawater sluicing off her sodden clothing and did a quick check for returning porters. Again, no movement, so Alicya dashed across the harbour frontage to what looked like a ruined church, the heaviness of her wet clothing and now-squelchy boots making her extremely uncomfortable and cold.

There was no glass in the church windows, and the front door and roof were both long-gone, but it offered sanctuary. It also got her out of the cutting wind. As Alicya dripped in through the gaping door, she took in the devastation inside. The remains of the collapsed roof were spread across the floor and the ancient, rotting pews, although the stone pulpit had survived more-or-less intact, as had the bell turret at the rear of the church, although it had now been largely claimed by ivy. Most importantly, though, all four walls were intact to help conceal her, while she could peep out of any of the gaping windows at the front from which she could see the stern of the body porters' boat, as well as the full length of the jetty and the approach to it from both sides.

In the meantime, she needed to do something about her clothing, but her options were either bad or worse: either keep her wet clothing on and freeze; or take her wet clothing off and freeze. Given it was only springtime, the chances of her clothing drying quickly were remote. However, something was nagging at her conscience. Something she'd seen on her sprint across the harbour.

Checking that the distant captain had his back to her, Alicya cautiously edged out of the church doorway, looking right then left. And there it was. An incongruous greatcoat draped over a low wall. One of the porters must have dispensed with it, probably after the heavy work of lugging the bodies into the cart. Alicya briefly thanked the heavens, and then sprinted left to grab the shabby greatcoat before bolting back into the church.

Once inside, Alicya shrugged off her peasant's outfit, squeezed more water out of her hair, and then donned the grey greatcoat. It was several sizes too big for her, so after buttoning it up, she pulled the belt tight such that excess material overlapped. The coat was rough against her skin but felt wonderfully warm and dry and, after a bit of arm-rubbing, Alicya soon felt some body-warmth return. She then picked up the dripping clothes, first checking the apron for the bread and water. Miraculously, both had remained in-place – although the bread was horribly soggy. Alicya parked them on top of the church's stone font and began to squeeze out as much water as she could out of her clothes. Satisfied, she flapped a bit of air into them, and then dusted down the nearest set of pews before draping the damp clothes over them.

She then grabbed the water and the soggy bread and sat down with her back to the front wall of the church. She eyed the first of the two hunks of soggy bread, dubiously, and her thoughts wandered to Mrs Alsnow's magical Sunday roasts. "Not much use now," whispered Alicya, glumly, as she raised the bread to her lips – but then stopped, her hand still in mid-air.

Had she seen movement to the right of the church aisle? She stared hard. Was that a hint of orange fur? Not a person, then – although she didn't much fancy being attacked by a rabid dog, either. Alicya waited patiently, bread still in mid-air. After about thirty seconds, a long orange and white snout with a black nose peeped out nervously. "Hello," said Alicya, gently. "Are you sheltering in here as well?"

The fox cub continued to look at her intently, its penetrating eyes searching for something. Then Alicya realised what it was. Alicya broke off a bit of bread and tasted it. It was obviously soggy – and excessively salty too. But it wasn't that bad. It was certainly still edible. She therefore broke off another piece and held it out for the inquisitive cub to see. "Would you like some manky bread, darling?" she asked – once again using that gentle, coaxing tone.

The fox cub still looked unsure – but put a tentative paw forward. Then another.

"That's it, come on you beautiful little thing," said Alicya, her heart melted by the large black and amber eyes and beautiful markings of the cub. "Are you all on your own?" she asked, continually coaxing the cub towards her. "Have you lost your Mummy?"

It took another two or three minutes of gentle coaxing before the cub finally arrived at Alicya's fingertips. It sniffed the bread several times, and then, satisfied it was edible, snatched it out of Alicya's hands and ate it greedily, licking its lips profusely afterwards.

"There you go," said Alicya, encouragingly. "Welcome to Alicya's Gastronomic Banquet. Would you like some more?"

The cub's eyes were flicking from Alicya's eyes to the bread and back again – and so Alicya broke off some more.

Despite being ravenous herself, Alicya made sure that she shared her meal fifty-fifty with the cub. She then took the water flask, uncorked it and sampled the contents – in case it was wine or spirit. It wasn't. It was refreshingly cold spring water. Having taken several swigs herself, Alicya poured some into her other cupped hand and held it out for the fox cub. It sniffed her hand, and then its long tongue slurped thirstily at the water. Alicya repeated the action three more times – and each time, the cub drank all the water.

With their simple meal devoured, Alicya was pleased to note that the fox-cub had remained with her. It just stood there, looking at her intently, occasionally licking its lips, savouring the aftertaste of the salty bread. Alicya put her hand out to the cub, and this time it came straight up and nuzzled her hand. Alicya's heart melted. "Oh, you are so beautiful," she said, as she gently began to stroke the cub's head. The cub tilted its head to one side, clearly enjoying the affection. "But where is your Mummy, hey? Has your Mummy abandoned you?"

The cub responded by licking Alicya's hand with a rough tongue. Delighted with this return of affection, Alicya risked moving her face closer the cub. Far from being intimidated, though, the cub then licked Alicya's face, too. Alicya laughed delightedly – but then cut off her laugh, sharply. She'd heard horses' hooves and voices.

Quickly adjusting, Alicya moved across to the nearest front window and peeped around the side of it. Two horses were passing the church, pulling two empty carts, with the horses being ridden, saddleless, by two of the body porters. Alicya recognised both of their faces from her playing dead exploits in the hold, earlier. Once they had their backs to her, Alicya sat down cross-legged under the window where she was at just the right height to peep over the ledge. Seconds later, she felt movement to her left. The fox cub had followed and was nuzzling her left arm. The action touched her heart again, and so Alicya gently picked up the cub and placed her (she was now sure she was female) into her lap – where the cub pulled at the greatcoat material with her front paws for a few seconds to make a nest, before settling down.

Alicya smiled before returning her attention to outside. The two men were tying up the two horses before they began to make their way down the jetty towards their moored boat. For the next half an hour, the two porters shuttled back and forth along the jetty, up the ramp and back again, ferrying another twenty bodies over to the two waiting carts under the watchful eye of the white-haired captain on the deck.

Half-way through this activity, Alicya glanced down at the fox cub in her lap. She was fast asleep. A strange noise caught in Alicya's throat, a bit like an "Oh!", and her eyes filed up with tears. *She had a friend.*

Just before they departed, the two porters passed close enough for Alicya to tune into their conversation. "He said he'd left it here – two buildings down from the church on a low wall. That wall," said the younger of the two porters, pointing to where Alicya had grabbed the greatcoat. Alicya's heart went cold.

"Ah, give over, Ty," replied the older porter. "That bloke'll lose his head one of these days! He probably never even brought it with him. Now come on, else we'll not be away from here before dark."

Alicya breathed a sigh of relief. She was also pleased with her assessment, so far. Other than her initial fear over the Shield of Crenac, she'd called everything pretty much right since then. She now had to plan her next move, though. Despite having avoided the captain and the porters, it would still be a weird feeling to see them depart – leaving her as probably the only human being alive on the entire island. That said, she'd heard rumours about weirdos, grave-diggers, necromancers, and the like – none of whom she was keen to make the acquaintance of. But at present, the Body Boat was her only means of escape from the island, apart from an eight-seat rowing boat that Alicya had spotted moored in the harbour, and which probably also belonged to the body porters for use at low tide.

Alicya had formulated half a plan to take the rowing boat herself the following morning. Her geography was imperious, and she knew that in daylight, she just needed to steer the boat to the south-west and she would eventually arrive at the Wrenko peninsula – far enough from Ghantiss to avoid Magnus' men. What would happen then was anybody's guess. But she had to get there first.

Rather than disturb the sleeping cub, Alicya gently moved to one side of the window and then rotated her position through one hundred and eighty degrees so that her back was to the rough stone wall. The cub barely stirred. Alicya smiled and decided that she should name her. She began turning appropriate names over in her mind but had only come up with Vixey before she'd slipped into a fitful doze.

CHAPTER 23 — DAVY

6th Tertiar, 1789   Day 97, 06:15

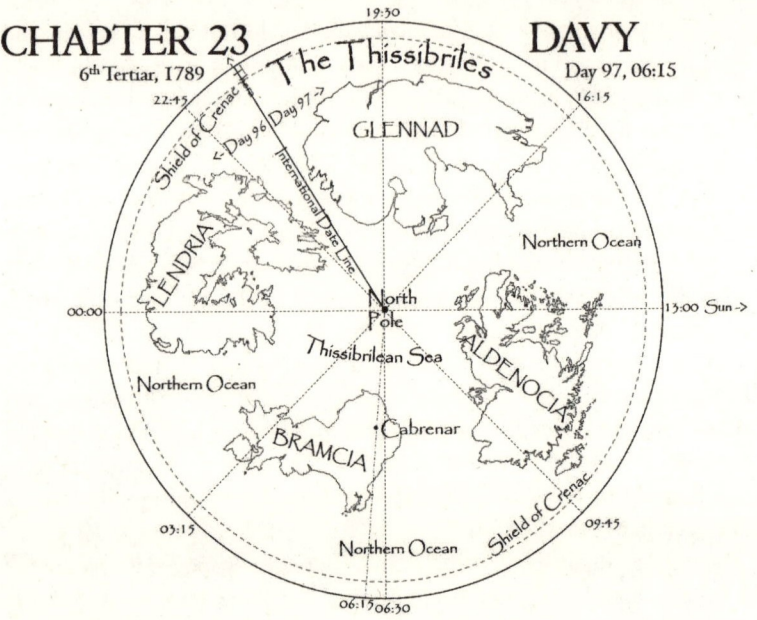

Davy and Will had just started the early shift which ran from 06:00 to 14:30. Unfortunately, given the 'tosser encounter' with Eckersley two days ago, poor Robbie was having to work back-to-back shifts to make up for his loss of earnings, including a follow-on 'late shift', from 14:30 to 23:00. Will was also working back-to-back shifts, an early with Davy and a late with Robbie – on the grounds that his Mam could use the extra money. Had it been anyone other than his best mate, Davy would have talked Will out of the punishing seventeen-hour undertaking, but he knew he could trust Robbie to look after him.

As Davy lifted another shovel-load of coal into the waiting wagon, he was instructing young Will. "You see, this that we're doing here," he said, thrusting his shovel back into the coal pile and lifting out a new load. "It's the most important job, not just in Bramcia," he said, emptying his load into the wagon, "but in the whole of the Thissibriles." And in went the shovel again, gathering its next load.

"Why do you say that?" asked Will.

Davy paused with his next shovel-load in mid-transition. "Because it provides heat for every home in Bramcia and fuel for cooking." He dumped his latest load into the wagon and turned around for his next load. Again, he paused, mid-transition. "And it's also the fuel that runs most of our factories and our engines and our iron-smelting works. Without it," he said, dumping again into the wagon, "we'd still be in the Dark Ages." He then looked Will in the eye and said: "Now you tell me, Will. What job is more important than that?"

"But it's not just us, though, is it?" asked Will.

"Well, us and people like us – in mines all over the Thissibriles."

"No, I meant – it's not just about the miners. What about the navvies who transport our coal via the canals to all of our towns and cities?"

Davy stopped shovelling coal and looked at Will again. "You really are a proper little thinker, aren't you?"

Will shrugged his shoulders. "Well without the navvies, none of those things you mention would happen."

"True enough," admitted Davy. "But we're the ones who risk our lives every day to get the coal in the first place. The worst that can happen to a navvy is he falls in the canal having had too much ale!"

"Fair comment," came Robbie's contribution from the next bay.

"You see!" said Davy. "Now then," he began, gathering his last shovel-load and dumping it on top of the pile in the wagon. He turned to face Will. "Over to you again, young man."

Will gave him one of his beams, and then attached the chain from his leather gurl belt to the front of the coal wagon. Will then put his fingers in his mouth and gave a shrill whistle – the sign for other apprentices further down the roadway to come and push the wagon from behind, a role known as a thruster. There was the sound of scurrying feet and then two very grimy young boys appeared out of the gloom – even younger than Will – and took their place behind the laden wagon. "Ready lads?" asked Will. The two boys assented. "Let's go then," said Will, forcing his head forwards, body at almost forty-five degrees and then pushing down into his legs with all his twelve-year-old strength. His face creased with the strain, but as soon as the other two lads pushed from behind, the wagon creaked into life and very slowly began to move forward. After around twenty seconds, the lads faded from Davy's sight, although he could still hear them puffing and straining. Once they got some momentum, though, Davy knew the task would become much easier.

Davy turned back to the coalface and held his lamp up into the cavity or goave that had been created by his earlier mining. The flame remained unaffected, so Davy was safe to carry on. He reached down for his pickaxe, lifted it, and swung it effortlessly at the coalface, loosening more and more coal with each swing. He'd been at it for around twenty minutes when he paused and laid down his pickaxe. Frowning to himself, Davy took his lamp and raised it in the direction that Will had disappeared. It usually took Will up to ten minutes to haul the wagon to the shaft station where men, materials and services entered and exited the lift shaft. Then it would be around one minute to load the laden wagon into the empty wagon-bay of the lift-cage, and another three minutes to pull the empty truck out of the other bay and push it all the way back to Davy – usually with the two younger thrusters sat inside and enjoying the ride.

Parking his concern, Davy went back to hacking more coal from the seam he was working, but when another five minutes passed without Will's return, he began to worry about an accident. Hurriers had been known to be run over by their own wagons before, particularly when they had over-enthusiastic thrusters. Thankfully, just as Davy was about to raise an alert, he heard the rumbling of the empty wagon returning – although Will didn't flash him his usual beam on arrival.

As the two oblivious thrusters jumped out and disappeared further up the gallery in readiness for their next wagonload, Davy put his hand on Will's shoulder. "Is everything all right, lad?"

Will looked at Davy. "I'm worried about my brother. I've just seen him at the shaft."

"Why, what's up?"

"I knew there was something wrong yesterday. Turns out Jack Musson has been laid up with the flu, so Dylan's working with some other bloke."

"Oh aye," said Davy. "Who's he with then?"

"Some bloke called Nate."

"What, not Nate Turner?"

"Yep, that's him."

"Robbie!" shouted Davy.

"What's up, mate?"

"Come here a minute."

"You serious? If Eckersley catches me in your bay again, he'll sack me on the spot, man."

Davy thought about that and realised he was right, so he walked further down the roadway to Robbie's bay. "What's up, mate?" asked Robbie, when he saw him. His grimy face was wet with sweat.

"Will's twin brother, Dylan – Jack Musson's got the flu, so Dylan's been paired with Nate Turner."

"No way!" exclaimed Robbie, putting his pickaxe down. "I thought they'd decided he'd have no more apprentices…after them rumours…"

"Yeah, well – nothing was ever proven. But there's plenty reckon that Nate Turner's a wrong 'un, for sure."

"What can we do?"

"Well, *you* can't do anything, mate, as you're on a double shift. *I'll* sort this out. I'll pay Nate and Dylan a visit, and then take Dylan up in the cage with me. I'm not having him work a double shift with Turner."

"You be careful, Davy. There's plenty down here reckon he's a psychopath when riled, never mind his age."

"Oh, I've heard he's a bit of a bully who can look after himself, Robbie. I just hope that's all he is."

"Well," said Robbie, picking up his pickaxe again and leaning on it. He looked Davy in the eye. "Whatever you do, don't go hinting at anything like that, Davy. I mean it! The last bloke got beaten to a pulp."

"Aye, probably because he'd touched a raw nerve!" said Davy, worriedly. "But you know Will's a bright lad, and if he says something's wrong, then something's probably wrong."

"What are you going say to him then?"

"Not sure yet, Robbie. I'll probably just say his Mam's sent a message down that she wants him home – and then I'll take him up with me."

"Sounds like a plan," agreed Robbie. "Trouble is – what we gonna do tomorrow?"

"Let's worry about that tomorrow. I'll have a think overnight -."

Davy had broken off suddenly as they had both heard the tones of Stan Eckersley coming down the roadway. By the time Eckersley reached Davy's bay, though, Davy was savagely hacking away at the coalface, as was Robbie next door.

Eckersley stood silently and watched first Davy, then moved on to Robbie before issuing one of his most-frequently uttered phrases of satisfaction. "There's lovely!"

CHAPTER 24   EMILYA
6th Tertiar, 1789   Day 97, 18:45

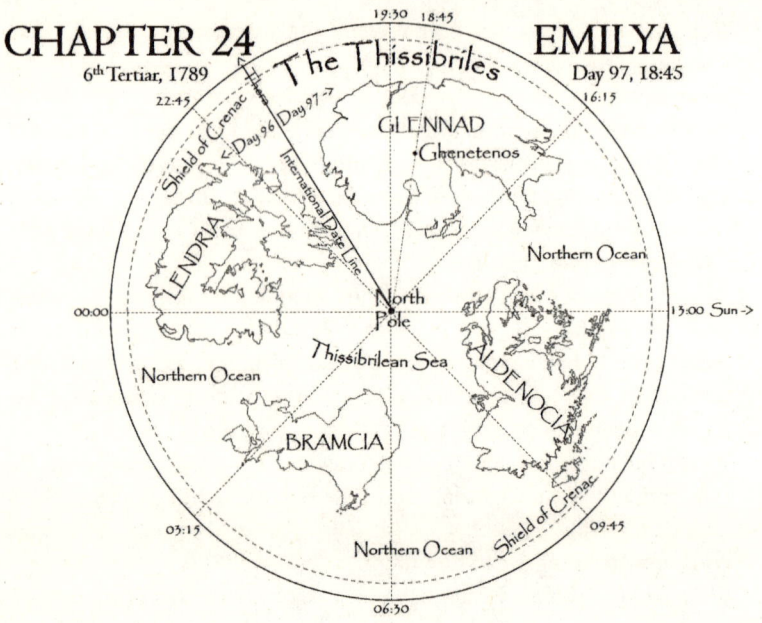

The communal home where the druids of Ghenetenos lived had been converted from an abandoned 15th century monastery. They had done a splendid job of restoring it and fitting it out with every kind of room you might find in an aristocrat's stately home – kitchens, pantries, bathrooms, bathing rooms, living quarters, bedrooms, dining rooms, a library, a games room, a study and even a very large banqueting hall.

Emilya, Elyse and Jake had been welcomed as honoured guests. Their horses had been stabled, Theo had been given a comfortable dog bed and was being fussed over by the communal dogs, and now, as they stood with Emrys in a lovely courtyard full of plants, flowers and tinkling fountains, they had just been offered use of a private bath (Emilya had declined the communal bath), and to have their clothes washed, dried and pressed. In addition, Emrys had offered Emilya and Elyse access to the commune wardrobe to dress for dinner, this being a custom of this rather strange community, once every week.

At first, Emilya had declined, but Elyse was having none of that. "For one night only, we are going to turn you into a beautiful young lady."

Emilya had screwed up her nose. "Erm, look at me," she replied, holding out her hands and indicating her dusty breeches and boots. "Not to mention this," she added, tugging at her wild, curly hair.

"I do like a challenge," responded Elyse, mischievously.

"Huh, thanks a lot!"

Elyse looked at her, the ghost of a smile on those delectable lips. "You know, you really are a very pretty girl, Emilya."

"I am not!" she responded. "And I'd rather give dinner a miss completely than be made up like a dainty princess."

"I admit, you are most certainly not a dainty princess."

Emilya couldn't help but smile at that. Elyse knew how to play her just right. "All right," she conceded. "But don't make me look stupid."

"Stupid?"

"Yes, stupid. Like stupid girls who spend hours in front of the mirror combing their hair and plucking their eyebrows."

"Emilya, I promise not to make you look stupid."

"Good. Well," said Emilya. "I admit that a bath and hair-wash wouldn't be a bad thing."

"Yes, dear," agreed Elyse. "It will be a good start."

Emilya looked hard to see if Elyse was making fun of her. Elyse, for her part, kept an innocent expression.

"Yes, well, if you ladies are all sorted then," said Jake, "I might as well make use of the facilities myself."

"Let me show you to your guest-room," said Emrys, "and I'll also show you where you can bathe privately – assuming you're not the communal type?" asked Emrys, wickedly.

Jake's face remained wooden, bar a slight raising of an eyebrow. "I think that my communal bathing days are well behind me, sir."

"Oh, you disappoint me, Mr Oscom," responded Elyse. "I was hoping for company."

"Elyse!" exclaimed Emilya, quite shocked by her brazenness.

Elyse reacted with a typically musical laugh, Emrys with a rich guffaw... and even Jake had a resigned smirk.

An hour later, Emilya was sat in a chair in Elyse's bedroom, clad in a white towelling bathing robe, while Elyse was stood behind her brushing out her hair, similarly garbed.

"Well, that seaweed shampoo of Emrys' certainly seems to have got the lugs out," said Elyse. "And your hair has got a real shine to it, now. It's particularly brought out those lovely dark-red hues."

Emilya briefly looked in the mirror. "Perhaps he can give us a supply before we leave," suggested Emilya.

"I'll ask him."

"I was joking."

"I'll bet you were," said Elyse, now taking care to brush Emilya's dark-auburn waves so that they framed her face and fell across the top of both of her shoulders. "There, that should do it. That will look beautiful in around twenty minutes when it's dry. Now for the face."

"The face!" exclaimed Emilya, alarmed.

"Yes, Emilya, the face," said Elyse, coming around to face Emilya with what looked like a pencil in her hand.

"What's that?" asked Emilya, her face aghast. "Are you going to draw on me?"

"In a way," agreed Elyse, that perennial ghost of a smile in place. "My goodness me, you do have beautiful eyes, my dear."

"Beautiful! Pah! They're muddy brown," objected Emilya.

"Elyse chuckled. "Just you wait, my little swan. Just you wait." And with that, Elyse moved the pencil towards Emilya's eye. Emilya automatically flinched, so Elyse gently put her hand on top of Emilya's head to steady her. "Keep still," she commanded.

Emilya tensed and remained stock-still as she felt Elyse draw a gentle outline around the base of her eyes, whilst imagining all sorts of hideous results. "Are you making me look like a clown?" she asked.

"Ooh, you are hard work," coaxed Elyse.

Having completed her work with the pencil, Elyse reached for something else in her little bag. "Now, look at me," she commanded.

"What are you doing now?" asked Emilya, warily eyeing the little brush in Elyse's hands.

"Eyelashes, dear."

"Eyelashes?"

Elyse took a step back, brush raised in her right hand, and looked at Emilya, quizzically. "Do you repeat everything, dear?"

"Repeat everything, dear?" asked Emilya, with mock concentration.

Elyse's tongue emerged slightly from her smiling mouth as she reminded herself that this girl was smart. "Keep still," she commanded again, and applied the little brush to Emilya's eyelashes, lifting them slightly and enhancing their darkness with iron oxide. With her eye-work completed, Elyse put away the brush and took out a pad of some kind. "Now for the cheeks," she said.

"You really *are* turning me into a clown."

"I might do, dear, if you don't stop resisting."

"Resisting?"

Elyse was smiling again but chose not to respond as she powdered

Emilya's cheeks, bringing out a lovely rosy colour that looked very natural. Apparently satisfied with the result, Elyse straightened up. "Right, my turn now. Watch how easy it is to do this for yourself."

Elyse then proceeded to brush out her own lustrous brown-blonde tresses, that needed very little encouragement to bounce and fall perfectly into place. The eyes and rouge followed, all done in less than five minutes, and to devastating effect.

Emilya's curiosity won out over decorum. "How old are you, Elyse?"

Elyse raised her eyebrows. "How old do you think I am?"

"I don't know," responded Emilya. "You're so beautiful, it's impossible to say."

"Well, do you think I'm over fifty?"

"No way!" exclaimed Emilya, laughing.

"Under twenty-five then?"

"Nobody under twenty-five offers a forty-seven-year-old man a communal bath. No one that I know, anyway!"

"Ah, you think you know people then, do you?"

Emilya paused before answering. Then: "I know that all the men look at you and wish that you were theirs."

"They do not."

"They do so."

Elyse laughed delightedly at that. "Well, I can see that a certain young man has got his eye on you," she came back with.

"What!" exclaimed Emilya. "No way! Who?"

"A certain young man with shoulder-length sandy hair."

"You are joking! He wouldn't look twice at me if I was the last girl in the world. And in any case, he's got girly hair."

"Hmm," said Elyse, annoyingly – like she didn't believe a word of what Emilya was saying. "Right!" said Elyse. "Time to dress you."

"Must we?"

"Stand!" commanded Elyse.

Emilya did as she was told.

"Now, wait there. I took the liberty of selecting dresses for both of us," she said, as she crossed to a large wardrobe. She opened the door. "And I thought that for you, with your beautiful auburn hair and brown eyes," she said, reaching in, grabbing the dress and then presenting it in front of her own form, "that pale blue would be perfect."

Emilya's jaw almost hit the floor. She was so aghast that she was even struggling to raise a pointed finger. "I am not…" she began.

"Oh yes you are," sang Elyse.

Half an hour later, Elyse led Emilya into the banqueting hall, with its thirty-foot-long oak table which glittered with silverware beneath two candle-laden chandeliers. Emilya was relieved to see the previously robe-clad druids were dressed for the occasion and could quite easily have passed for wealthy gentlefolk of Ghantiss; meaning she didn't feel quite so out of place. It didn't help when the conversation died down, though. Those assembled were looking at her and Elyse; well, mainly Elyse, conceded Emilya – and she was quite happy with that.

Elyse was wearing a stunning and daringly low-cut red dress, that at times, threatened to not be up to its containment job. Emilya could sense the pupils of all the men jiggling up and down as they approached the banqueting table. Except for one with sandy hair, though – who was looking directly at her. Their eyes met briefly and then flicked away.

They were invited to take seats near to the head of the table where Emrys was seated, and it took Emilya a moment to realise that the suavely-dressed man to her left was Jake Oscom. As she sat, he smiled at her and told her that she looked beautiful. Emilya found herself thanking him and telling him that he looked very smart – which indeed he did in his dark brown hip-length coat over a dark grey waistcoat with two sets of buttons, a white stock and dark breeches, while his dark hair with grey flecks at the side was immaculately swept back.

Emilya then became aware of the smells, and she suddenly realised how ravenous she was. Looking towards the back of the hall, she could see a whole pig being roasted on a spit inside a cavernlike fireplace, and she voiced her thoughts to Elyse. "I am so hungry.

Elyse was looking at her, eyeing the pig. "Of course, you don't have to eat animals, you know."

Emilya looked at her, not understanding what she meant.

"I gave up eating meat twenty-five years ago," said Elyse. "When I was about your age."

"Ah!" said Emilya, sharp as ever. "So, you're forty then."

"I didn't say that," said Elyse, for once caught off-guard. Then she laughed. "Dear Emilya," she said, touching her hand to Emilya's cheek.

Emilya felt a wash of affection at the gesture. And perhaps a little emptiness, too, for her dearly departed mother. She pushed those feelings aside. "So, what do you eat, then?"

"Lots of fruit and vegetables. And you can also make mushroom taste like meat, with the right consistency, all complimented with the right spices and seasoning."

Emilya pulled a face at that.

"Well," said Elyse. "You can look at me like that if you want. But that poor piggy," she said, nodding to the back of the hall, "was running around perfectly happy with the world, yesterday."

"Oh, Elyse!" cried Emilya, as the words sunk in.

"I mean," coaxed Elyse, gently. "What right do we have, really? They've as much right to live as we have."

Emilya looked at Elyse in horror, as if she'd had her eyes opened for the first time in her life. "Why is it that I don't feel hungry anymore?"

"Trust me, Emilya. Have what I have – and then if you don't like it, you can go and chew on a bit of piggy instead."

Emilya was now gawping at Elyse.

"Close your mouth, dear," said Elyse. "Otherwise, you'll catch flies."

"Don't take any notice of her," said Jake leaning across and interceding. "You eat what you want, girl."

"I'll not waste my breath on you, Jake Oscom," said Elyse. "But Emilya Luca here isn't yet a lost cause."

"Oh, so that's what *I* am is it?" asked Jake, wryly.

Elyse ignored him. "All I'm saying is, Emilya, what's the difference between a pig or a lamb…and poor little Theo, for example?"

"Oh, that's *way* below the belt, Elyse," said Jake, showing his first ever display of annoyance.

It hit the mark with Emilya though, and she found her eyes filling up. Jake was about to remonstrate further when Emilya stopped him. "It's all right," she said. "She's right. How can we?"

Jake started to tut but was distracted as his glass was filled up with red wine. Emilya turned to him. "Please don't be cross with her, Jake. I don't want us to fall out. But Elyse understands me – that's why she did that."

Emilya then dabbed at her eyes with a handkerchief and turned back to Elyse. "I'm definitely having whatever you're having. You can educate me as we progress through our journey."

Elyse took hold of Emilya's hand and patted it. "Good girl," she said. "You won't regret this. And I've already checked with the head chef. Especially for me, he's cooking a vegetarian dish comprising broccoli, peas and pine nuts combined with a fresh cream and mustard sauce."

Elyse then laughed at Emilya's dubious face. "And yes," she said, squeezing Emilya's hand. "I am forty."

CHAPTER 25 — DAVY

6th Tertiar, 1789 — Day 97, 22:00

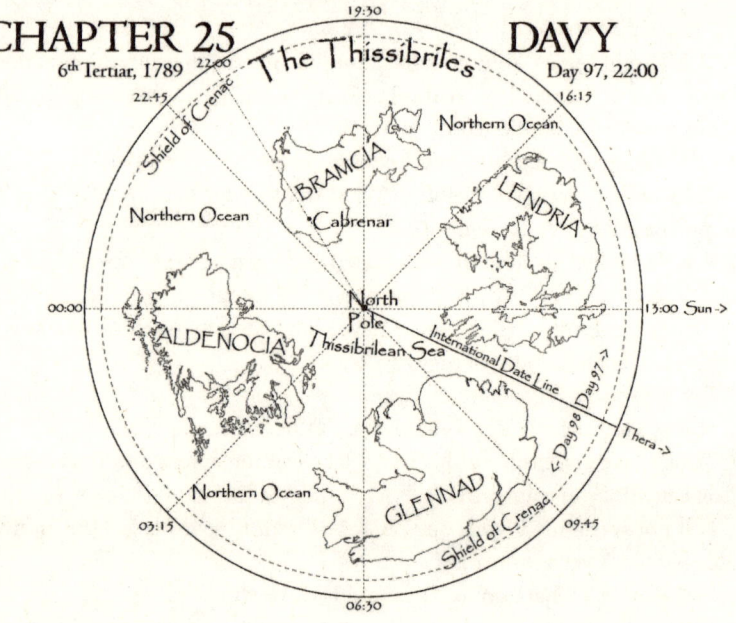

"Hey, look who's here," said Davy to Daisy, as Robbie and Carys approached their table, tankards in hand.

Daisy's freckled face lit up, and Carys smiled back, revealing a set of perfect teeth – a trait which both sisters shared. "What are you two doing here?" asked Daisy.

"Old Eckersley let us finish two hours early, didn't he?" said Robbie.

"Ah, he's not such a bad old stick after all, then," said Davy."

"Huh," responded Carys, as she took a seat. "Poor Robbie's just worked a fifteen-hour shift, thanks to that 'old stick'. Well," she reconsidered, "thanks to Eckersley and Robbie's own big mouth; that is."

Robbie rolled his eyes whilst Davy smirked. Carys still hadn't let go.

"You sort out Dylan?" asked Robbie, before taking a big slurp of ale.

"No, I didn't. Bloody Eckersley wouldn't let me go up the main offshoot to where they were working. Said it 'wasn't orderly'. Oh yes, and I got the usual threat about having my wages docked, too."

"And you think he's not a bad old stick, do you?"

"Well, he's a stickler for rules, to be fair? You have to respect that."

"I take it you didn't call him a tosser, then?"

"Only you're stupid enough to do that, dear," said Carys, sweetly.

"All right, babe," moaned Robbie. He looked at Davy, widened his eyes and nodded his head towards his wife. "You taking note, mate?"

Carys elbowed him in the ribs.

"Ow! Physical abuse, too! You saw that didn't you, mate?"

"Oh, put a sock in it, Russell," said Carys. She saw his hurt look, so draped an arm around his shoulders and kissed him on the cheek. "It's a good job I love you, you old whinger."

"It's a good job I love you, too…you old battle-axe!"

"Why you…" Carys was lost for words as the two of them started a playful tussle which was threatening to knock their table of drinks over.

"Oi, you two!" shouted Eric, the landlord. "Keep your domestics for behind closed doors please."

For a second, Robbie thought Eric was serious. Then he saw the smirk on the landlord's face – so he raised a single finger, suddenly realising that his wife had issued the same gesture at the same time. All four of them laughed, while Eric just wafted his hand at them, playfully.

"So, seriously, mate," said Robbie, his face now straight. "I get you didn't tackle Turner, or take Dylan back with you. But did you tackle Eckersley about Dylan being reassigned to me?"

"I tried to," said Davy, shaking his head, ruefully, "but when I got up top, he'd disappeared for some meeting with the local council."

"Will's going to be really disappointed, Davy. He was proper worried, all afternoon and evening."

"Thanks, mate," said Davy, his face sinking. "I feel bad enough as it is. But I am planning to collar Eckersley tomorrow morning, before we go on-shift. If he won't speak then, I'll demand a meeting after-shift."

"Well, if you do, Davy, just remember this: Nate Turner is Stan Eckersley's brother-in-law."

"Aye, I know. And I also know he doesn't believe the rumours, either, so I'll not even go there. But old Eckersley's got a soft side, we all know that, so I've a plan on how to turn him."

"If anyone can do it, mate, you can," said Robbie.

"And don't go facing down Nate Turner, either," said Daisy, slipping her hand into her fiancé's. "You keep your boxing for the boxing club."

"I know, love," responded Davy, squeezing Daisy's hand. "But I will get it sorted tomorrow," he added, draining his tankard. "In the meantime," he said, facing Robbie, "it's your round, pal!"

CHAPTER 26 — MAGNUS

7th Tertiar, 1789   Day 98, 09:00

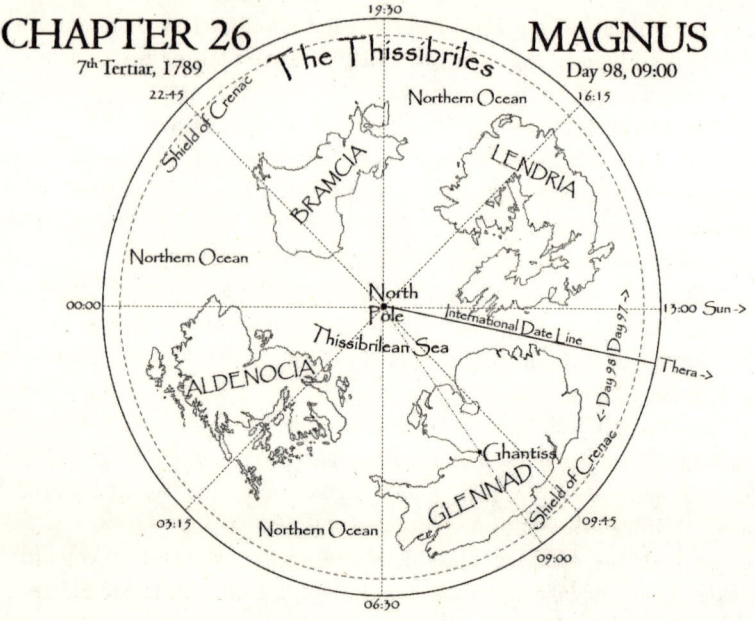

Magnus had a large audience and a golden opportunity for salvation. Despite flutters within, he regally mounted the shallow steps to the dais in the palace Council Room, dressed in his official uniform of blue and gold, while his bicorn hat of office had been suitably layered with felt, conveniently hiding his raw scalp-wound. Behind him, sat the forlorn figures of his father and mother, King George and Queen Maud.

A hush fell across the room as Magnus scrutinised those assembled before him. Nash's men were all here – his private army of around forty spies, largely former soldiers, all straining at the leash to repay those who had murdered their employer. Then there was the Palace Guard – another thirty soldiers, aching to overturn the shame of having Princess Alicya kidnapped from under their noses *and* the Head of Royal Security murdered in the corridors of the palace they were supposed to be keeping safe. Also present, was Dolly, James Cecil, the grizzled Lord Chamberlain, John Russell, the solemn Lord High Constable, and a dozen-or-so magistrates and local JP's. Finally, there was Magnus' own little force of thieves and cut-throats, led by the brutish-faced Hoskyns and the one-eyed Marler – both of whom knew considerably more about recent history than the rest of the audience facing Magnus.

They didn't know everything, though, thought Magnus, smugly.

Magnus began, all steely-eyed and acid-tongued. "Magistrates apart, everyone here has let me down. You have also let down my grieving mother and father," he said, turning and holding out his hand so all could see the misery caused by their collective failure. "And more than anything, you have let down your princess."

Amid much bottom-shuffling and shame-facedness, Magnus knew that he already had them all.

"But I, my mother and father, and especially my sister, will forgive you, if you make amends by capturing the villains who have done this."

There were varying noises of encouragement issued from those desperate to make amends.

"I will tell you now, what I know. For, alas, I also played a significant role in precipitating the events of the last forty-eight hours – something for which I am deeply repentant. But I am willing to be completely open and honest with you about those events, because I want to give you the very best opportunity to apprehend the people who abducted my sister and murdered John Nash…and the very best opportunity to get our beloved Princess Alicya back inside the palace, unharmed.

"Before I start, though, I want to make one thing very clear. Everything that is said in this room is in the strictest confidence. If *any* of this gets out, I *will* find out who blabbed, and I *will* personally execute any guilty persons myself. For high treason. Do I make myself clear?"

This time, there was a more audibly positive response.

"Excellent," snapped Magnus. "We must not alert the general public to the fact that Princess Alicya has been abducted. Not yet."

Magnus scanned his audience again. "So, what of our quarries? Well, alas, six days ago, at around dawn on the 1st of Tertiar, myself and my good friend Dolly Prew, were engaged in an activity that I am not proud of. We had been out all-night drinking to celebrate the end of our semester – as all students of Ghantiss University were. We were also engaging in an activity that is known as…" Magnus paused, and swallowed, as if utterly ashamed of himself, "…Let Us Prey."

Queen Maud looked away from her son, furious with him. However, Magnus knew very well that a large percentage of those assembled would not judge him so hard, as many had indulged in the pastime themselves, a number of them – like him – during their university days.

"Now I deeply regret this activity, not only because it is inhumane, but also because it triggered events which led to the abduction of my sister." Magnus paused again to ensure that everyone was listening. As anticipated, they were all riveted. "What happened, is that at around 07:00 am, our bout of Let Us Prey was gate-crashed by a wildcat urchin, who savagely set about Dolly's dog, impaling the poor beast through his right eye with a six-inch nail attached to a plank of wood."

Magnus paused to view his audience. They were all suitably shocked and completely hooked.

"Now I could have set my dog on the girl. However, I decided to spare her any immediate retribution. After all, the girl couldn't have known who was orchestrating the bout, and to be fair to her, she had gate-crashed because she had the interests of the Prey at heart. Indeed, we should perhaps justify her actions as commendable.

"Now, had things stayed like that, I would probably have told her to take the Prey and go, and leave Dolly and I to care for his injured doberman. Unfortunately, it was at this point that a man came upon our scene. An opportunist and anti-Royal. Someone who instantly recognised me and his opportunity. Mr Nash later admonished me for putting myself into such a vulnerable predicament in the first place. And he was right. I will *never* do that again. But we all live and learn.

"What happened next, is that the sailor had his cutlass drawn and pinned to my neck." Magnus pulled aside his white stock to show the now largely-healed nick. "After sending the girl away, he then proceeded to slash my breeches to rags, totally exposing," Magnus paused, and raised his eyebrows, "shall we say, the Crown Jewels."

Magnus spotted one or two lips twitching in the audience – but he allowed them that. This was all part of the trap. He even had the ghost of a smile on his face himself. Others in the audience, though, were frowning, raging that such an upstart could be so impudent towards his prince. As Magnus had hoped.

"He then proceeded to blackmail me," continued Magnus. "He requested a thousand guineas to buy his silence. In other words, if I paid him the ransom by thirteen o'clock on 2nd Tertiar, he promised to keep quiet about our illegal bout of Let Us Prey, and the exposure of said Crown Jewels. For the record, the thousand-guinea drop was to take place at the harbour-front inn known as the Fisherman's Cot.

"Now, here is where I made my second mistake – although this, ironically, was on the advice of the trusted John Nash. John advised me *not* to pay the ransom, and to call the sailor's bluff. He claimed we could pass the story off as a pack of lies, and although the tale might gain *some* traction in the pubs of Ghantiss for a few days, it would all soon blow over without any hard evidence. In the meantime, Nash engaged his men – you men here," said

Magnus, gesturing towards some of Nash's men at the front, "to hunt down this sailor, who he believed would go on the run, once the drop on 2nd Tertiar didn't take place.

"For those of you in the room *not* in Mr Nash's employ, I can tell you that the sailor in question did indeed go on the run, and next showed up in Boserentua on the evening of 2nd Tertiar – where he slit the throat of one of our royal magistrates – Mr Humphrey Horrocks."

A great outcry greeted this latest revelation, particularly from the assembled magistrates and JP's who were now vocalising unswerving support for him. Marler – the real cut-throat – kept his face impassive. When the hubbub died down, Magnus continued. "Mr Nash personally informed the devoted and now bereft Mrs Horrocks of his murder."

Magnus paused, closing his eyes in apparent pain and remorse before opening them and continuing. "As I have said several times, I deeply regret my actions and their consequences, and spend much time praying for redemption. However, I could not have known that such actions were going to entangle me with a blackmailer and cut-throat, and neither could Mr Nash have known the lengths to which this villain would go to get back at us for not paying that ransom of a mere one thousand guineas."

Magnus paused, grim-faced. "So, what do we know about this man? Well, I had already circulated his description to Nash's men, which they will gladly share with the rest of you, later. However, in the last twenty-six hours, we have uncovered his identity. His name is Jake Oscom. He is a native of Bramcia, and served in the Bramcian Navy for nearly thirty years, rising to the rank of captain for the final six years of his career. So, he is no ordinary adversary, gentlemen. However, three years ago in a bar in Byastwerthy, he killed a man following an altercation. He then went on the run – setting up a new identity and life for himself here in Ghantiss where he is known as Jack Moose, sometimes Jack Morse – the former, an anagram of Jake Oscom, would you believe?"

"I know him!" said Tom Drake, one of the palace guards. "He was a regular at the pubs in the harbour – including the Fisherman's Cot. Dark hair, sports an off-centred nose," he said, tapping his own.

"You'd have thought he'd have had more sense than to use one of his old haunts to receive his ransom package, though," said Ted Codd, one of the magistrates.

Magnus thought quickly on his feet. "I suspect this only gives us a further insight into Oscam's conceit and arrogance, Mr Codd. Similarly, the off-centred nose hints at his belligerence."

"Aye, I reckon you're right," agreed Codd. General agreement followed. Magnus had all on to stop himself from laughing. However, he composed himself, and continued with his beautiful charade.

"I suspect you can guess the rest. Having been denied his one thousand guineas, this former naval captain has returned to Ghantiss to teach us royals a lesson. He clearly has accomplices, too, because we now know how he got Princess Alicya out of the palace grounds. The Princess was known to be with her stablemaster, Maddox, at around 15:30 on 5th Tertiar, and was seen shortly afterwards in the palace by one of our butlers. But she hasn't been seen since. However, we had an unscheduled laundry collection at around 17:30 that same afternoon – admitted by two palace guards. You two, I believe," said Magnus, nodding towards two pasty-faced and desperately unhappy-looking young men. He then put on his best compassionate face. "But please understand, men, you are not alone in making mistakes during this terrible episode. I actually started it all, none of the palace guard challenged these two imposters, and the normally infallible Mr Nash under-estimated Oscom's threat and ended up paying with his life. We're not all perfect."

General sympathy greeted Magnus' most reasonable stance.

"Thank you, Your Highness," croaked one of the pasty-faced men.

"You can count on us to do anything you ask of us," said the other.

"I know I can Lester, Jenkins. And thank you. Now, back to the evidence. I'm sorry to have to tell you, that we also found a chloroform pad in the Princess's bedroom."

Another round of shock rippled through those assembled.

"So, the abductors clearly gained entry to the palace grounds posing as laundry men, chloroformed the Princess, and then carried her off the premises in one of those two laundry baskets. However, whilst they were executing this task, Nash must have come across them. He knew the faces of every worker within the palace and its grounds and the faces of those who have access to it from outside. He almost certainly, therefore, did *not* recognise those two laundry men – and paid for his vigilance with his life. I'd wager a large amount of money, that one of those two laundry men was Jake Oscom himself – and it was probably Oscom who stabbed John Nash to death. It was, after all, Oscom who slit the throat of the esteemed Humphrey Horrocks, and Oscom has clearly killed at least once before. I suspect, though, that he has the blood of dozens of men on his hands."

The response in the room was now starting to ramp up. Around fifty people under this one roof were beginning to crave the guts of Jake Oscom.

Magnus, however, continued cranking up the pressure.

"At present, we have yet to receive a ransom note from Oscom. But we will. He is currently making us sweat. Making *me* pay, for not paying him the first time around. Of course, when the ransom note does come, it will be for considerably more than one thousand guineas, as the stakes have escalated. We will, of course, not put the Princess's life at risk. We *will* pay the ransom. If Oscom then returns the Princess, we will rejoice." Magnus paused. "And then we will hunt this dog down."

This time a barrage of aggressive assent greeted Magnus' carefully delivered bait. He tried his best to not start self-congratulating just yet.

"That's not quite all, though," said Magnus, when the hubbub had died down. He reached for the glass of water on his lectern and took several sips before setting the glass down. "There are other innocent individuals involved in this terrible episode. I have already mentioned the first – a 'wildcat-urchin' was the term I believe I used. Remarkably, it turns out that she was actually a fifteen-year-old baker's daughter, who has a great love of animals. And the incident with the plank of wood and nail was most definitely in self-defence – as Dolly's doberman was in the process of attacking her – isn't that right, Dolly?"

"Absolutely right, Prince Magnus," agreed his strawberry-blonde friend. "I was deeply unhappy with her at the time and remonstrated most vociferously, but shortly afterwards, I reflected that she had not meant to injure my dog and was only trying to protect first the Prey and then herself. I, too, am deeply repentant for my part in this whole episode and will never again be indulging in that activity."

Again, a wave of sympathy greeted Dolly's repentance, particularly from those former students in the room. This could, they were no doubt reflecting, have quite easily been them, but for the grace of God.

"Thank you, Dolly," said Prince Magnus. "Now, I mention this baker's daughter, because once we'd found out Oscom's true nature, we became concerned for her well-being. So, I sent my men," he paused, indicating Hoskyns and Marler, "to search for her. My instructions were that if they found her, they were to apologise on my behalf, and to invite the girl to the palace to speak to my sister with a view to being offered a post as an apprentice lady-in-waiting to Princess Alicya. My reasons for this were again, partly due to repentance, but also because the girl had shown remarkable courage, character and moral fibre in attempting to rescue the Prey. I felt this offer was the least she deserved."

Once again, a buzz of approval towards the Prince's generosity was proffered forth.

"Alas," continued Magnus, "this is where I'm afraid that yet more mistakes were made, were they not, Mr Hoskyns?"

Hoskyns straightened up, and put on his best repentant face. "I'm afraid, your honours," he said, nodding towards the magistrates and JPs, "that we'd worked out that she was a baker's daughter by this stage." Hoskyns' dialect and vocabulary were in stark contrast to Dolly's. "We then found a baker's daughter matching the description given by Prince Magnus and Dolly Prew. Unfortunately, I had misunderstood my instructions, and instead of *inviting* the girl to come to the palace, we thought that we had to *bring* her to the palace." Hoskyns closed his eyes. "We then went and brought in the wrong girl."

"Yes, and not entirely of her own free will either, eh, Hoskyns?"

"I'm sorry, Your Royal Highness," said Hoskyns, his eyes downcast. "We thought you wanted to identify her at the palace…"

"Thank you, Hoskyns." Magnus then gave a deep sigh, now appearing to have the weight of the world on his shoulders. "Alas, this is where events get darker, gentlemen," he began. "Obviously when Hoskyns brought her in, I immediately identified her as the wrong girl – a poor girl by the name of Freya Colin, the daughter of Rex Colin who runs a bakery on Sadler Gate. I was therefore deeply apologetic to Freya and told Mr Hoskyns to return her to her parents immediately, and even offered financial recompense for her inconvenience. However, the girl refused the money and flew off in a huff, stating that she would find her own way home. The problem is, gentlemen," Magnus paused, his face deeply troubled, "she never made it home."

A collective intake of breath was heard.

"And, of course, this all happened on the afternoon of the 5th Tertiar – the same time that my sister was being abducted."

"So," said a middle-aged magistrate with iron-grey hair and a lofty bearing. He rose to his feet. "You think that this girl – this Freya Colin – bumped into this Oscom character on her way out of the palace?"

"I do, Mr Percy. She may even have seen Mr Nash's murder. And if that was the case, then Oscom and his accomplice couldn't afford to let her talk…or even live. I therefore fear that she ended up in the second laundry basket, and Lord knows what happened to her from that point onwards. We're currently asking the body porters who do the weekly run to Cemetery Island to let us know if they transported anyone matching Freya's description. Alas, you know as well as I do, that they usually transport around eighty bodies at a time – so the chances of them remembering Freya are extremely remote. I haven't yet closed down the idea, though, of exhuming the latest batch of bodies."

"I must say, Your Highness," said Magistrate Percy, who was still on his feet, and was now somewhat pompously holding on to the lapels of his jacket, "that your conduct in this whole matter, since acknowledging the error of your ways on the 1st of Tertiar, has been wholly humane, considered, and exceptionally mature."

A rising hum of agreement went up from the assembled men, and even Magnus' mother looked considerably cheered by the reaction.

Magnus waited for the approval to die down. "Thank you, Mr Percy," he responded. "I fervently wish I could do more – but I thank you for your support and understanding. I just wish the circumstances of me seeing the error of my ways could have been less punishing."

"What about the original baker's daughter?" asked one of the JPs.

"Ah yes, I was coming to her," said Magnus. "Her name is Emilya Luca. She is the daughter of Danny Luca who runs the bakery on Irongate – and who serves the most delicious meat pies, I might add."

A slight titter greeted this last line.

"Yes, I visited him three days ago, and made my offer to apprentice Emilya to Alicya. Unfortunately, the poor man had packed young Emilya off to his sister's in Dominniul. Turns out she'd told her father all about the Let Us Prey episode. When she told him what she'd done to Dolly's dog," Magnus paused, shaking his head in amused disbelief, "poor Danny Luca was terrified that I would seek her out and punish her!"

A round of laughter ensued, although a look from the Queen soon brought them all back into line.

"Yes, sorry mother," said Magnus. "But where in the world do people get these notions from? Anyway, I've been assured that Emilya is coming back to Ghantiss, and my offer to her still stands. Because we *will* get our beloved Alicya back – whether we have to pay the ransom or not. And maybe, just maybe, in a few years' time, myself, Alicya and Emilya will all be able to have a good old chuckle about how this all panned out."

Reassuring noises of agreement greeted this last comment.

Magnus took another drink from his glass of water. "So, finally," he began. "A summary for you. Princess Alicya has been abducted. It is almost inconceivable that this has nothing to do with Jake Oscom. He is therefore our primary suspect – a proven murderer and someone who has already attempted to blackmail me and has probably blackmailed countless others. Our number one priority, therefore, is to track him down – ideally *before* he sends his ransom note. Although I have to say, that I will be exceptionally relieved when that note arrives, as it will confirm that my dear sister is still alive and well."

Another chorus of agreement greeted this latest statement.

"Anyway, we are *not* going to sit around and wait for Oscom's ransom note to come to us. We are going to try and find him first. So, our next steps are to divide you men up into teams. We will first comb Ghantiss to pick up any leads on where Oscom might be hiding out. We need to complete that operation before close of play on the 9th of Tertiar. So, in two days' time. After that, we start to spread out, looking for his trail. Once we have it, we pursue relentlessly. Is everyone clear?"

Another surge of assent.

"Good. We will now have a ten-minute break. We will then re-convene in the Council Room at 10:00, where I will oversee the creation of four search brigades and appoint each brigade leader. By 11:30, each brigade will have their search plans in place for their quadrant of Ghantiss." Magnus paused for effect. "We will then start heading out into the city…to hunt this dog down."

The floor burst into a spontaneous round of applause for Magnus. Then, as the mixture of Palace Guard, Nash's private force and Magnus' ruffians, along with magistrates and JPs all headed off for their short break, Queen Maud stood and approached Magnus, tears in her eyes but a smile on her face. She squeezed his hand. "I always knew you would come good, Magnus. I'm so proud of you, my love."

"Thank you, mother. I have learned a painful, but valuable lesson. But above all else, I realised that I needed to grow up."

His father then patted him on the back. "One day, you'll make a fine king, son."

CHAPTER 27   ALICYA

7th Tertiar, 1789   Day 98, 09:30

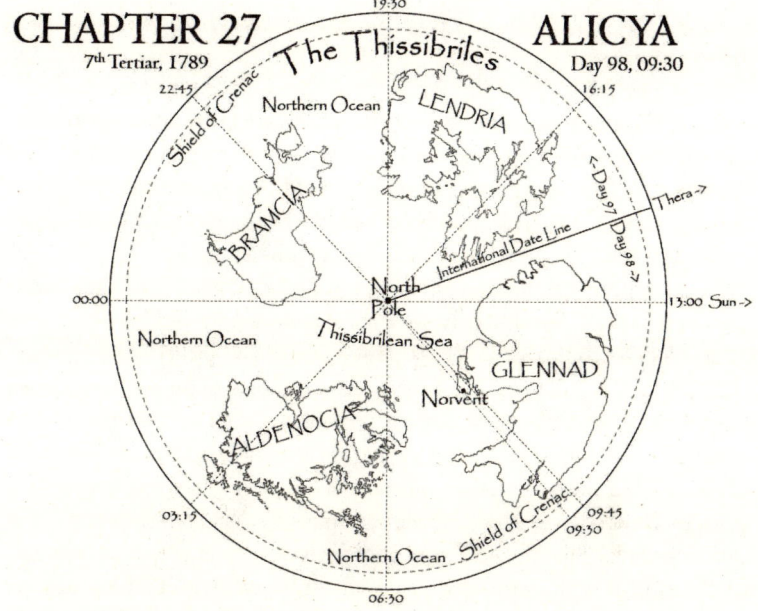

Alicya woke with a start, briefly puzzled by her ruinous surroundings – but her desperate predicament soon came flooding back. Catching her breath, her eyes darted right and left. She still had her back to the wall alongside one of the windows in the shell of a Norvent church on the Island of the Dead – and as far as she could tell, she was still very much on her own. She listened carefully for any signs of human presence, but there were none: just the ever-present sound of seabirds and the lapping of the waves in the harbour across the road from the church.

Happy she was in no immediate danger, familiar sensations of loss and injustice closed in as the constant cycle began to re-play in her mind: what her brother had done to Freya Colin; what Magnus had done to her; the likely impact upon her parents; whether she should or even *could* return to Ghantiss. And then there was the loneliness. Alicya had grown up with people around her every day of her life. Once again feelings of profound loss were invoked…until Alicya remembered her most recent companion.

"Vixey!" she whispered. Then she remembered she was on a deserted island! "Vixey!" she called out louder. Alicya held her breath, listening for the slightest sound, afraid she might be on her own again. She then heard a scuffling from the back of the church in what had once been the chancel – and there she was, trotting towards her with something held in her mouth.

As Vixey drew closer, Alicya was disconcerted to see that it was a mouse – dead, thankfully.

Nevertheless, Vixey trotted right up to Alicya and dropped the mouse at her feet. Alicya immediately understood what Vixey was doing; just as she had with the fox-cub the night before, Vixey was offering to share her meal with Alicya. "Oh, you clever, loyal girl," said Alicya, reaching out and touching Vixey's face. The fox-cub licked her hand, and then lowered her head and pushed the mouse towards Alicya with her snout.

Alicya couldn't help but laugh. She placed a hand gently to Vixey's face. "I'm sorry, darling, but things haven't got that desperate yet!"

Vixey looked confused, so Alicya steeled herself and picked up the mouse. Trying her hardest not to gag, she pretended to eat some of the mouse and then passed it back to Vixey. The fox-cub eyed her rather strangely, but then proceeded to lie down and started tearing at the poor dead rodent. When she had finished her meal – crackly bones and all – Vixey lay down at Alicya's feet.

"Right," said Alicya, after a while, causing Vixey's ears to shoot up. "The plan for today?" She looked out of the window. It was grey and overcast, and the tide was in, with her potential escape vehicle bobbing around against the harbour wall, attached by a single rope. The rowing boat didn't look as big or sturdy as it had when beached, yesterday, and so her enthusiasm for Plan A was waning rapidly. The Wrenko peninsula was around forty leagues away. It was all very well plotting a course across St Humo's Bay, but out there in the middle of the bay, it might as well be open ocean. It certainly wasn't fair to take Vixey and risk her life, as the fox-cub would likely survive on Cemetery Island perfectly well without her on a diet of small animals, berries and fresh water.

Unable to bear leaving Vixey just yet, Alicya deferred her decision, and instead, decided to spend the day looking around Cemetery Island for a stock of food and fresh water. She reasoned that if she didn't find anything, then she would have no choice but to take the rowing boat tomorrow, head in a south-westerly direction, and pray hard for safe delivery to Wrenko. Or take the safer, nearer route to Port St Humo, but with the greater risk of being spotted by Magnus' men.

Alicya stood, still clothed only in her stolen greatcoat, and stretched her cramped limbs. She looked down at her attire. The coat had kept her warm enough throughout the night, but she didn't fancy wearing it as an only item of clothing on her planned sortie. She walked over to the pews where she had draped her peasants' garb, but was dismayed to find that the garments were still way too damp to wear.

Sighing, Alicya made for the church door, Vixey padding along beside her, looking up at her. Alicya smiled. They really were a team, weren't they? "Good girl," she said to Vixey, as they walked out into the deserted and ruined street. "Now, which way to fresh water?"

Vixey just looked intently back at her.

"Hmm," said Alicya. She turned her back on the harbour and lifted her hand to shade her eyes as she looked inland towards the morning sun. There was a road of sorts which the body porters used to access the burial ditches. Alicya decided to walk along that route for a while, but keeping her eyes peeled to the left where there was a low range of hills to the north of the shallow valley. The chances were that there would be at least one freshwater stream running down a gulley from there. As for the burial channels, these ran due-east, inland, for as far as the eye could see.

"Hmm," considered Alicya again. "No wonder it took them so long."

Alicya's foray eastwards was rewarded after fifteen minutes, when she came across a small wooden bridge to her left. It was in the middle of some old grave channels but had been built to enable the porters to cross a small stream that, sure enough, ran down from the hills to the north. "Come on Vixey," said Alicya, crossing the bridge and walking up one of the grassy paths between the grave channels.

After another five minutes, the ground began to climb and had become too uneven for burials. However, in the valley heading east, the burial channels still stretched away for as far as she could see. It would be interesting to get up into these low hills and see just how far they went.

Within a minute, Alicya was following a hedgerow that was climbing up the hill, and immediately spotted flashes of red towards the ground. "Well, well," said Alicya, delightedly. She bent down and turned up one of the plants growing under the hedge to reveal wild strawberries, and although the berries were only tiny, they looked perfectly ripe. Alicya pulled one free and popped it into her mouth. She chewed and considered. It wasn't as sweet as the much larger strawberries both grown and served at the palace, but it was certainly pleasant enough – and her empty stomach certainly welcomed it.

Alicya picked two more, popped another into her mouth and offered the other to Vixey. The fox-cub sniffed at the berry, and then lapped her long tongue over Alicya's hand, taking the berry with it.

"There, that wasn't too bad, was it?"

Vixey just stared back, her tongue smacking all around her lips.

"The problem is, Vixey, I've not brought a basket with me. I'm obviously not conditioned to survive, am I?"

Alicya bent down and started picking lots of wild strawberries, sharing the first twenty-or-so with Vixey. Thereafter, she stuffed them into what were thankfully very large pockets on her greatcoat. She kept on moving upwards alongside the hedgerow, until eventually, the pockets of the greatcoat were full. Seeing that there were plenty more, though, Alicya decided she would return later with a container.

Carrying on uphill, the ground soon began to climb more steeply, and the hedgerow soon came to an end. Now, there were just occasional trees, while the stream was tumbling more freely. At a convenient point, where there was a mini waterfall of around two hand lengths, and a tiny plunge pool at its bottom, Alicya stopped, crouched down, and cupped her hands into the water. She tentatively lapped up some of the water and swallowed. The water was cool and fresh.

"Well, that's another crisis averted," said Alicya to Vixey – who was also now busy lapping at the water.

This time, Alicya did have an object with which to collect, as she'd had the foresight to bring along the now-empty water flask that she'd stolen from the body porters' ship. Once that was filled, Alicya bent down to have another drink, and then turned around to observe the plain below. What she saw took her breath away. She could see Norvent's harbour and the ruined town away to her right, and beyond that the vast grey stretch of St Humo's Bay. But beneath her and stretching for miles to her left in an easterly direction, were hundreds of grave channels. Even at her current elevation, Alicya couldn't see where they ended. She had no idea where the body porters had been shuttling back and forth to, yesterday.

"What a place," she whispered. She dropped her eyes and sighed. Poor Freya Colin was out there somewhere. No doubt Magnus would have woven a suitable story by now, with Nash backing him to the hilt. The poor Colins would never know what happened to their daughter, would never lay her to rest, and would spend the rest of their lives waiting for Freya to walk back into their bakery, still aged fifteen and fresh-faced.

Alicya looked up to the heavens and blew out a long breath of air. It was that same dilemma again. For the sake of Mr and Mrs Colin, should she change her chosen course of action – and instead, return to Ghantiss on the next Body Boat? Go straight to her mother and father and tell them what their son was? What the heir to the throne was?

"Pah!" she exclaimed. She was being naïve. Magnus had now had two days to plan his cover-up. He would never allow her to get within a hundred yards of the palace, and certainly not dressed like this. But then again, he probably thought she was dead, right?

Alicya sighed. Truth be told, how could you second-guess someone who functioned without compassion? That said, Magnus had stated at one point, two days ago, that he would never hurt his sister – although that had clearly been conditional on her keeping his terrible secret. But was that still an option? To return to Ghantiss and promise Magnus she'd keep his secret? If she did that, she could soon be riding Sebastian or Tabetha again and bantering with Maddox in the stables. Such thoughts brought on pangs of loss and longing. She hoped that Maddox was all right and had kept his head down, knowing how much the gruff stablemaster cared for her, and how little he thought of Magnus.

Eventually, Alicya shook her head. No, she could never return to Ghantiss. Not as Princess Alicya, anyway. And although that was effectively selling out people like Mr and Mrs Colin, Alicya was determined that she would one day avenge herself and Freya, one way or another. She had no idea how, at the moment – but hopefully she had a long lifetime ahead of her, during which there would be many twists and turns, with new opportunities presenting themselves.

So, it was back to Plan A. Or was it Plan B? Either way, she had to get off this island. There were enough strawberries and fresh water to sustain her here for a while, but if she settled for this existence, then her brother would have won – and Alicya was determined that her brother would not win – at least not in the long-term, anyway.

It took Alicya and Vixey another fifty minutes to return to the harbour at Norvent – at which point Plan C presented itself.

Alicya ducked back behind the wall of a crumbling house, heart thumping. She had got so used to being the only living human being on Cemetery Island – even though she'd only been here for around twenty-six hours – that she hadn't taken any precautions to hide her presence on her return to the ruined port of Norvent.

"Vixey!" she hissed, calling the fox-cub to her. The cub sauntered across, completely oblivious to whatever was troubling Alicya. Once Vixey sat down next to her, Alicya slowly moved her head towards the edge of the wall she was hiding behind and peeped around it.

The new vessel in the harbour was a cutter. An attractive one at that. Whoever owned it was wealthy. It was dominated by pristine white sails, fore-and-aft-rigged, which were attached to a single mast, while its long bowsprit enabled one of the fore-sails to be stepped farther forward on the hull. There was also the incongruous presence of a single horse which appeared to be tethered to the main mast.

Ignoring the horse puzzle, Alicya soon realised this was a golden opportunity to get away from this grim island far earlier than she had hoped for. She scanned the ship for potential stowaway places – but the vessel was considerably smaller than the one used by the body porters. It had a cabin, but Alicya couldn't tell from here if it even *had* a hold in which to stow away. It didn't look like it from this distance.

She then saw a well-dressed, tall man with fair hair appear to rise from somewhere just under the cabin, and Alicya felt hope surge again. There may well be a small hold, after all. The man appeared to be relatively young, but as Alicya observed, it became clear that he was also the man in charge, and therefore the boat likely belonged to him. His companions were two significantly less well-dressed men, both older and thicker set. As Alicya watched, they manoeuvred a ramp into position like the one that the body porters had used yesterday, so that both they and the horse could disembark and then traverse the jetty.

Alicya frowned, wondering what in the world they were up to, but as they reached the promenade and began walking towards her, she looked around, frantically. Unlike the church that she had sheltered in last night, this building was still part-roofed and clearly unsafe. However, she had no choice. Silently scooping up Vixey, and crouching all the way, she moved further in to the house and found a convenient internal wall to hide behind. The *clip-clop* of the horse got closer, along with the occasional sound of human voices – and then the sounds began to recede as the horse and the three men drew further away.

With Vixey still tucked under her arm, Alicya moved back outside and crouched behind another external wall. The party had stopped further down the harbour road, opposite a former wooden stable. She could see the tall fair-haired man and one of his lackeys, but the other man was nowhere to be seen – until he suddenly emerged from the wooden building pulling a cart. Intrigued, Alicya watched the two lackeys hitch up the cart to the horse – and then the party proceeded to head back in her direction.

This time, there was no chance of ducking back into the house because they would see her. Alicya took the only action she could. She put Vixey down and lay flat on the floor, side-on to the low brick wall facing the men with the horse and cart. She also kept a calming hand on the back of Vixey's head to stop her from moving away, or worse, from barking. The horse and cart kept coming towards her, but then instead of heading back past her towards the boat, the party took a right-turn inland – along the path that Alicya had just returned on; the same path that the body porters had shuttled back and forth along, yesterday.

As Alicya watched their figures recede into the distance, she was already formulating some unpleasant thoughts. She was far too well-educated to believe in necromancers, voodoo and that sort of thing, and the young, fair-haired gentleman certainly didn't look the type for any of that business. But there was another rumour which made more sense. It was illegal in Glennad to perform post-mortems on bodies without consent of the next of kin. And if the next of kin believed in souls and an after-life, they rarely gave permission. So, it was rumoured that some doctors and surgeons, for small sums of money, paid the body porters a few back-handers to 'lose' the odd body prior to heading off to Cemetery Island. Those bodies were then used to help further knowledge of human anatomy. Of course, this activity was illegal, so it was taking an enormous risk to acquire such a body in Ghantiss. But how much safer would it be to come to Cemetery Island, unobserved, on a non-body-porting day…and help yourself to fresh cadavers?

The trio of men with their horse and cart were now almost out of sight. The more Alicya thought about it, the more she was convinced the fair-haired man was a doctor or a surgeon who was about to pick and choose his fresh corpses like a punter might choose their fruit and veg from Ghantiss Market.

Alicya shuddered. She had come pretty close to being on the fruit and veg stall, herself!

Offering up a quick prayer that Freya would not be selected, Alicya put aside thoughts of cadavers and prepared to check out the cutter and see if there was anywhere for herself and Vixey to stow away. But first, she headed briskly for the church, her greatcoat billowing, whilst Vixey skipped along beside her. To Alicya's dismay, the garments that she had so unpleasantly had to purloin were still damp, so she folded them into a bundle and exited the church. She then picked up Vixey and tucked her under her left arm, with the clothes wedged under her right, and quickly traversed both jetty and ramp. Dropping down into the cutter, she stood still for a few seconds – just in case there was anyone else on board. It soon became apparent that there wasn't.

Alicya then turned around to observe the ruined port of Norvent in case the boat's crew were returning prematurely or any other eyes were watching her. Satisfied she was unobserved, Alicya turned back around and moved cautiously forward, ducking under one of the booms – and was delighted to see a flight of shallow steps leading down to a hold of sorts underneath the cabin, albeit a semi-open-air hold. She slowly descended the six steps, each of them creaking alarmingly, and found herself in a fairly airy space, with lots of daylight shafting through the slatted wood to the sides and the front. The hold, however, was empty. And there was nowhere to hide.

Alicya's heart was already sinking when she noticed the cupboard. Putting Vixey down, she moved silently across to it and pulled the door open – and screamed as something fell towards her. She then cursed herself for being so loud when it was only a fishing rod. Alicya quickly ascended the six steps to see if her scream had alerted anyone – knowing full-well that she and the three men were likely the only living human beings on the island. Satisfied, Alicya dropped down into the hold again. She picked up the fallen fishing rod and put it back inside the cupboard, where it joined several others, as well as nets and other fishing equipment. She then started to move equipment to one side, having already worked out that the space would be large enough to house both herself and Vixey.

All the time, Alicya's hopes were increasing thanks to her lucky break. With growing excitement, she began to wonder where the fair-haired man had sailed from. Was it too much to hope that this destination could become her new home, too?

Inevitably, that thought triggered a fresh round of guilt about her parents and the Colins…and then anger at Magnus…and the whole hopeless thought-cycle began to circulate again.

It was another hour and a half before Alicya heard the horse and cart return. Steeling herself, she crept up three of the six steps to peer out. Her suspicions had been spot-on. The cart had four or five figures on-board, but which Alicya was pleased to note had been wrapped in appropriate shrouds. She quickly dropped back down into the tiny hold, picked up Vixey, and then squeezed them both into the corner-space that she had created inside the cupboard. She then pulled the doors towards her, which closed with a satisfying *click*.

Holding Vixey close to her, Alicya could only hear the pounding of her own heart in her ears as the boat bobbed gently on the harbour swell. A thousand different conversations ran through her mind as to what she would say if the tall, fair-haired man discovered her. It wasn't beyond the realms of possibility that she would tell the truth and order him to take her back to Ghantiss. But what then?

Those thoughts disappeared the next instant, when the men began to re-embark.

CHAPTER 28   MAGNUS

7th Tertiar, 1789   Day 98, 11:45

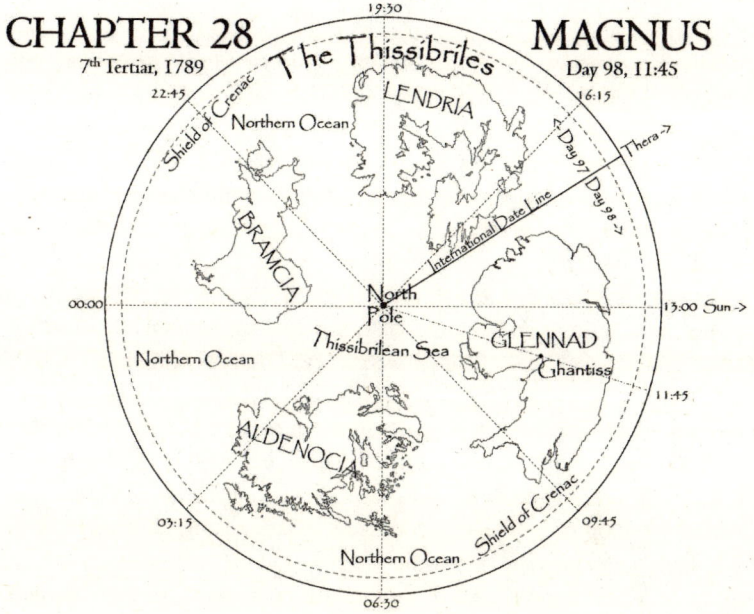

Magnus' four brigades which were comprised of a mixture of spies, Palace Guards, magistrates and JPs, were now out combing different quadrants of Ghantiss in their search for Jake Oscom. He was now holding another conference with his own private team of thugs and cut-throats in the Games Room. There were five of them in total. As well as Hoskyns and Marler, there was also Skinner (a former pick-pocket), West (a former sailor thrown out of the Glennadian navy for constant brawling) and Gage (the oldest of the five men, and who had spent most of his adult life in prison for various types of theft).

"Well, gentlemen," began Magnus, picking up the wine decanter and filling a glass just for himself. "How did you think this morning's conference went?"

The one-eyed Marler responded straight away. "It went pretty well for you, Sir."

"Yes, I thought your ruse to place everything at Oscom's door was inspired, Sir," added Hoskyns. "Particularly given his past record."

"Ruse?" questioned Magnus. He put his glass down. "Ruse?" he repeated, advancing on the now-alarmed Hoskyns. "There was no ruse, Hoskyns. Oscom murdered Nash, and he has also kidnapped the Princess Alicya and Freya Colin. Has he not?"

"I'm sure that he has, Sir," agreed Hoskyns, hastily.

Marler, however, was less intimidated by the Prince. He focused his one eye on Magnus. "I am, of course, very happy for Mr Oscom to take the rope for Mr Nash."

"I'll bet you are, Marler. For Humphrey Horrocks also, no doubt."

"But" continued Marler, ignoring the barb, "I would like you to answer just one question for me, please, Sir."

"Just one, Marler?"

"Yes, Sir. Just the one."

"Fire away then," said Magnus, deliberately standing right in front of Marler, two paces away. Both men were tall, so they were looking at each other, eyes-to-eye.

Marler took a deep breath. Magnus' stomach quivered. Marler was afraid of nothing, but right now, he was looking like a man who knew that he was about to step onto dangerously thin ice. "The two girls that Williams and Hauberker took out in the laundry baskets," Marler said. "Neither of them would have been…royalty, would they, Sir?"

Magnus didn't reply. Instead, he channelled pure venom at Marler's single eye. Marler, to his credit, remained stock still and held Magnus' gaze. At the same time, Magnus' mind was working overtime. He had underestimated Marler. He still trusted his hold over him though; he had, after all, stabbed Nash to death two days ago, the latest in a long line of transgressions, many of which would see him go to the gallows. But this question: it either spoke of over-confidence and insubordination, or it hinted at a line in the sand regarding his levels of loyalty; perhaps it even spoke of a previously-hidden conscience, maybe even regret. Nevertheless, it was still Marler and Hoskyns who had organised the despatch of those two laundry baskets to Cemetery Island, making him an accomplice to a royal murder at the very least. Maybe that didn't sit well with Marler. Meanwhile, realisation had now dawned on the dim-witted Hoskyns, and a look of horror slowly manifested across his brutish features.

A good thirty seconds had now passed since Marler had asked his question. Magnus decided to break the silence himself. "What are you getting at, Marler?"

There was another long pause before Marler answered. "I just want you to understand, Sir, that we're *all*," he paused and glanced around, before looking back at Magnus. "We're *all* in the same boat, here."

Magnus narrowed his eyes. "Are you threatening me, Marler?"

"Aye, Sir, I think that perhaps I am."

Once again, Magnus' mind was in overdrive. What should he do with such open impertinence? The problem was, that without actually stating it, Marler was very cleverly making the other occupants of the room aware that he, Magnus, had murdered Alicya and got Marler and Hoskyns to dispose of her body by deception, along with the body of Freya Colin. What the other three men in the room didn't know, though, was that the fake laundrymen, Williams and Hauberker – the only other witnesses – had joined the two girls on the same Body Boat. Magnus did not believe in loose ends. Meanwhile, the silence endured – until Magnus took the only course open to him. He started to laugh. Marler, also visibly relieved, started to laugh as well – after which the other four thugs joined in, but with only Hoskyns truly understanding the full nature of the exchange that had just taken place.

When he had stopped laughing, Magnus walked back to his crystal decanter and filled another glass full of wine. He indicated that Hoskyns should do the same for himself, Skinner, West and Gage. Magnus then took his second glass back to Marler along with his own. Marler took the proffered wineglass. Magnus then turned around alongside Marler and looked at the rest of his private lynch mob, raising his glass in a toast. "To being in the same boat," he said, and promptly drained his wine. The other five men did the same.

Magnus still had a smirk on his face. He turned to Marler. "I can't believe you just did that, Marler."

"I figured we needed to get things straight, Sir – as I'm guessing we still have some work to do."

Magnus was already back at the decanter, filling another glass. He then appraised Marler again. "You really are a shrewd one, aren't you?"

Marler decided not to respond to that question.

"All right," said Magnus, now business-like. "This is how we're going to play this from here. Please, all of you, take a seat."

Magnus waited for his five henchmen to sit before he began. "At present, we have firmly on-side, my mother, father, the Palace Guard, Nash's private army and, most importantly, all of the key magistrates and JPs in Ghantiss. Now the chances are, that with that small army, they will turn up some key information about Oscom either today or tomorrow. And if any of those leads turn up Oscom himself, then Oscom's position will be hopeless. Because, will he be able to produce either the Princess Alicya or Freya Colin as witnesses, Hoskyns?

"That would be most unlikely, Sir."

"Yes, it would, wouldn't it," agreed Magnus, happily. "At which point, instead of being accused of kidnapping them both, he will be accused of their double murder. Treble murder if we include Nash – which no one is in any position to cast doubt upon. And even quadruple murder if we include Humphrey Horrocks. I will see to it, *personally*, that the hatred against Oscom is ramped up to such a degree, that he will be more-or-less executed immediately. And thankfully," he said, briefly thinking of Williams and Hauberker, "dead men can't speak."

Magnus paused to sip his wine before continuing. "However, if they *don't* turn up Oscom in Ghantiss, but they *do* manage to pick up his trail, that's where *we* come in, gentlemen. Because it will be the six of us, along with a small squad of soldiers, that will hunt Oscom down."

Magnus waited for them all to get used to the idea and was pleased to see plenty of anticipation.

"Of course, our stated objective will be to bring in Oscom alive so that he can stand trial for either kidnapping, abduction, murder, or whatever. However, I surely don't need to explain to you men what will happen if we find him, do I?"

"Sadly, killed in an act of self-defence?" suggested Hoskyns.

"Quite so," agreed Magnus.

"I will happily perform that deed for you, Sir," said Marler, dryly. "So that we continue to remain in the same boat, you understand," he added, without any hint of mirth.

"Well, Mr Marler, I thank you for your commitment. But if anyone is going to be running through Jake Oscom," he said, pausing to scratch the vague scar on his neck. "Then that will be me."

"Of course, Sir," agreed Marler.

"All of which leaves one unresolved problem."

Marler looked at Magnus. "Emilya Luca?"

"Exactly, Marler. Although she is far less of a problem than Oscom, Nash, Alicya or Freya Colin. But she is a loose end. Danny Luca lied to me. Luca's sister was baffled when Nash's men turned up at her house in Domminiul. And just in case *she* was lying as well, Nash had a man watch the premises, but there is no evidence of Emilya Luca being there. Which means that she is very likely still in Ghantiss, in hiding."

"And you've got Nash's men watching the bakery in Irongate?"

"Naturally, Marler. But again, no sightings in the last two days."

"May I offer an opinion, Sir?" asked Marler.

"Of course."

"May I suggest that we leave that loose end alone. As you said yourself, tying up Oscom with the murder of Nash, the Princess and Miss Colin is our main goal. I don't think you'll have any trouble from Danny or Emilya Luca. They're both clearly too scared to do anything. And the only thing that Emilya Luca has actually seen, is a session of Let Us Prey – which everyone knows goes on, and you've already publicly confessed to it, anyway. So, Emilya Luca isn't a big deal."

"I'm inclined to agree with you, Marler. And actually, Miss Luca didn't actually *see* anything either; she just *heard* the bout."

"Weren't you about to set your dog on her when Oscom turned up, Sir?" asked Hoskyns.

"I was," agreed Magnus. "But I didn't – ironically because of Oscom's intervention! So, again, there is nothing to defend."

Happy with the situation, Magnus drew their discussion to a close. "We shall continue our planning later, gentlemen, when we shall see what our teams have turned up. Let us hope that there is game afoot tonight. In the meantime, I believe a mini-billiards contest is in order."

As they set the billiard table, though, Magnus' blasé façade belied his inner concern. Marler had shaken him to the core. *Might he need a new henchman to kill his current one?* The sooner Oscom was charged with those three murders – alive or posthumously – the sooner Magnus could relax. He would *never* put himself in this position again. He'd been foolish and naïve, and for two days, he had been staring into an abyss. He'd also been spinning too many different deceptions and it had become mentally exhausting to keep them all going.

A loud rap on the Games Room door took Magnus by surprise. When he opened it, he was even more surprised to see the very serious face of James Cecil, the Lord Chamberlain. "What is it, Cecil?"

"There's a disturbance at the palace gates, Your Royal Highness. A Mr and Mrs Colin are there with a magistrate, demanding to see you."

"With a magistrate?"

"Yes, Sir. They're making some rather unpleasant accusations."

Magnus felt his heart sink. There were more loose ends than he'd anticipated.

CHAPTER 29   EMILYA
7th Tertiar, 1789   Day 98, 12:30

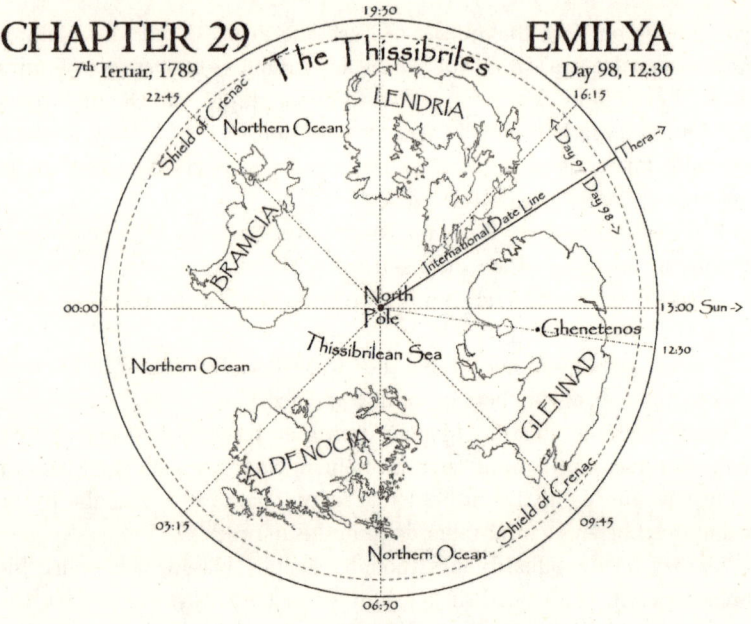

Emilya yawned again. It had been a late night, but Jake had insisted on an early start, as progress would be slower once they began ascending the foothills of the Bleaklow Hills. Thanks to the gentle up-and-down motion of the horse's gait, Emilya found herself half-dozing, whilst little Theo was fast-off, tucked up against her chest in his harness. Back in her dull travelling clothes again, Emilya's thoughts were constantly on an evening she would remember with warmth for the rest of her life.

She allowed herself a little smile as she recalled how awkward she must have been for Elyse to make-up and dress. Despite all her protestations, Emilya would never forget the moment she had first seen the stranger in the mirror; the dress and Elyse's expert make-up had been so transformational that she hadn't recognised herself. Of course, she had been forced to wear dresses at school – but they were plain, formal affairs, made for children. This pale blue dress had showed her off as a woman, for the first time in her life. Just the memory of it gave Emilya butterflies. She probably wasn't ready for womanhood just yet, and it was certainly not in her nature to show herself off – or even think that she *had* anything to show off.

The other thing Emilya recalled, was how the whole ensemble had made her *feel* different. She had moderated the way she walked, the way she looked at people, the way she addressed people. It was like that dress and her hair and make-up had conditioned her to act as a lady; as if she had no other choice. It was all a far-cry from school days when the rotten boys in her class had nicknamed her Miss Mouseface – because her nose had a tendency to twitch – and so the boys would squeak several times in unison whenever they saw her. That memory usually made her flush with embarrassment, but not this time.

And then there was the effect on the sandy-haired Edwyn. Also aged fifteen, she had caught him looking at her often. Around about the dozenth occasion, they had both laughed, shyly.

The evening had started off very seriously, though, with Jake and Elyse filling in Emrys and his family – which included Emrys and Elyse's mother, Martha – as to why they were here, and effectively on the run. They had all been stunned; and angry, too. Most people in Ghantiss were aware of Prince Magnus' reputation; Emilya now knew that this reputation extended well beyond the capital, too.

Martha's reaction, in particular, had interested Emilya. Even though she was in her sixties, Martha was upright, elegant and strikingly attractive, despite her greying hair. Like Elyse, she was blessed with high cheekbones and large blue eyes which shone with warmth and intelligence whenever she smiled. Like Elyse, those eyes also looked right into your soul, seemingly all-knowing. And there was one thing she had said, which even though it had been about Magnus, had sent a chill down Emilya's spine. "His time is near." When pressed to explain further, Martha had effortlessly deflected the conversation elsewhere.

As for taking Emilya out of harms' way, the consensus had been that it was the correct decision – despite the fact that her 'offence' was ludicrously tame. Conversely, it was thought that Prince Magnus would soon forget about Emilya and Jake and find a new target to ease his boredom. After that, the conversation had progressively relaxed, and as the wine had flowed, it had become increasingly more adult, too. Communal baths were one thing, thought Emilya, but they were starting to look like the tip of the iceberg in these parts.

Finding herself uncomfortable, Emilya had excused herself and gone and stood on the veranda which the banqueting hall opened onto. The cool night breeze had felt refreshing on her face, and Emilya had closed her eyes, listening to the sounds of the countryside at night, still very aware that she was dressed like a woman in a beautiful pale-blue dress. When she'd heard a stir of the curtain, she had known who it was. "May I join you?" Edwyn had asked, quietly.

Surprising herself at how relaxed she felt, Emilya had replied: "Of course."

Edwyn had moved alongside her, looking out over the courtyard where its fountains still tinkled away. Neither of them had said anything for a while, then Emilya had turned to Edwyn, and had managed to hold eye contact for the first time. "Do you go to school?" she had asked.

Edwyn had smiled at that. It was a nice smile, Emilya had decided. "Of course," he had confirmed. "But not like you."

"What do you mean?" Emilya had asked, curiously.

Edwin had paused before answering. "Hmm," he began, smiling at Emilya. She smiled back, shyly. "So, like all the other children here, I am home-schooled. We don't follow the national syllabus."

"You mean, you don't have to do mathematics?" asked Emilya. Maths was her pet-hate.

"Oh, we do maths," confirmed Edwyn. "My father teaches that; he's an absolute wizard. And we also do science and history and geography and… other subjects." Emilya was intrigued to notice Edwyn's eyes dart a little at that last statement.

"Other subjects?" she pressed.

"Yes," confirmed Edwyn, the word rather drawn-out.

"Would you care to expand?" asked Emilya.

"Well," began Edwyn. "They're not really approved of by the authorities."

"So, what are they?" asked Emilya, aware that this was her third attempt to elicit a response.

Edwyn sighed before looking Emilya fully in the face again. Emilya's heart did a tiny flip. "They're called Earth Studies," said Edwyn.

"Earth Studies? You mean, like physical geography, mountains, rivers, seas, that kind of thing?"

Edwyn smiled at that. "No, not really."

"But 'earth' is like the ground that we walk upon, isn't it? As are the rocks, mantle and core beneath us. Or is your 'Earth' something to do with that fabled planet on the opposite side of the sun?"

Edwyn laughed at that. "No, definitely not that Earth."

"OK," said Emilya, disappointed. "You don't have to explain them to me if you don't want to."

"I don't mean to be rude," said Edwyn. "I would tell you. It's just…"

Emilya waited expectantly, and then prompted when nothing was forthcoming. "Yes?"

"It's just that…you would probably be put off – you know – of me…"

"Well, if it's any comfort, Edwyn," she'd said, her first use of his name causing another tiny flutter, "we have some very strange customers back at our bakery, too."

Edwyn smiled again at that. "So, who is your strangest customer?"

Emilya considered this for a moment or two. "Well," she began. "There's old Mr Trimble. He always comes into our shop with a dog lead – but there's no dog on the end of it. Apparently, he lost his dog, Mabel, a black-and-white collie, a few years back, but has never had another one because no dog could ever replace Mabel. And then there's Mr Cratchett – he's old as well – and sometimes, he doesn't even bother to get dressed before he comes in for his morning sausage roll; he sits at one of our tables in just his greatcoat, vest and long-johns and eats. Then there's Mrs Willets. She's as loopy as a fruit bat. She talks all the way through her queuing – to anyone or no one, really – and even talks whilst she eats – with her mouth full – even though no one is listening. And not forgetting Jo-Jo No-Go. I don't know what *his* surname is, but my father christened him 'No-Go' as he's always trying to get Dad to buy items that he's convinced aren't totally legal, shall we say, and -"

Emilya stopped, realising that she had become rather breathless in her monologue, and that Edwyn was looking at her rather oddly. "What?" she asked.

"Nothing," said Edwyn, innocently. "It's just that…"

"What?"

"There's no one else here quite like you, Emilya. And that's a good thing," he added, hurriedly before Emilya took offence.

"Huh!" she responded. "My Dad loves me to bits, but he still tells me that I'm an odd-ball. Or whacky. Or a Tom-Boy."

"You don't look very much like a Tom-Boy tonight, Emilya."

Emilya looked down at her pale-blue dress. "Hmm," she began. "Well, this really isn't me, you know."

"I know that."

"How do you know that?"

"I saw you ride in. That's more the real Emilya, isn't it?"

"With scruffy boys' clothes and dusty hair."

"It was nice dusty hair though."

"But not the clothes?"

Edwyn's approach suddenly changed and it made him look like a startled young boy. "Oh, I'm sorry, Emilya," he said, his hands raised in defence. "I didn't mean to…"

Emilya smiled at his response. "It's really fine, Edwyn. I don't mind what you say. And it's nice to speak to someone of my own age."

"Is it difficult with Jake and Elyse?"

"Oh no, they're both lovely. But they're so much older. And, you know?"

Edwyn looked at her quizzically, obviously not knowing.

"You know?" said Emilya, widening her eyes.

"Are they an item?" asked Edwyn, with great surprise. It was his aunt, after all, considered Emilya.

"No, no, no, not at all. But I *think* they like each other. You know… maybe…like that. And they're both constantly making comments that they both seem to understand but I don't. And I also catch them smiling at each other or winking whenever they think I'm not looking – usually after they've been teasing me."

"My Mam and Dad do that all the time."

They had then fallen silent for some time, before Edwyn had asked her if she really needed to go tomorrow.

"Did you hear why we're travelling?" Emilya had asked.

"I heard. It made me want to punch Prince Magnus' lights out."

Emilya laughed at that, and briefly put her hand on Edwyn's arm. Surprised, he looked down at it. Immediately self-conscious, Emilya removed her hand. To hide her awkwardness, she said: "Why thank you for your chivalry, my Lord."

Edwyn had bowed to her. "It was really nothing, my Lady."

Emilya had giggled at that. She liked this affable boy with sandy, girly hair…but the giggle had elicited a pang of loss for Freya Colin.

Edwyn had noticed the change in her expression. "Is something wrong?"

"Oh, it's my friend, Freya – you know, the one the palace thugs took in my place. I'm worried for her."

"I'm sure she'll be all right," Edwyn had consoled. "Once they realise they've got the wrong baker's daughter, they'll send her home, surely."

"Penny for them."

Emilya blinked as she came out of her reverie. Elyse had moved her horse alongside Emilya's, her expression gentle, humorous and caring, triggering a flush of warmth for someone who had rapidly become her surrogate mother. "Oh, I was just thinking of last night," she said.

"Yes, it was lovely, wasn't it? And you looked lovely, too, Emilya."

Rather than rail against the comment, Emilya found herself thanking Elyse – to which Elyse just gave her the warmest smile back.

"You have the loveliest family, Elyse," responded Emilya. "Even though they are a little different."

"Different?"

Emilya offered Elyse a wry look. "You know exactly what I mean."

Elyse's response was that musical laughter again.

They trotted on for another thirty seconds in silence, and then Emilya asked: "What are Earth Studies, Elyse?"

"Ah," responded Elyse. "You've been talking to Edwyn, I take it?"

Emilya immediately blushed. Elyse laughed again, and then took Emilya's hand in hers – a familiar trait now, which Emilya adored. "I saw you two out on the veranda. Is my nephew still impeccably courteous?"

"Oh yes, Elyse," responded Emilya, enthusiastically. "He was…"

"Hmm?" prompted Elyse, both eyebrows raised.

"Lovely," replied Emilya, quietly. She was quite amazed at her own honesty and bravery.

"Yes, he is, isn't he?" responded Elyse, warmly, whilst also giving Emilya's hand an encouraging squeeze.

Emilya looked across at Elyse, as they released hands. "Earth Studies?" she asked again, this time raising both of *her* eyebrows.

Elyse gave in. "All right," she said. "Let's see how open-minded you are, then."

"I'm very open-minded, actually," said Emilya.

"Do you mind if I learn a little, too?" asked Jake, falling in the other side of Emilya.

"Ha!" responded Elyse. "You're so open-minded, you'll probably be disappointed!"

"And how, pray, does the lady know this?"

"The lady knows considerably more than the gentleman realises."

Emilya rolled her eyes at this latest typical exchange. "Earth Studies, please, Elyse," she requested.

"Of course, dear. So, you will have realised by now that my family and friends can loosely be termed 'druidic', yes?"

Emilya nodded.

"Well, we druids, I'm afraid, do not believe in religion, or mainstream gods, or a higher authority. Although that said, our schools do still teach Religious Instruction – so that we can understand what others believe."

Emilya nodded again. Although looking straight ahead and holding her reins to steer her horse, she was listening avidly to every word.

"However," clarified Elyse, "despite this absence of an omnipotent god in our lives, we are still a very spiritual people."

Again, Emilya nodded. "Yes, I can see that; I *feel* that."

Elyse smiled. "Good, Emilya. I felt sure that you would. Because, you see, our beliefs simply promote harmony and connection and reverence for the natural world; for everything around us: the animals, the trees, the hills, the fields, the flowers, the rivers, the seas. We are all connected, Emilya. We all contain the same energy."

"I can definitely understand that," encouraged Emilya.

"Well," said Elyse. "Here's where you're going to need to stretch your understanding."

Emilya looked across at Elyse, and Elyse winked back at her. Emilya smiled before returning part of her concentration to steering her horse.

"The natural world – the earth beneath our feet – it has," Elyse paused for effect, "certain powers."

"Powers?"

"Yes, powers. An energy which runs through Mother Thera, or Theraea as we know her, and every organism on her surface – including every person on the planet, if they deign to search for it."

"So, I have this energy in me?" questioned Emilya.

"Of course," confirmed Elyse. "It's even in Mr Oscom here," she added, nodding towards Jake. Jake vaguely raised his eyebrows at that, but Emilya could tell that he was listening avidly, too.

"The problem is, Emilya," said Elyse, now looking intently at her charge, "that people today are brought up in a society that is unnatural."

"Unnatural?"

"Yes, unnatural. It's a society created on the basis of money, economy, profit and greed. People are conditioned to think 'rationally', for want of a better word – and so they fail to engage their intuitive capabilities; the energy side of us. This is why there are so many unhappy people – because they are natural beings, but living in an unnatural society. Again, for want of a better phrase, they are soulless."

Emilya was totally transfixed, and could feel something stirring deep within. "And this power?" she questioned, eventually.

"Is available to all, some more so than others. Like my mother. She has what is commonly called the Second Sight – generally by those who don't understand the nature of the power."

"She's your High Priestess, isn't she?"

Elyse smiled. "Very perceptive, Emilya."

"Does that mean that you will be one day?"

Elyse smiled again. "That is the plan."

"So, you feel this power within you as well, then?"

Elyse looked directly at Emilya with those intense blue eyes of hers. "Of course. But hopefully not like my mother for many, many years."

"And this power comes from beneath us? Mother Thera, you said?"

"Very good, Emilya," said Elyse, appreciating her student's desire to understand. I just wish that we could have demonstrated that to you amongst the stones. One day, I promise you that we will – if you will allow us to?"

Emilya was immediately nervous about that; perhaps it was just a fear of the unknown. "I'm not sure, maybe," she said, non-committally.

"Anyway," continued Elyse. "Earth Studies are concerned with how we can *recognise* those powers, how we should *respect* those powers…and how we can *harness* those powers."

"You mean magic…or sorcery?" asked Emilya, slightly disappointed.

"Those are words invented by non-druids, Emilya. To explain what they cannot explain!"

"Hmm," said Emilya, trying to understand.

"Take medicine, for example," Elyse continued. "How is little Theo doing this morning?"

Emilya looked down at her adorable little terrier, sleeping peacefully in the harness strapped around her chest. "He's doing very well. You've done a wonderful job…"

Elyse raised her left eyebrow, quizzically.

"Ah," responded Emilya, while at the same time, feeling a tingling sensation at the top of her spine. She looked back at Elyse. "My father said you were…"

"Yes?"

"Well, to quote him word-for-word: 'She's a wizard of a healer.'"

They walked their horses on in silence for a few seconds as Elyse let this new line of thought sink in. "So," said Emilya, eventually. "Medicine is one branch of your Earth Sciences, then?"

"It is."

"What else is there?"

"General things. Respect and veneration. For all other human beings, all other creatures, the environment. And veneration of our ancestors, too. Especially our ancient ancestors. For example, how did they have the wherewithal to build Ghenetenos? You, yourself, were asking the very-same question on our approach, yesterday. What did they possess that enabled them to build such structures, many thousands of years before we invented engines?"

"You're suggesting that they tapped into this energy?"

"Without question they did. And they likely had help from the very objects that were erecting, too, as they are also part of Mother Thera."

"You're saying that the stones, *themselves*, collaborated in the build of the temple?"

"Ah, you've become a sceptic again."

"I haven't," corrected Emilya, quickly. "It's just that…the *stones*…"

"Mother Thera's power is everywhere, Emilya. But especially at Ghenetenos. And there are also many other places around the world where Theraea's power is tightly concentrated. You see, there are lines beneath the surface, Emilya. Energy lines. And, inevitably, these energy lines cross each other – and where they do, they create a vortex. The Ancients knew this and felt it, too – hence the building of stone circles in The Thissibriles and the pyramids in Epanaga. Structures that precisely align to heavenly bodies at certain times of the year. But, you see, the thing is Emilya, whatever that energy was that they tapped into – it is still with us, beneath us. We can still feel that energy, we can absorb it…we can *use* it.

"Of course, later, some of our greatest abbeys were built on these vortexes as well; sacred sites which are pure energy amplifiers. And if you just stopped, for one minute, at any of these sites, and searched within, for who you are, naturally…"

Emilya suddenly realised that she was holding her breath, whilst the hairs on both arms were standing upright. She gently let out her breath. "OK, so you've moved me," she admitted.

"Good. I recognised promise in you when I first saw you, Emilya."

"In me?"

"In you."

Emilya laughed, breaking the spell. "All right," she said. "So, what's the communal bathing about, then?"

"Ah, now that's a lesson for a later date."

"Well, how does that relate to Earth Studies," said Emilya, not giving up that easily.

"The human body is a powerful thing, Emilya. Especially when it is at one with nature."

Emilya looked hard at Elyse – who promptly raised her eyebrows again. Jake, meanwhile, carried on looking straight ahead, his features as implacable as ever.

CHAPTER 30 — MAGNUS

7th Tertiar, 1789 — Day 98, 12:45

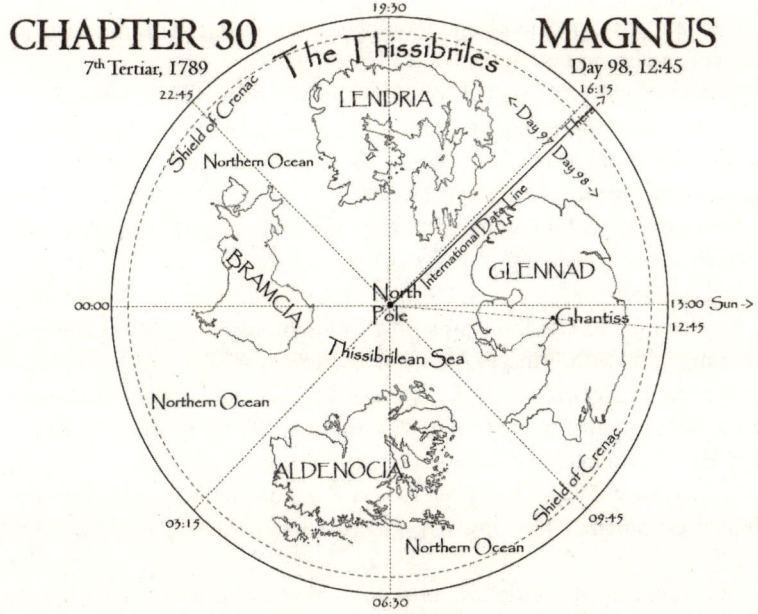

Magnus' first instinct had been to order James Cecil to tell the Colins to go away – and to use force if necessary. But he'd stopped himself, and instead, guided Cecil out of the Games Room and into the corridor. There was no love lost between them, but Magnus needed Cecil as an ally, and if this issue blew up with the Colins, he'd lose all the advantages he'd worked so hard to gain earlier that morning.

"How far does your loyalty to the Crown stretch, Lord Chamberlain?" he'd asked, in a low voice.

Cecil looked back at him. Hard. Magnus held his breath. Cecil's shoulders then sagged. "My loyalty is absolute, Your Royal Highness."

"Then take me to your office please, James," said Magnus, holding out his hand to indicate the way, and hoping that use of his first name would clinch the deal. Cecil shook his head slightly, clearly not happy with the way things were panning out but did as he was told.

Three minutes later, Magnus was seated across the desk from James Cecil. The grizzled Lord Chamberlain was looking tired. Magnus had concocted a dozen different ways to commence this conversation on their silent walk through the palace corridors, and had eventually decided on the repentant approach. "I've been an idiot," he began. "More than that, I've been a monster."

Cecil put his right thumb and forefinger to the bridge of his nose, closed his eyes and began massaging. He said nothing.

Unnerved, Magnus waited for a few seconds and then continued. "I know you don't approve of me, Lord Chamberlain, and these last two days, I've come to disapprove of myself too. I hope it isn't too late for me to mend my ways, and avoid a catastrophic scandal."

James Cecil held up his hand to stop him. "Please just answer me one question, Prince Magnus."

"Of course."

Cecil leaned forward, his forearms resting on his desk. "Have you had anything to do with Princess Alicya's disappearance?"

Magnus also leaned forward, keeping his expression earnest. "Only what I told those gathered in the Council Room earlier. That my actions with the Prey and Emilya Luca and Jake Oscom on 1st Tertiar, may have inadvertently led to Oscom abducting my sister. I swear that I had nothing to do with the abduction myself. I love my sister, Lord Chamberlain. I love her very dearly."

Cecil continued to look at him, searching his face for any sign of falsehood. Magnus kept his face earnest, knowing his future might be hanging by a thread. Eventually, Cecil sighed and sat back in his chair. "I can't tell you how relieved I am to hear that, Prince Magnus."

Some of the tension had already disappeared from Cecil's face. He had obviously feared the worst. Part of him perhaps still did. Cecil issued another big sigh. "So," he began. "Tell me why you've been a monster, and I will do my best to help you."

"You are a loyal servant, Lord Chamberlain," responded Magnus.

"But" said Cecil, raising a forefinger. "You must change your ways."

"I already have," said Magnus, his face and voice still sincere, and at least part of that genuine – albeit from a self-preservation perspective. "These last two days have been the worst of my life. I've examined myself a thousand times and seen everything that was wrong with me. Arrogance. Conceit. Bullying. A belief that I could do as I pleased."

James Cecil continued to regard Magnus, wearily. Eventually, he spoke. "So, what do we need to cover up?"

"Freya Colin," he said, simply.

"You killed her?"

"It was an accident."

"But she's dead?"

"Yes."

"And the body?"

"Disposed of."

"Where?"

"Cemetery Island. No questions asked."

"Who else knows."

"Just Marler and Hoskyns. Both totally reliable."

"And they did the disposing?"

"They organised it. Their associates did the disposing. The associates are now also on Cemetery Island."

"Meanwhile, Marler and Hoskyns are implicated, too. This is good. This is salvageable."

"You heard what I suggested this morning?"

"That Oscom killed Freya Colin after a chance encounter?"

"Yes. It is believable, isn't it?"

"It will be if we can silence Oscom."

"My thoughts entirely," agreed Magnus.

"So," began Cecil. "Our priority – as you outlined this morning – is to capture Oscom. Ordinarily, I'd say dead, rather than alive – as we can't afford for him to stand trial."

"What do you mean by 'ordinarily'?"

"Because we need to get the Princess back first, obviously," said Cecil, looking hard at Magnus again. "Don't we?"

Magnus briefly despaired at the effort required to keep so many deceptions spinning at once. "Of course we do," he began, with the utmost sincerity. "But the best-case scenario for us…" Magnus stopped, flicked his eyes upwards to meet Cecil's and then flicked back downwards again. "The best-case scenario for *me*," he corrected, "is to receive the ransom note, pay the ransom, get Alicya back…and then hunt Oscom down and kill him. We then try him posthumously and find him guilty of the abduction of Princess Alicya, and the murders of Humphrey Horrocks, John Nash and Freya Colin – in that order."

"Well," said Cecil, wearily, sitting back in his chair once again. "If it turns out like that, I, for one, will rejoice."

You and me both, thought Magnus.

"But we have another more immediate problem, don't we?" suggested Cecil.

"Yes, and hence my admission to you, Lord Chamberlain. So, what do we do with the Colins?"

Cecil sat back in his chair, deep in thought. Neither man said anything for a full minute, and the only sound in the room was the steady tick-tock of Cecil's grandfather clock in one corner. Eventually, Cecil spoke. "What were you planning to do with the Colins yourself, Prince Magnus – given you know full well that their daughter's body is never going to be turned up, much-less ransomed by Oscom?"

Magnus shifted awkwardly in his seat.

"You can be honest," suggested Cecil.

"Well, I'd rather hoped they would just accept that Oscom had taken her and killed her -."

"Never going to happen," interrupted Cecil. "Freya was their daughter. They would have loved her dearly."

Magnus put his head in his hands in a false show of grief and agony. "I *am* a monster," he cried.

"This could bring down the monarchy, Your Royal Highness," said Cecil, testily. "This is no time for self-pity."

Magnus almost bit back at that, but he was learning new strengths. Penance, self-reproach, restraint and deference, were clearly useful qualities to utilise – in certain situations.

"So, what was your plan?" asked Cecil again.

Magnus sat back in his chair and regarded Cecil. Cecil regarded him back. "Well, that would be me being a monster again, James."

"Hmm," pondered Cecil, and left it at that – and so Magnus bit the bullet. "I was going to get Marler and Hoskyns…" he paused and licked his dry lips, "…to torch their bakery. A tragic accident. And not one so uncommon for such an establishment."

Cecil lifted his hand to his chin and rubbed it thoughtfully. He then looked at Magnus, his eyes penetrating. "It's as good a solution as any I can come up with."

Magnus' eyebrows went up in surprise at Cecil's ruthlessness.

"The monarchy must not fall. Whatever my private thoughts are on this, I have to lift myself above them. The ends justify the means."

"And the magistrate."

James Cecil chuckled, mirthlessly. "You can leave him to me. John Nash, John Russell and I worked closer together than you might think."

Magnus' thoughts flicked back to when he had found all three of them colluding in Nash's office. He raised his eyebrows questioningly.

"The man's name is Wragley. He frequents certain institutions without his wife's knowledge. I will persuade him to cease his interest in the Colins."

"And you want me to initiate my plan, as you put it?"

"Well, let me add my suggestion as to how this could play out – firstly regarding our current dilemma at the palace gates."

"Please," suggested Magnus. "Do continue."

"We invite in Wragley on his own. I encourage him to play along, making clear the alternative. We then send him back to the Colins, advising we are already doing everything in our power to bring to justice the man that we believe has apprehended their daughter. We could even fob them off by saying we'll have an announcement by tomorrow. Any longer, and they'll likely not leave us alone, today."

"Is it worth telling them that we believe the same man has abducted the Princess Alicya?" asked Magnus, speculatively. "And to have them swear their silence? Even get them to sign a disclaimer. Wragley, too?"

"Well," said Cecil, rubbing his chin again. "It would suggest a certain solidarity between us all. They may even feel privileged to be in our confidence. Then again, if it was me, I'd just want my daughter back."

"Let's do it, Cecil," said Magnus. "Get Wragley in now. Tell him everything and emphasise that we've already got a hundred men out searching Ghantiss for Oscom, Alicya and Freya Colin. We then make him sign the disclaimer. If he baulks at that, play your blackmail card."

"Agreed," said Cecil. "You let me deal with Wragley, but you must deal with Mr and Mrs Colin yourself. Are you happy with that?"

Magnus sat back in his chair. "'Happy' isn't the word I would use. But needs must. Send them up to the Games Room when you're done with Wragley. I will receive them in there."

"I don't believe a word of it," said Rex Colin, his eyes like stones as he glared at Magnus.

"Excuse me?" responded Magnus, trying to reassert his superiority.

"You heard me! I know all about your encounter with Emilya Luca. Danny Luca told me. You took our Freya thinking she was Emilya."

"That's all true, yes," admitted Magnus, as he surveyed the odd couple before him. It would appear that Freya inherited her height from her father and her dark-red hair from her small and rotund mother. "But you will also know from Danny Luca that I intended to apprentice both Emilya and Freya to my sister, Alicya – as compensation for my poor behaviour."

"But if you'd left her alone, none of this would have happened in the first place," sobbed Peggy Colin.

"I deeply regret everything that has happened, Mrs Colin. I was trying to make amends."

"That won't bring her back, will it?" snapped Rex.

"May I remind you to whom you are addressing," said Wragley. *Cecil had obviously brought him fully onside.*

Magnus held up his hand. "It's fine, Mr Wragley. Their daughter is missing. I would feel exactly the same way if my sister was missing."

"Now would you really?" sneered Rex Colin.

The sneer pushed Magnus' buttons and he couldn't help himself. He jumped to his feet, wild-eyed. "I invited you here to offer to help find your daughter," he raged.

Rex Colin flinched backwards from Magnus' anger, whilst Peggy Colin was now also on her feet, her plump hands flapping. "Oh please, Prince Magnus," she begged. "Rex isn't himself. He's beside himself with worry for our Freya. He doesn't know what he's saying."

"I know exactly what I'm saying," snarled Rex, now recovered and beyond reining in. "I know who Jake Oscom is. He's a decent man. He doesn't go around abducting young girls."

"How-how-how do you know Jake Oscom, Rex?" stuttered Mrs Colin, now confused.

Rex sighed, looking like a man who needed to tell the truth. "Jake Oscom is the real name of that furniture merchant who was in our shop the day our Freya was taken. He was using an alias, Jack Morse. He was the ex-navy captain who saved Emilya. From him," he said pointing accusingly at Magnus.

Magnus remained on his feet. "Jake Oscom is indeed an *ex*-naval captain," he said, coldly. "Before he was dismissed from the Bramcian navy and sentenced to execution for killing a man in Byastwerthy, three years ago. Isn't that so, Mr Cecil?"

"You have my word on that, Mr Colin," responded Cecil.

"Since then, he's been on the run from the authorities. Hence his alias of Jack Morse; sometimes Jack Moose. As recently as the 2nd Tertiar, he has murdered another man – a Ghantiss magistrate called Humphrey Horrocks – a colleague of Mr Wragley's, I believe."

Wragley looked shocked. "Humphrey Horrocks!" he exclaimed.

"Yes. Oscom slit his throat five nights ago in Boserentua."

"Good God!" exclaimed Wragley, genuinely shaken.

"Again, this is the truth," confirmed the Lord Chamberlain. "Oscom is currently our most-wanted criminal."

"Mr and Mrs Colin. I understand your worry and concern, but this is my last peace offering," said Magnus, now looming over the pair of them. "I am now going to take you into further confidence of events that are known only to a few – to demonstrate my authenticity and understanding of your worry and grief."

Rex Colin's face was now a kaleidoscope of confusion, clearly no longer sure of his daughter's fate, and so Magnus hit them with his monster lie. "Jake Oscom has kidnapped Princess Alicya!"

Two jaws dropped open before him.

"She disappeared two days ago. We then received a ransom note from Oscom. For ten thousand guineas. A large sum – but for which we are currently arranging payment." Magnus then lied through his teeth to the Colins about the original blackmail based on the Let Us Prey session, and how Freya had been with his sister two days ago when they had both disappeared. By the time he'd finished, Rex Colin had his head in his hands. "But he was a good man. He rescued Emilya. He…"

Magnus looked at Rex Colin sharply. "Do you know where Oscom has gone, Mr Colin?"

The tables were completely turned. Rex Colin now looked like a startled rabbit.

"Mr Colin!" encouraged Magnus, firmly. "Is Jake Oscom with Emilya Luca, right now?

"Rex, what's going on?" wailed Mrs Colin. "What haven't you told me?"

"Mrs Colin," said Magnus, now determined to turn the screw on the weakest link. "Jake Oscom is a highly dangerous man. A murderer, thief, blackmailer and someone who has a fetish for young girls. He is also a very clever predator, a natural liar and a confidence trickster to boot, which is why he has so easily duped your husband and Danny Luca. If he has Emilya Luca in his care – and I used the word 'care' ironically – she is in *very* grave danger. He has most definitely kidnapped the Princess Alicya, my sister. We are assuming that he has also kidnapped your daughter, and now Mr Colin is suggesting that he has kidnapped Emilya Luca as well."

"It wasn't a kidnap!" stammered Rex Colin, his hands now almost out of control with the shakes.

Magnus approached the seated Rex Colin and went down on his haunches. Inside he was exulting. This was a most unexpected bonus. Outwardly, he put on his sincerest expression. "Mr Colin. I'm sure that Jake Oscom would have been *very* convincing, because that's what he does: role-playing. But he has played you and Danny Luca for fools. And I promise you, that if we find him, not only will we be able to rescue Emilya Luca, but we will almost certainly rescue your daughter, too."

Rex Colin continued to look at the floor in total turmoil. His mind was made up by his wife, with an out-of-the-blue slap across the top of his head. That brought Rex around.

"How *could* you?" she shrieked. "You're actually implicated in our daughter's disappearance. You!"

"I'm not -."

"You tell them," Mrs Colin demanded, amid falling tears and an accusing pointing finger. "You tell them everything that you know. You tell them now. Because if our Freya dies as a result of this, I will hold you personally responsible."

"Oh, my Good Lord!" exclaimed Rex, putting his head in his hands. He actually began to sob.

"Oh, you snivelling wretch," said Mrs Colin, her face screwed up in disgust. She raised her hand to strike him again but was stopped by an unlikely source. Magnus had gently stayed her arm.

"Please, Mrs Colin. We're all desperately working towards the same goal, here. Let Mr Colin tell us everything he knows, and then we'll redirect our search parties appropriately."

"You tell them Rex," commanded Mrs Colin again, her voice now dangerously calm.

And tell them he did. He told of their introduction to Oscom when Hoskyns and Marler had taken Freya. He told of Oscom's warnings to Danny Luca that Emilya was in danger. And then he told of the agreement for Jake to take Emilya to a place of safety, and of how Emilya had said goodbye to her father three days earlier.

"And they were heading south?" asked Magnus.

"Somewhere on the south coast. I know Danny Luca has a sister in Dominniul."

"She's not there," said Magnus. "We've already checked. Are there any other clues as to their destination?"

"I just remember Jake Oscom mentioning the south coast, because you wouldn't expect him to go over land, and certainly not south."

"And was there any indication that he had anyone else with him?"

"None whatsoever," said Rex. "But of course, this all happened on the 4th. You're saying that he kidnapped the Princess and our Freya on the 5th. So maybe he's taken all three of them to some hideout near here – and he's not heading for the south coast after all. Then again," he said, his face falling, "Oscom also talked of taking poor Emilya to Lendria. Said she'd be safe there." He turned to his wife; his expression now hapless. "How could I have known, Peggy? He was so believable."

The meeting wound up shortly after that, with Mrs Colin now eternally grateful for having the palace on her side whilst reasonably optimistic that they would get her Freya back. The Prince had even agreed to pay any ransom for Freya and Emilya on their and Danny Luca's behalf, courtesy of his unwitting role in their twin abduction. Meanwhile, Rex Colin was now consumed with guilt, believing he had played a crucial role in condemning Emilya Luca to goodness knows what, and dreading having to tell Danny Luca the awful truth.

"That was extremely well played, Your Royal Highness," said Cecil, approvingly, after the Colins had been escorted out. "But it doesn't solve the problem that their daughter isn't going to show up."

"I'm fully aware of that, Cecil," said Magnus, some of his old arrogance back now that the immediate situation had been dealt with. "There will be no loose ends. They die tonight in the fire."

Cecil merely inclined his head. "Will that be all from me?"

"Yes, thank you Lord Chamberlain," he replied with a little more respect. "You have been exceptionally helpful and understanding."

"Yes," agreed Cecil. "But I won't be next time."

"There won't be a next time."

"Good. Let us hope that once this nightmare is over and we've got our princess back, we can start training you for the duties that lie ahead."

Magnus gave the Lord Chamberlain a weak smile. Cecil nodded once and turned to leave.

"Oh, Cecil?"

"Yes?"

"I suggest we cover aspects of this meeting in tonight's debrief. In the meantime, I am going to use the same story we just used on the Colins with Danny Luca. Scare the living daylights out of him. See if he crumbles and reveals all. They may not have headed south, after all."

"That sounds like an excellent plan, Sir, given Oscom has likely got all three of them."

As soon as Cecil had exited, Magnus turned to the waiting Hoskyns and Marler. He quickly ran over the plan for their little arson outing which he told them had to happen tonight. "You need to make certain they both die," said Magnus, his eyes blazing. "But we can't afford any post-mortem give-aways – like slit throats or embedded musket balls. Make sure they die by the fire. You can manage that, can't you?"

"Leave it with me, Sir," said Marler, an evil look in his single eye.

"Good man," said Magnus. "And this magistrate, Wragley. He now knows too much – but he regularly whores in Ghantiss. Work out his routine and then slit his throat in a dark alley at the first opportunity."

"Again, that will be no problem," said Marler.

"Thank you Marler. However, before any of that, I need you two to accompany me on another little trip to Luca's Bakery.

A few hours later, Magnus retired to his room. The first thing he did was to remove his hat and look at his ugly scar in the mirror. It was still a mess. His face twisted in anger, his only satisfaction being that the perpetrator was somewhere on Cemetery Island, and would be joined there, shortly, by her parents. Magnus then threw himself onto his bed, still frustrated. He'd got nothing out of Danny Luca. Unlike the Colins, Luca wasn't buying the Oscom story; he clearly believed his daughter was safer with Oscom than she was at the palace. And much as he would love to torture the truth out of Danny Luca, Magnus couldn't afford any more loose ends – or another burned-down bakery, for that matter. And in any case, Luca had nothing on him, whilst the pending arson of his friend's bakery would likely cow him into submission for the rest of his life, given he had two other younger children to bring up on his own. All being well, Magnus now only had the absence of a ransom note to worry about, which would be resolved by the capture and death of Oscom before he could talk. He was, as yet, undecided on whether to spare Emilya Luca. Much depended upon her stance when they eventually found her.

Magnus yawned, suddenly realising how tired he was. He also had a nagging headache. The de-brief was planned for 19:00. It was now 17:00. He had instructed Marler to wake him at 18:45.

Magnus closed his eyes – and within seconds, was sleeping soundly.

CHAPTER 31 — ALICYA
7th Tertiar, 1789   Day 98, 15:00

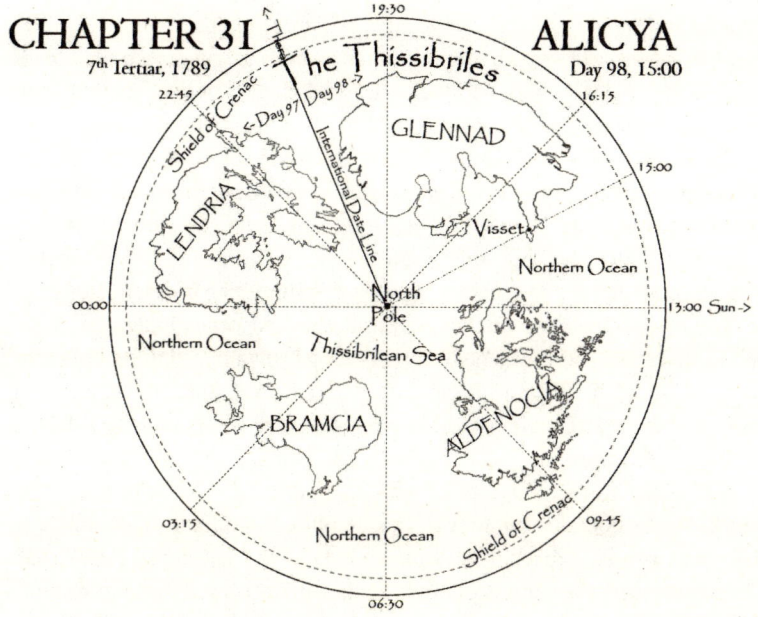

Alicya awoke with a start – and was immediately confused. Fortunately, the gentle rise and fall and the thin slats of light coming through the louvred door before her, soon reminded her where she was. Also fortunate was the fact that little Vixey was curled up asleep in the folds of her greatcoat...and the fair-haired man clearly hadn't fancied any fishing, either.

Composing herself, Alicya took stock. The motion of the boat told her they were still sailing, but her little nap had ruined any chance of working out distance sailed. Given it wasn't yet dark, though, they were surely still in Glennadian waters?

Earlier, in Norvent, she had felt the boat list to port when the men started bringing their cargo on board, and then the creak of the six steps as they populated the hold. The pungent and now familiar smell which followed confirmed Alicya's suspicion about the cargo. Given they had almost certainly selected fresh cadavers, Alicya was fairly sure she had just been reunited with some of her former shipmates!

Shortly afterwards, she had heard the clip-clop of the horse mounting the ramp, while a minute later, had come the calls of the two-man crew as they had cast off and sailed out of Norvent's harbour. Listening hard to snatches of conversation and occasional shouted orders, Alicya was sure the accents were Glennadian, but certainly not Ghantissian. There was a strange intonation to their wording and phrasing that sounded oddly familiar. It had taken another ten minutes before she had placed the accent. One of the palace chefs sounded just like that – and he hailed from somewhere on the Wrenko peninsula.

Alicya had been to Wrenko before, but only for brief royal visits to coastal ports. She was well aware of its stunning scenery, though; a mountain range running down the middle of a long peninsula surrounded on three sides by tall cliffs leading onto endless miles of gorgeous sandy beaches, with spectacular waves crashing against the shore. Such descriptions had always stirred the romantic in her, and she had often imagined riding Sebastian across those beaches, with her long brown hair flying out behind her and some handsome suitor keeping her company. It would seem, though, that the circumstances of her first visit would be somewhat different to the imagined ones.

Alicya remained alert for the rest of the voyage, although it felt like another three hours before they docked. Unlike Norvent, though, this time, there was plenty of background noise. Lots of human noise, for starters. Then there were the sounds of other boats – many other boats – the shouts of fishermen bringing home their catch for the day, dogs barking, the ubiquitous seagulls. Next, Alicya heard a church bell chime, and that one sound of civilisation was so sweet; the little over twenty-six hours that she'd been isolated on Cemetery Island had felt more like twenty-six weeks. Alicya also noted the number of chimes – eighteen. It was therefore five o'clock in the afternoon on the 7th of Tertiar – a little over two days since she had been 'murdered' by her brother.

Noises of disembarkation soon followed, but they were too slow for Alicya's liking as she was desperate to move her cramped legs. When the men came down for the fifth and final body, Alicya's leg made an involuntary twitch and caught the inside of the cupboard door. Vixey also began to stir at the movement.

Alicya went rigid with fear. She could swear the men in the hold had stopped what they were doing, as the silence lasted for ages. Then, she heard one of them say something and the next thing she heard was the creak of the six wooden steps as they hauled their cargo up onto deck. She then heard the cultured tones of the man she had taken to be a doctor. "Right, thank you very much gentlemen. I suggest you go and take some supper now and meet me back here at twenty-thirty with full stomachs and the cart."

The men agreed and then Alicya felt them disembark, one-by-one. Strangely, Alicya hadn't heard the horse alight, and so it was presumably tethered to the mast as it had been in Norvent. Perhaps the doctor had also gone for his supper. It certainly made sense that they weren't going to transport their cargo until dark.

Wracked with indecision on what to do next, Alicya did at least manage to straighten out her legs, bringing great relief. The action also woke up Vixey, who began to stretch herself, and then issued a huge yawn. "Alicya tickled the fox-cub's tummy. "Did you have a nice sleepy?" she whispered.

Vixey's response was to lick the hand that was tickling her tummy. She then righted herself onto all fours and started sniffing about in the tiny space, before turning and looking at Alicya.

"What?" whispered Alicya.

Still Vixey just stared at her – until the penny dropped.

"Oh, you need to do a wee-wee," whispered Alicya. "You and me both!"

Alicya remained undecided. It was still light. She was dressed only in a man's greatcoat that was two sizes too big for her, and mismatching boots. *And* she would be carrying a fox-cub! It was not the most unobtrusive way to disembark from a boat in a bustling harbour. But their needs of nature were becoming urgent.

Her mind made up, Alicya screwed her face up and then cautiously applied pressure to the cupboard doors until they parted with a very audible *click*. She paused for a few seconds, and then pushed open the doors. Light filtered in from above the six steps, temporarily blinding her. Alicya put her hand out to shield the worst of the brightness. Something else was blocking the light as well.

With a start, Alicya realised it was the figure of a man, sat on the steps, looking directly at her. It was the tall, fair-haired doctor.

"Good afternoon," he said. "I suspect we both have a great deal of explaining to do."

CHAPTER 32 — EMILYA

7th Tertiar, 1789 — Day 98, 18:45

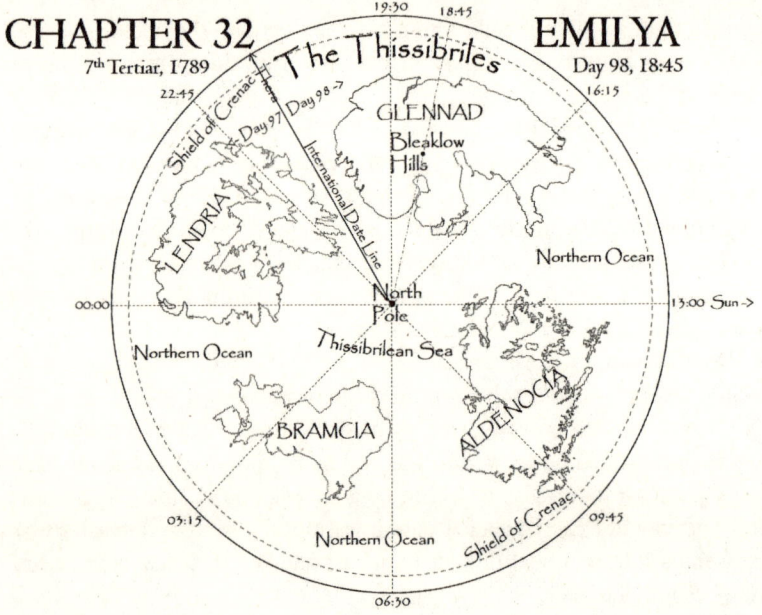

"We'll need to push on for another half-hour or so," said Jake. "The hostel I was talking about is located in a small village called Ghintarton, around a quarter of a league from here."

They'd been riding slowly uphill for several hours through dense forest, Emilya's thoughts constantly revolving around Mother Thera, energy lines and the power that they allegedly held, whilst periodically searching with her mind for something, anything out there, but not making a connection of any sort.

"*I recognised promise in you when I first saw you, Emilya,*" Elyse had said. Perhaps she had been wrong. Or perhaps none of it was true, more like. Either way, Emilya was strangely disappointed.

As they journeyed uphill, every now and then, the path would wind to the left or the right and afford a spectacular view between the pines and firs, looking back towards Ghenetenos on the plain below them to the south-west. Whenever the path straightened north-eastwards, all Emilya saw were more trees, although she knew they would eventually reach the treeline. Apparently, the Bleaklow Hills had earned their name thanks to a number of bleak plateaux at around 2,500 feet above sea level, meaning they weren't hills in the traditional sense. As a result, the wind was said to constantly howl across them, particularly in winter, and hence why they were uninhabited by man or anything else other than a few hardy bushes and even hardier sheep.

Thoughts of the howling wind made Emilya think of her grandfather and his collapsed aqueduct, the remains of which would be some fifteen leagues east of here, on the other side of the Bleaklows. She wondered if they would get the chance to visit. As for the Bleaklow Hills, Jake had explained that the 'low' part of the name was derived from the Old Glennadian word *hlāw*, meaning 'tumulus or burial mound'. Apparently, the Bleaklows were covered with Bronze Age and Prehistoric barrows which Emilya was looking forward to seeing. For now, though, she was enjoying the arboreal habitat, with its busy, scampering red squirrels and the numerous scarlet-crested woodpeckers, drumming away industriously at their trees. Her sinuses were also totally clear at this altitude and Emilya felt sure she would miss the rich smell of the pines once they left them behind.

As their path hairpinned to the left again, another gap in the trees afforded a view back south-west. The stone circle was now only just visible from eight leagues away on the plain far below, while the silver ribbon of the River Yew snaked away beyond it on its route towards Ghantiss and the home and bakery she had left behind. The thought made her wistful, and she felt sure for a second or two that she could smell freshly baked bread amidst the resiny pines. That thought made her stop her horse and gaze back longingly towards her homeland, which brought a lump to her throat and a hotness to her eyes.

Lost in her thoughts, she had failed to notice that Elyse and Jake had drawn up silently behind her. She was eventually pulled out of her reverie by a dramatic drilling sound from immediately behind them. She turned and saw her concerned-looking companions. She managed a watery smile before the sound came again, enabling her to focus on the exact spot – where she saw a bright red crest pneumatically drilling into a pine. "Don't they get headaches?" she asked.

"Apparently not," replied Elyse. "They have very sturdy skulls, but if you watch him, he moves his beak ever-so-slightly around as he drills, and that helps to minimise the impact to the head."

Emilya dismounted to get a better look, the action helping to push the feelings of sadness away. Elyse also dismounted and joined her, putting her arm around Emilya's shoulders. Emilya gave her a sad smile and then leaned her head towards Elyse, the top of her dark-auburn hair nestling against Elyse's cheek. The healer put her hand to the back of Emilya's head and stroked her hair. No words were spoken.

After a couple of minutes, Emilya pulled back. "I'm all right now," she said, simply, with a weak smile. By the time they set off again up the path, the woodpecker had disappeared on other business.

As was the norm, Emilya was riding in between her companions, with Elyse to her left and Jake to her right. She decided to learn something more about Earl's Leet, which Jake estimated they would arrive at in three days' time. "Jake," she began.

"Yes Emilya," he responded, turning to look at her, his face typically implacable.

"You were going to tell me more about Earl's Leet."

"Ah, yes. Earl's Leet and the Isolationists."

"The Isolationists?"

"Yes. I'll come to them shortly. First, though, the town. Did you know that Earl's Leet is the remotest town in Glennad?"

Emilya thought about that and shook her head.

"In fact, thinking about it," said Jake, pushing out his lower lip. "Earl's Leet could be the remotest town in all of the Thissibriles."

"So, it's more remote than Kifsel Place?" asked Emilya.

"Kifsel Place is just a village, Emilya. And a small one at that – made up mainly of visiting climbers and monks from the nearby monastery."

"Ah, I see, you said 'remotest *town*'. Earl's Leet is quite large then?"

"Yes. It has a population of around eighteen thousand. All the facilities you'd expect from a lowland or coastal town: multiple shops, banks, schools, an infirmary, a theatre, government offices, a renowned market, and so on. Doesn't have a brothel, though."

"Trust you to know that!" interceded Elyse.

Jake looked at Emilya and gestured towards Elyse with his head. "There she goes again. That woman has got completely the wrong idea about me."

"This woman knows men!" retorted Elyse.

A light smile played about Jake's lips. "I mention it, because Earl's Leet is the *only* town in Glennad without one."

Emilya pursed her lips, choosing not to dwell on this new piece of trivia. "Why is it called Earl's Leet, then?"

"Ah!" exclaimed Jake, refocusing on Emilya's education. "Well, that's a good question and is directly related to its history…and the Isolationists. They were a group of disenchanted nobles, wealthy tradesmen and professionals from all over the kingdom, who formed an exclusive club around two hundred years ago. It appears the one thing they all had in common, was their tiresome dealings with liars and cheats – who they claimed were prevalent in every walk of life; in politics, business, local government…even the clergy.

"Yes, I know," said Jake, spotting Emilya's rolled eyes. "Nothing much has changed. Anyway, the aim of their club was to provide support and backing to each other whenever any of them were in need. But this didn't stop the liars and the cheats from blighting their professional and sometimes private lives. So, after the club had existed for around twenty years, they came up with this idea of creating their own society – where everyone abided by the laws of the land, where there were no liars and cheats, and certainly no thieves or murderers. And to do this, they decided they would need to create their society from scratch – in a brand-new town, built by themselves, and located far away from the bad influence of other towns. The location chosen was a valley in the eastern Bleaklows, which as well as being one of the remotest parts of Glennad, is also notorious for inclement weather throughout the year – and hence likely to deter the kind of people they were trying to extricate themselves from."

"Sounds pretty sensible to me," said Emilya. "And presumably there were no princes in Earl's Leet, either?"

"Absolutely not," agreed Jake, a half-smile on his face.

"So, why Earl's Leet then?"

"Well, firstly, do you know what a leet is?"

"I didn't know that 'leet' was even a word," confessed Emilya.

"Well," said Jake. "A leet was a yearly or half-yearly court that certain medieval lords of the manor held. It wasn't granted to every landowner, but those who were granted leet privilege had the power to try and sentence people who lived in their manor who had committed an offence. Now, when the Isolationists broke away and first founded Earl's Leet, one of the leading protagonists was the 6th Earl of Bryde, Albion Gurch. He was one of only four Isolationists who held a leet status. However, Gurch was confident that they would never need to hold a leet court in their new settlement, because criminality simply would not exist. They therefore decided to be ironic when they named the town, and hence it became known as Earl's Leet – after the Earl of Bryde's unrequired privilege."

"And are there any liars and cheats in Earl's Leet today?"

Both Jake and Elyse laughed at that.

"Ah, what a pity," responded Emilya, genuinely disappointed.

"To be fair," said Elyse. "It's still a nicer and fairer place to live than anywhere else in Glennad – and probably the world, too. But they have had a few high-profile cases over recent years."

"Yes," agreed Jake. "Because unfortunately, when you promote your society as the most civilised in the world, you can guarantee that any perceived misdemeanour will be gleefully exposed by outsiders."

"Yes, and probably exaggerated beyond reason," added Elyse.

"Well, it still sounds like a good place to go to if you're trying to escape from psychopaths!" said Emilya, mirthlessly.

"Aye, that's what we figured, too," said Jake, giving Emilya a little wink. "Now then," he said, facing forwards. "Let's get us to this hostel in Ghintarton, have ourselves a nice supper, and then I'll show you on the map where we're going tomorrow."

CHAPTER 33 — ALICYA

7th Tertiar, 1789   Day 98, 15:10

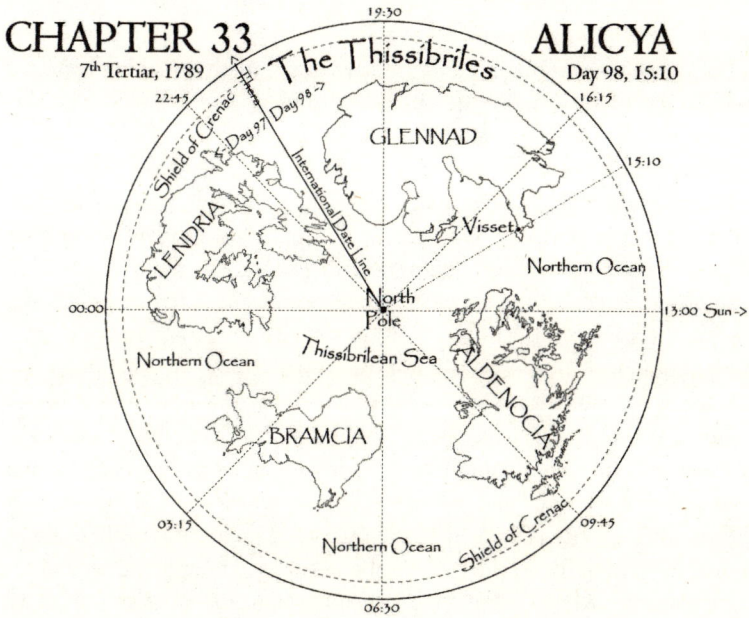

"Good afternoon," he had said. "I suspect we both have a great deal of explaining to do."

Alicya almost began to hyper-ventilate. At the same time, Vixey began to yap at the fair-haired man – at which point he held up his hands. "Whoa," he said, a half-smile on his face. "I come in peace."

His relaxed attitude helped to calm Alicya's breathing a little, and she bent down to shush and calm Vixey. She then protectively picked up the fox-cub and held her close, but was still unable to form words.

Seeing this, the man smiled at Alicya. "My name is Gawain Piran. This is my cutter, *Morwenna*," he added, gesturing around them.

He had a cultured voice, thought Alicya. Well educated. And his beige three-piece suit was expensive.

"I'm sorry if I startled you," continued Gawain. "Would you like a drink? Some food perhaps? You do understand me, don't you?"

"Yes," breathed Alicya. The word hardly came out. "Yes, I understand you," she confirmed, more clearly.

"Are you hungry, thirsty?"

"Both," said Alicya, her hand going to her greatcoat pockets and feeling a mush of crushed wild strawberries.

"Does the baby fox have a name."

"Vixey," responded Alicya.

"I suspect Vixey is hungry and thirsty, too, then. I'm just going up to my cabin where I have wine, water and some mini sausage rolls. Please come up and join me when you're ready." With that, the man unfurled his long legs and disappeared upwards.

Alicya could scarcely believe her luck. The boat-owner could have had her thrown into the cells of wherever this place was and what was her defence? That she was the daughter of the King and Queen of Glennad? A stowaway dressed only in a man's greatcoat and mismatching boots! But instead, the owner of the boat – Gawain – seemed pleasant and educated. Things could have been a thousand times worse.

Steeling herself, with Vixey still tucked under one arm, Alicya slowly mounted the steps and exited the tiny hold. The first thing that grabbed her attention was the new surroundings. They were in a bustling harbour and were one of seventy or eighty boats either moored to the stone harbour walls or with anchors dropped in the middle of the harbour. There was a slipway in front of them, and some stone steps inset into the wall where the cutter was moored which led on to a broad promenade. Above that, Alicya could see a row of houses or shops, all three-storeys high, made from brick and stone, all with startling terracotta-tiled roofs, with more terracotta roofs above them, and more above those. In the middle of the riot of terracotta rose the four-square tower of the church from where she had heard the bell, earlier, and which sported four splendid pinnacles at each corner. And there were people everywhere – normal and civilised people – walking up and down the harbour frontage.

Alicya then turned to look into the cabin, where Gawain was busy pouring white wine into two glasses. Hearing her footfall, Gawain turned around and gave Alicya an encouraging smile. "Water or wine?"

"Sausage roll!" responded Alicya, with a shy smile. She didn't know where that had come from.

"One moment, Miss," said Gawain, as he uncovered a plate to the side of the ship's wheel. "They're obviously cold," he said, as he brought the plate towards her.

As she looked at him, Alicya noticed that Gawain had startling green eyes. Alicya kept her eyes on Gawain's briefly, and then tentatively reached out and took a sausage roll. "May I take one for Vixey?"

"Of course. You can have them all," he said, nodding at the six remaining snacks.

Alicya fed the first one to Vixey, who tentatively sniffed it first, before deciding it was edible. From that point, the sausage roll didn't touch the sides. Whilst Vixey smacked her chops, Alicya shoved the whole of the second sausage roll into her mouth. She wasn't on royal view now, so no need to stand on ceremony.

It tasted divine. Even though it had only been two-and-a-half days since she'd last eaten a proper meal, it felt like much longer. The taste of civilised food also set her tummy rumbling. They both laughed at the noise, and Alicya inadvertently sent puffs of pastry fluttering out of her mouth, too. She held her hand up. "Sorry," she said, after she had swallowed her food. "That was so rude."

"Someone with manners, I see," replied Gawain. "Intriguing."

"And great fashion-sense," replied Alicya, warming to Gawain's manner, whilst also reaching out for the next two sausage rolls.

"So I see," said Gawain, eyeing her greatcoat up and down. "Did I see a change of clothes down below, as well?"

Alicya waited until she'd swallowed this time before replying. "Of sorts," she responded, ambiguously.

"Well, I must say," said Gawain, smiling and folding his arms, "I am very much looking forward to hearing your story."

"You'll not believe a word of it. Do you mind?" she asked, indicating the last pair of sausage rolls.

"No, please go ahead." He paused. "So, I won't believe you then? Is that because it will be a tall story?" His eyes narrowed. "Or because it is totally true, but off-the-scale ridiculous?"

Alicya nearly choked on her third sausage roll.

"I'm sorry," said Gawain. "Tell me in your own time. Or not at all, if you don't want to. But I think I should maybe explain myself first."

"You're a doctor?" suggested Alicya.

Gawain's eyebrows shot up at that. "My, we are a sharp one."

"It's not difficult to deduce," said Alicya. "I saw your, erm…cargo."

"Ah!"

"Well, I smelt it too."

"Hmm!"

"You take cadavers for human biological research. You do so because it's difficult to get relatives to donate bodies due to superstition – or human emotional attachment, I guess, not wishing to have their loved ones cut up, even after death – at a time when their loss is still raw."

"Are you sure you're not a government official in disguise? Well, I say disguise," he added, nodding at her greatcoat. "If that's the latest spy-wear, it's not exactly inconspicuous."

"A spy might be easier to explain than the truth," said Alicya, wryly.

"Well, it's going to be a fascinating story, I'm sure. A young girl – how old are you, by the way?"

"Eighteen."

"An eighteen-year-old girl, alone on an island reserved exclusively for the dead. A girl with a big heart," he said, nodding at Vixey. "And also exceptionally well-educated; naturally intelligent too. There can only be foul play at the heart of this," he finished, the smile having now vanished from his concerned face.

Alicya didn't respond immediately. "May I have a sip of your water, please?" she asked, eventually, whilst also setting Vixey down.

"Oh, of course. Sorry," said Gawain, turning around, grabbing a silver-plated flask engraved with GP, and passing it to her.

The water tasted very pure. Alicya then prepared to water Vixey, but the fox cub had already moved to the side of Gawain's boat and squatted down. A long trail of urine began to run backwards along the wooden deck towards the stern of the boat, and through the legs of the still-tethered horse. Alicya was mortified. "Oh my God, Vixey!" she reprimanded. "Oh, I'm so sorry!"

"It's absolutely fine, miss," said Gawain, now smiling again. "I'll soon clean that up. When you consider my cargo, a little fox urine doesn't concern me at all!"

"You're very kind," said Alicya, glancing apologetically at Gawain before pouring water into the palm of her hand and enabling Vixey to have a drink. She pondered on Gawain's words about foul play, prior to the interruption. "I'm thinking," she said, as she poured more water into her palm and let Vixey lick it up.

"Thinking?"

Alicya stood, took another long swig from the flask, and then passed it back to Gawain. "I'm thinking that I'll not be telling you the whole truth," she said. "Just so we're straight."

"All right," said Gawain, slowly.

"I will tell you an approximation," said Alicya.

"I'm all ears."

"GP!" exclaimed Alicya, the penny suddenly dropping.

"I'm sorry?"

"The initials on your flask. Both your initials and profession?"

"Ten out of ten," said Gawain. "I do believe you're the cleverest spy in a greatcoat I've ever spoken to."

Alicya laughed out loud at that. It was a weird sensation. She'd been all-but murdered two days ago by her own brother and left for dead on the *island* of the dead. The phrase 'surreal' wasn't really adequate.

"An approximation?" nudged Gawain.

"Ah, yes. Right. Well. Excuse me if this takes some time – as I'll be constantly translating the real into the cover story."

"Cover story? So, you are a spy then?"

"I am definitely not a spy," confirmed Alicya. "I do, however, come from a wealthy family. I have been privately educated all of my life, and was due to start at Ghantiss University later this year."

"Studying?"

"Ah, you'll be disappointed. History. It's my passion. History and horses."

"History is a grand subject. Dear to my heart, too."

"So, we can test each other," said Alicya, her eyes lighting up at the thought. She'd then blurted out her next sentence before even vaguely considering its appropriateness. "Are you married, by the way?"

"Well, my word -."

"Sorry, sorry. I didn't mean -. I mean, I'm not fishing. I'm just wondering if I'm keeping you from…"

"I'm not married, no."

"Right. I'm not fishing," reiterated Alicya.

"I would have been flattered if you were."

"What, seriously? Men's greatcoats and hair like a rat's nest work for you, do they?"

At that, Gawain let loose a great bellow of laughter. When it had subsided, he regarded her. "You are the most intriguing person…"

"Anyway," said Alicya, after an awkward pause. "You're right. Foul play." Her eyes went distant. "Inconceivably foul play. From an inconceivably foul brother."

"Your parents must be frantic with worry."

Thoughts of her mother and father weakened her when she least expected it. She could have kicked herself, but the tears had welled up before she could abate them.

"Here," said Gawain, offering his pristine white handkerchief. As Alicya dried her eyes and blew her nose, he asked: "Might I know your name?"

"Al-." Alicya stopped herself, just in time. "Freya," she said.

"Freya?"

"Yes."

"All right, take your time, Freya."

"He tried to kill me."

"Your brother?"

"Yes." Alicya nearly lost it again. "Because he'd already killed Freya."

"You mean, he killed you – metaphorically? Or is Freya someone else…"

"Freya is someone else. A poor baker's daughter. I found her. Found *them*. He had obviously…" Alicya tailed off, unable to say the words.

"I'm very sorry, erm, Freya," said Gawain, eventually. "Listen, can I call you something else. Freya no longer sounds appropriate. You were about to say Al-something."

"Right. You can call me Al, then."

"Al?"

"As you have so shrewdly guessed, it is part of my name – but far from all of it. Please," Alicya said, holding up her hands. "Please don't try and work out the rest."

"As you wish. Al."

Alicya couldn't help but smile at that. She'd never been called Al before. Magnus used to call her Lissy. Her smile tightened at the thought of her brother. *What was he doing now?* What lies had he spun to save his skin and hide the fact he'd carried out one murder and attempted another? And how many others before that?

Alicya refocused and looked at Gawain. "What are you going to do with me?"

Gawain considered the question. "I really don't know," he said. "But you have nothing to fear from me. I will do anything I can to help you. And Vixey, of course," he added, nodding at the baby fox who had settled down on the decking at Alicya's feet.

Alicya stared at Gawain and cursed herself for the umpteenth time as she felt yet another hotness well up behind her eyes. "I can't believe I could be this fortunate."

"What, me?" said Gawain. "Fortunate! Everyone thinks I'm a crackpot. I do nothing but work and study. My surgery all day and my study all night."

"Except for today."

"Today is my day off."

"And what do you normally do on your day off?"

"Study."

"I've a feeling I wouldn't want to be around when you're doing your 'day-off studying'."

"I've a feeling you could be right."

"Why do you work so hard?"

"Because one day, I intend to be the royal physician."

Alicya just stared at him for a full five seconds. Then she began to laugh. Hysterically.

"Well, it's not that much of a stretch, surely?"

Alicya continued to laugh.

"But you don't even know me," said Gawain, now looking quite hurt.

"I'm sorry," said Alicya. "I am too rude for words. And here I am, laughing at you when my life is totally in your hands."

"Well, indeed. I was about to threaten you with the local JP."

"You weren't?"

"No, I wasn't. But I should like to know why you find what I said so funny."

"It was the earnestness on your face," lied Alicya.

"Really?" queried Gawain, dubiously.

"I suspect that one day, you will make the finest-ever royal physician, Gawain Piran."

That cheered Gawain up a little. "As to your question, I own two apartments in Visset. This," he said, gesturing around the harbour, "is the Wrenkish port of Visset by the way. I suppose you didn't know that, given your mode of arrival."

"Would you believe me if I told you that I'd guessed we were headed for the Wrenko peninsula."

"From what I've witnessed, so far, I very much would believe you."

"Why thank you, sir."

"Anyway, as I was saying. I have two apartments, and a housekeeper, Mrs Baker, who keeps everything spick and span. I will ask her to put you up in the guest apartment."

"You would do that? For a complete stranger?"

"I *am* doing that. And I'm even doing it without having heard your full story. Al."

Alicya felt herself smile again. This was beyond her wildest expectations. "I'll tell you my story, Gawain Piran. But first, you know *my* age. How old are you?"

"I'm twenty-four."

"And what are you going to do with those?" she asked, nodding towards the five shrouded forms at the other end of the deck.

"My associates will deal with them once it gets dark. They have their instructions – and two crowns apiece. I shall remain here on guard until they arrive. Once they have loaded the cargo up into my cart, they'll hitch up Samson here," he said, indicating the horse, "and we can leave. They will then stable Samson, while Mrs Baker will have left plenty of dinner for the both of us."

"Thank you," said Alicya, simply. "And in the meantime, I guess I had better tell my story. And then you can tell me yours."

"Well, mine will be very much after the Lord Mayor's show."

Alicya laughed again. Gawain appeared to have an ability to make her laugh, regularly. She then remembered something. "Before I start, may I ask," she said, her head nodding warily towards the five shrouded figures. "Are any of those a young girl?"

Gawain frowned. "Why do you ask?"

"I'll explain later, as part of my story."

"Very well. No, as it happens. Four men and a middle-aged woman."

Alicya exhaled with relief. "Oh, thank goodness."

Gawain's frown deepened.

"I'll explain, shortly," repeated Alicya. She moved aside a strand of dark hair that had been hanging down over her left eye, and then began her story. "So, I grew up in a large house on the eastern outskirts of Ghantiss, the daughter of a gentry family…"

CHAPTER 34   EMILYA
7th Tertiar, 1789   Day 98, 19:30

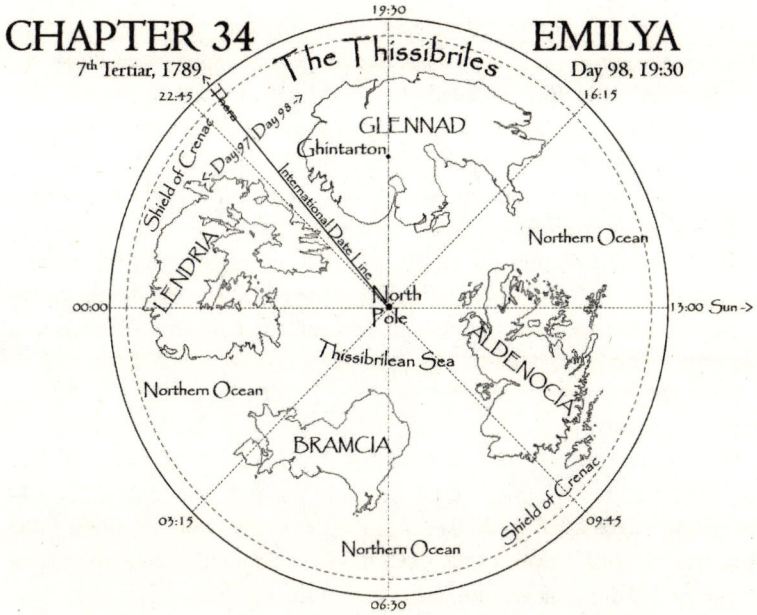

The innkeeper was a stooped, irascible old man, bald on top with huge bushy white whiskers covering both cheeks. "There are two garrets left on the top floor, that's all. It's either that or the stables." His voice creaked like his joints, thought Emilya, wryly.

"We'll take them," said Jake, opening his drawstring moneybag.

The innkeeper took each coin and bit them to check authenticity. "Can never be too sure," he said, catching Elyse's withering look.

"What time is supper served, please?" asked Jake.

"Half an hour or so," responded the innkeeper.

"Perfect. Just enough time to get settled in then."

"Boots off first," ordered the innkeeper.

"I'm sorry?" questioned Jake.

"I don't take kindly to scrubbing the dirt off the stairs every day of my life, fella. Boots off, and stick 'em under there," he said nodding towards a row of two wooden racks that were already populated with an odd assortment of footwear – and, to be fair to the innkeeper, most of them were far-from clean.

The innkeeper didn't wait to watch them remove their boots, though. He'd already pocketed his payment and was heading back to the kitchen, muttering under his breath.

Boots removed, Emilya led the way up the narrow stairs – every one of which creaked to varying degrees as they took her weight. With Elyse and Jake following behind, it sounded like a hideously discordant concert. The garrets were tiny, both low-ceilinged, with a single small square window, and each had room for one single bed and a small table populated only by a largely-spent candle. "I hope you don't snore," said Emilya, cheekily, to Elyse.

"I hope *you* don't have cold feet," responded Elyse.

Emilya looked around the cramped quarters, perfectly happy, though. Her misfortune in Ghantiss was leading to the adventure of a lifetime. "To think, that only twenty-six hours ago, you actually had me togged up in a pale-blue frock!"

Elyse laughed her musical laugh. "Yes, it does seem rather a distant memory, doesn't it?"

Emilya unbuttoned her coat to reveal the previously concealed Theo. She lifted him gently out of his harness and put him down on to the far-from-fresh rushes that had been scattered over the wooden floor. Poor Theo tried to walk, yelped as he remembered his injured back leg and then compensated, hopping around. He soon got the measure of it though, and as Emilya sank to her knees, he hopped playfully up to her and buried his muzzle in her hands and then began licking them. "Good boy," she said.

"He's definitely chirpier," said Elyse.

"Thanks to you," said Emilya, looking up at her travelling companion with great affection.

Elyse ruffled Emilya's hair in response.

"What should we do with him during supper?"

"We'll have to leave him here. That innkeeper will likely throw us out if he thinks we've got a dog."

Emilya thought of the innkeeper's grouchy countenance, and knew it was true. "He'll have to stay on the floor. I don't want him falling off the bed and re-breaking his leg." Emilya shrugged off her coat. "He'll likely settle down and go to sleep on this."

It took a while to coax Theo to relax, but eventually he settled down, albeit with sad eyes as he watched Emilya wave to him as she closed the garret door. She then wedged her back-pack against the door to prevent any chance opening, just as Jake emerged from the adjoining garret, stooping to avoid hitting his head on the low ceiling. He winked once at her, before all three of them creaked their way downstairs.

The common room was a large, smoky space, low-beamed and populated with long benches, most of which were already hosting a diverse bunch of travellers: farmers, locals, merchants, a curate and even a couple of soldiers in their red and white Glennadian liveries. There was a huge open fireplace at one end of the room, and down one side were a dozen enormous kegs, which Emilya assumed held gallons of Glennadian ale. A serving boy was moving between the benches with skewers of meat, the smell of which was making Emilya's mouth water.

Jake found them a space at one of the benches near to the kitchen, opposite the two soldiers. "Evening," he said, nodding at them.

"Evening," they replied. They didn't seem to be the chatty type.

Emilya looked out of the window alongside her. Dusk was falling now, and all she could see was the road and the black shadow of trees all around. She was about to turn back when she heard a low howl. It lasted for several seconds. The cry was then taken up by several others.

Noticing her disquiet, Jake just winked at her. "Wolves," he said, simply. "Just big dogs. Nothing to be scared of."

"Well, you say that," said one of the soldiers. "But I wouldn't advise going anywhere on your own at night around here."

Emilya regarded him. He was young – twenty at most. Clean-shaven, too; no whiskers. "You mean they're dangerous in packs? For people?"

"Very much so," responded the other soldier. This one was a good ten years older, with a dark moustache and dark sideburns. He also had the markings of a sergeant on his tunic. "They're very bold up here in the hills. Even bolder on the plateaux – mainly because those packs are hungrier; less prey up there."

"Nothing for us to worry about," said Jake. "We only intend to travel by daylight."

"Very wise," said the sergeant.

"Although there's bandits during both night *and* day up in the hills," added the younger soldier.

"Bandits!" exclaimed Emilya, concerned.

"You're from Ghantiss, I believe," said the sergeant. Emilya nodded. "Things are a little different in the wilds, lass. Looks like your Dad can look after himself, though," he said, nodding at Jake. "I assume you've stashed your cutlass and knives," he added, a twinkle in his eye.

Emilya frowned.

"I saw you arrive," said the sergeant. "The eye gets trained over the years, and your old Dad isn't looking as bulky now as he did when you arrived."

"You're not going to say anything?" questioned Elyse.

"No, Miss," said the sergeant. "You've every right to defend yourself up here. But a word of warning. We were dispatched here to confirm reports that Harry Black is in the area. We're on our way back to Ghantiss now to confirm that is the case. Seems the old brigand thinks the soft folk of Earl's Leet are easier pickings than the turnpike from Dominniul to Ghantiss."

Even Emilya, from the safety of law-abiding Ghantiss, knew who Harry Black was: the most prolific highwayman Glennad had ever known; and the most flamboyant, too, if the many stories about him were to be believed.

"He's been quiet for the last two or three years, though," said Elyse.

"Aye," responded the older soldier. "But rumour has it that he's spent all of his loot now."

"Ah, and hence he needs to top up the Bank of Brigands again."

"Exactly."

They were interrupted as their supper arrived. The serving boy was carrying and balancing on his arm five trenchers of bread. He then returned thirty seconds later with chunks of medium-rare meat, dripping with hot juices. Emilya looked at Elyse and saw the look of disapproval on her face as she held up her hand to say "no" to the meat, whereas Emilya couldn't find it within to also decline. Elyse's face cheered up, though, when the next skewer arrived, and the serving boy deposited onions, peppers and mushrooms onto their trenchers. Emilya, however, was still gazing longingly at the meat, so Elyse put a hand on her arm. "Eat it," she said. "Converting to vegetarian doesn't need to happen overnight. Once we are settled, I'll make sure your mouth waters at every meal, and there'll be no need for you to be tempted by meat."

Emilya looked at Elyse, realising that the older woman was hinting at their relationship extending beyond their arrival at Earl's Leet, and she felt a wonderful warmth well up within. Elyse's response was to wink once at Emilya, and then put her finger to her lips.

CHAPTER 35   ALICYA

7th Tertiar, 1789   Day 98, 21:30

Gawain had left the apartment at around 7 o'clock (20:00), just as dusk was falling, to move his five illegally acquired corpses to his 'laboratory' as he called it – a separate room which he rented out from the local authorities. Alicya had offered to join them, but Gawain wouldn't hear of it. "Too ghastly an operation for a lady," he had said. Instead, he had left her alone in his adjoining guest apartment, free to eat his food, use his bath, and – in the absence of any female attire – to dress in whichever of his clothes she felt the most comfortable in. Having heated up and eaten some of Mrs Baker's delicious chicken in white wine sauce (with greens and new potatoes), and soaked for an hour in a wonderful hot bath, Alicya had rifled through Gawain's spare wardrobe in his guest apartment, and selected a white silk shirt that drowned her and a pair of dark trousers that she had to turn up three times – and which now looked ludicrously bottom heavy. Nevertheless, mused Alicya, these clothes were preferable to damp, deceased farmer's wife-wear or an over-sized and scruffy male greatcoat!

Vixey was also very happy and now fast-off – having devoured a whole haunch of ham that Gawain had kindly provided, followed by an hour-or-so of gnawing at the remaining bone. The result had expanded the fox-cub to almost twice the size of the scraggy pauper Alicya had met in the ruined church at Norvent. That swollen pink belly was now rising and falling with a blissful contentment that mirrored Vixey's beatific smile, whilst her whiskers blew up and down in sync with her gentle snoring.

Alicya smiled. She had no idea how long their good fortune might last, but Vixey had at least known pampered comfort for one night in her life. Alicya was a good judge of character, though, and Gawain Piran was undoubtedly a good man. He was also a single man and very good-looking – but Alicya refused to let any thoughts develop along those lines. She had never been much of a dreamer, and pragmatism had served her well, so far, particularly over the last two days. She was more concerned about what the people of Visset might think of her and, more particularly, of Gawain for putting up a young *female* in his guest apartment!

As she awaited Gawain's return, Alicya had begun to read by candlelight. The first book she had chosen was a medical anatomical volume by the foremost anatomist and surgeon of the day, Harry Gyne. She had been determined to improve her knowledge of the human body, given her gracious host's profession and ambition, but after an hour of studying *Gyne's Anatomy*, she had tired of the subject and gone in search of something historical. Her eyes had soon fallen on Andrew Dobbig's 1781 version of *Thera: Our World, Not An Empire*. She had a copy of her own back at the palace in Ghantiss and had already read the volume from cover-to-cover twice before. Being particularly familiar with the period that covered the Theran occupation of the Thissibriles up until 410 AT, she decided to re-read about the Dark Ages that followed – so-named, because very little was known of this period in history. This was primarily because once the educated Therans had been ousted from the Thissibriles (and ousted in a manner which still made Alicya feel ashamed, some 1,379 years later), the largely uneducated Thissibrileans had not been able to record their history. Dobbig, however, understood Old Thissibrilean, and had therefore studied later *Thissibrilean Chronicles* of the 7th, 8th and 9th centuries to help try and fill the gaps from the 5th and 6th centuries.

His first assertion was that the Theran 'departure' in 410, had a severe effect on the Thissibrilean economy which didn't return to similar levels until the late 9th century, and that the Theran bureaucratic system designed to maintain Theran laws and to levy taxes, soon disintegrated. Naturally, this had a negative effect on trading and the Thissibrilean economy reverted overwhelmingly back to agriculture.

Dobbig believed that the Glennadians were the first to form a kingdom of sorts in the late 6th century, as this infant kingdom is referred to in the 7th century *Thissibrilean Chronicle* as the kingdom of Nyaxos, and was centred around Bryde in central Glennad. Given Bryde was not too far from the famed stone circle at Ghenetenos, and which was still of great importance at that time to the older tribes, Alicya mused that the theory was not unreasonable.

The author then devoted a whole chapter to the recorded wars between the kingdom of Nyaxos and the tribe to the west, known as Mnonudia, and of a famous earthwork constructed in the mid-8th century to keep the Mnonudians out of Nyaxos. Known as Affo's Dyke and named after King Affo of Nyaxos (757-796), this large linear earthwork ran all the way from Ghantiss to Dominniul in the south-west. It was up to sixty-five feet wide when including its flanking ditch, up to twelve feet high in places, and was constructed across low ground, hills and rivers, always traversing around hills to the western, Mnonudian side.

Alicya's mind began to wander. She had visited the section of Affo's Dyke in Ghantiss many times but was aware that more impressive sections remained in central Glennad, half-way between Ghantiss and Dominniul, traversing up and down valleys. Indeed, Affo's Dyke was considered the most impressive memorial in the Thissibriles from the time known as the Dark Ages. Perhaps she could use her new-found anonymity to visit those central sections, ideally with Gawain.

Next, Alicya read how during the early 9th century, the kingdom of Nyaxos became splintered into several sub-kingdoms, of which Swexes became dominant during the mid-9th century. It took until the 10th century for the whole island to be united for the first time, taking the name Glennad – or *Glynnat* as it was known then – with the name deriving from the Old Thissibrilean words *Glyn* (meaning 'brotherhood') and *Nat* (meaning 'clan', where *Nad* is the plural definition); hence Glennad, the brotherhood of the clans.

As Alicya's book moved into the late 10th century, her eyelids were becoming heavy. She didn't remember falling asleep – but was awoken by a soft footfall, nearby. All of her trauma from the last three days came crashing in and she shrieked, panicked…and also fell off the sofa.

"It's all right, it's all right," said Gawain, hands held up in front of him, a look of panic on his face, while Vixey was suddenly stood alongside Alicya, wide awake and snarling at him.

Alicya rapidly gathered her composure, calmed Vixey and got bashfully to her feet. "I'm so sorry!" she said, putting her hand on her chest. "I must have dropped off. I didn't hear you come in."

"I was trying to be quiet," he said. "Thought I'd succeeded, too."

"Well, after what's happened to me…"

"Well, quite," agreed Gawain. "Anyway," he said, now smiling at her. "You found some clothes, I see?"

Alicya looked down at her attire and they both laughed. Like on the boat earlier, Gawain's demeanour was so disarming that Alicya was soon relaxed again.

"Yes," said Alicya, doing a little curtsey. "This apparel is all the rage amongst the young ladies in Ghantiss."

"Really?" asked Gawain, looking amusedly at the triple turn-ups.

Alicya waved her left foot around. "It's very fetching, don't you think?"

"Hmm," responded Gawain, dubiously. "I see you found some books too," he added, nodding at the two upside-down volumes on the living room floor. "Which one sent you to sleep?"

"Well, it was the Dobbig, actually," said Alicya, pleased to note that Vixey had relaxed and was now curled up on her mat again.

"Having already given up on the Gyne, presumably?"

"I didn't give up on the Gyne," protested Alicya. "I found him extremely interesting. All those spleens, ventricles and alveoli."

"I would test you on those, but I somehow suspect it would be unnecessary."

"I know what they are and where they are and what their function is, yes. I wouldn't much like to hold any of those in my hand, though, much less dissect them. Or any other organ or body-part, for that matter."

"You think that makes me weird?"

"No, not at all," said Alicya. "I completely understand why you have to learn that way."

"But you eventually got drawn to your favourite subject?"

"Ah, yes. Mr Dobbig is an interesting read, for sure."

The two strangers looked shyly at each other as the conversation dried up. "Erm, I will be taking to my bed shortly," said Gawain. "Early surgery at the infirmary; starts at seven. I will look out a night-shirt for you. Is everything else to your taste. The bedroom, the bathroom…"

"Everything is perfect, Gawain," responded Alicya with a sad smile. "I don't know what I've done to deserve your kindness."

"It seems to me as though you've been in short supply of kindness, recently. And in any case, it is my pleasure. I have thoroughly enjoyed our conversations."

"Even the ones where you know I've been lying?"

"Especially those," said Gawain, with a warm smile. "But I do hope that you can learn to trust me enough to, well, perhaps one day, to tell me everything."

Alicya looked back at the handsome, fair-haired doctor. "I have a strong feeling that day will come, Gawain. Although the chances are that you'll think the truth a lie!"

"I look forward to it immensely," said Gawain. "Now, please, erm…Al. I will bid you good night. I will probably have left for work when you awaken, but I will leave a note for Mrs Baker to explain everything. Well, as best as I can," he said, issuing a quick and bashful smile. "And please feel free to use this place as your own until I return. I take it you will share dinner with me tomorrow evening?"

"Well, let me think," said Alicya, tapping a finger to her lower lip. "I do have several other compelling invitations…"

"This is exactly what I'm talking about," said Gawain.

Alicya laughed. "Of course I will share dinner with you tomorrow, Gawain. That would be lovely."

"Excellent," said Gawain. "Oh, and here," he said, handing Alicya a key to the apartment. "If you feel up to exploring Visset tomorrow, please take this, and come and go at your leisure."

Alicya took the key from Gawain, but also put her other hand on top of his and held it there for several seconds. "I will never forget what you have done for me," she said, earnestly.

"It's the least I can do. Al," responded Gawain, shyly. "Until tomorrow then?"

"Goodnight, Gawain."

And with that, he nodded at her and exited the guest apartment for his own.

CHAPTER 36　　　　　　　　　　DAVY
7th Tertiar, 1789　　　　　　　　　　Day 98, 13:30

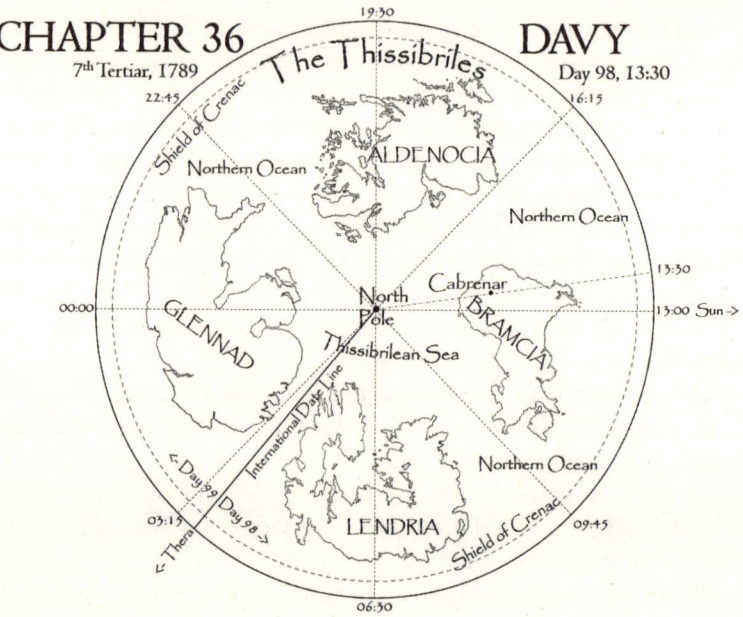

"Now look," said Stan Eckersley to Davy. "I'm not an unreasonable man, but we can't talk about it here, can we?" he said, gesturing around the dimly-lit gallery.

"So, when can we talk about it?"

Eckersley shook his head. "You've got it all wrong, Sheerin."

"So, humour me."

"All right. We do this by the book then – in my office, after shift."

"But that's -."

"After shift, all right? And that's my final word on it. Now get back to work before I dock your wages as well."

Davy was about to object further when Robbie intervened. "Leave it, Davy. It's a start. Speak to Mr Eckersley after shift. But for now, we need to get back to work."

"Good God, Russell!" cried Eckersley. "Are you feeling all right, man?"

Robbie half-smiled at Eckersley. "What I'm feeling like, Mr Eckersley, is a bit of a pauper."

"Give over, man," he said, before heading off towards the main shaft. "You'll have my heart bleeding, you will," he threw back over his shoulder.

Robbie looked at Davy ruefully. "It's fine, mate. We get this sorted in – what – around an hours' time."

"If he listens," responded Davy, mournfully.

"He'll listen. Like he said – he's not that unreasonable."

Davy patted Robbie on the shoulder. "You're right. And blundering about accusing Turner isn't going to achieve anything."

"I can't hear any pick-axes," floated Eckersley's voice up the tunnel.

The two friends smirked at each other, clasped hands, and then set back to work. A minute or so later, Will returned with another empty wagon. He was still out of sorts, worried for his twin brother. Davy briefly paused, looked Will in the eye and said: "We're all sorted, lad. Me and Mister Eckersley are having a chat after shift, and he's going to re-assign Dylan to Robbie's bay. Hopefully later today."

All the tension visibly left Will's body and he gave Davy one of his best smiles, thanked him and called him a superstar. Davy was still on edge, though, feeling guilty at stretching the truth with a twelve-year-old. He still had his work cut out to pull this off.

For the next hour, Davy pushed aside his misgivings and concentrated on filling up wagons with coal. Eventually, the bell sounded to indicate end of shift. Davy patted Will on the back and shook hands with Robbie. "Leave it with me, fellas. We'll have young Dylan down here with you in no time."

"Thanks again, Davy," said Will, holding out his hand.

Davy took the tiny hand in his own sooty paw and couldn't help but smile. "Who's all grown up now then?" he said, lifting Will's felt hat and ruffling his hair.

Five minutes later, he, Stan Eckersley and another forty miners were rattling up the shaft in the lift, with another forty-or-so coming off-shift waiting down below for the second run. When the lift arrived at ground level and the cage door was pulled open by an attendant, Davy followed the flow into the bright daylight, before peeling off with Eckersley for the pit-head office – where Eckersley's replacement, the rather gaunt Dai Morgan, was already at the desk, filling in his log book.

"All right, Dai?" said Eckersley as he breezed into the office.

"Fair to middling," came Morgan's standard response. "Anything to tell, Stan?"

"Nah, it's all working like clockwork, mate. I've even got an honest shift out of both Russell and Sheerin here!"

"Get away! You'll be wanting a medal next, man! He in here for a pay rise, is he?"

"Nothing for you to worry about, Dai. You cut along now and keep the troops honest."

Dai Morgan grinned at Eckersley's standard line. The two supervisors shook hands warmly, and Morgan headed off to begin his shift.

"Now then," said Eckersley, flopping down into the single office chair. "Let's see if we can get this thing all straightened out."

"All right," said Davy, clasping his hands together. He decided to cut straight to the chase. "I know you've heard the rumours."

"Oh, for God's sake man, not that again," cried Eckersley with frustration. "He's my brother-in-law, for pity's sake. Do you think I wouldn't know if he was…well…*that* way inclined?"

"You're right, Mr Eckersley," said Davy, attempting to play a different card. "There's probably nothing to worry about. Maybe it's just that young Dylan is missing dear old Jack Musson."

"Well, there you go then," said Eckersley, as if that wrapped everything up.

Davy was having to think quickly now. "You're a good man, Mr Eckersley," said Davy, looking Eckersley in the eye. "A bit of a slave-driver, mind, but essentially a good man."

"Well thank you very much, Sheerin," said Eckersley, scratching the end of his pointed nose. "You really *are* after a pay rise, aren't you?"

Davy laughed. "No," he said. "Not at all. Please. Humour me, Mr E."

"Humour you?"

"Put Dylan Lowe next to his brother – put him with Robbie Russell."

"What, so I can have the four of you having a picnic in mid-shift?"

"Mr E, please. That was out of character – and we genuinely were teaching Will about safety lamps. Although," re-considered Davy, "it was probably Will teaching us, to be frank. He's a bright lad. But he also asked us about '79 – as you know, his old man was, well…"

"I knew Alf Lowe very well, Davy," said Eckersley, his eyes briefly distant. "He was a good man."

Davy was surprised that Eckersley had used his first name, and so he pressed on. "So, what about it? Putting Dylan next to his brother? I bet that's what Alf would have wanted."

Eckersley looked at Davy, his expression unreadable. "You aren't going to give up on this are you?"

"No Mr E. It's important. No offence meant – to you or Nate Turner. But please. Put Dylan with Robbie. At least until Jack Musson gets back."

"Well," said Eckersley closing his eyes and pinching the top of his nose with his thumb and forefinger. "If what I'm hearing is true, poor Jack Musson won't be coming back to work."

"I thought he just had the flu?"

"Wishful thinking, I'm afraid. It's bad pneumonia. But don't you go saying anything to anyone, lad."

"I swear to you, I won't. Poor Jack. But this means it's even more important that -."

"Yes, yes, yes, I know what's coming next. All right. You win, Davy. I'll tell Nate tomorrow morning that we're moving Dylan to work alongside his brother."

"Tomorrow morning!"

"Don't push your luck, Sheerin," snapped Eckersley, now clearly at the limit of his benevolence.

"All right," said Davy, holding up his hands. "You're a gentleman, Mr E. And I'm not just saying that. I mean it. I really appreciate this."

"Go on with you. Bugger off home. It'll all be sorted when you come back on-shift." And with that, Eckersley opened the logbook and pulled out some battered old spectacles from the single draw in the desk.

Clearly dismissed, Davy thanked Eckersley again and exited the pit-head office. He looked around at the unsightly slag heap towering above the colliery to the north, and the considerably more picturesque hills and mountains behind it – but his thoughts were elsewhere. He hadn't got exactly what he'd wanted. But given the circumstances – Eckersley's compunction to call the shots, and it being a fairly clear slur on his brother-in-law – it wasn't such a bad result. Will would feel let-down when Dylan didn't show up for the afternoon shift, but he'd soon come around when he learned they'd all be working together tomorrow. And maybe they'd all got it wrong about Turner, anyway. But at least they were now playing safe. Pulling his cloth cap out of his rear pocket, Davy put it on and began his walk home towards the rows of terraced houses at the bottom of the hill, already wondering what his Mam was cooking for dinner.

As he walked, he met old Walt Garcroft hobbling up the other way. Walt had been half-crippled since he was nine years old, after getting his left leg trapped by a runaway wagon full of coal. The buffer had forced his leg up against the jagged coalface and had nearly sheared through. The doctors had wanted to take his leg off, but Walt's Mam wouldn't let them. He'd walked with the aid of a stick, ever since, but never once complained – and it hadn't stop him working the mine for another fifty-six years, either.

Davy always had time for Walt, and Walt had time for everyone, especially fellow miners. The pair were soon exchanging stories, with Walt telling tales of days of old that Davy had heard several times before – but they were always worth another hearing. No one else told tales quite like Walt.

CHAPTER 37 — WILL
7th Tertiar, 1789 — Day 98, 15:00

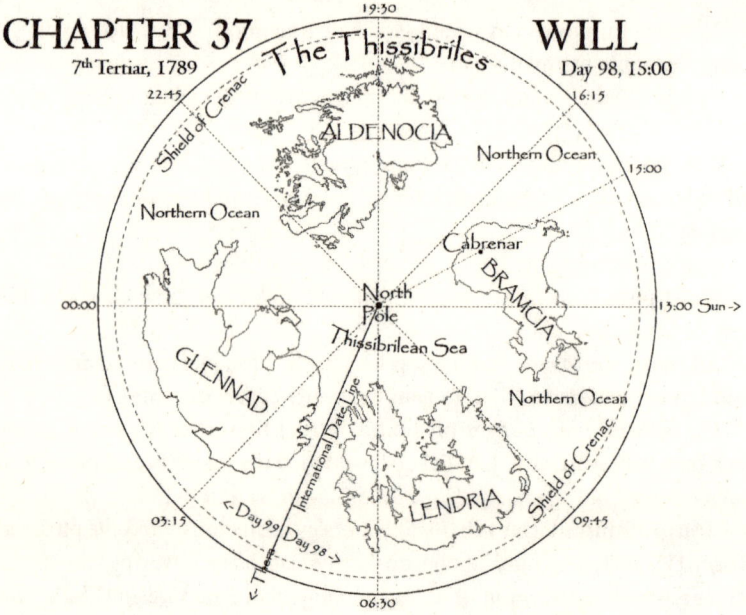

Will Lowe had moved a bay further down the current gallery but had his back to where Robbie Russell was hacking away at the coalface. He had his safety lamp held up and was straining his eyes in the direction of the lift shaft, but there was no sign of his brother, Dylan.

Robbie paused to take a breather and saw what was happening. "Still no sign then?"

Will shook his head, disconsolately, but then held his hand up. He'd heard something. He strained to hear more – and then his face fell in disappointment as the tones of an approaching Dai Morgan grew gradually louder. Robbie immediately got back to work at the coalface.

"You all right there, Russell?" shouted Morgan above the noise, a minute or so later.

Robbie stopped hacking and turned around. "Yes thanks, Mr Morgan."

"Only I think you're close to loosening a whole section there, son. I can hear it. Thirty years of experience, that is."

"I was wondering myself," agreed Robbie. "As in, maybe it's not solid behind this section."

"Well, you'll soon find out, son," said Morgan before moving on. "Keep up the good work," he added. "Oh!" he said, turning around and coming back. "I've got some good news for you two. I had a message passed down from Stan Eckersley. Will's brother will be joining you tomorrow as your apprentice, Russell. Told me to tell you – so as to stop his twin brother from worrying," he added, with a wink at Will.

Will's face immediately cracked into a smile. "Thank you, Mr Morgan," he said. "You're very kind."

"Kind, am I? I need to have a stern word with myself, then," he joked, chuckling to himself as he went.

Robbie laughed at that. "Thanks, Mr M," he shouted after him, as Morgan carried on down the gallery.

Morgan just raised his free hand in acceptance and was then busying himself fussing over the next bay.

Robbie turned back to Will. "Told you Davy'd pull it off."

"Hmm," said Will, wistfully. "Wish it had been now though."

"Listen," said Robbie, gently knocking on Will's felt hat with his knuckles and making the young apprentice smile. "It's a great result. We'll have a ball, the four of us together, you'll see."

Bang on cue, Will issued one of his best beams.

"Now then," said Robbie. "You might want to stand back and bit, young Will – as I reckon this whole section is about to drop."

Will did as he was told, reversing up the gallery by a few feet, but holding his lantern in front of him to make sure he saw all the action. He watched Robbie hack once with his pick-axe – and sure enough, there was a little movement. He then hacked again, and Will observed a crack suddenly form at the top of the coalface and then zig-zag part of the way down. Robbie spotted it a split-second too late and was already swinging the pickaxe for a third blow. The whole overhanging section came loose, making a ghastly noise as it all clattered to the floor. Robbie flung himself backwards as great black clouds billowed out towards him.

Will shielded his eyes, and began to choke, but still managed to hold up his safety lamp – which suddenly went blue and then went out. "Gas!" shouted Will. "Fire-gas!"

Dai Morgan suddenly appeared out of the dust and took in the scene. He raised his voice. "All right everyone, turn your safety lamps down to minimum. We need to get this place ventilated as soon as possible."

"Shouldn't we be getting out, Dai?" asked Robbie.

"Yes, but we're going to do this in an orderly way, right? No panicking. Now then -."

Morgan broke off at the sound of rapidly approaching feet from the direction of the lift shaft. With half of the safety lamps turned off and the other half turned right down, it was impossible to see into the gloom, with visibility worsened by the still-settling dust from Robbie's coal-face collapse. Then, all of a sudden, a small figure burst out of the gloom – carrying a naked flame in front of him.

Will recognised his brother instantly – albeit wild-eyed, his blackened cheeks tear-stained. There was no time to shout a warning.

Time stood still.

And then their darkened world exploded.

CHAPTER 38　　　　　　　　　　　　　DAVY
7th Tertiar, 1789　　　　　　　　　　　　Day 98, 15:05

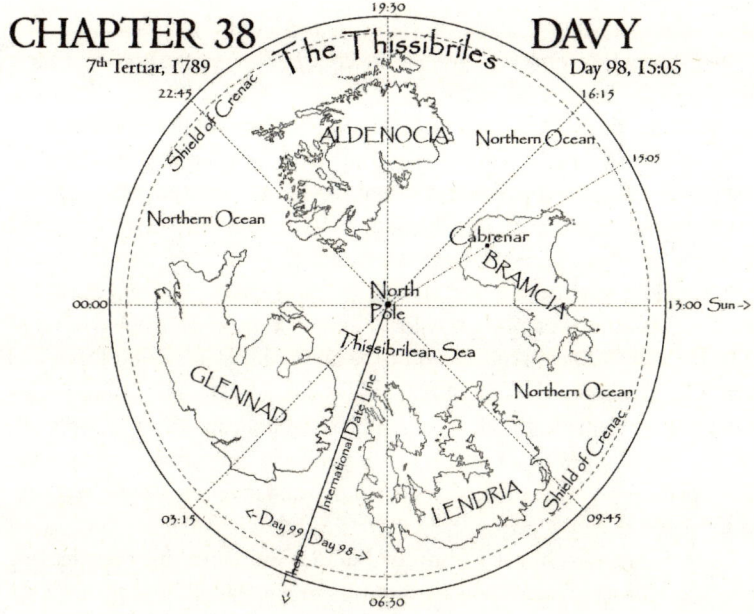

Walt Garcroft was still regaling Davy with tales of his mining youth when both of them felt the ground lurch. At the same time, their ears sang to a surge of pressure. Walt stopped talking immediately. They looked at each other, terror present in both sets of eyes. A split-second later, the whole valley was rocked by a mighty underground explosion. Both Davy and Walt staggered a little, and then whipped their heads around to the pithead. Already, smoke was being emitted from No 1 Shaft.

Only seconds had passed, but Davy quickly gathered his wits. "I'm going to help," he said, before turning and sprinting for the pithead. Halfway there, the colliery's steam-whistle blared for the first time, although there was little need to signify that an emergency was in-force. By the time Davy reached the top of the lift-shaft, his worst fears were confirmed, with roiling, dense smoke billowing out of No 1 Shaft, whilst the steam-whistle continued to blare out its desperate message.

At first, Davy thought there was no one around, until he heard a groan from ground level. Looking down, he saw Stan Eckersley, blood gushing from a cut on his forehead. Davy rushed over to him and helped him to his feet. "Blew me into the door-frame," gasped Eckersley. "I managed to sound the alarm and then…must have blacked out…"

Davy helped Eckersley back into his office and his chair, making sure he was all right. "I'm going down there," he then announced.

"Don't be a fool, Sheerin," gasped Eckersley. "No one can go down there now. Not for a long time."

"But Will's down there! Robbie! Dai Morgan!" wailed Davy, wild-eyed.

"Son, I know," said Eckersley, struggling to his feet. Davy tried to help the staggering Eckersley back into his seat, but Eckersley resisted, grabbing Davy's arms. "I'm so sorry, son," he said. As he looked Davy in the eye, Davy could see that Stan Eckersley's eyes were moist.

"Oh God!" responded Davy, the enormity of it now crushing him. His hands went to his head, his eyes wild, his chin taking on a life of its own, just as Walt Garcroft limped into the office. Walt put his arm around Davy, and then Eckersley joined them in a brief huddle, the two older men continuously patting backs. Outside, the alarm continued to sound, and the first of the off-shift colliers along with a number of villagers were now haring up the wide grassy path towards the pithead. Men, women and children. Wives, mothers, brothers and sisters.

Davy disengaged himself from the huddle, and wiped his eyes, leaving two clear skin-coloured streaks around them. He patted both men on the back simultaneously and then ran out to meet the newcomers. In their vanguard was Vin Ellis, the chief engineer, and Jed Morris, the colliery manager. Both were as white as sheets. "Mr Morris, Mr Ellis," said Davy, walking now with them towards No 1 Shaft. "Count me in for the rescue team. Use me however you see fit. I've got dear friends down there."

"Aye, we all have, lad," said Morris, grimly. "But thanks for the offer. You can be sure we'll need brave lads like you once Mr Ellis has completed his assessment."

For the next hour, Davy tried to remain positive. *Everyone was alive down there and would remain so.* But even as a relatively young miner, he knew how crucial the next few hours were. For the moment, though, all he could do was hang around the fringes of Ellis and his team, numbly shaking hands with fellow-off-shift miners who had also come to help. Few words were spoken. They all just wanted to get on with the rescue as soon as possible. It was clear the main shaft was out of the question, though. Thick smoke was still billowing out of it, and on the one occasion he had ventured within ten feet of it, Davy had felt the heat from the flames below. That didn't augur well. Although, at least there hadn't been any secondary explosions – not yet, anyway.

"Right, gather in," Vin Ellis eventually called out to the rescue volunteers. Happy that he had their attention, he continued. "As you can see," he said, nodding at the shaft opening, "the fires won't be burning themselves out any time soon, and there may not be any survivors within two hundred yards of the bottom of that shaft."

Davy tried his best not to dwell on the word 'survivors', before trying to calculate the distance from the foot of the shaft to his and Robbie's bays. Was it two hundred yards? Surely it was nearer four hundred, wasn't it?

"Also, the lift is totally done for," Ellis was saying, "as we've tried to haul it up and it won't budge. It's likely buckled and twisted, so, there'll be no rescue party down the main shaft – not today, anyway. Instead, we're going to hike over the hill there," he said, thumbing behind him, "to the upcast shaft and see if we can get down by cable and kibble. We're hoping that the ignited gas just blasted eastwards along the main roadway towards the bottom of the main shaft – meaning survivors will have gone westwards, deeper into the mine, towards the upcast shaft – which is just under half a league west of the main shaft. We need to get them out before they get critically poisoned by the after-gases."

Vin paused to wipe his sweating brow with his white handkerchief, before continuing. "So, it's all about speed now, boys. Mr Morris is organising the rescue equipment – kibble, rope, masks, spare cable, a cable drum, cutting gear and such like – along with medical supplies. He estimates that will take another ten minutes. As soon as he's ready, we'll head off. In the meantime, I'll take a rollcall of all miners who will be in the first rescue party. I've already got Job Law, Josh Goose, Davy Sheerin, Pat Martyn and Daff Duncan. We'll also be taking Doc Evans – for obvious reasons. So, with me and Mr Morris, that's eight. We'll need a team of around twenty so I'll grab another dozen of you now, and I would like the others not selected to go home, have some dinner, get some rest, and then come back here for about ten o'clock tonight nice and fresh, and we'll start swapping you in for some of the first twenty. Is that all understood?"

There was a firm round of assent from all.

"Right then. Those names I've already called out, please go and stand by the gate behind the engineering shed, as that's where we'll head off from. The rest of you, I'm going to recruit now."

As Vin Ellis started collecting the rest of the first rescue party, Davy and the other named miners, plus Doc Evans, headed off in the direction of the engineering shed. "What do you reckon the chances are?" asked Josh Goose, his eyes downcast as he walked. Josh was about Davy's age.

"In my mind, they're all still alive, mate," replied Davy.

Pat Martyn turned to look over his shoulder. "I like your sentiments

Davy, lad," said the older miner, "but you need to prepare yourself for the worst, and then celebrate every life we manage to save."

Davy closed his eyes at the logic of the older miner. Pat had been in the rescue party of '79, for starters. But Davy couldn't bear the thought of Robbie or Will being dead. A hideous image of the twelve-year-old burned to a crisp forced itself into his mind. Then the face of Robbie's Carys as she was told the worst. And then poor Edyth Lowe. She'd already lost her husband to the mine, but to lose one or both of her bairns, too…

Daff Duncan saw all the emotions passing across Davy's face, so he moved across and put his arm around him as they walked. "Hang in there, kid," he said, patting him on the back, just as they arrived at their appointed meeting place.

The enormity was closing in again, and Davy's chin began to wobble. Pat Martyn stopped him and took hold of both of his arms. "You're OK, son," he said. "Let it out now if you want, so you can focus on saving lives later. None of us here mind. I cried like a baby back in '79 before we went down for 'em."

"Thanks Pat," said Davy, wiping his grimy cheeks and runny nose with even grimier hands and somehow producing more clear skin on his face. "It's just the thoughts – they're unbearable!"

"I know, son, I know. That's why we're the closest family on this planet, isn't that right lads?"

The others all agreed, taking it in turns to pat Davy on the back or give his arm a reassuring squeeze.

"When this is all over," said Pat, "we'll have a private do. We'll celebrate those that we've saved, and we'll mourn those that we've lost. As brothers."

It wasn't much, but Davy felt some comfort in those words.

CHAPTER 39   WILL
7th Tertiar, 1789   Day 98, 16:00

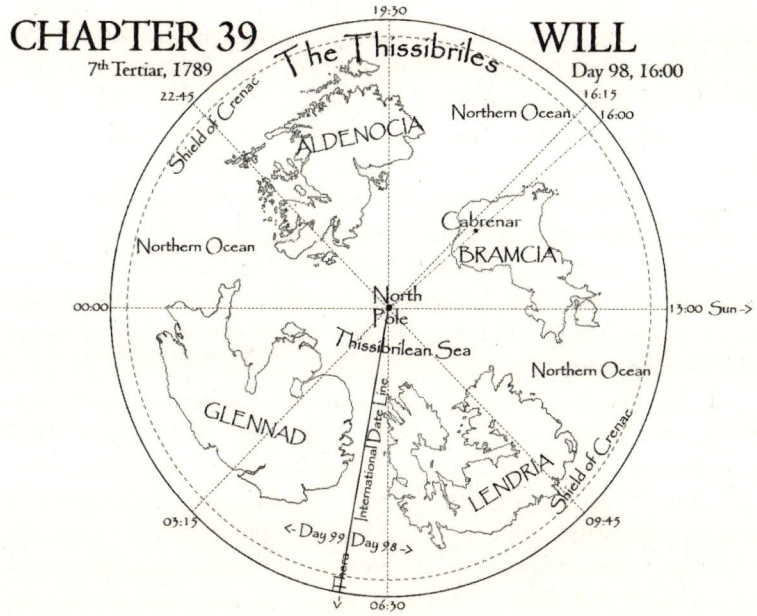

Will Lowe was floating above ground, looking down on Cabrenar Colliery. It was like an ant's nest; men in black scuttling about all over the place. The reason was clear: thick black smoke was belching out of No 1 shaft.

Despite a headache which was impairing his vision, and the absurdity of his position, Will bowed to a subterranean compulsion, bore to his left and then spiralled down in a dive towards the opening of No 1 Shaft. He took a deep breath before plunging into the thick, pulsing smoke, then shut his eyes as he felt the approach of the heat from the flames. Defying elemental science, he did not catch light as he zoomed towards the bottom of the shaft, before pulling a ninety degree manoeuvre to his right and missing banging his head on the main pit prop by a whisker. Will noted that the pit props and seams were also ablaze, as well as noting the smell of singed hair (his own, no doubt), but then he was speeding along the main roadway, through the flames and past abandoned, overturned and burning wagons that appeared to have been blown about like leaves in the wind, past blackened men and boys lying on the ground, none of them moving…until he began to slow, around four hundred yards in…and found himself looking at a familiar face, staring up at him.

It was Robbie Russell. And he was *really* staring…

Will came to with a start. It was pitch black, and yet he somehow knew he was lying face-down on the roadway floor, his left cheek pressed hard to the still-warm ground. The only thing that was sustained from his strange dream was the hideous throbbing in his head.

As he regained consciousness, other noises gradually began to filter through – coughing, moaning, crying and a number of men actually screaming. It was the sound of nightmares.

Will tried to take a deep breath but the action caused great discomfort in his chest. He tried breathing more shallowly, giving himself time to take stock and remember: the collapse of the gallery wall that Robbie was working, his safety lamp blowing out…and then his brother, Dylan, racing towards them with a naked flame.

Will had been looking directly at Dylan when the gas had ignited with an intense flare, and he had also been vaguely aware of Robbie throwing himself towards him. That had all happened in a split-second. After that, it was a blank. He couldn't even remember hitting the ground, much less being burned by the ignition.

Will began to tentatively check himself out, all the while accompanied by the sounds of men in agony. He was aware that the left side of his face was tender, and there was a lot of pain from his left arm and hand. A blistering sort of pain. Satisfied he was at least still in one piece, Will sought out the sound of his brother's voice – but none of the nearby noises were being made by a twelve-year-old boy.

Will managed to raise himself onto his knees. "Robbie," he tried to say – but the words came out as an unintelligible croak, and also exacerbated his shortness of breath. His mouth was full of dust, too. He spat it out. Then he tried again. "Robbie," he croaked.

He heard a moan beside him, and then a pain-wracked voice: "Will."

"Robbie," repeated Will, feeling to his left towards the voice. As he touched what he took to be Robbie, the form beside him yelped in pain.

"Sorry," cried Will. "How bad are you?"

Through his pain, Robbie managed to wheeze a jocular response. "I think I'm well-cooked, Will."

"What do we do?" asked Will, holding his hand up right in front of his face – but still unable to see anything.

"You need to get away from here, Will," gasped Robbie. "Deeper into the mine, away from the fires. Make sure you keep low. The air's less poisonous low down."

"But what about you? What about Dylan? Where is Dylan?"

"I can't move, Will. I'm burnt to a crisp. All I can do is wait until the rescuers come. Davy will come for us. I know he will. They'll come down the upcast shaft. It's about a third of a league west of here."

"But I can't leave you and Dylan," cried Will.

"Yes, you can, son, and that's an order," gasped Robbie. "Now go. Can't keep talking to you. Need to conserve my breath. And Dylan will need help as well. Go and find the rescue party. Like I said, they'll be coming down the upcast shaft. Now go."

"But which way? I can't see anything."

"Can't see!" cried Robbie, both astonishment and caution evident in his voice, despite his pain. "Back towards the shaft, son…we're lit up by the fires of hell!"

Will's heart leaped into his mouth. He was blind.

CHAPTER 40   DAVY

7th Tertiar, 1789   Day 98, 16:05

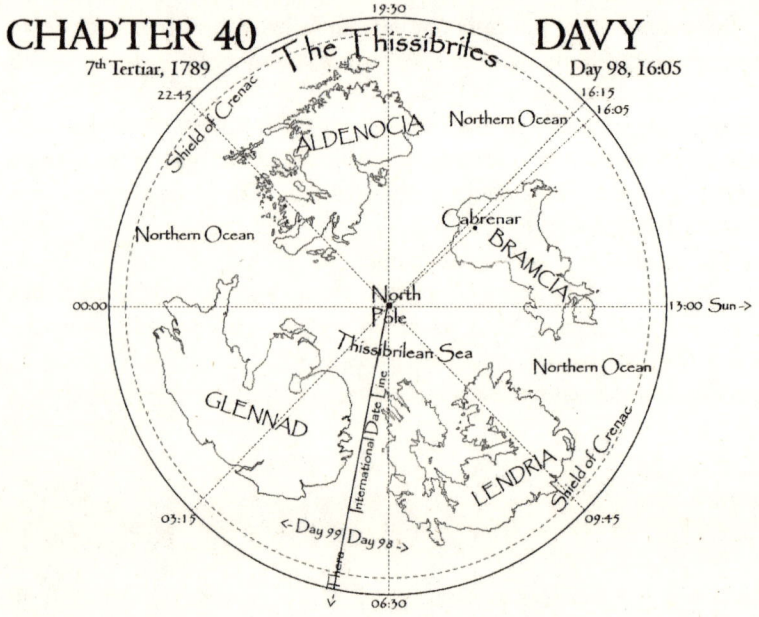

Davy was currently sixth in a line of around twenty miners striding up Axe Edge, following the well-worn path to around half-way up this valley, before dropping down the other side into the next valley. He had a great roll of rope over his right shoulder and was carrying an enormous wooden toolbox with his left hand. In front of him Pat Martyn, Daff Duncan and Doc Evans were carrying the medical supplies and some heavy cutting gear, while leading the way was Chief Engineer, Vin Ellis and mine owner, Jed Morris, carrying the plans of the mine and other equipment. Bringing up the rear, some dozen-or-so miners further back, were Josh Goose and Job Law who were rolling an enormous cable drum up the slope before them, while just in front of them were four sweating miners pulling and pushing an iron wagon that was bearing an enormous, strapped-down kibble – a cast-iron bucket capable of carrying six or seven miners at a time. With all of them breathing heavily, conversation was limited.

With the summit of Axe Edge rising to his right and to the north, Davy squinted up towards the sun to the south-west. At least that was shining on them today, as traversing this ground in a downpour would have been a nightmare, and the kibble wagon would have had no chance. And whereas straight along the main roadway at the foot of the mine measured around half a league, up and over the hills was at least twice the distance.

Five minutes later, they reached the stone wall and stile that delineated the two valleys. There was much huffing and puffing as equipment was hauled over the wall, especially the cable drum, while the kibble had to be unstrapped and lifted separately, followed by the wagon – before the kibble was strapped back down again. They were all ready to go, but Vin and Jed were stood looking at the wall, both rubbing their respective chins in thought.

"We need to widen that gap, Vin," said Jed.

"Aye, it'll be a nightmare getting casualties over that." Vin turned around and called over young Charlie Pritchard. "Charlie, I've got a job for you, lad. I need you to run back to the pithead and grab some lump hammers and a couple of men. That stile needs to go and a foot of wall on either side. We need a gap large enough and flat enough to wheel the trolleys through when we start bringing back the casualties."

"Will do, Mr Ellis," said Charlie.

"Good lad," said Vin and Jed in unison.

That sorted, the rescue crew headed off downhill, soon becoming spread out in a long line once again. This time around, though, Josh and Job were leading the way with the cable drum butting up behind them – no one was taking any chances with a runaway drum at their rear. Meanwhile, the kibble crew were alongside them with two men positioned at the front with their backs to the trolley, and the two men at the rear taking the strain, digging in their boots and angling their bodies back at almost forty-five degrees.

After another ten minutes, the wooden hoist mounted above the upcast shaft came into view down below them. It took them another ten minutes to reach it, at which point Davy marvelled at the size of the four oak struts which formed the main frame, with giant bolts holding it together at the cross-braces and securing it to the ground, while the enormous iron hook hanging from the top of the hoist looked to be nearly as big as he was. Davy then looked down into the gaping black maw directly beneath the hook: the upcast shaft. Ordinarily, he would have been able to feel the air coming up the upcast, as that was how the mine worked: air being drawn down through the downcast shafts (of which there were two further back up the hill), through the two leagues of mine workings – and then exhausted out through the upcast shaft. To force air *through* the underground workings, ventilation was handled by induced draught from a pair of furnaces that were located around seventy yards from the base of the upcast shaft. Given the lack of an upwardly mobile air current, Davy suspected that the furnaces had been blown out.

Meanwhile, each of the miners had gratefully released their burdens, and Vin Ellis was already setting up their makeshift rescue base, ordering miners about, offering words of encouragement here and a pat on the back there. Vin had been mighty relieved about the state of the hoist. It hadn't been checked for six months, but he was satisfied the cable was in decent working order, and expressed his hope that they wouldn't need to use the cable drum that Josh and Job had hauled up and down Axe Edge – for which they'd given Vin quite a bit of friendly stick. After another half hour of preparation, the kibble had been mounted upon the enormous hook by the same four sweating miners who had hauled it up and down Axe Edge. Vin then went to the huge iron winding lever and turned it in a clockwise direction. The hook and kibble moved downwards by a few feet until the kibble was at the right height for mounting.

Satisfied with the set-up, Vin called everyone into a huddle. "All right," he began. He quickly checked his pocket watch. "It's 16:45, so it will be getting dark in two or three hours. So, a quick summary for you before we go in. Now we don't know for sure, but it is highly likely that the explosion was caused by the ignition of gas by either a faulty safety lamp, a spark or a naked flame. I know, I know," he said, raising his hands as the men around him began to object. "No one's daft enough to expose a naked flame, and the boys know they can't go past the caution boards with one. But lamp, spark or flame is the likely cause."

Vin paused to lick his lips. "Now as you know, fire-gas is the name given to several flammable gases, but especially methane. It's found in areas where the coal is bituminous – as it is in our mine in large quantities. This gas accumulates in pockets in the goaves behind the coal. So, chances are that a miner has exposed a goave full of methane, and something has triggered the explosion," said Vin, gravely. "But if that's the case, there's a good chance the fire-gas is now burnt out and dispersed, so further explosions are unlikely. But not impossible. So, we still need to be very cautious."

Vin paused, making sure that everyone was paying attention. They were rapt, to a man. Satisfied, he continued. "Now, the explosion will have caused significant damage to the mine's main roadways, certainly close to the bottom of the main shaft. Given the amount of fire and smoke we were seeing up top, I'm guessing that coal seams have been ignited along with supporting timber structures. That's not good. It means that even if the main roadway isn't still alight, or it's still filled with smoke and poisonous gases, the structure itself – pit props and the like – are likely unstable and liable to collapse. On top of that, the wood-burning will also have filled the roadway with carbon-based smoke as well."

Good old Vin, thought Davy. He was giving it to them brutally straight.

"Even more dangerous," continued Vin, "is carbon-monoxide, another by-product of these type of explosions. High levels of carbon-monoxide kill miners. This is because it stops the blood pumping freely around your body and your heart eventually gives out. Which is why we must get those lads out, and fast. Not to mention minimise the risk to ourselves. But what makes carbon-monoxide so lethal," Vin paused, to ensure all were clear, "is that you can't smell it, you can't see it; you can't even taste it."

The levels of nervousness within the group increased at that point, and there was a certain amount of feet-shuffling. But, thought Davy, proudly, there was still a total resolve from them all.

"So," continued Vin, "we're each going to be wearing one of those facial guards that Jed is now demonstrating."

Everyone turned to look at Jed Morris, who had tied a thick woollen grey scarf around his nose and mouth so that only his eyes were visible.

"They're not foolproof, I'll grant you that. But it's more than the lads down there have got."

Davy and his colleagues managed a round of sombre head-nodding.

"So, I hope that's all clear. We will be going into an *extremely* dangerous environment. You obey me and Jed at all times. And if any of you are not happy going down there," said Vin, jerking his thumb behind him, "now is the time to speak up." Vin looked slowly around him, seeking every miner's eye, but they all nodded their support.

"We're all with you, Vin," said Pat Martyn.

"Aye, count me in," added Daff Duncan, before his voice was joined by everyone else's assent.

"Good lads," said Jed Morris, quietly. The mine owner's eyes were moist. He was taking this very personally. "Brave lads to a man," he added, a little louder.

"As for our safety lamps, we've treble-checked them all, and they're functioning perfectly. Therefore, when we get to the bottom, we're going to proceed at walking pace, with our safety lamps turned down to the lowest flame. We hold them out in front of us, like this," he said, demonstrating, "and we look out for any sign of a blue flame."

Everyone murmured their understanding.

"So, this is what we're going to do," Vin said, glancing down at his notes and clipboard. "I'll be going down with the first rescue party, which will also include Job Law, Josh Goose, Pat Martyn, Davy Sheerin, Doc Evans and Daff Duncan. There's twenty of us here, so we stick to rescue teams of seven, all right? Me or Jed plus six of you lot?"

Murmured assent again.

"Each team initially searches for a total of thirty minutes – although as the search moves further afield, we'll have to extend those times. Jed and I will adjust the timings as necessary and keep you all informed. But to start off," he said, checking his pocket watch again. "We'll be going down at 16:55 pm exactly, and we'll be coming out as close to 17:25 pm as possible. Jed will then be leading the next team of six which he will select shortly. To minimise crossover, Jed's team will descend at 17:20 to make sure we handover at the bottom of the shaft. I'll brief Jed on where we've been and what we've found, so that his team can carry on from where we left off. Jed's first shift will run from around 17:25 to approximately 17:55 and then he'll hand back to me – as in the meantime, I will have picked a new team – the last six of you – to go down in the kibble with me at around 17:50."

"Hang on," said Davy. "That means that you and Jed are getting exposed to the gases and smoke more regularly than the rest of us."

"The price of being the mine owner and Chief Engineer," responded Jed, wryly. "And I take that responsibility willingly."

"All right then, boys, I'll get in the kibble first," said Vin, turning around and moving to the edge of the shaft. He handed his safety lamp to Jed, and then pulled the kibble towards him, hauled himself up with both hands and over the edge, whilst a couple of other miners held the kibble relatively stable. Vin then took his safety lamp back off Jed who also passed him two functional sacks that contained their medical kits. Vin then turned his attention to Davy. "Now you, Davy, lad," he said.

Davy briefly checked out the massive hook and drum hanging over the kibble about twelve feet above them which, in turn, was suspended from the top of the hoist. It looked sturdy enough. He then copied Vin, handing his safety lamp to Jed and hauled himself up and over into the kibble. Josh, Pat, Daff, Doc and Job followed, along with their medical supplies, and then they were ready, each clutching their safety lamps and looking out at the cluster of miners at the top of the shaft. There was a brief round of back patting from those in the kibble, and then Vin gave the command to lower them down.

One of the other miners who was standing by the enormous winding lever, began to turn it in a clockwise direction. Davy felt the kibble lurch, forcing all seven of the miners inside to grab the edge with their free hand. Davy's stomach had lurched as well – as had a few of the others judging by the wry looks being passed around. And then they were descending. As his eyes became level with the ground, Davy looked up at the nearest miner and gave him a brief nod and a wave. The miner nodded back and gave Davy the thumbs-up.

Twenty seconds later, accompanied by the constant crank and creak of the moving cable, Davy was looking up at a receding circle of light, and could just make out the shadows of faces looking down on their descent. After another twenty seconds, the darkness began to crowd in, and after another twenty they were all hitting the striker bars on their safety lamps, and then turning the flame down to the lowest level, as instructed.

As the kibble continued to descend, relatively smoothly, Davy found himself constantly sampling the air with his nose, trying to detect a difference; smoke, gas, he wasn't sure what. He smelt none of those things; just an increasing mustiness as they descended.

"How far down is it from the top of the upcast?" asked Daff of Vin.

"It's around six hundred feet, Daff – as we're quite a bit higher up here than at the top of the No 1 Shaft."

Five minutes later, they hit the bottom of the shaft with a meaty thud – all of them being slightly off-balanced again. The chain above them kept paying out for another two or three seconds – but then the landing impact telegraphed itself back up top to the operator, and the slack cable was reeled back in.

"Right, here we go then boys," said Vin, climbing out of the kibble first. "Just wait here a second whilst I check the furnaces. And put your scarves on, too," he added, tying his own in place. He then headed off to the right, which Davy figured must be a dead end as it was in the opposite direction to where the main shaft was.

Whilst they waited, Davy lowered his scarf and sniffed the air again. There was a new smell, now. "You smell that?" he asked of Pat Martyn.

"Aye," agreed Pat, glumly. "It's a sort of scorched smell, isn't it?"

"That's what I thought," said Davy. The others agreed.

Sure enough, Vin returned after a minute or so. "The furnaces are out," he announced. "That's good news and bad news."

"What do you mean?" asked Josh Goose.

"It means that the blast carried right the way along in this direction. That's probably what put out the furnaces, starving them of oxygen."

"And would that blast have been preceded by its own inferno?" asked Davy.

"Aye," agreed Vin. "If you look at these pit props, they're all scorched. So, I don't think the flames burned up here for very long. Maybe just seconds when passing through."

"But it does account for the smell," stated Davy.

"Aye."

"And the good news?" asked Job Law.

"Well, it's not major good news. But whatever flames were conveyed in this direction, they were soon exhausted due to lack of oxygen. It's what gases they've left behind that we need to worry about."

"And I don't suppose it's good news that there aren't any miners already gathered here," said Davy.

Vin looked at him, his brow creased, and he nodded once. "I think we need to be prepared for a lot of casualties, men. Those burned and blasted by the initial explosion, and those suffering from oxygen starvation. Now, get those scarves up over your noses," he said, adjusting his own. "The plan is to head straight up the main roadway, ignoring the offshoots, and treating casualties as we go."

CHAPTER 41   WILL
7th Tertiar, 1789   Day 98, 17:00

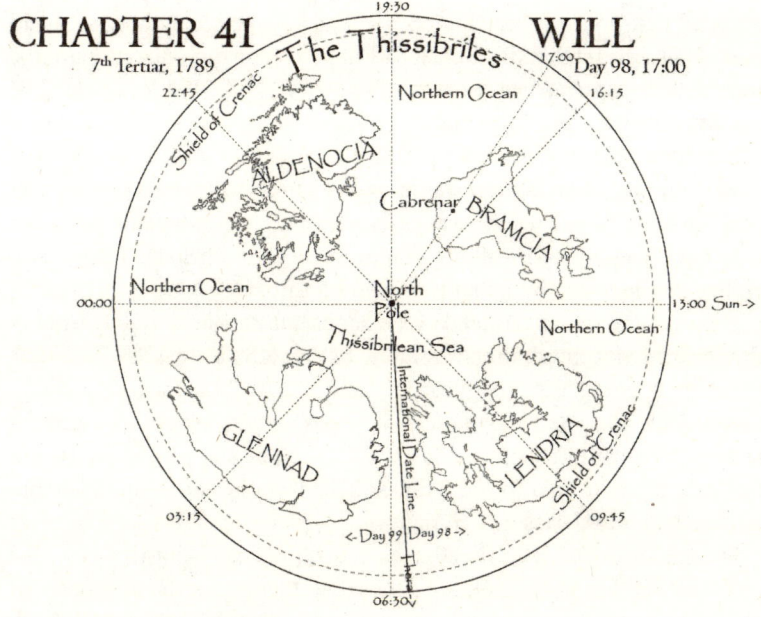

Will was stumbling down what he believed to be the main gallery in the opposite direction to the main shaft, in line with Robbie's instructions. "Help me!", came the constant plea from stricken miners on the ground. The pleas tore his heart out. But what could he do?

"I'm blind," he would reply. "But I'm going for help. The rescue party is coming down the upcast shaft."

On at least four occasions, Will had stumbled into stricken miners, causing them to cry out in pain. On other occasions, he would kick bodies on the ground and no sound would emerge.

Maybe he should be grateful for his lack of sight.

Although Robbie had also given him hope as well. "You were looking right at Dylan's candle when the gas ignited," he'd said. "That's what's blinded you. But it will only be temporary."

Will wondered if Robbie was just being kind. Nevertheless, Robbie and these other stricken miners were relying on him. And it was thanks to Robbie shielding him that he was better off than everyone else. Will reasoned that a split second after the gas ignited, he was already being taken down by Robbie's dive, thereafter smothered by his mentor, protecting him until the inferno blew over them and blew itself out.

Given the casualties heading further away from the main shaft, Will reasoned that none of these miners had had anyone or anything to shield them. It also meant that the fireball had ripped out in both directions of the main gallery. Even at twelve years of age and blind, Will knew that the casualty rate was going to be high.

Blindness wasn't Will's only problem, either. The air was smoky and acrid – although Will knew it was the gases you *couldn't* smell or taste that were the most dangerous. He was certainly struggling to breathe normally, so he tried keeping his breathing shallow – which did help a bit, but it still felt like someone had both hands around his throat.

Will's reverie was interrupted by his hands hitting a stone wall in front of him. He'd been feeling all the way along to the right, so he knew he hadn't missed an opening. But now, the right-hand wall was walking him round in a semi-circle. Despite his blindness, Will was certain he was now walking back in the same direction he'd just come. Then he stopped, as realisation dawned. He was in an offshoot. This explained why he hadn't stumbled into another miner in the last five minutes.

Frustration and despair flared. How much time had he lost?

It took another five minutes to get back to the start of the offshoot, and Will felt the right-hand wall now veer sharply to the right. He must be back in the main gallery again. Then, Will stopped dead. He had heard something over the sound of stricken miners. He kept quite still. There it was again. A shuffling sound back down the main runway in the direction of the main shaft. Will rejoiced. Another miner had survived and was making his way towards the upcast shaft. The man would be Will's eyes.

"Hello," called Will. "Who is there please?"

"Dylan, is that you," gasped a voice that Will didn't recognise.

Will frowned at mention of his brother's name. Maybe it was another Dylan, though. "My name's Will. Will Lowe," called back Will.

"Dylan," wheezed the voice again. "Oh Dylan, son, you're safe. Thank the Lord."

"I'm not -," began Will, and then broke off. He knew who this was.

The man was close now. He could hear his chest wheezing. He didn't sound good. "Dylan, son. Why did you run? Why? I didn't mean to upset you, son."

Will was paralysed with fear. What should he do? If he'd had his sight, he could have outrun this wheezer in seconds. Then it was too late as two strong hands gripped his upper arms. "Dylan, was it you? Was it you who set off the explosion?"

"I'm not Dylan!" shouted Will, accusingly exaggerating his brother's name. "He ran because of *you*, didn't he?"

Silence followed this accusation – other than the man's wheezing. Eventually, he spoke. "You're blind, aren't you?"

"Robbie says it's only temporary," cried Will.

"What did you see?" asked the voice.

Will felt a great anger boil up inside him. "He's dead!" he shouted.

"Did you see Dylan die?"

"I saw the explosion. That's the last thing I saw."

Will heard an exclamation of great anguish, and then silence for several seconds. Then the man asked: "So why?" he gasped. He then paused to compose himself. "Why aren't *you* burned to a crisp, Will?"

"Robbie protected me. He needs me to get help. I've got to get help, otherwise he will die as well."

That got no response other than the continual wheezing. Then, he felt a breath at his ear, and the man spoke. "We can't do anything for Dylan, son, if he was at the source of the explosion." Will then felt the man straighten up. "God rest his little soul." Was that a sob? "But let me help you get out of here, Will."

Will felt paralysed for a second. Then he vented. "I'll not team up with you," said Will, bitterly. "You're the one who caused all of this."

"And what makes you say that, boy?" asked the voice, sounding angry for the first time, whilst he also shook Will as he spoke.

"Because you upset him. Something you did…were doing…"

Another long pause. Then the voice in his ear again. "If I were so-inclined, why are you unmolested – blind and helpless as you are?"

Will's skin crawled. But he had no answer to the question.

"We're all alone here, Will Lowe. We're the only two able-bodied survivors. I've walked past at least fifty dead or dying, and I can hear more in the next gallery. The explosion blew out in all directions, igniting gas, coal, wood. Its fire took everyone – except you, who was sheltered by your precious Robbie. And me."

Curious, Will couldn't help himself. "So how…how did you…"

Another pause. Then in his ear again. "Because I'm clever."

"In what way? How did you survive?" persisted Will.

The man finally released Will's arms. Ten seconds passed. Then he responded. "I've been a miner for thirty years, Will. I was in the rescue party in '79. This time, I felt the shock from the explosion seconds before it ripped through the main shaft and then ignited its way back along the Level Z offshoot. By the time the flames consumed my gallery, I was underneath an upturned wagon. I got cooked a bit, mind. And where my skin touched the metal sides, I've got some rare blisters. And now, having sat for an hour under the wagon until the gas burned itself out, I've got carbon-monoxide poisoning, too – as have you, son.

"Anyway, I was able to use the cross-cut flat to get back to the main gallery, beyond the fires. The rescue party will come down the upcast shaft, see. They'll be here in the next hour. God willing, they'll find and rescue Dylan. But we'll be going up in the first batch of survivors."

There was another long pause. Then the man – clearly Nate Turner, in Will's opinion – made clear his intentions. "Or rather, we'll be going up in the first batch…*if* you promise to keep your wild accusations to yourself."

CHAPTER 42 — DAVY
7th Tertiar, 1789   Day 98, 17:05

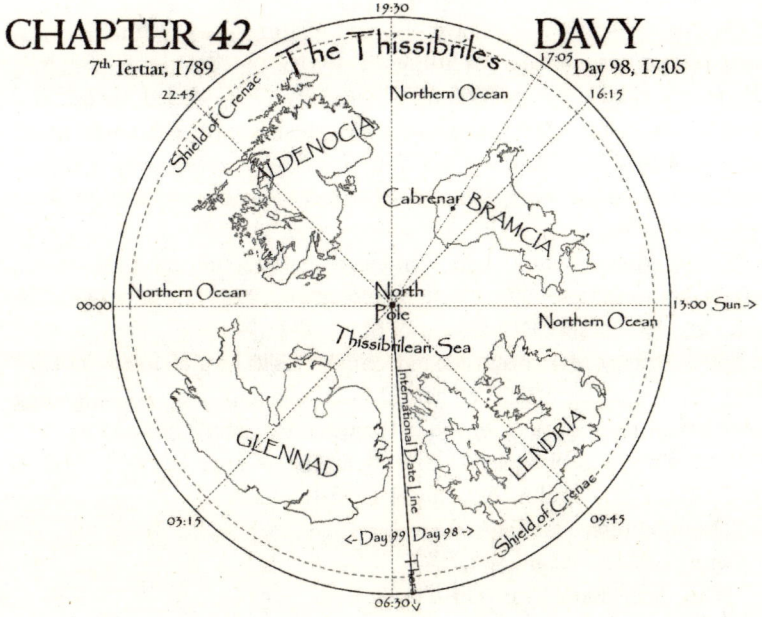

Davy and his fellow rescuers had just found their first casualties. They were in the furthest bay along the Level Z main roadway from the main shaft, and the signs were about as bad as they could be. Most of the forms lying on the ground were unmoving. Davy lifted his safety lamp so that the flickering light played across the form lying at his feet – and he recoiled in horror. The man was lying on his back, his clawed hands raised in a futile defence. There was little remaining of his face.

Davy's stomach lurched, so he quickly turned to his left – only to projectile vomit over the body of another dead miner. When he had finished vomiting, he began to hyper-ventilate. "I'm sorry, I'm so sorry!"

Vin Ellis was with him in an instant, gripping his right arm with his free hand. "It's all right, Davy, lad. It's a natural reaction. Take a deep breath. That's right. Now, breathe out slowly. That's it."

Vin kept his hand on Davy's arm but turned his head around to face the others. "How's everybody doing?" he asked, loudly.

He got a mixture of responses, but the other four miners were generally handling matters better than Davy, which made him feel ashamed. He pulled himself upright and looked Vin in the eyes. "I'm all right Vin, I'm all right. I'm sorry."

"Don't apologise, lad. Just try and stay composed and let's see how many of these poor souls we can save," he said, patting Davy's arm. Vin then moved over to a slumped form sitting with his back to the side of the gallery. The man was alive but mumbling incoherently. Davy steeled himself and lifted his safety lamp. The man was badly burned across the face which was both blackened and blistered. He then opened his eyes – which looked starkly white compared to the rest of his face. Those eyes suddenly went wide with terror.

"Shush, shush, Denny," said Vin, clearly recognising the poor miner, despite his condition. "We're here to rescue you, boy. You're going to be fine. Here you go, son. Drink some of this."

The wildness began to subside in Denny's eyes as he took the water flask from Vin in shaking, blackened hands, and began to drink, rivulets spilling down his blistered chin. "Can you tell us what happened?" asked Vin.

Despite his evident agony, Denny attempted to describe events. "Felt it first," he croaked, handing back the water flask to Vin.

"The compressed air?" asked Vin.

Denny nodded. "Came so fast."

"What did?" asked Vin. "The flames?"

Denny nodded again. "A second or two later. We had no chance."

Davy noticed a single tear slide out of Denny's left eye.

"It's all right, son," said Vin again. "You're doing great."

"I'm a terrible person, Mr Ellis," gasped Denny.

Davy gritted his teeth. He could see how much the talking was hurting Denny, with the cracks around his mouth opening up to reveal hideous red sores.

"You're not a terrible person, Denny," Vin was saying. "You've always been a good boy."

"I grabbed Marcus Griffiths," sobbed Denny. "I grabbed him…"

"What do you mean, Denny? I don't understand."

"I grabbed him – to shield me. I don't know why…" he tailed off, the tears flowing freely now.

"Listen to me Denny," said Vin. "Instinct is all that was. Nothing can prepare you for a situation like this. None of us react normally."

"But he took the full brunt."

"Listen, Denny. It is what it is. But we need to move fast here, lad. There'll be time for reflection later, but there'll be no recriminations from me." Vin turned to Doc Evans who was stood alongside them. "Can we get him to stand?"

"We've no choice, Vin," replied Doc, unslinging his medical kit. "We need to get the survivors away from the lingering gases as soon as possible.

But I'm going to give him some opium first," he said, pulling a large glass bottle out from his kitbag along with a metal tablespoon. With Vin and Davy holding up their lanterns for light, Doc uncorked the bottle, emptied out a half-tablespoon of black liquid and then knelt down before Denny. "Here you go, son. This will help take away some of the pain."

Denny's white eyes opened wide but he also opened his mouth to take the medicine. It must have tasted bad, as even amidst his terrible pain, Denny screwed his face up in disgust.

"Good lad," said Doc. "In five minutes, you'll be whistling with the fairies, son!"

Incredibly, Denny even managed a half-smile at that.

"Is it worth giving him a scarf?" asked Vin.

Doc shook his head. A woollen scarf around poor Denny's blistered face would just compound his agony. "We need to get him up top, Vin. As fast as we can."

Davy's head and heart were struggling to take it all in, but he found himself wondering if poor Marcus Griffiths was one of the burnt husks at his feet. Meanwhile, Vin had turned back to Denny and crouched down again. "Can you stand, lad?"

"I can try."

Vin went to offer a hand, but Denny put both hands up to stop him: "Please! Please don't touch me."

"All right, lad," said Vin, backing off, but still holding his hands out, wanting to help.

Despite his unfathomable agony, Denny managed to haul himself slowly to his feet, whimpering from the pain it caused him. Davy forced himself to look at Denny's clothing, which was a mass of burnt rags that were hideously melded with blistered, congealed flesh.

"I've got another one over here," came Pat Martyn's voice. "Tommy Spencer."

Davy snapped out of his stupor and rushed over to Pat. "What do you need me to do, Pat?"

"Give him a drink of water, then half a tablespoon of Doc's opium. Then help him stand. Same drill as for Denny. Then start walking him back to the upcast, if you can."

"Josh," commanded Vin. "Same for you with Denny please. Doc, what's the status of the men on the ground?"

Both Davy and Josh paused to hear the diagnosis.

"They're all gone but two others, Vin. First degree burns. And these two here – I'm not sure we can move them, Vin."

"We've got no choice, Doc. We can't leave them here to die."

"It might be kinder, Vin," said Doc, quietly.

Vin Ellis put his hands to his head for a second, and then made his mind up. "We stick to the plan, Doc. Josh and Davy are walking Denny and Tommy to safety. Me and you'll take one of these poor souls, give them the opium and carry them back between us; Pat, Job and Daff will take the other survivor." Vin held up his lamp and took out his pocket watch. "It's 17:15 now. By the time we get back to the bottom of the upcast, Jed's team will be on the way down. This is how it works, boys. This is how it works."

"The thing is, Vin," said Daff, walking over to him. "If they're in this state here…"

"I know, Daff," said Vin as he walked over to the side of the gallery. He took out a piece of chalk from his pocket and marked a big X on the wall – so Jed Morris' team would know how far the first party had got. He'd expect another X further down from Jed when he returned in another half an hour or so. Vin turned back to Daff. "But we go on until we've tended every man. We treat and rescue those nearest the upcast, as statistically, they'll have the best chance of survival. Now come on. Let's get these boys out of here."

Vin's statistical reasoning was pretty much what Davy had been in denial about, preferring to think that Robbie and Will had found somewhere to shelter. Yet somehow, he dealt with the news. He'd already shown weakness back at the pithead and again on seeing his first casualty. There was no way he was going to let anyone down again. And he was determined to remain part of the rescue team until he'd found his best friend and twelve-year-old apprentice, no matter what that took or what it meant seeing first.

CHAPTER 43
WILL
7th Tertiar, 1789 — Day 98, 17:15

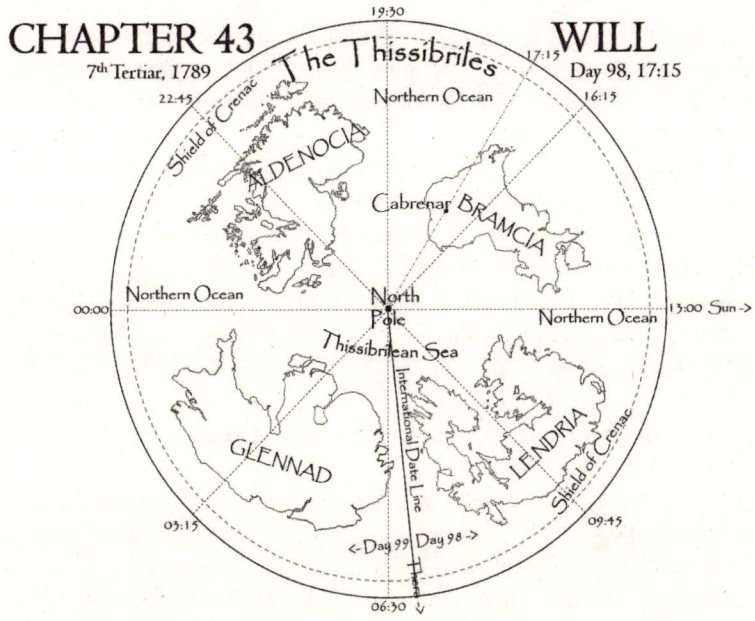

Will held his hand in front of his face for the umpteenth time and waved it about. Still nothing. His shoulders slumped.

"It'll come back, young Will," wheezed Nate Turner. "The same thing happened to Alf Lynn way back in '54. He was blind for three days before his sight returned."

"I don't care about my sight. It won't bring Dylan back, will it?"

Another anguished sound came from Turner's direction. "We don't know that Dylan's dead." Turner's voice was cracking.

Will stopped walking. "He was the one holding the naked flame. Of course he's dead, you idiot!"

Will felt Nate grab his arm again, more roughly this time. "I could just leave you, you know."

"Do it then. I was doing fine before you came along."

"Oh yes, you were doing fine – up a blind alley!"

"I'd already worked my way back to the main gallery. I'm not stupid."

"No, you're not, are you?" Will noted a change in Nate's tone.

They had both stopped walking – but Will was sure something had changed. Twenty seconds of silence passed, then thirty. "Shouldn't we keep on moving?" asked Will.

There was another long pause. Then finally: "I'm thinking not."

"Well, I'm thinking we should," said Will, starting to walk forwards.

Nate then grabbed Will even more roughly, and the next thing Will knew, he was pinned against the gallery wall. "There's no way you're not going to call me out, is there?"

Will struggled briefly, before realising there was no point. "He was my brother," he said, his voice heavy with grief.

"He may still be alive, son. Yes, he'll be burned. But I've seen miners beat similar odds. What's more, the rescue party will be down here soon. At the very worst, they'll take his body back up top, so we'll know one way or the other."

"Right, so let's get moving then."

"No," repeated Nate.

"Why? Don't you want to live?"

"I do," whispered Nate. "But I don't trust you. You're going to sell me out. You're going to blame me."

Will kept quiet. He was determined to sell Nate Turner out if it was the last thing he did.

"Thought as much," said Nate, slyly.

Will could feel himself beginning to shake. He knew where this was heading. And yet, he still couldn't bring himself to beg, or promise Turner that he'd keep quiet. "You're going to kill me."

Will heard a hiss of anger from Turner. "I'm not a murderer, boy. I'd never hurt you. But I can see I'm going to have to prove that to you."

"You don't have to prove anything to me. I know what you are."

Will felt the whistle of wind a split-second before a blow landed across his right cheek. Turner had slapped him. Hard. For a few seconds, Will saw stars. Then everything settled back to pure blackness again.

"I will prove it to you, Will Lowe, that I am no molester of young boys. But I can't give you the opportunity to sell me out. That would be too cruel for words."

"So, what? We hide down here, with the after-gas – which will kill us. Or we wait for another explosion – which will kill us."

Nate Turner fell silent again.

"Look, we can't go back via the main shaft because of the fire, and the only other way out is via the route the rescuers will be coming in."

"Except that it isn't."

"What isn't?" asked Will, confused.

Another long pause and then: "It's not the only way out."

That simple reply turned Will cold. He knew in an instant that if he didn't get to safety via the upcast shaft, he would be held prisoner by the very same man who had likely molested his twin-brother and driven him to a level of desperation that had brought about not only his own death, but the deaths of dozens of miners. He might only be twelve years old, but Will was a good reasoner. He therefore tried to run – but Turner had anticipated it and grabbed him again. Now desperate, Will began to shout for help at the top of his voice.

This time, it was a fist instead of a slap. This time there were no stars.

Will had no idea how long he had been unconscious. He tried to moan but the only sound he could make was a weird, muffled groan. He then felt the gag, pulled tight about his mouth.

"Good, you're awake. That was foolish. Now, you listen to me. I'm going to get you out of here, and I can do that faster than the rescuers, if you play along. Will you play along? Just nod."

Will could feel his lungs hurting. They needed to get out of here soon, otherwise he felt they'd likely be impaired for life. He therefore nodded. He suspected he had little choice, anyway. And so long as he lived to fight another day, he might still get justice for his brother.

"Right, now, do as I say."

Will nodded again.

"Firstly, I'm just going to hook your lamp onto your belt like this." Will felt the weight of the lamp as it was hung from the right side of his belt. "I'm now going to lift you up."

Will felt the strong Turner lift him upwards by holding onto his hips.

"Now, reach out with your left hand. That's it. You feel that groove?"

Will slid his left hand upwards and then felt it. He nodded.

"Good lad. Now, reach out with your right hand – further up. That's it. You got that groove?"

Will nodded again.

"Good lad," repeated Nate. "Now, I want you to thrust yourself upwards, and put your left foot where your left hand was and your right foot where your right hand was, and grab whatever you can, higher up, with your hands."

Will shook his head, convinced he'd be knocking himself out on the gallery roof.

"It's all right, kid. I'm lifting you up into the old downcast shaft. It runs all the way up to the surface on Axe Edge. I know every single handhold, footrest, and old bit of rope in this shaft. Spent years running around this old mine when I was a kid. Then decades mining it. No one else knows this mine like me. So, do as I tell you – and every minute climbing takes us away from the poison."

Will still hesitated. He knew this action would take him away from his rescuers, and probably closer to another kind of poison. But the rescuers weren't here, Turner wasn't going to hand him over, and he desperately needed to find better air.

"Go on, Will," encouraged Nate. "This'll work, you'll see."

Will would have loved to have retorted that he couldn't 'see' anything, but made do with a muffled grunt of defiance, and then thrust upwards as Nate had suggested. His left hand grabbed the next handhold, and his foot automatically slotted into the previous hand-groove, but his right hand missed its target and his right leg was left flailing – until Turner grabbed him from beneath and pushed him up. Will gratefully grabbed a new right-hand groove, then secured his right foothold. He paused, relieved to be properly balanced, although his heart was still pounding. His lungs were also beginning to scream.

"Good lad," gasped Turner. "You're a natural."

Will issued another muffled grunt by way of reply.

"Now, you need to do the same manoeuvre. Just reach up with your left hand – that's it – you feel that next handhold? Good. So, same again – and don't worry, I'll catch you if you don't make it."

Once again, Will had trouble on his right side, but once again, Turner supported him and pushed him upwards so that he ascended by another couple of feet. Will's heart wasn't pumping quite so wildly this time. And he had to admit, Nate Turner's presence beneath him was comforting, although he couldn't understand how the old miner was keeping pace with him. "How…" he tried to ask through his gag.

Somehow, Turner understood his question. "I'm standing on two… upturned trucks, son, one on top…of the other," answered Turner, gasping in between talking. "Got my lamp around my neck. Like I said earlier…I know this mine inside out."

A pause then ensued as Turner got his breath back. "Now," he began. "Here's a little secret for you. Reach up this time with your right hand. That's it. A little bit more. There."

Will felt his right fingers brush against something dry. He immediately recoiled.

Turner laughed – the first time Will had heard him laugh. "You're all right, son," he said. "It's just the bottom of a length of rope. It's been there a long time though. So, test if it'll take your weight."

Will reached up and grabbed the rope with his right hand. He then deliberately released his other three points of contact, demonstrating a somewhat irrational faith in his companion, given what he knew – and then he swung his left hand over to the rope as well. The rope held. He then found footholds and felt secure.

"Now, use the rope to pull yourself upwards, but go slowly as that length of rope runs out after another twelve feet.

Will did as he was told, finding the ascent much easier with the rope. He was also well aware that the exertion was forcing the discomfort in his lungs to transition to outright pain. By the time he got to the top of the length of rope, though – perhaps twenty feet above the main gallery floor – Will was convinced the air didn't taste as bad, and the pain in his lungs might just have eased off slightly. Meanwhile, below him, he heard the clatter of the topmost truck as it fell off the first – indicating that Turner had pushed off and was hauling his considerably heavier frame upwards.

"Right then, Will," gasped Nate, eventually moving up just below him. "We're back to manoeuvre number one. Left hand first, then right hand, then left foot, then right foot. That's it. Good lad."

They continued like that for another fifty feet or so, making faster time whenever there was rope to hand, before the heavily wheezing Turner called for a breather. Will did as he was told – but already knew the pain in his chest had begun to recede. The sensation of being able to breathe relatively normally was wonderful. *He would never again take fresh air for granted.* As for Turner, though, his breathing problems were clearly as much age and health-related as they were gas-related. Neither was going to impede Will – and he was already formulating plans. He just needed a bit more information. He therefore waggled his gagged mouth at Turner, hoping the middle-aged miner was looking. Much to his surprise, Will felt Turner grab the gag and then remove it.

"Thanks," said Will. "I'll not shout again."

Nate Turner just grunted by way of a reply.

"How far up have we come?" asked Will.

"We'll be about halfway between Levels Z and Y," answered Turner.

"How far is that then?"

"About fifty feet."

"So, Level Y is a hundred feet above Level Z then?"

"One thirty, maybe."

"And how far down is Level Y."

"You planning on making a dash for it?"

"No," said Will, rather too quickly and petulantly.

"Ha!" responded Turner. "We need to trust each other, Will. You know I'll get you out of here, don't you?"

"It's what you'll do then that worries me," replied Will, surprising himself at his own frankness.

"I've not decided myself yet," snapped Turner. "But I can promise you, boy, I won't be hurting you. And I certainly won't be molesting you, either."

Will didn't know what to think of that, but he still didn't trust Turner. And he still planned to make a dash for it when the time was right. He just needed his sight to return. If it did between here and the surface, he had every chance of getting away from Turner. If it didn't, then maybe his best option was to stick with Turner, after all – at least until he heard the presence of someone else.

"Right," said Turner, now wheezing less than before. "Let's press on to level Y, young man."

CHAPTER 44 — DAVY

7th Tertiar, 1789   Day 98, 17:45

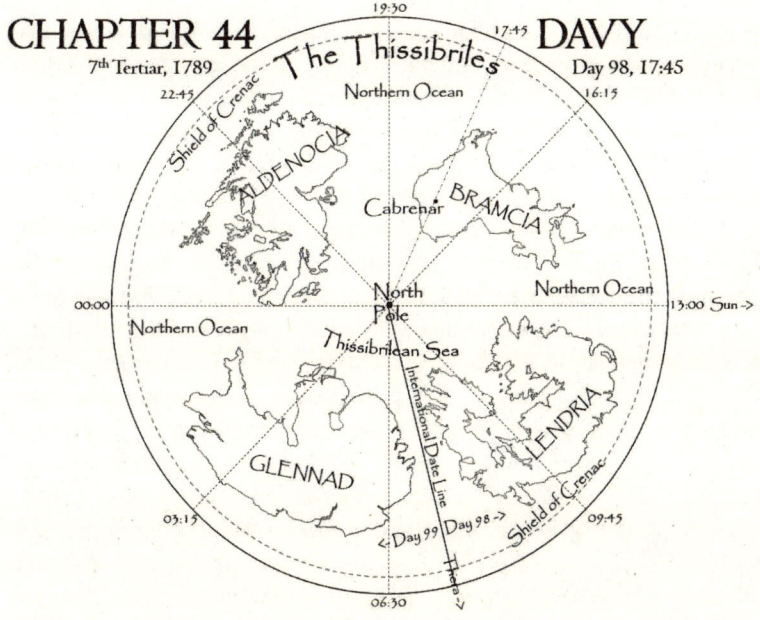

The sun was beginning to set to the west of Axe Edge and the hills beyond, the sky ablaze with yellows, oranges, pinks and even a deep purple. Davy briefly enjoyed the spectacle, and then diverted his attention back to their busy camp at the top of the upcast shaft, where an array of candles had been lit in preparation for the evening shift. The area was bustling with extra bodies, as helpers had arrived with trolleys and wheelbarrows to ship the stricken miners back to the pithead. From there, they would be taken by horse and cart to the infirmary at Craffid – although it was clear to Davy that some of them would not get there alive. Despite this, he was still refusing to believe that Robbie or Will were dead. Or Will's twin brother, Dylan, for that matter. They were just too young to die.

Some of the thrusters were younger still.

Davy's thoughts were interrupted as he spotted Vin Ellis. He jumped off the low wall he'd been sitting on and intercepted the engineer. "I need you to take me down with you at 17:50, Vin."

Vin looked at him. "It's not your shift, Davy. You're going down again at 18:20."

"I need to go down with you, Vin. By my reckoning, Jed's team will have got to my mate's bay."

"Sorry, Davy, lad. Jed and I are responsible for everyone's safety, and we're not sending you boys down in anything less than one in three shifts."

Vin noticed Davy's disappointment. "Come with me, son," he said. "Let me show you the plan of the mine. I know where Robbie Russell was mining, and I think your 18:20 shift will be bang on for finding him."

Davy followed Vin across to his pile of documents that were weighed down by a large stone on top of one of the trolleys at the rear end of the hoist. Vin un-scrolled one of the documents across another trolley, using the stone and a miner's lamp to pin it down at both sides. "Right, here's the bottom of the upcast," he said, pointing at the bottom left-hand side of the plan. "And here's where we found our first casualties," he added, pointing to an area some way to the right, marked at roughly four hundred yards. "Now, you apply that same distance for Jed's team, minus a bit for the extra distance, and you're here," he said, pointing to an area a few yards west of the Level X, Y and Z downcast shaft. "When I go down, I'll get to about here," he said, pointing to an area a few yards before the cross-cut flat between the main gallery roadway and the main offshoot. "Assuming we've not hit fires, of course. And if we haven't, that means that your next shift will get to around here," he said, pointing to an area further right. "Now you weren't mining west of the cross-cut flat, were you?"

"No, we were roughly a hundred yards east of it," confirmed Davy.

"Well, there you are then, son. Let's stick to Plan A. Now, if you don't mind, I need to gather my troops." And with that said, Vin was off, roll-calling before his group descended, on schedule, at 17:50. Between 18:00 and 18:10, Jed's first team came up in the kibble in two shifts, supporting more miners. All of the casualties were in a bad way, but Davy took heart from the fact that they didn't look any worse than Denny and Tommy whom his team had rescued an hour earlier. Davy then busied himself, helping the casualties onto their makeshift transport, offering water and encouragement, and helping some of the porters get the trolleys up the first and steepest part of the hill. By this stage in their rescue journey, most of the stricken miners were as high as kites and babbling like loons as the opium took its merciful effect. Then Jed Morris was running his next rollcall, and Davy was back in the kibble. This time, there was no trepidation; only eagerness to get on with the rescue and find his friends.

As the kibble descended, Davy was hoping he would see more casualties in a similar state to the earlier ones, and he held his breath as he saw the approach of the gallery floor. He could hear voices, and sense movement. And then…there they were. Rescued miners. Still alive. Davy's heart soared. Quite apart from the improving chances of Robbie and Will's survival, he was ecstatic at how many miners they were saving. Four from his team's first foray, five from the next, and then…will counted them as the kibble hit the gallery floor – five more. Fourteen miners with a chance of survival. If he could just find Robbie and Will in the same state, he would truly rejoice.

Davy's thoughts flicked to Carys. She would know by now that Robbie was in the middle of this. Davy then felt a pang of guilt at not passing on news that he was unharmed to his own Mam and Daisy. Of course, Stan Eckersley would have put their minds at ease by now, although being part of the rescue team still put himself and his comrades in danger. Carys and Daisy would be amongst a large crowd of terrified, anxious, grieving relatives at the pit head. In fact, the whole village would be there – including poor Edyth Lowe who would be frantic for news of her two boys.

Davy shook his head, forcing himself to focus on rescuing miners. He stepped out of the kibble and listened hard to the handover, with Vin telling Jed that they needed to move faster and stay down for five-to-ten minutes longer, as the rescue parties were travelling increasingly greater distances. He also heard Vin say that he was finding breathing harder than his team – presumably due to his extra half-hour or so of exposure to harmful gases. Davy, along with the same crew of Job, Josh, Doc, Pat and Daff, were also about to extend their time below ground to an hour. At present, Davy felt he wasn't breathing any different than he would on a normal shift, but he still pulled his grey scarf up and over his nose in readiness.

With their handover complete, Jed led his team up the main gallery at a brisk pace, whilst Vin and his team took the latest casualties up in the kibble. They soon reached the point at which they had conducted their first rescue. Davy spotted the X that Vin had marked on the wall, and then looked across to where he'd found his first dead miner – the poor soul lying on his back with his clawed, charcoal hands in front of his face. But the bodies had gone. Jed Morris read his mind. "They've been stored where the furnaces are, Davy. We'll be bringing the dead out last, son – assuming this mine doesn't blow again, that is."

Davy didn't know what to say to that. He was part-horrified with himself for thinking they would have just left them where they had died. Not that he would be leaving Robbie. But he mustn't think that way. Robbie would be alive – like the fourteen men they had rescued already.

Five minutes later, they passed the second downcast shaft and were approaching the cross-cut flat. It was here that they found the third X – the furthest point that Vin's last party had got to. Davy could see that there were more bodies on the ground in front of him, and again, some of them were moving and breathing. Just up ahead was the narrow exit from the cross-cut flat.

As the others set to tending the injured, Davy couldn't help but look a little further on. Jed Morris noticed, but allowed it. As Davy passed the cross-cut flat, he began to traverse a curve in the gallery. After a few more paces, his heart nearly stopped. He could feel heat. And he could see shadows flickering; he could hear a distant crackling, too. It was his worst fear. But how far ahead were the flames?

Torn between going on and doing the right thing by Jed Morris, Davy forced himself to turn around and report back to Jed. As he approached, Jed looked up from where he was tending a stricken miner. "There are flames up ahead," said Davy, simply.

"I know, son," was Jed's response. Vin told me. We'll not be able to go much further."

"Can I…"

Jed Morris looked at him – and then just motioned with his head that it was all right for Davy to go and look for Robbie and Will.

"Thanks Mr Morris," he said, before turning and hurrying around the curve, a terrible dread gripping his heart. A stricken miner groaned as he passed and reached out to him. "I'll be back in two minutes," said Davy, numbly. "I promise." Davy felt terrible leaving the man; truly terrible. But then he recognised Robbie's bay as he approached, and his sense of dread increased with every step. There were figures strewn around all over the ground. But no boys. No Will.

Then Davy recognised someone. Despite the blackened state of the figure, Davy recognised Dai Morgan's ravaged supervisor overalls. He knelt by the body and felt for a pulse – but it was way too late for Dai. Davy bowed his head and said a brief prayer for Dai, then he gently closed Dai's staring eyes, knowing the action would haunt him for the rest of his life. Steeling himself, he moved on to the next body. Also dead. As were the miners sprawled to the left and the right. This was looking bad. Given the flames up ahead, this was possibly where the explosion had originated.

Davy then heard a rattle of breath from just up ahead. Despite the blackened state of the figure, Davy knew it was Robbie. He was still alive. *Strong as an ox.*

"Robbie," he sobbed.

The figure on the floor opened his eyes. "Davy," he rasped. "Knew you'd come."

Davy rushed to his friend's side and proffered his water flask. "Here you go, mate," he said, pulling down his makeshift mask as he spoke. "Get some of this down you?"

Robbie opened his mouth and let the water flow in – but too fast. He began to choke.

"Easy, easy," said Davy.

Mercifully, Robbie stopped choking after a few seconds – but Davy could see the agony the action brought to his ruined body. "Water!" Robbie managed to blurt out. "You bastard!" he gasped. "Should've been…ale!"

Davy laughed, despite his tears. "Robbie," was all he could say.

Robbie offered him his hand. It was blackened, blistered and hideously sore – but Davy still took it. It was hot, too – but Robbie didn't let go, despite the pain it must have brought. "You're my…best friend," he gasped.

Davy was unable to respond. Both his eyes and his nose were streaming, now.

"You make sure…you marry…Daisy…Davy," said Robbie, before his chest became wracked with coughing.

Davy was beside himself. This was torture. Then he suddenly remembered something urgent. "Will," he said. "Where's Will?"

Robbie's coughing subsided after another twenty seconds. Davy gave him another drink – this time at a shallower angle. Finally, Robbie stabilised. "He got out, Davy."

Davy's eyes widened in disbelief. "He got out! What do you mean?"

"Saved him. Smothered him. Sent him…to find you." Robbie suddenly looked alarmed. "You haven't seen him?" A new choking fit set in, and hideous rasping noises issued from poor Robbie's throat and chest.

"Robbie, easy, easy," responded Davy, helplessly, his mind racing. "I'm an idiot, mate. I saw two boys go up in the last kibble," he lied. "One of them must have been Will – but we were just too focused on our mission to notice."

"Thank God!" exclaimed Robbie, settling his head back on the floor. Then he seemed to remember something, and he raised his head again, painfully. "He was blind. Will was. The flash. Should be…temporary though."

Davy's mind was a wash of emotion and questions. Will was in relatively good health. But as far as he knew, no one had found him either. This was another massive worry. More imminently, his best friend was dying before his eyes – and yet he still had a duty to perform.

"What happened?" he asked, simply.

Robbie began coughing again. Davy waited patiently for him to stop. "It was Dylan!" he gasped.

"Dylan!" exclaimed Davy. "Here!"

"Something was wrong. He was running…towards us…with a naked candle -." Robbie broke off. This time the coughing was violent, and at the end, Davy saw his friend cough up blood.

"All right, Robbie, easy Robbie, easy. Don't talk any more, mate. I'm going to get you out of here."

As Davy tried to rise, Robbie just held on to his hand, and looked back at him. They both knew what that look meant. Davy knelt back down again, a fresh tide of emotion catching his throat and weakening his chin.

They remained there in silence for a minute or so, Robbie with his eyes closed. *What unbearable agony must he be in?* Then he spoke again. "You're my…best friend," he repeated – this time barely more than a whisper.

"I know," sobbed Davy.

Robbie's eyes then opened and looked straight into Davy's. His voice was still only a whisper. "Tell Carys…that I love her. Tell me Mam…too. And you…Davy. I…love you too. Brother."

Davy was stunned. He couldn't think what to say back. And then it was too late. Robbie's hand went slack.

Davy just bowed his head as an immense grief began to well up, threatening to consume him – but he knew that he couldn't succumb to it. He had other responsibilities, not only to the other stricken miners, but to Will, especially. He therefore lifted his head and looked at Robbie. "I've got to go now, mate," he said softly. He gently disengaged his hand from Robbie's, which flopped to the gallery floor. Davy then gently closed Robbie's eyes and said a prayer for his precious soul. He then stood and looked at his friend for one last time. "God bless you, Robbie. We'll be back to lay you to rest. I promise."

Davy then turned and re-traced his steps to the stricken miner who had reached out to him earlier. He was in better shape than Robbie. Davy handed him his water flask and watched as the miner drank, gratefully.

"Sorry about that," said Davy, nodding in the direction of the main shaft.

The miner reached for Davy's hand, which caused a further swell of grief at the memory of a minute earlier. "I heard you, son," said the miner. "Down there," he nodded. "I'd have done the same."

That gave Davy some strength. "Well," he began. "I'm not going to lose you as well, mate. What's your name?"

"Dai," he responded. "Dai Probert." Davy knew the name – one of the older miners.

"Well, Dai Probert. Are you able to stand?"

"Aye, with your help, Davy lad."

Davy raised his eyebrows. Dai knew who he was.

"Your reputation precedes you, son," said Dai Probert with a pain-filled grin.

Davy helped Dai to his feet. Like all the other survivors, he was in a bad way, but Davy already instinctively knew when a miner was or wasn't going to make it. Dai Probert was going to make it.

As he led Dai Probert back towards Jed Morris' rescue party, Davy glanced back once towards the main shaft, and whispered what he'd said earlier. "God bless you, Robbie."

CHAPTER 45 — ARRAN

7th Tertiar, 1789 — Day 98, 19:00

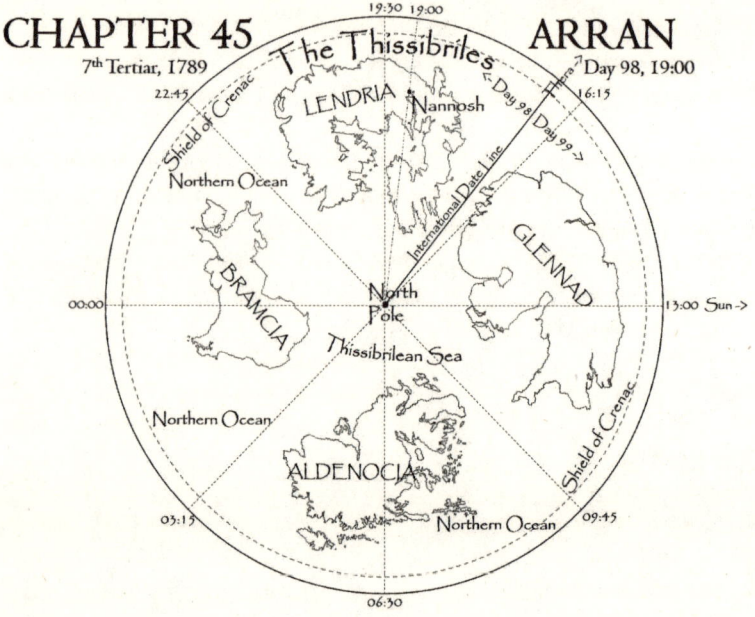

At thirty-seven, Arran Reed was the second youngest Astronomer Royal in Lendria's history. There were many who had cast doubt on his appointment, feeling that old Farrell, or long-serving members of the Royal Observatory like Doyle and Mullins had better credentials for the role. None of them had had a civil word to say to Arran in the six weeks since his appointment.

Arran pulled his eye away from the eyepiece of Old Grand, and ran a hand through his straight, collar-length brown hair. *This was why he had to be sure.* He looked down the outer casing and long brass barrel of the most powerful telescope in Nannosh Royal Observatory – but his cornflower-blue eyes weren't focused. Like his mind, they were millions of miles away.

Arran had first spotted the object around twelve weeks ago. Unconcerned, he had felt it was either an asteroid forced out of the asteroid belt by the strong gravity field of the gas giant, Rufus Macula, or it was a meteoroid which was a fragment of one of the asteroids created following a collision with one of its fellows. Either way, it appeared to have been jettisoned out beyond the asteroid belt towards the inner solar system.

It was another eight days before Arran had sought out the object again and another nine after that – by which time the object had bypassed Tarmia and its gravitational field and was headed towards Thera. By this stage, though, Arran was confident it was a small asteroid and not a meteoroid and therefore probably wouldn't burn up in another planet's atmosphere. Thereafter, he had felt compelled to track its course on a daily basis. This had enabled him to work out its likely trajectory for the following months, which predicted it would pass Thera by several million miles. But seven days ago, the asteroid had started to veer slightly on its trajectory, bringing it into line with Thera's orbit around the sun – and against odds of several million to one, to a point in Thera's orbit where the two objects would likely arrive simultaneously.

Having now reviewed the asteroid's course from the last twenty-six hours, Arran began adding these coordinates into his overall model, hoping against hope that it would show a trajectory veer back towards its original course. But it didn't. Within seconds, Arran was sweating profusely. It was becoming ever-more certain that – at best – the asteroid was going to pass dangerously close to Thera.

Arran's dilemma remained. Did he risk raising the alarm, only for the thing to pass millions of miles beyond Thera and make him a laughing stock, or did he remain cautious and risk being vilified for not calling out sooner? Caution had been well-founded so far, as there was little point terrifying the world over something that might never happen. Neither would it have been wise to raise a potential false alarm which could lead to widescale anarchy. But now that he had strong evidence, he had a responsibility to the world and could not procrastinate any longer.

Arran stood, grabbed his cloak and then began placing his rolled-up charts into a large satchel bag. He knew to whom he must go first. It would be a major slap in the face for the incumbent sages – but then they should have treated him with more respect, shouldn't they?

The house of his former mentor, Professor Erasmus Doran, was in the hills, a good three leagues east of Nannosh, but Arran reckoned he could make it in less than an hour on Rum Dearg.

Two minutes later, Arran was tapping his heels to the flank of his dun stallion with the red dorsal stripe and was soon racing down the hill on which the Royal Observatory was set. He then had to slow down as he weaved his way east out of the busy streets of Nannosh, which were packed with people, carters, other riders, and numerous horse-driven carriages, before pushing Rum Dearg as soon as they hit the outskirts. By the time he was climbing into the hills, the sun had disappeared, and Arran was thankful for the moonlight. Eventually, he slowed his dun down to navigate the narrow path around the north face of the range, some two thirds of the way up.

As ever, smoke was pumping out of the chimney of Star Cottage; Professor Doran always kept a good fire. Arran quickly trotted Rum Dearg into the professor's stables, secured him in an enclosed bay, draped a handy cover over him, and fed him some hay. Then, with his satchel over his shoulder, he jogged around to the front of the cottage and rapped loudly, five times, on a front door of thick oak. Arran heard movement and an irascible voice within, but when Doran didn't appear, he rapped again, even louder.

"I'm coming for pity's sake," the voice inside grumbled. "What ungodly hour do you call this for a visit?" There was further chuntering as Arran heard a large key turn in the large lock. The door creaked open to reveal the grizzled face and straggly long grey hair of Professor Doran, Arran's immediate predecessor as Astronomer Royal – and now very much retired.

"Oh, it's you m'boy," said Doran when he saw Arran, his voice softening. "What the deuce are you doing here at this hour?"

"Very urgent business, professor. Lendria needs you."

"Oh, she does, does she? Well so long as that business can be conducted here, you might as well come in," said Doran, opening the door wide to admit Arran.

As the door shut behind him, Arran took off his satchel and cloak and whistled, loosening his collar. "Are you trying to cook yourself, Prof?"

Professor Doran led Arran into his sitting room. "The north winds here cut right through you, son. Now then. What dire emergency has brought you three leagues out of Nannosh on a cold Spring night?"

"I need your help, Professor," said Arran, now very serious. "I fear I have the gravest of news – but I need a second opinion."

"I don't much care for the sound of that, m'boy. Sit down, sit down…and tell me all about it."

Arran opened his satchel and took out his charts, spreading them out over a low table. A Grandfather clock chimed once in the corner. "Before we start, is Aoifa still in good working order?"

"She certainly is," confirmed the professor.

"Good – as we're going to need her shortly."

Arran smoothed out his top sheet, which plotted the course of the asteroid close-up, with no reference to where it currently resided in the heavens. "Now, this is my problem, Professor. I first spotted this beastie twelve weeks ago, when you were still with us. A distant asteroid or meteoroid. Didn't think anything of it at the time, but after a couple of weeks of recording its course, I started to get vaguely concerned."

"Go on," encouraged the professor.

"As you can see, the first sheet is the course of an asteroid way out beyond our orbit." Arran then took the first chart off the table and placed it on the floor, revealing the second chart. This one showed the same plotted course, but tiny when compared to the first sheet and hovering in the top right of the chart. In the foreground was the planet of Thera marking its location in eighty-five days' time – and between Thera and the asteroid was a dotted line – linking one with the other. "And this, after twelve weeks of plotting," said Arran, "is my estimate for its trajectory up to Midsummer's Day."

Professor Doran stared at the chart, transfixed.

"Now I obviously don't want to go ringing any alarm bells this early in my tenure for something that isn't going to affect us. But I also need a second opinion – from someone who isn't looking to stab me in the back."

Professor Doran looked up at Arran, his face grave. "You've done the right thing, m'boy. Come on – let's go and fire up Aoifa, and you can show me where this little beastie is."

Half an hour later, Professor Doran finished drawing his own orbital interpolation, using Arran's figures from the last twelve weeks, all mapped onto a rough outline of Thera's inner solar system in eighty-five days' time. He also had the asteroid striking Thera.

The two men sat in heavy silence for a while, both fully aware of the appalling responsibility that they now had. Eventually, Arran spoke. "And you agree that it's about half a league wide?

"We'll know better in another three or four weeks. But yes, that's my estimate, too."

"And you agree, that on current trajectory and speed, it's going to hit on the first of Quinar?"

"I do."

"So, we've got less than ninety days then?"

Professor Doran didn't answer that. "So much for a long retirement," he said, morosely.

"You will come with me to explain this to the Ocateshia, won't you?"

"Of course, m'boy," said Doran, snapping out of his melancholy. "But not tonight. I'll put you up in my spare room – and I promise I will ride with you to Parliament House, first thing tomorrow morning."

"Thank you, Professor. I really appreciate that."

"It's the least I can do. And well done, m'boy, well done. It may not be the happiest news for Thera, but at least we can now prepare for it. And that's thanks to you, m'boy. It will most-likely be known as Reed's Rock, by the way, you do realise that don't you?"

"No thank you," responded Arran, briefly alarmed that his name might be associated with such a potentially devastating event, before switching his focus. "Do you agree with me, though, that until that thing is a few weeks out from Thera, we'll have no idea *where* it's going to strike?"

"I do indeed agree."

Arran thanked the professor, and then wandered over to one of the bedroom windows which looked out onto the northern sky. Professor Doran walked over to join him, his pale blue eyes looking in exactly the same place. They stood in silence for a few minutes before Arran spoke. "The question is," he said, turning to face his former mentor. "Are we the first to spot it…or are there other eyes, right now, gazing up at it as we speak."

CHAPTER 46 — CALIDIUS

7th Tertiar, 1789 — Day 98, 19:00

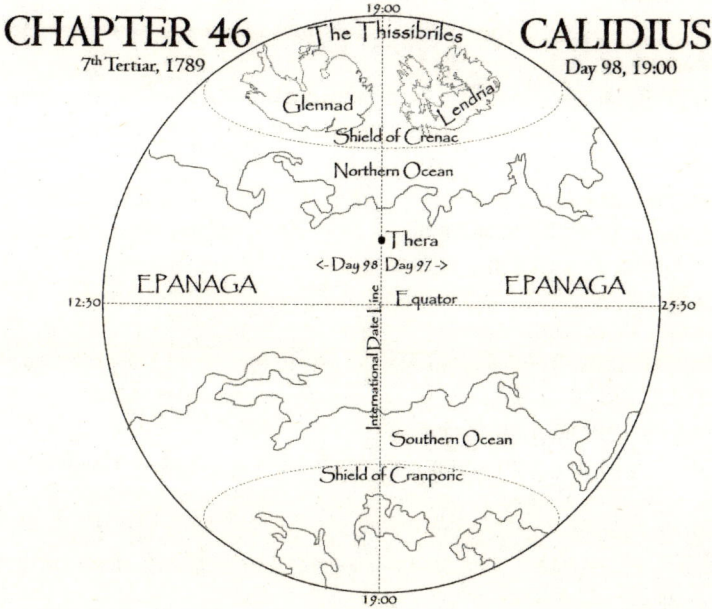

Four hundred leagues to the south, Calidius Antoninus Dominius eased his eye away from the giant reflector telescope in the Imperial Observatory at Thera, and turned to face those gathered, his mouth a grim slit. Aged thirty-one and the heir to the Theran throne, he had never been anything less than one hundred per cent certain he would be crowned the 316th Emperor of Thera – a line which stretched back over 2,100 years. But from what his Chief Astronomer, Gaius Maurus, had just told him, his father – Vitasian Flavius Dominius – now had a very good chance of being the 315th and *last* Emperor of Thera.

"You're now certain?" he asked of Gaius, a short and skinny fellow in robes a size too big.

The Chief Astronomer's constant tic in his left eyelid went into overdrive. "It will strike our world in around eighty-five days, Your Majesty," came the reed-thin response. "Of that, there is no doubt."

"And we cannot yet forecast where?"

"Not yet, Your Majesty."

"Valerius?" commanded Calidius.

"Yes, Your Majesty," asked a quietly-spoken and saintly-looking white-haired man, with a closely-cropped white beard and wearing the white robes of a senator.

"I want a meeting of the Senate in the *Curia* in one hour. I do not care that the hour is late."

"Yes, Your Majesty. I will have them gathered immediately," he concurred, before turning and sweeping out of the observatory.

"Gaius?"

"Yes, Your Majesty."

"I will need you there for council."

"Of course, Your Majesty."

"How many charts do you have which demonstrate trajectory?"

"Just the three, Your Majesty."

"How many can you and your team create in one hour? They don't need to be painstakingly accurate."

"Will fifty suffice, Your Majesty?"

"Fifty will be fine, Gaius. One between four. Now, please hurry along."

"At once, Your Majesty".

"Lucinius?"

"Yes, Your Majesty?" responded a swarthy-looking man in his forties, with carefully oiled dark curls.

"Is there any chance you can drag my father away from his...*companions*?" sneered Calidius, the last word loaded with distaste.

"At once, Your Maj-."

"Wait! Don't bother. He can find out second-hand, tomorrow. All of you. Leave me now. Give me some time alone. I will address you all shortly in the *Curia*."

Calidius watched them all file out, one-by-one, after which a profound silence descended upon the ancient, but opulent observatory. He sat down wearily on one of the marble steps and put his head into his hands. The one thing he had always yearned for was power. True, he ran the Empire in all-but name, but it wasn't absolute. Meanwhile, his lazy, fat, deviant father pleasured himself all day long with girls and boys, whilst eating and drinking himself into a stupor – and with little discretion, either.

Calidius drew back his lips in fury. The humiliation of his mother, Messalina, was remorseless, and Calidius was watching her shrink before his eyes as month followed month; occasionally, he would also spot excessive concealer on her face, too.

Calidius blew out a long and weary breath. He now had two monumental problems on his hands, although the problem of the asteroid vastly outweighed the problem of his father. The former also now gave him a reason for removing the latter – which he would resolve personally –

perhaps even tonight, after announcing to the Senate the peril that the whole world faced. By that stage, no one would care about the sudden murder of his father; he may not even need to deny being the murderer.

Calidius turned to his left and saw his reflection looking back from a highly-polished copper urn. His was a cold, hard and cruel face, with a thin mouth, hawk-like nose and eyes as black as onyx. It was a face which struck fear into all those around him, exactly as he wished.

"Well," hissed Calidius, to his reflection. "Eighty-five days is better than never." And with that, he stood, and began to make his way towards the *Curia*, his mind already turning over the possibilities under which his world might still survive.

Fifty minutes later, Calidius raised his hands for silence, attempting to quell the numerous remonstrations.

"What's the meaning of this?"

"Why have we been called at such short notice?"

"What's so important that I have to give up my evening?"

When the hubbub had died down and all two hundred pairs of eyes were on him, Calidius paused, and slowly rotated through three hundred and sixty degrees. He coldly took in the five stacked but well-spaced rows of occupied wooden benches arrayed around the dais upon which he stood, this being the centrepiece of the *Curia*; a dais encircled at ground level by a beautiful mosaic floor of red, blue and cream. Elsewhere, the circular perimeter of the room was marked by high, vaulted windows, and beneath them – behind the assembled senators – were armed soldiers. Calidius was taking no chances.

Continuing his slow rotation, Calidius began his speech, eyeballing each and every senator. "Honoured members of the Senate of Thera," he began, before cutting straight to the chase. "I have called this emergency session, to inform you of the gravest threat that our Empire has ever faced."

A stunned silence greeted his delivery. It was not like Calidius to exaggerate. He was far too pragmatic for that. As the message sank in, Calidius imagined all sorts of conclusions being jumped to, most of them involving Thera's many enemies – pretty much all of whom were subjugated states. He decided to put them straight on that, immediately. "I regret to inform you, that this is not a human threat. This is not war. Neither is it a biological threat – in the form of pestilence or plague. Nor is it a geographical, geological or meteorological threat; there will be no devastating fires, earthquakes or rains for forty days. This threat," he said, pausing for effect, and then pointing a finger beyond the *Curia's* vaulted windows, "comes from beyond our world."

A genuine disquiet fell upon the Senate. Calidius did *not* make announcements of this type. His announcements and proclamations were about war and victory and conquest, and his policies were usually about *funding* war, victory and conquest. He had little time for anything that didn't further the might of the Neo-Theran Empire.

Calidius waited for silence, and then continued to rotate slowly as he delivered his chilling message. "I have with me, our esteemed Imperial Chief Astronomer, Gaius Maurus." Gaius got shakily to his feet, eyes darting left and right, nose twitching and his eyelid tic back in overdrive. "Gaius came to me some eleven weeks ago now, concerned about an unchartered object which had appeared in the night sky to the north. I am a pragmatic man, so I offered him all the assistance that he needed to be able to chart the object's progress and to attempt to predict its future trajectory."

Calidius paused before continuing his rotation. "As you all know, we have had meteoroids before. The majority burn up in Thera's atmosphere before they make planet-fall – becoming meteors. Occasionally, some land – and these are meteorites. Some of them – perhaps the size of a man's head – can cause considerable destruction. So," he paused, making sure everyone was paying attention. "Imagine what destruction an asteroid could do… that is half a league wide?"

This time an outpouring of consternation greeted Calidius' message. He was expecting that, so he let his senators express their misgivings. Eventually, one deep voice rang above the rest. "And you think this asteroid is going to strike Thera?" asked a large senator in his thirties, sporting a big black bushy beard. A hush fell, immediately.

Calidius turned to Gaius Maurus and nodded. Gaius cleared his throat, nervously. Despite his reedy voice, Gaius' response was very clear. "We *know* it is going to strike Thera."

If consternation had greeted Calidius' message, Gaius' message was greeted with absolute pandemonium. Calidius noticed two or three senators – for reasons he couldn't fathom – attempt to head for the exit. They were forcibly denied exit by the sword-drawn guards Calidius had posted before being firmly re-directed to their seats. No one was to leave the *Curia* without Calidius' authorisation.

Calidius picked up his staff of office and banged it on the mosaic floor. The hubbub gradually settled down. He deliberately waited until silence had fallen again. "May I remind you, gentlemen, that you are all Therans. Therans do *not* panic."

The man with the bushy beard spoke again, in similarly resonant tones. "Might we know what the Senate plans to do about this, Your Majesty?"

"Thank you, Eugenius. A sensible question. I will attempt to answer. But for anything that I say that is inaccurate," he said, looking at his Chief Astronomer, "Gaius, please do not hesitate to interrupt and correct me."

"Your Majesty," acknowledged Gaius.

"Half a league-wide or not, this potential destroyer – which we have named as Nessemi after our goddess of retribution – will not necessarily bring an end to our civilisation."

A few previously catatonic faces began to look more hopeful.

"It all depends where Nessemi strikes Thera," said Calidius. "If it strikes us here in north-western Epanaga, then I won't mislead you. We are all dead. The impact and resulting shockwave will destroy us outright. But the reality is, that if this asteroid strikes land *anywhere* in Epanaga – north, south, east or west – then we are probably all dead, too. This is because the impact will throw millions of tons of debris into the atmosphere, thus blocking out the sun's rays for years – hence all trees die, hence there will be no oxygen, and hence all animal life dies."

This time the rection was muted. Calidius almost felt sorry for them, struggling to take in the scale of it all. An hour ago, they had been eating supper, playing with their children or cavorting with their concubines.

"And," continued Calidius, "even if Nessemi hits land in the Thissibriles at the North Pole, or whatever land may lie towards our South Pole, the result will almost certainly be the same."

Calidius watched the dawning realisation spread across the assembled Senate.

"Yes, that's right," he nodded. "Conversely, if that asteroid strikes the Northern Ocean – or even better, the Southern Ocean, if there is such a thing – then life goes on."

Genuine hope began to filter around the room.

"And do you know where the asteroid will strike?" asked Eugenius.

Calidius turned to Gaius, who cleared his throat again. "Not yet, Senator Eugenius. We will have more idea when Nessemi is closer."

"And do you know *when* impact is likely to be."

"We do," confirmed Gaius. "Nessemi will hit Thera in eighty-five days' time, on the 1st of Quinar. Midsummer's Day."

Another great outpouring of consternation was released, with so many questions being asked simultaneously. Calidius allowed that. As the hubbub died away, an elderly senator on the front row stood up. "But we won't know the point of impact for another, what, twenty, forty, sixty days?" he asked.

"No, Praxus. We won't," confirmed Calidius, evasively. "This is a game of dice."

"Dice!" exclaimed Praxus.

"Yes, Praxus. A game of dice – in which the die has already been pre-loaded. In other words, there is nothing we can do about where and when the asteroid impacts. But what we *can* do is prepare for both the best-case scenario and the worst-case, too."

Once again, he had everyone's undivided attention.

"That is the purpose of this emergency Senate. We will begin to put my plans into preparation, starting first thing tomorrow morning. However, I want to make one thing very clear to each and every one of you." Calidius paused for effect. "News of Nessemi stays in this room, at least for the time being. If word gets out, I *will* find out who talked, and they *will* be executed. Cruelly. No matter who you are."

"But we can't not tell our wives," cried an elderly senator.

"You will *especially* not tell your wives," snapped Calidius.

"How are we supposed to carry on as normal?" asked another.

"You *will* carry on as normal," demanded Calidius. "We have much work to do, much preparation, and you will bury yourselves in that preparation, and this will help make it easier for you all to cope. If news of Nessemi gets out, there will be anarchy. That cannot happen. So, I say again. Any senator caught talking about Nessemi *will* be executed. I will *personally* execute you. Do you understand?"

A murmur of frightened agreement greeted Calidius' question, albeit with one or two exceptions. One of the objectors, a greying middle-aged man with a permanent sneer on his face, stood from his position on the third row. Ganatus was a long-time opponent of Calidius. "You can't possibly expect two hundred senators and one hundred legionaries," he said, sweeping his hand towards the occupants of the perimeter, "to keep news of this magnitude a secret. Such a notion is beyond naivety."

Calidius smiled in anticipation. He had prepared for this eventuality. The fact that it was Ganatus who had walked into the trap made it that much sweeter. "It's very simple, Ganatus. Anyone who leaks this secret is a traitor to the empire." Calidius paused for effect, before pinning Ganatus with an icy glare. "And we all know what happens to traitors, Ganatus." Calidius nodded at the two legionaries flanking him on the dais.

The soldiers immediately moved in on Ganatus who had already turned as pale as his robes. "What is the meaning of this?" he demanded, as he was seized roughly by the arms and dragged out on to the dais. "I demand you -. Unhand me -."

His protestation was cut off by the hilt of a sword, smashed into his nose by one of the soldiers. Between the two of them, they then shredded his white robes and ripped the strands of cloth free, leaving the terrified senator crouching naked on the dais, blood dripping from numerous fresh cuts. Meanwhile, any thoughts of remonstration from the assembled senators were curtailed as the one hundred legionaries arrayed around the outskirts of the *Curia* drew their swords and stepped up behind the back row of the assembled Senate.

"Remain still, all of you," commanded Calidius. "And witness how we Therans deal with traitors."

In response, the two soldiers on the dais pulled Ganatus upright and pinned his hands behind his back. Calidius, meanwhile, had drawn his wicked eight-inch curved dagger, and calmly drew a line across Ganatus' lower abdomen. Steaming snakes spilled out. Ganatus looked at the floor in disbelief, his eyes as wide as saucers. Then the pain hit, and Ganatus began to scream – at which point Calidius drew another line across his throat. Ganatus' body flopped to the floor like an abandoned sack.

Calidius sheathed his dagger and moved to one side to avoid the spreading blood and viscera. He turned back to face the Senate. "Sit down!" he commanded.

Every last senator obeyed.

Still icily calm, Calidius continued as if nothing had happened, whilst the two soldiers began to drag Ganatus' body from the *Curia*, taking a leg each and leaving a slimy trail behind them. "Now, the plans," began Calidius. He paused to ensure that everyone was paying attention. Satisfied, he continued. "Our best-case scenario is for the asteroid or comet to strike the Southern Ocean – if there is a Southern Ocean. This would result in zero impact on our culture here in Northern Epanaga. Southern Epanaga and whatever lies towards the South Pole, that's a different story. Their coastal towns, villages and cities would be totally destroyed by monstrous waves – maybe one or two-thousand feet high. I doubt anyone would be safe twenty leagues inland either, or even further inland along valleys through which rivers run to the coast.

"Exactly the same applies to the Thissibriles and Northern Epanaga, if the comet lands in the Northern Ocean. That is our second-best scenario. This we can prepare for, though. If we learn a mere two weeks or even ten days before impact, that the Northern Ocean is the point of impact, we will alert all Northern Epanagan settlements and we will evacuate everyone inland by at least thirty leagues. Anybody foolish enough to disbelieve us, and remain, deserves to die. Having said that, as the weeks roll by, that asteroid is going to become increasingly dominant in the night sky. So, unbelievers will make for a very special kind of fool."

Calidius paused in his monologue, taking stock of the reaction in the room. He couldn't tell whether they were more shocked by news of the asteroid or by Ganatus' brutal death. It made no difference to him. The main thing was that he had their undivided attention.

"For a Northern Ocean strike," he continued, "we also need to make plans for our boats, particularly our warships. For our most important ships, we will build land-rafts to help us portage them inland. For others, we will cluster them in the safest places along the northern Epanagan coastline. For example, the Gulf of Alglia is likely to be the most protected area of coastline due to the configuration of the coast there – an enclosed gulf accessed by a narrow channel. So, boats might survive here – particularly if the point of impact is thousands of miles away in the east.

"We then have the final scenario – a land strike. The further away from Thera, the better. But to stand any chance of survival, we need to start building underground shelters now. These shelters will be built at least a hundred leagues south of the northern Epanagan coastline, and we will build them in a line, twenty leagues apart – from Cabetia in the west to Acahea in the east. If later, we don't need them because the asteroid has struck the ocean, then nothing is lost. On the contrary, we rejoice – because our planet and our civilisation and our Empire will have survived. And, no doubt the shelters will be converted to other uses in the future.

A stunned silence descended upon the *Curia*. A good twenty seconds passed before anyone was brave enough to speak.

"I have a question about scenario number 3," said Eugenius, shakily.

"Please ask away, Eugenius," responded Calidius. "All constructive questions and opinions will be welcomed by me, so do not fear to ask."

"Of course, Your Imperial Majesty, thank you. There is no affront or negative connotation intended by this question. But how do we keep the building of the shelters quiet for such a long time?"

"Because we build them in remote places, Eugenius. They will all be closer to the Desolation than the coast, and far enough away from civilisation when the truth is revealed – otherwise they would be overrun in hours. Of course, we will guard them heavily and repel anyone unauthorised who approaches. I realise that the build activity will be spotted by a few nomads – and there will be questions asked. The response will be that the work is top secret, and in the interest of the Empire. Which is completely true, of course. And by the time those nomads make the correct connection, it will be too late for them."

"Another question for scenario three," said the aged Valerius. "How many people are we going to accommodate in each of these shelters, and who will be selected?"

"An excellent question, Valerius. Our initial estimates are that each shelter will be able to accommodate five hundred people for a timespan of two years."

"And how many shelters will there be?" asked swarthy Lucinius.

"Our initial estimate is twenty," replied Calidius, watching his Senate now doing some mental arithmetic. He spared them the brain-ache. "That's approximately ten thousand people."

A stunned silence greeted this revelation. Eventually, Valerius voiced everyone's fears. "But Thera alone is home to half a million people. Northern Epanaga, sixty million. Only ten thousand people will survive?"

"Yes, Valerius. And I can't even guarantee that those ten thousand will survive, either. These are unprecedented events."

"You never answered Valerius' question about *who* will be selected," pointed out Lucinius.

"Well, to put your mind at rest, Lucinius, all two hundred of the Theran Senate are included, as are their immediate families. We estimate that to be around one thousand people. The remaining nine thousand will be those required to build a new world. Scientists, medics, architects, builders, shipbuilders, and so on." Calidius almost smirked as he observed a synchronous reaction of selfish relief sweep around the room.

"What about our soldiers?" asked Lucinius.

"Our generals, such as Macrinus and Theodosius will be recalled from their Eastern Epanagan campaigns, starting tomorrow. Senior soldiers will be selected, as will some of our best warriors and gladiators, along with all the legionaries present in this room and who have all been pre-briefed ahead of this session. Their families will be accommodated, too. But let me be clear, gentlemen. If the worst-case scenario happens, and we need those shelters – and by some miracle, most of the ten thousand survive – we won't be needing too many soldiers, thereafter."

Calidius let that sink in.

"You mean…"

"Yes, Lucinius. There will be no one left over which to rule."

It had been a very long night, but it wasn't yet over. The Senate session had been wound up half an hour earlier. Tomorrow would see the commencement of their plans to start building the shelters.

Calidius felt nothing but frustration at this infernal asteroid, but one positive thing was that it had brought forward his father's fate. His previous preference had been for a gradual poisoning over a period of six to eight weeks. But in this new doom-threatened world, taking six to eight weeks to poison him to death meant six to eight weeks less of his own reign as Emperor. That, Calidius would no longer allow.

Calidius briskly approached his father's private room, passing torches mounted in golden sconces attached to the wall every three paces, and which were casting flickering shadows upon the walls and ceiling. He noted that at least there weren't the usual disgusting noises of indulgement emanating from behind the large white double doors. That meant they were probably all asleep – which would make his task considerably easier. As did the fact that his father's two guards were no longer present – both offered sanctuary within the selected ten thousand along with their families.

Calidius drew his sword gently so as not to give out a tell-tale rasp. He then kept walking, didn't even break his stride before pushing open the unlocked doors and striding over to the bed.

It was the boy who saw him first – a second before Calidius thrust his sword right through the youngster's heart. Calidius' strength and fury was such that the tip of his sword punched out of the boy's back, bits of heart and spine splattering the wall behind. Calidius rapidly withdrew the sword with a hideous sucking noise and then lifted it high, ramming it down with both hands through the chest of his befuddled, naked father. This time, he left the sword in place and quickly grabbed the girl by her long and lustrous black hair before she could run away. Calidius hadn't quite timed everything to perfection, though, as the girl had managed to get out one horrified shriek, but the second died in her throat as Calidius pulled her to him, his knife already drawn and at her throat – and still spattered with the blood of the unfortunate Ganatus. "Keep quiet, or die."

With the girl's naked body taught against him, Calidius felt himself responding. He'd been determined not to do this. He really had. It was supposed to be three quick thrusts of his sword and out. But he was Calidius. The Emperor's son -.

No, thought Calidius, breaking off that line of thought with growing exultation. He was already Calidius Antoninus Dominius, the 316th Emperor of Thera. And as such, he would claim his first prize. She was certainly beautiful. But then father always picked them beautiful – both boys and girls.

Ten minutes later, the girl was dead and Calidius was sated. The day after tomorrow, he would be crowned Emperor.

CHAPTER 47   MAGNUS
8th Tertiar, 1789   Day 99, 18:30

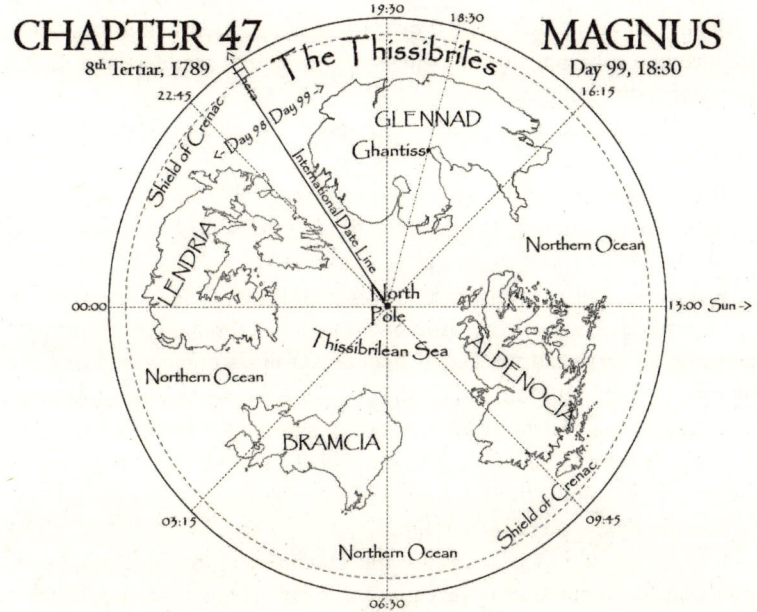

Prince Magnus stalked into the Council Room. He had been in a foul temper since the previous day, following the failure to come up with any firm leads on Jake Oscom's whereabouts. Despite his black mood, though, he was still resplendent in his dark blue and gold three-piece ensemble. As ever, a hat – a navy tricorn, today – hid the raw scar on his scalp.

Silently, he took his place at the head of the long set of tables that had been laid out for their daily updates. To his left was James Cecil, the Lord Chamberlain, and facing Cecil to his right was John Russell, the Lord High Constable. Other high-ranking officials were seated towards the top of the table, while further down there were the forty or so agents that they had working for them in Ghantiss.

Magnus looked for empty seats. There were a couple. *They had better be the bearer of good news.* In the meantime, Magnus started going down the table for updates, one-by-one, each getting 'the look' when they disappointed. They were about half-way through when the door opened – framing a thirty-something, ginger-haired, fresh-faced official called Willis – one of Nash's former agents. All eyes turned towards Willis, Magnus' searching the man's face for good news. The agent's face broke into a wide grin.

"You've got him?" asked Magnus, hope surging.

"Not got him, Sir," said Willis. "But I know where he went. *And* where he's going."

Magnus stood up and walked over to Willis. A good half a foot taller, Magnus put both hands on the ginger-haired man's shoulders and kissed him hard on the forehead.

"Please," said Magnus, steering Willis towards the table. "Take a seat and tell all."

Flushed with embarrassment, Willis took the nearest empty chair, while Magnus moved back to his place at the head of the table. Willis cleared his throat. "It was Mr Hoskyns who put me onto them."

Hoskyns looked as surprised as anyone at this news.

Willis nodded at Hoskyns. "You mentioned that Oscom rescued Emilya Luca who, in turn, had rescued a small dog. You also mentioned that the dog was found by Mr Marler at Danny Luca's bakery. So, knowing there was an injured animal, I decided to look up healers. This eventually led me to the home of Elyse Dolmen. She's forty years of age, and has a reputation as a healer who uses unorthodox methods."

"Unorthodox?" questioned Magnus.

"Lots of herbal-based remedies and concoctions that doctor's frown upon. But her reputation is very good; she gets results. Anyway, when I called at her cottage, no one was in. One of her neighbours told me she'd not been home for days. This aroused my suspicion, so I asked her point blank if she'd had any visits from a baker, recently. 'Oh yes,' the neighbour said. 'Danny Luca, from Luca's Bakery on Irongate.'"

Magnus leaned forwards his attention focused on every word.

"That neighbour couldn't tell me anything more, but when I visited the old gentleman on the *other* side, he told me that he'd seen Elyse Dolmen leave on the road to Ghenetenos, four days ago – accompanied by a young girl with a tiny dog...and a middle-aged man who fits Oscom's description."

"Ghenetenos!" said Magnus thoughtfully. "So, they went inland. Were they mounted?"

"They were, Sir, but the old gent reckoned that the girl with the dog couldn't ride, and the other two were laughing at her attempts to mount her horse. He reckoned it was her first time in the saddle."

"Excellent. They'll not have got far then. This also proves that Danny Luca was lying to me all along – he knew damn well his daughter wasn't in Dominniul. What more do you know, Mr Willis?"

"I did some checking up on Elyse Dolmen. Her family actually *comes* from Ghenetenos. They're druids – and hence the alternative medicine. In fact, her brother, Emrys, is the Head Druid, and her mother, Martha, is a High Priestess and is supposed to have the Second Sight."

"Pah!" sneered Magnus. "She'll not see us coming! Anything else"?

"Yes. I mean, they'll probably have stopped off at Ghenetenos, maybe for more than one night. But the old fella back in Ghantiss – Ms Dolmen's neighbour – was sure he heard them mention Earl's Leet."

"Ha!" exclaimed Magnus. "They probably think they'll be safe up in the Bleaklow Hills, particularly in prim-and-proper Earl's Leet. This is excellent news, Mr Willis. And excellent work, too."

"I'm just happy to have been of service, Sir," responded Willis, still grinning with delight. "Oh, there was one other thing, Sir."

Magnus looked at him expectantly.

"I asked the old gentleman if there was anything else that he could recall, and he said he heard Lendria mentioned twice."

"Lendria!" mused Magnus. "Maybe Earl's Leet is just en-route to an east coast port, then. Well," he said, eyeing his audience, his earlier tension now gone. "This news changes everything. I'm tempted to grab a horse and head for Ghenetenos tonight, but given what Mr Willis has told us, a four-day head start is nothing if Emilya Luca can't ride. And even if they beat us to Earl's Leet, we'll soon root them out once we get there. So, I suggest that we set out first thing in the morning."

A rumble of agreement circulated up and down the long table.

"I will lead the expedition myself," said Magnus. "I will take you, Mr Hoskyns, and you, Mr Marler, and three of your men. Please choose three whom we can trust and can handle themselves."

"You should take four or five of my soldiers with you as well, Sir," suggested John Russell. "We're all aware that bandits operate in those hills beyond Ghenetenos, and there are now tales about Harry Black accosting travellers on the road to Earl's Leet as well."

"Harry Black," mused Magnus, setting aside the notion that the Lord High Constable was trying to keep him observed and in-line by taking his own men along. "Can you imagine if we get Oscom *and* Black?"

"Maybe there's a connection between the two," suggested Marler.

Magnus narrowed his eyes. "Indeed," he mused. "From what we know of Oscom's past, they'd make perfect partners in crime. Anyway, Mr Russell, I agree to your offer – please assign me five of your best men. Other than that, I propose that we draw this meeting to a close and call off the search in Ghantiss. Feel free to have a couple of drams tonight, everyone. And thank you very much for your assistance over the last two days."

"We're not quite done, yet," said James Cecil, the Lord Chamberlain, his searching eyes all over Magnus' face.

"What do you mean?" asked Magnus.

"What about the Princess Alicya?"

Magnus managed to keep his face neutral, but inside he was cursing himself again – although his response was smart and quick. "Our only current route to my sister is through Jake Oscom, Lord Chamberlain," he began, haughtily. "That's why he is our number one priority. According to Willis here, he clearly didn't have Alicya with him when he left for Ghenetenos, and nor would any of us expect him to; it would be impossible to smuggle her out of Ghantiss. So, the man must have accomplices, here in Ghantiss. I'm *convinced* that Alicya is being held somewhere nearby."

"Very well," said Cecil, coldly. "I just thought our main priority was to find the Princess. Not to arrest Oscom."

"It amounts to the same thing, Mr Cecil, surely you can see that?"

"There's been no ransom note then?"

"No, there hasn't. Oscom is playing with us. He's hidden her away in Ghantiss, with accomplices, and plans to send the ransom note from the safety of Earl's Leet. But when we apprehend him, we will force him to reveal the names of his accomplices and the whereabouts of Alicya. I shall willingly torture the truth out of him myself. So, we *need* to take this opportunity, Lord Chamberlain – starting tomorrow. In the meantime," he began, fully aware that he was about to contradict himself from a few seconds earlier, "I suggest that you and Mr Russell continue leading the search for Alicya in Ghantiss."

James Cecil continued to regard Magnus, coolly. "Of course, Your Royal Highness," he said, eventually.

Sixty minutes later, Magnus was lying on his bed, a full glass of wine on the table beside him, and his scalp wound freshly treated. He was getting closer to playing his way out of this mess, although he was also finding it hard to forget the look of suspicion in James Cecil's eyes. And he really couldn't afford another murdered palace official!

The situation was clear, though. All he had to do was to track down Oscom and kill him. Emilya Luca was less important, but if she died in the crossfire, it wouldn't harm his cause. He would then maintain that Oscom's secret of Alicya's whereabouts had died with him – and hence Magnus' mother and father would never know what had happened to her, and Cecil's likely suspicions would be baseless without any evidence. Oscom would be charged posthumously, and Magnus could get on with his life – albeit making sure he never killed anyone again…at least not on palace premises, anyway.

Naturally, he didn't spare a second's thought for Freya Colin, who had died in this very bed just three days earlier. Or for her parents who had followed her to the afterlife last night in a tragic bakery fire…

CHAPTER 48

8th Tertiar, 1789

DAVY

Day 99, 12:30

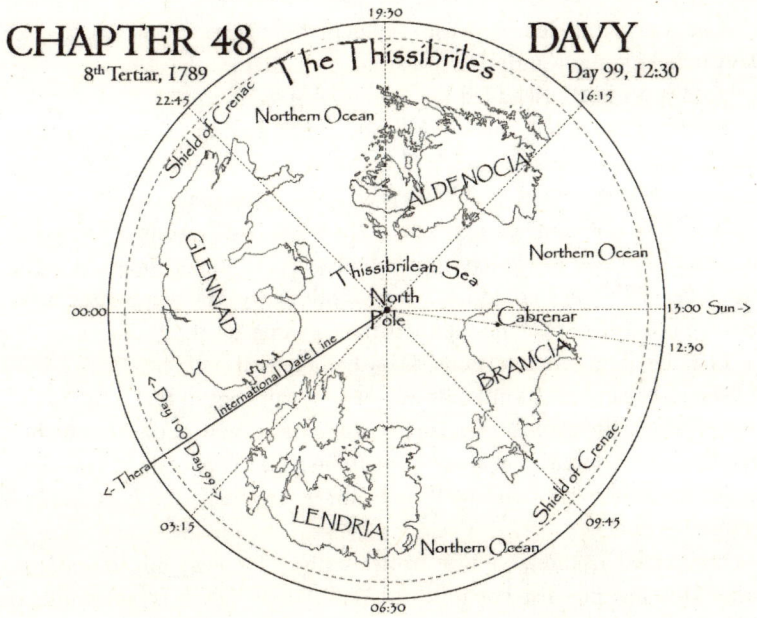

Davy Sheerin quickened his pace as he headed up the slope towards the pithead. He had remained on duty the previous night until well after midnight, travelling up and down the upcast shaft numerous times. Both Vin Ellis and Jed Morris had eventually ordered him to go home and rest, but he'd refused point-blank until they'd found Will Lowe. He'd even argued with Jed Morris – which under normal circumstances would have landed him in hot water. However, Jed was a good man, and understood what was driving Davy.

"Robbie Russell told me that Will was fine," he'd argued, at around 01:30 am.

"Listen, son," Jed Morris had replied, his hand on Davy's arm. "Robbie Russell is dead. You saw him die. I helped you bring his body out. When he was speaking to you, the poor soul was in unimaginable agony. He probably didn't know what he was saying."

"I'm telling you Jed: Robbie was lucid. He told me it was Dylan Lowe who caused the blast, with a naked flame. We know that's likely true, as we found poor Dylan's body twenty feet from where Robbie died. Survivors have told us of a commotion just before the blast and hearing a boy's voice. Robbie called it right, I know he did. He also told me that he'd shielded Will so that he only suffered minor burns to his face and arm. He knew exactly what he was saying, Jed. He wasn't hallucinating. He even told me that…" Davy tailed off, not wanting to reveal Robbie's final words.

"Told you what?" asked Jed.

"He asked me to tell Carys that he loved her. And to tell his Mam, too. And he also asked me to find Will and take care of him. Yes, he was in unimaginable pain – but he still knew what he was saying."

"But we've not come across Will," Jed Morris had reasoned. "If he was alive and well, we'd have seen him. You checked all the offshoots, *and* the cross-cut flat. No one could have done more, Davy. You're a bloody hero, man. You've helped save more miners than anyone."

"I need to help save one more," Davy had pleaded.

"Davy," began Jed. "Will Lowe was categorically not in that mine to the west of where the explosion occurred. I'm sorry, Davy, but as no one has seen him since yesterday at around 14:30, we have to presume he ended up *east* of the explosion – and we'll find him when the flames have burned themselves out."

Davy pulled his thoughts away from last night. He *was* going to find Will today. He'd just promised as much to Will's Mam, Edyth Lowe, who he'd spent the last hour with, trying to console her. Her grief was a terrible thing, having lost one son and the other still missing; grief laced with guilt for letting them both do a double shift, just for more money. Davy was desperate to find his young apprentice alive, but knew if he couldn't, the next most important thing was to find Will's body, so that Edyth could at least bury her sons together and properly grieve for both of them. The poor woman.

As Davy drew level with the pit office, he spotted Stan Eckersley sitting in his office chair, staring at the wall, unseeing, his normally sharp features somehow softened. Davy was reminded of Dai Morgan, Stan Eckersley's fellow foreman. Stan and Dai had worked together as boy and man for thirty-five years.

Davy popped his head around the office door. "You all right Mr Eckersley?"

Eckersley seemed to come out of his stupor. "Eh? Yes, yes, I'm fine, Davy, my boy," he responded.

Davy smiled inwardly. Stan Eckersley had rarely used his first name until yesterday. "Has the fire abated enough to start thinking about tackling No. 1 Shaft?"

"Fires are still burning, Davy. We'll not be going down No 1 today."

"Any news on Will Lowe?" asked Davy, hopefully.

"No, I'm sorry, Davy. I know you were fond of the boy. I won't deny him being missing has got us very concerned, but we've got to assume that he's ended up on the wrong side of the fires."

Davy winced, but then re-focused. "And what about Nate Turner?"

"Please, Davy, I know you're upset, but you've got to stop jumping to conclusions."

"I'm only asking if we've found him or not."

"No, we haven't. But then again, we've still not found thirty-one miners in total – and that total is including both Will and Nate."

"I know, Mr E, I know," said Davy, rubbing a hand over his face and dragging the skin downwards under his tired eyes. "Is there a team over at the upcast right now?"

"Yes," confirmed Eckersley. "Vin Ellis is leading. The emphasis today is on putting out the fires. Vin's got an idea about re-directing the water from the old lead mine sough into Level Z, somehow."

"Right, I'll get over and help, then. Speak later," said Davy, about to exit the office. Before he did, though, Stan Eckersley called him back.

"Oh Davy?" he said.

"Yes, Mr E?" said Davy, turning around.

"I'm so proud of you, my boy," he said, his voice briefly catching. He then controlled himself. "They're all saying you've saved more miners than anyone. We'll be making sure Mr Grey-Doogell knows."

Davy shook his head and looked Stan Eckersley in the eye. "Thanks for that, Mr E, but I don't want any fuss. Least of all from the Prime Minister. Right now, I just want to find those thirty-one miners. And particularly Will Lowe."

"Aye, Davy," agreed Eckersley. "We all do, son."

When Davy arrived at the upcast shaft, half an hour later, Vin Ellis had more plans laid out on a temporary bench and was addressing a group of around twenty bleak-faced miners. Vin paused when Davy approached. There was no back-slapping. They'd all carried out far too many of their colleagues, more dead than alive, with several of the latter having since succumbed to either their horrific burns or blood poisoning. "All right, Davy?" asked Vin.

"At your service again, Mr Ellis."

"Good lad," said Ellis. "Now then," he began, moving the plan around so that Davy could see. "We're looking to re-direct a handy water supply. You've just walked past it on your way down here."

"Aye, Stan Eckersley mentioned the old lead mine sough."

"That's right. It still pumps out thousands of tons of water a day, but at the moment, it all finds its way into Blackdale Ghyll, here," he said, pointing at the map. "But if we can get that flow re-directed to the downcast shaft, we'll have a steady supply of water for Level Z."

"Thousands of tons, though," said Davy, dubiously.

"Aye, it's dangerous, Davy. But we've got a plan. We've already got the biggest iron coal bucket that our colliery owns at the bottom of that shaft, mounted inside one of the wagons, and another bucket on the way. We need to control the flow of water, and as soon as the first bucket fills up, we switch the second one into place. We then haul the wagon down Level Z to the edge of the fires, and we unseat the bucketful of water into the face of the flames. There's no guarantee it will put the fires out, but it's worth a try. We don't have a better plan."

"I assume we're not going to re-direct all the water out of the sough?"

"Not initially. We're planning to build up in stages by cannibalising stone walls to help re-direct the flow."

The next hour was spent further up the hillside. The day was overcast and the wind was whipping at their clothing, but at least it wasn't raining. They had soon partially dammed the man-made sough that had been built to drain the old lead mines, and which emerged from the hillside amidst ferns, bracken and bramble as a low, brick-arched tunnel. Their damming efforts, using limestone purloined from nearby stone walls, had re-directed roughly a fifth of the flow so that it cascaded down the hillside towards the secondary downcast shaft, while the other four-fifths continued to flow down to Blackdale Ghyll. Looking into the blackness of the downcast, Davy could hear the water more than five hundred feet below, slapping into the iron coal bucket.

Satisfied with the volume of water, Vin selected six miners, including Davy, to head down the upcast shaft in the waiting kibble. On reaching Level Z, Davy was immediately struck by the purer air compared to yesterday – this thanks to Vin having reactivated the furnaces which had improved the circulation of air and gone some way to nullifying the poisonous gases. By the time they reached the foot of the downcast shaft, though, there was water everywhere and the iron coal bucket was four-fifths full. It took another ten minutes before the bucket began to overflow, by which time the second team had arrived, pushing a second coal bucket on top of another wagon – this one empty.

"Right, lads," said Vin, moving around to the rear of the first wagon. "Let's get this first bucket moving."

Davy joined him at the rear of the wagon, and between them, they managed to get it rolling, albeit with water sloshing over the sides of the bucket and soaking their trousers and boots. When a third miner joined them, they started to move faster, but were also losing more water. Vin put his hand up to stop anyone else joining them. "It's all right lads, just follow us. Any faster and we'll lose the bloody lot."

It took them fifteen minutes to reach the place where Robbie had died, and another minute to get to the fires. "I reckon this is further back than it was last night, Mr Ellis."

"I think you're right, Davy. Let's hope it's burning itself out."

"Lads!" called out Josh Goose, the urgency in his voice causing everyone to turn around. "We are further in. Look!"

They followed Josh's pointing finger. It was impossible to say how many charred bodies there were, huddled by the side of the wall. Even when they all moved across and held up their safety lamps, you still couldn't tell where one body ended and another started.

Eventually, Davy spoke. "How are we supposed to know who…" he tailed off.

Vin put his hand on Davy's shoulder and patted it. He didn't have a response. Eventually, Vin rallied his troops. "Right, men," he said. "We take them back in the wagon once we've emptied the bucket of water. It'll likely need all of us to carry the bucket, though.

So it was that seven sweating and straining men, managed to lift the huge bucket – which by now was only half-full – and shuffle painfully slowly towards the wall of flames. When they were twenty feet away and unable to get any closer because of the intense heat, they stopped, their muscles screaming in torment.

"Right," gasped Vin under the strain. "On the count of three. One, two, three."

All seven men flexed their muscles and helped to sling the water towards the fires. There was instant sizzling, and lots of steam. The water seemed to briefly cut a path through the flames, but they soon closed up again. The disappointment was palpable.

"Well," said Daff, voicing their thoughts. "This isn't going to work."

"I'm not giving up so easily, Daff," said Vin. "Look. I can still see water on the floor." But even as they watched, it began to evaporate.

"Well, we've got to at least try," said Vin. "I'll admit that if we're not making any headway after five or six trips, we'll have to have a re-think; try and fix up a pipe from the downcast, maybe."

"Or," began Davy, "if that doesn't work, and those fires just rage on, we could always re-direct the entire sough and flood Level Z."

Vin looked at Davy, approvingly. "Aye. That was my fall-back plan for a worst-case scenario."

Davy nodded, but still felt guilty at the ramifications for the remaining bodies. "Shouldn't we?" he said, indicating the charred remains of men; men who had been down here twenty-six hours ago, animate and alive, laughing and joking and discussing what they were going to eat for tea.

"Yes, come on boys," said Vin, and with that he started organising who should do what.

Ten minutes later, Vin and Daff were pushing the wagon with its grisly cargo back towards the upcast shaft, and Davy was one of five miners struggling with the iron coal tub – but which was considerably easier to carry without water in it. They were about halfway back when Davy felt his safety lamp come loose from his belt and fall to the floor.

"Sorry lads," he said, as he went to retrieve it. The other miners carried on without too much difficulty.

As Davy knelt to pick up his safety lamp, he noticed something glinting on the floor. He moved across to it and picked it up. He recognised it immediately. "Mr Ellis!" he shouted, urgently.

The crew up ahead stopped and turned around as one. "What you got there, Davy?" asked Vin Ellis.

Davy held it up. It was a penknife. "It's Will Lowe's," he said.

There was a stunned silence. Then Vin asked: "Are you sure?"

"I know it's his, Mr Ellis…because I gave it to him."

Vin Ellis started walking towards Davy. "All right, so he must have dropped it."

"Exactly," said Davy. "Which means he *did* head off west of the fire, after all.

"He might have dropped it before -."

"No," interrupted Davy. "He always worked back there with me and Robbie," said Davy, nodding his head back down the gallery towards the fires. "He must have come this way *after* the explosion. Just like Robbie said. So," paused Davy, dramatically. "Where is he now?"

Davy had everyone's attention, but no one spoke, so he repeated his question. "Where is he now? And how did he get out?"

As his fellow-miners tried to digest this new information, Davy became aware of a vague draft. He stared at the flame in his safety lamp and, sure enough, it was gently leaning. Davy lifted the lamp and immediately spotted a gap in the roof above them. "What's this?"

"The original downcast shaft," said Vin Ellis. "We still use it for ventilation."

Davy lowered his safety lamp as he turned to look at Vin Ellis. They were clearly thinking the same thing. "Can you give me a leg up, Mr Ellis?"

"Course I can," said Vin, "putting down his safety lamp."

"What are you doing?" asked one of the other miners, curiously.

"Testing a theory," said Davy, as he put his left boot into Vin Ellis' cupped hands. Vin then gave him a shove up as Davy launched himself into the narrow shaft. He failed to find any handholds, and Vin had to grab him to prevent him from falling to the runway floor. As Vin released him, Davy grimaced at what he needed to ask. "Mr Ellis," he began. "I need that wagon."

Vin looked at him and then nodded. They needed to know. Between them, the miners gingerly lifted the brittle corpses out of the wagon and placed them gently onto the ground. They then positioned the wagon underneath the old downcast shaft. Davy and Daff turned the iron coal bucket upside down inside the wagon, and two other miners helped Davy up onto the wagon and then onto the coal bucket. Davy's head and shoulders were now inside the shaft. "Pass me a safety lamp, please."

Daff passed his up. Davy took it and lifted it above his head. "Well, I'll be…"

"What is it, Davy?" asked Vin.

"There's handholds and footholds. And it goes up for miles."

"I know, son. It goes all the way to the surface – although it's a bit overgrown up top, these days."

"I can see rope as well," said Davy. "Along the sides. Why is there rope in here?"

"It was once used by miners to take a short-cut between levels X, Y and Z. But that was all stopped when a miner fell to his death. It's been out of bounds for nigh-on fifteen years."

Davy lowered his head and shoulders out of the shaft and then dismounted from the bucket and wagon. "And did Nate Turner know about this?" he asked directly.

Vin Ellis closed his eyes before responding. "Almost certainly."

"Well then," said Davy, his face creasing with anger. "We now know where they went, don't we? I bet if I climbed up that shaft, I'd find more objects dropped by Will. That penknife was a message. For me."

"OK Davy, I'm not going to argue with your logic. But we need to get back to the active downcast, otherwise Level Z will start flooding."

Davy just looked at him. "Vin, he's twelve years old, and probably badly burned."

Vin stared back as Davy watched him wrestling with his moral dilemma. "You're right," he decided, eventually. "But you can't go up there alone in case you get into trouble."

"I'll go with him," said Daff.

"Thanks Vin. Thanks Daff. Are you sure this is OK?"

"We'll get more men down to replace you, and you can come back down yourselves when you're ready."

It was another two hours before a tired Davy and Daff climbed out the top of the old downcast shaft. As Vin had suspected, the entry-point was overgrown with a dense thicket of tangled thorn bushes. Soon covered in scratches, Davy spotted more evidence of recent activity: torn bits of cloth on the thorns. He could add that to the left-hand glove he'd found on Level Y and the right-hand glove on Level X. Both Will's.

"So," said Daff. "There's not much doubt, then."

"None. Do you know where Turner lives?"

"I'll show you," said Daff. "Vin will understand if we shoot off."

"Good man," said Davy.

They slowly and carefully fought their way out of the thorn bushes, both picking up a network of scratches on their arms and faces along with tears to their own clothing. Once they were free, Daff put a staying arm on Davy's. "If he's there, at the house – let me talk to him."

Davy looked at Daff intently, and then breathed out, nodding his head. "I'll not make a scene. Truth be told, finding him alive and possibly well is more than I ever expected. We'll cross the other bridges when we get to them."

Twenty minutes later, Davy and Daff were back at the pithead. As they walked past the office, Stan Eckersley poked his head out. "Oi, you two! Where do you think you're going?"

Davy winced. This was going to be difficult. He walked up to Eckersley who was regarding him with a frown. "We think we've found Will Lowe."

"Well, where is he then?" asked Eckersley, looking all around them.

"We found this," said Davy, taking out Will's penknife, "on Level Z at the bottom of the old downcast shaft. Will Lowe's."

Eckersley looked at the penknife, still not clear what Davy was getting at.

"And then we found this," said Davy, showing Eckersley Will's left glove, "on Level Y. And this," he said, holding up the right glove, "on Level X. All Will Lowe's stuff. And then at the top, we've found evidence of someone coming out of that shaft very recently."

It was dawning on Eckersley where this was going.

"Now, you tell me, Mr Eckersley. What's a twelve-year-old boy doing in a shaft that's been disused and out-of-bounds for three years longer than he's been alive?"

Eckersley was just staring at Davy, his sharp features going through a range of emotions. Eventually he came to a decision. "Right, wait there. I'm locking up the office." Twenty seconds later, Stan Eckersley came out of the office and was shrugging on his coat. "Come on then."

"How do you mean?" asked Davy, confused.

"I'm coming with you, Davy. I need to know for myself." Their destination remained unsaid, but understood.

Fifteen minutes later, they were stood outside a typical miner's cottage on a steep cobbled street which ran parallel to Cabrenar's High Street. Eckersley knocked loudly on the dark green door. There was no answer, so the three of them started looking in windows.

"Can we get around the back?" asked Davy.

"Round here," said Eckersley, leading them three houses down the road and then right, up a narrow covered brick alleyway. They then turned right again onto an open alley which ran back up and across the rear of Nate Turner's house. The wooden door leading onto Turner's back yard was locked. "Needs must," said Eckersley, and he kicked the door clean off its hinges.

Davy was taken aback. This was a very different Stan Eckersley to the one who fussed over every rule and regulation back at the colliery. They followed him up the back yard and looked in through the rear window. The place looked empty. "In for a penny," said Eckersley, and with that, he kicked open the back door to the property – although this one was much sturdier, and took six kicks to shatter. He then led them into Nate Turner's musty-smelling kitchen. All the cupboards were empty.

"Where does he keep his clothes?" asked Davy.

Eckersley nodded, understanding Davy's line of thought. "Follow me."

They climbed a very narrow and steep staircase, without any handholds, before emerging onto a narrow landing. "In there," said Eckersley, indicating the dingy first room on the right. They went in. Again, largely empty – as were most of the cupboards and drawers. The room was also a mess; someone had clearly left in a hurry.

Eckersley was rubbing his chin, deep in thought. Eventually, he looked up. "I'm very sorry, Davy," he said. "Very sorry indeed. It looks like you were right all along. It's just that…"

"That's all-right Mr Eckersley. We just need to find him."

"Chaps!" said Daff, his tone immediately alerting Davy and Stan. They turned. Daff had picked something up from behind the bedroom door. He held it up. It was Will's felt hat.

"Well, that clinches it then," said Davy, his lips drawn in.

"Dear God!" was all Stan Eckersley could say, his right hand rubbing the back of his head in anxiety.

"I'll rip that man apart," threatened Davy.

"No!" commanded Eckersley. "You leave this to me."

"I'm coming with you then."

"You're needed back with the rescue team, Davy. You leave this to me. I'm going straight to the JPs. I'm going to tell them everything. It will sound much better coming from me. I'm afraid you might just compromise matters if you go in too hard."

Davy was about to argue when Daff stepped in. "It's the right thing to do, Davy. Mr Eckersley's held in very high regard by the JPs, and Nate is his brother-in-law – so they'll take what he has to say very seriously."

"Well, they've already got their hands full at the moment with the disaster," mused Eckersley. "But I'll make them take this seriously and put out a description for Nate and Will that will go to every special constable and magistrate in northern Bramcia. We'll find them, Davy. And please God, we find them alive and well."

CHAPTER 49 — ARRAN

8th Tertiar, 1789
Day 99, 05:30

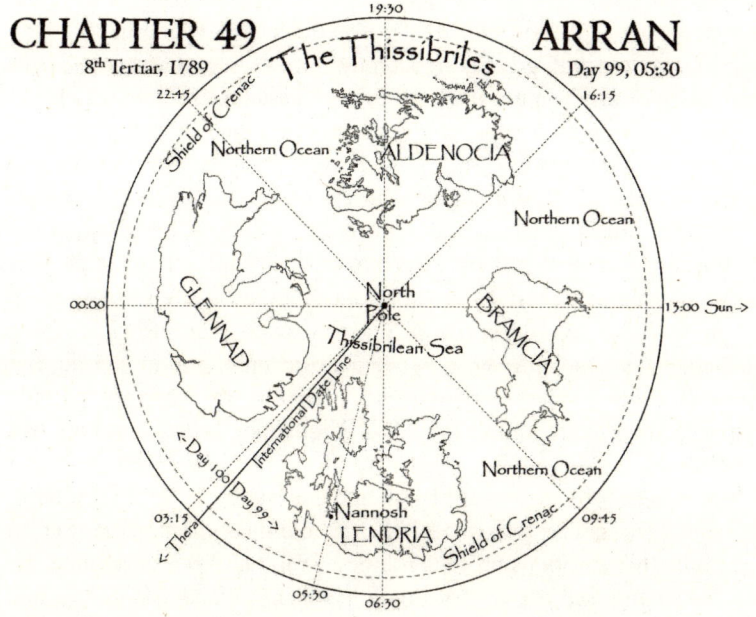

Professor Erasmus Doran's spare bed was very comfortable – but Arran Reed was wide awake. As had been the case every night for a few weeks now, he had two things on his mind. Once he'd awoken – usually between 04:00 and 04:30 – his roiling thoughts meant that there was no chance of going back to sleep. The first cause of this insomnia was, of course, the asteroid – or Reed's Rock, God forbid. The second cause was Ella Degan: the love of Arran's life.

Ella and Arran had met as teenagers on holiday in Bramcia, nineteen years ago. Although Ella lived in Olindo and Arran in Gwyala they had both fallen so deeply in love with each other that, once they had returned to Lendria, the distance between them hadn't mattered. Fortunately, both of their hometowns were ports in the Sound of Ekilek, so although they lived over sixty leagues apart, and a tortuous three hundred leagues by land, they were only a ten-hour steamer trip apart and they soon began to see each other every other weekend.

Arran had loved Ella from the moment he had first seen her – sat at the back of a concert hall in Natterspy where the Royal Bramcian Philharmonic Orchestra were performing. Most girls of her age wore their hair long, but Ella's was short. Short and blonde and soft, and often complemented by a fashionable and sometimes quirky hat; it had been a soft, raspberry beret on that occasion. She had smiled at him on that night, so long ago; a warm, sunny smile, and with great expression from the eyes; eyes that would later turn mischievous in an instant, but which always looked at him with love.

Happily, they were besotted with each other for the next year. There was a depth of understanding that went beyond their shared hobbies and interests; they were almost like two halves of the same person. A year on, though, now aged nineteen and eighteen, they had begun to take their relationship further than they should have for an unmarried couple. But they couldn't marry as Arran was at Nannosh University in the first year of his Applied Sciences degree, and Ella was due to commence studying Medicine later that summer at her hometown university in Olindo. But they still saw each other every weekend, and both were certain they would marry in three years' time, after Ella's graduation. Arran's certainty had been absolute.

But then he had received 'the letter' in the summer of 1771. Inexplicably, Ella didn't feel as deeply as she had before and didn't think it was fair on Arran for their relationship to continue. Arran had been devastated. He had micro-analysed the previous months, trying to understand how and when things had begun to go wrong for Ella. The fact was, though, that they had never argued or exchanged a single cross word, and yet somewhere along the way, he must have done something wrong, or not done enough, or got too blasé. Or all three.

Foolishly, rather than travel to Olindo and discuss everything face-to-face, he had written back to Ella, telling her that he still loved her with all his heart – but if that was the way she truly felt, then she must follow her heart and not his. Adults back home had already coached him on that mantra. Of course, he had hoped she would change her mind on reading of his sadness – realising that no one would ever love her as much as he did. Perhaps the fact that she had not changed her mind was justification for Arran not taking a boat to Olindo and begging for a second chance. But having *not* done it, how could he ever know how it might have turned out if he had?

They had exchanged letters for another nine months after that, Arran always replying immediately to Ella; Ella's replies becoming increasingly delayed – until there was no reply at all.

All around him, Arran's family and friends had comforted him.

"*It wasn't meant to be.*"

"*There are plenty more fish in the sea.*"

"*You'll find someone else and you'll love them even more.*"

And he'd believed them – at the time.

But in 1773, after two years without Ella, and several girlfriends who hadn't *been* Ella, and now understanding that there would never *be* another Ella, he had been brave and written a letter to her, addressed to her parents' house where he hoped that they still resided. Nothing too strong, a few hints of how he missed her and how wonderful their time had been together. The reply took over three weeks to arrive – so Arran already knew the score before he read that letter. Only one line truly resonated, though – and it was delivered around three quarters of the way through, rather matter-of-factly. "I recently became engaged to a man called Mal."

After that letter there had been a handful more back and forth, discussing known friends and relatives and what they were doing, and probably the weather, too. Of course, the letters soon stopped.

Life had rolled on, though, and Arran had just buried himself in his studies. Not only did he graduate with a First-Class Honours degree in Applied Sciences in 1773, but he had continued to take a Master's and then a Doctorate, becoming Dr Arran Reed in 1778, aged just twenty-six. By this stage, he had come to terms with the fact that his first love would probably be his only true love. A cruel occurrence, of course; for how could you possibly know at the time, when you have nothing to compare it to? Instead, he had devoted his life to his career, recognising that it would not be fair to a prospective partner to marry.

Then, in 1779, a year after commencing his first post at the Royal Observatory, Arran had met Sarah who, at thirty-four, had been seven years older than him. Lady Sarah Mackinnon was a supremely wealthy heiress who also possessed a towering intellect. She had inherited from her landed parents who had both passed away in 1777, having been their only child, and also from her much older husband, who had died in 1778. She was therefore much sought-after by men, who knew very well that she was the wealthiest woman in Lendria. Sarah, of course, had seen these potential courters for the gold diggers they were, but when she had met Arran, she had seen someone totally different. He had no desire to marry, for starters, but their intellects and personalities were wholly compatible, too.

Despite living apart, their relationship became something of a Nannoshian institution, but marriage was never proposed, despite the odd hint from Sarah. For although he did care for Sarah, dearly, his feelings never matched those that he'd had for Ella. To marry Sarah would not be fair on her. And so, two years ago, he had ended their relationship, giving Sarah the chance to meet someone wholeheartedly committed to her. It was the hardest thing he had ever done.

Becoming Astronomer Royal, aged just thirty-seven, was never on Arran's agenda either, and was largely due to his total devotion to his role and the close relationship he had built with his predecessor, Professor Doran, both during his doctorate and from his eleven years at the Royal Observatory working alongside him. Arran's studies and his job had certainly helped him over the years to find solace from his teenage loss and, more recently, to overcome uncertainty at having ended his relationship with Sarah. Nevertheless, his teenage loss could hit him hard at any time, often without warning and when he least expected it. The look of someone else, the same perfume, an accent on a particular spoken word, a song heard, a place visited, a laugh that sounded familiar, a quirky look or comment…or perhaps a raspberry beret. It always cut to the bone.

But then, at the beginning of 1789, Arran had received a letter out of the blue. From Ella. It had been sent to his parents' house back in Gwyala, and they had forwarded it to his address in Nannosh. The letter had been mainly humorous and up-beat and joked about how he had had a narrow but lucky escape in 1771! It also mentioned her graduation in 1774 in Medicine, but how she had not extended that education any further, as she had intended as a teenager. Instead, she had immediately married the aforementioned Mal and by 1776 was a mother to two boys. It appeared as though Mal, six years her senior, and a wealthy banker, saw himself as the sole wage earner and, reading between the lines, saw Ella's place as being in the home. A not untypical stance, even in these modern, progressive times, but it still irked Arran; had Mal also smothered her intellect, her ambition, her quirkiness – and perhaps her sunny smile, too?

Naturally, Arran had replied, providing Ella with a summary of his career, and admitting that he had never married, having never met the right woman. *Except that he had, nineteen years ago.*

The response came to his new address in Nannosh within a few days – considerably faster than after their split in 1771. This time, there were a number of references to their time together, nineteen years ago, each remembered with such apparent affection.

"Do you remember that time when…"

"Wasn't it wonderful when we went to…"

"You used to make me laugh so much when you…"

It was only the second letter, but the message was coming through fairly clear.

The third letter contained elements of self-reproach.

"But I was stupid enough to let you go…"

"Someone else is going to be the lucky one..."

All delivered as apparently offhandish comments. Arran's hopes would soar, but he would then remonstrate with himself, firstly because of Mal, secondly for their boys, and thirdly for himself – because he could *not* handle going through losing her again.

It was the fifth letter that he would remember for the rest of his life. Both the letter and what it had done to him. The tone had been different right from the start. He only had himself to blame, though. His previous letter had asked Ella, quite bluntly, if she still loved him. He had surprised himself at his bravery, but he had been so desperate to know the truth. He had even stood for thirty minutes outside the Royal Post House with that letter in his hand. He'd walked away twice – only to return twice. At any of those points, it hadn't been too late to turn around, go home and burn the letter. But he had eventually handed it over to the Royal Postmaster who had arrived to attend the post box.

Ella's fifth letter had arrived six days later. "*I love you now as much as I loved you back then. I have always loved you and I will never, ever stop loving you.*"

How did those words make any sense?

He had taken the letter up to his bedroom to read it again, and after that second read, he had walked out of the bedroom on to the landing in something of a stupor before the full force of the grief had struck home. He had ended up on his back, wailing at the ceiling in anguish, totally out of character. It had been the rawest grief of his life, the sense of loss so profound – and his pain had felt genuinely *physical*. But the loss was also laced with a desperate sense of frustration. *Because it had all been so unnecessary.*

And there were so many whys. Why had she finished their relationship in 1771? Why would she do that if she had always loved him? And why had she courted and then married Mal, if Arran was the man she had genuinely always loved?

Of course, he had written back asking the questions. The response had been strange. She couldn't really remember. She had thought that maybe it was a joint decision to end their relationship – which had left Arran aghast, as it certainly had not been. She had also said something about 'not knowing how to take their relationship to the next level'.

Arran had been hurt and stunned. How could you not know why? How could you not remember why you had given up the most precious thing that any human being could ever have in their life? Again, Arran tried to analyse his own actions. He *must* have done something wrong himself to bring about their split. He simply must have. And yet, at the same time, Arran felt there was perhaps more to this than was coming across in the letters. But exactly what…he just didn't know.

That last letter had arrived seven days ago. Arran had not yet replied. He had started a good dozen or so letters since, but had ended up throwing them all into the wastepaper bin. The recurring theme in his aborted letters had been for them to meet. He just had to see Ella; to look again into those loving blue eyes again; to no doubt see his own depth of love reflecting back. Except she was married now. So, what right did he have to see another man's wife?

Then again, what right had he had to ask another man's wife if she loved him?

It was a bit late to be rueing that, now.

And on top of all of this, Arran now had the weight of his grim celestial discovery. Indeed, it may well be, that in just over eighty days' time, none of this would matter, anyway. There were odd moments when Arran felt that he perhaps cared more about losing Ella eighteen years ago than he did about the possible end of the world in 1789.

Arran shook his head to clear that line of thought away, appalled by his own selfishness. He had a duty to millions. Ella came after that duty.

But then again, if Armageddon was where they were all heading, didn't that make meeting Ella again all-the-more important? To feel those feelings again. To hold the woman that he adored again. And it wasn't as if he could actually *do* anything about the asteroid striking Thera. No one could.

Arran closed his eyes, knowing that sleep would once again be an impossibility when faced with such insoluble turmoil.

CHAPTER 50   DRAXAELEN
8th Tertiar, 1789   Day 99, 08:00

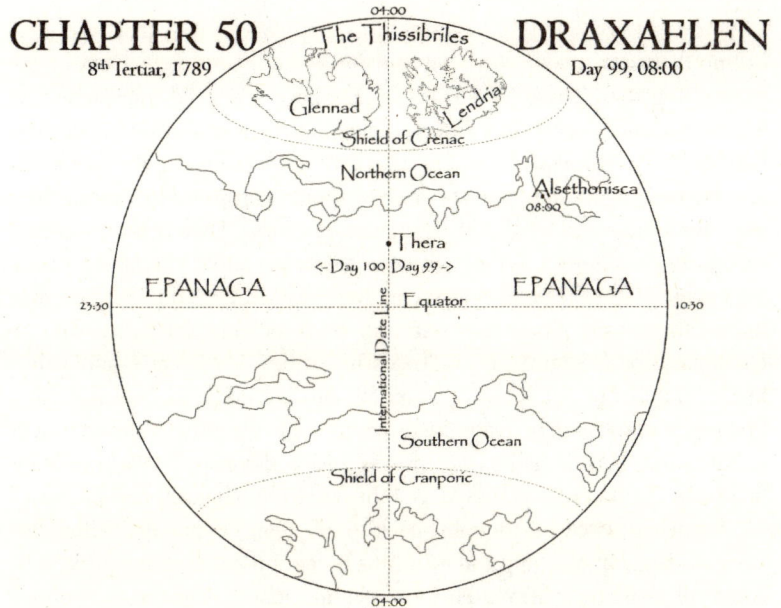

It was an azure sky morning in the market square of Alsethonisca, on the Gulf of Acahea, and although it was only eight o'clock, the sun was already beating down remorselessly. Draxaelen surveyed his men and his chest instinctively swelled with pride. A thousand of Demonacia's finest – the *Demonata* as they were both known and feared. Renowned for 'fighting like demons' and yet the majority of them just farmers or fishermen – each more at home in the rolling green valleys and fertile plains of Demonacia, or its myriad coves with white sand and clear turquoise seawater. Drax himself was the son of a farmer who lived in central Demonacia, in a typically rural home – white-walled with shuttered windows and terracotta roof tiles, surrounded by golden fields of wheat and barley in late summer.

Known as the Jewel of Epanaga, it was ironic that Demonacia had such a menacing name – although any glance at a map of northern Epanaga provides the answer, given its peninsula landmass rears out into the Northern Ocean for all the world like a twin-horned demon! Perhaps it was this name, combined with the idyllic beauty, that drove the *Demonata* to defend their lands so fiercely. Draxaelen's countrymen had certainly *earned* their reputation for fighting like demons, as they'd had plenty of practice over the last two thousand years of brutal Theran rule. Indeed, there had been twice as many rebellions in Demonacia as anywhere else in western Epanaga.

Draxaelen pondered on his brutal masters. *Neo*-Therans they were now calling themselves. *As if there was anything 'new' about them.* Drax's teeth ground together. These Neo-Therans may have advanced impressively in terms of science, technology and medicine in the last millennium, but there had been little ethical progress, still constantly at war, thirsting after conquest, always engaging modern and superior weaponry compared to their victims; well, modern, except for their fighting pits, of course. There, only traditional weaponry was allowed, as the fighting lasted longer and elicited greater gore. Meanwhile, technology advancements were deliberately confined purely to Liatia; there were no cotton-spinning mills or modern infirmaries in Demonacia or Nopannia, no railroads in Acahea or Maldatia, and only a limited number of canals east of Setteri, Praam and Edmano. That said, most Epanagan states east of Liatia were happy with the preservation of their cultures and their alleged backwardness, whilst also happy to acknowledge that their Theran masters should lead the way technologically and militarily.

Draxaelen pulled his thoughts back to his men. Despite their discipline since waking that morning and marching to the appointed meeting-place, he could still sense their nerves. He looked at his captain, Argaeus, and nodded a brief reassurance. Argaeus, his friend and companion since childhood, nodded back, then straightened up and thrust his chest out even further. The action sent a ripple of reassurance along the front line, which transmitted itself all the way to the back. All those impeccable dark green leather jerkins with the embossed golden demon over their hearts; tanned, muscular arms, bare apart from the brown manicae protecting their forearms, while brown-leather skirts, greaves and gladiatorial sandals completed the traditional ensemble. For sure, their armour and weaponry were no match for the Theran flintlock musket and twelve-pound canon, not to mention their ruthless cavalry, but the Eastern Alliance had planned their attack in the finest detail, and the *Demonata* wouldn't be unleashed until the fighting was hand-to-hand. That was when their lightweight circular shields, short swords, and lots of close-up technical know-how became lethal.

Draxaelen glanced across to the town hall clock, a relatively new addition to the ancient marketplace. Five past eight. He felt the first niggle of doubt – and then inwardly reprimanded himself, hoping nothing had shown on his face. Leonnatus' loyalty was without question. He'd known the Acahean for seventeen years since they'd commenced their Theran National Service together. Together, they had travelled the world, helped build cities and towns, helped to irrigate isolated desert settlements, helped save lives whilst serving in various medical roles; but they had also taken lives, too, an untold number – and, in quiet moments, they had shared their guilt, many times, at what they had been forced to do in the name of the expanding Theran Empire. Without doubt, they had loved each other like brothers. Meanwhile, the Acaheans had every bit as much reason to overthrow the Neo-Therans as the Demonacians and the Adcians did. This gathering, here in Alsethonisca's marketplace, was just the first part in what Drax was convinced would become the greatest shock in the history of Theran conflict.

By half past eight, though, Draxaelen was concerned. Eight o'clock, they'd said, following an overnight departure. Weather conditions had been, and still were, perfect for crossing from Nyvastrilana in western Adcia. Perfect weather to ferry three thousand Adcians across the Gulf of Acahea to their rendezvous with Draxaelen and his men in Alsethonisca. Their combined force of four thousand men would then march forty leagues south-west to Jarvaseo where they would join seven thousand Maldatians and ten thousand Acaheans, resulting in a combined Eastern Alliance force of at least twenty-one thousand men; thirty thousand if the Esomians and Nopannians joined.

Draxaelen kept his face impassive, his shoulders back and his chest out, looking straight ahead, and not eastwards towards the seaboard side of the marketplace, where his lookout would come running at the first sight of the Adcian fleet. Or Drax would look towards the church at the western side of the market place – a beautiful building enhanced by the sun shining gloriously across its ironstone walls and pristine terracotta roof tiles which graced both the nave and chancel as well as the turrets on its western tower.

The town hall clock struck 08:45. Draxaelen could now sense disquiet amongst his men. Even if the Adcian fleet appeared on the horizon -.

"They're coming!" cried a boy, his voice issuing somewhere from the east. Then he burst out of an alleyway and into the marketplace, all brown curly hair, tanned limbs and wild-eyed. "They're coming, General, they're coming!" he cried.

Sighs of relief and smiles broke out all around. Then, as one, the assembled soldiers began chanting – "Demonata, Demonata, Demonata" – whilst bashing their manicae against their shields in time with the first three syllables. After around two minutes of this, Draxaelen signalled his men to quieten down. "Argaeus, with me," he commanded. "Crateuas, take my place."

As Argaeus joined his general, a handsome giant of a soldier, with dark skin and a scar running down his right cheek took Draxaelen's place in front of the assembled *Demonata*. Draxaelen led Argaeus down several narrow, cobbled streets until they broke out into Alsethonisca's harbour with the vast blueness of the Gulf of Adcia beyond. And there, approaching from the north-east, were fifteen glorious Adcian warships, each flying the blue, yellow and red flags of Adcia, each carrying around two hundred soldiers apiece. The sight stopped Draxaelen in his tracks. Perhaps it was because it had all suddenly become so real. Argaeus, realising his general was no longer with him, whipped his head around with concern. "Drax?" he questioned.

"It's fine, Argaeus, it's fine." He nodded towards the approaching fleet, a half-smile now on his face. "It's just that I've waited all of my life for this moment. To avenge our fallen. To avenge our ancestors. This really is going to happen, Argaeus," he finished, his eyes now blazing exultantly. "We are going to make *history*!"

Argaeus looked his general in the eye with an expression of controlled venom. "Aye, that we are, Drax," he declared. The two friends regarded each other for several seconds before embracing.

Five minutes later, they arrived at the harbour, ready to greet their Adcian allies amidst cheering and waving townsfolk. Draxaelen was pleased to note that the early-morning crowds, as requested, were not blocking the route from the slipway. Nor were they blocking the south side of the harbour or the south-westerly road out of Alsethonisca – where the three thousand Adcians would soon march to rendezvous in a vast field with the one thousand Demonacians who, in turn, would be marched there from the market square by Crateuas. You could always rely on Alsethoniscans to behave in an orderly fashion.

Drax put both hands on the harbour rail, squinting as he looked into the early-morning sun. The leading Adcian ship was so close now, that he could see the faces of the men on board. He sought out the face of the Adcian general, Zyraxes, but couldn't spot him anywhere.

Two things then happened in quick succession. The first barely registered above the hubbub of the crowd, the sound of the surf washing up against the harbour walls and the ubiquitous squawking of seabirds. On top of that there were shouted orders between the lead battleship and the harbourmaster and his men on the harbour wall, who were there to steer the boats safely in to port. Nevertheless, the sound was unmistakable. It was the sound of marching feet.

Draxaelen had a split-second to contemplate reasons why Crateuas would be marching the *Demonata towards* the harbour – but then, as he searched for the face of Zyraxes on board the first ship, he spotted another that simply shouldn't have been there. Draxaelen gripped Argaeus' arm. "We have been betrayed!" he cried.

"Betrayed? How?"

Draxaelen pointed to a face at the prow of the lead ship. "Macrinus!" he snarled.

"But they're Adcians!"

"They're not Adcians, Argaeus. They're Therans. We need to get back to Crateuas. Now!"

But as they turned to run, the answer to the marching feet riddle was supplied – hundreds of Theran legionaries, still wearing the red and gold garb of antiquity along with their metal visored helmets and protective cuirass, but each holding sophisticated muskets with lethal-looking bayonets attached. A second later, Argaeus was spun around and thrown to the floor – by a musket bullet shot from the prow of the first 'Adcian' ship.

Draxaelen froze. What should he do?

Loyalty won out. He dropped to his knees to examine Argaeus. His childhood friend was writhing in agony, but Drax was relieved to see that the bullet had just passed through his shoulder. He pressed down to stem the flow of blood, as pandemonium broke out around him, with the townsfolk unable to comprehend why an Adcian ally had just shot a Demonacian officer, or why a *Legio* of the Theran army was marching on their town, seemingly destined for a pitched battle with the incoming Adcians. Others trusted to instinct and ran. Throughout this, Drax continued to staunch the blood-flow from Argaeus' shoulder, his mind rapidly turning over options. Meanwhile, Argaeus had phased back into consciousness and spoke through gritted teeth. "Drax, run," he gasped. "You can still get away. Get the troops away, re-group."

They then heard a barrage of musket fire, screams and war-cries from the direction of the market square, whilst at the same time, the Theran soldiers from the south-west had reached the harbour. Looking behind him, Drax saw that the first of the Therans wearing the blue, yellow and red disguise of Adcian troops had begun to disembark from the lead ship. Two of the other fourteen warships were also docking. Things were happening so fast.

"It's too late to re-group, Argaeus," said Draxaelen. "And if we fight here, we will we lose – and Macrinus will execute every man, woman and child in Alsethonisca for any perceived resistance."

The words were barely out of his mouth when the Theran land-force reached them and he was forced to stand and raise his hands at the prodding of a bayonet. There was nothing he could do but listen to the sounds of the rout in the market square, his head down, his shoulders slumped.

Swords against muskets. His men were dying. His *friends* were dying.

Eventually, the sounds of conflict in the market square began to diminish, perhaps thanks to a sensible Demonacian surrender – just as Macrinus came swaggering up to him, a baleful smirk across his tanned and weather-beaten face. "One of life's constants," he gloated. "A Demonacian with the brains of an ass."

"Leonnatus!" exclaimed Draxaelen, with sufficient malice.

"Of course. He's mine. *Everyone* is mine. It's Draxaelen isn't it?"

"General Draxaelen to you," hissed Argaeus, climbing shakily to his feet, in great pain, with his right arm held limply by his side.

General Macrinus Severus Vitellius said nothing. He let Argaeus stand – and then slowly drew his dagger and casually pushed it into the flesh around Argaeus' bullet-wound. Argaeus howled and fell back to the floor again, a fresh flow of blood now spilling from his wound. Instantly, Draxaelen launched himself at Macrinus – who leaped back and levelled his rapidly-drawn sword at Draxaelen's throat, having anticipated the attack. Two Theran soldiers then roughly seized each of Draxaelen's arms. "I'm afraid you won't be prompting me to kill you just yet, General," he hissed. "I have plans for you. And for your men. I also want you to see, first hand, what happens to traitors. Or rather more pointedly…to the *families* of traitors."

Draxaelen's blood ran cold. "What have you done?"

"No, old boy. What have *you* done?" exulted the Theran general. And with that, Macrinus walked fluidly over to the general leading the Theran land troops. They gripped arms and then had a brief conversation that involved a bit of pointing and gesticulating, before Macrinus returned. "Strip them of their tunics," he ordered the two soldiers who were restraining Draxaelen. "And you," he said to another trooper. "Go and get Maxi Zoninus. We have an early bonus for him."

Whilst all this was happening, Draxaelen's mind was in torment at the possible fates of his family. He cared little for whoever this Maxi Zoninus character was or what he was going to do to him – although it was of little surprise when he saw Zoninus walking along the harbour wall: not a soldier, but a wealthy, middle-aged individual, dark and swarthy-looking, dressed in the finest silks and dripping with golden adornments. Behind him, two dark-skinned assistants were hauling a red-hot brazier, whilst a third was carrying a branding iron. Drax should have been traumatised by what was about to happen, but he would gladly take whatever punishment Macrinus would mete out, just to have his family safe; equally, to keep the innocent inhabitants of Alsethonisca unharmed, who at present were being kept away from the drama by a chain of disembarked soldiers with muskets pointing at them, their fingers ready on the triggers.

Draxaelen was briefly aware that Macrinus and Zoninus were in conference, before they and the brazier-bearers came over to him. It was at this point that Drax noticed Maxi Zoninus' startling eyes for the first time; one brown, the other green. "Turn around," ordered Zoninus.

Despite his predicament, Drax registered the fact that the slaver had a long-tongued lisp…and imagined that anyone finding fun in it would likely be minus a tongue themselves, shortly afterwards. Nevertheless, he ignored the slaver's command to turn around – and so the two men holding his arms forced him to and then pinned him to the ground, face down. Drax managed to move his head slightly to one side so that his right cheek was pressed hard against the packed earth. He then braced himself. First, he felt a foot in the middle of his bare back. Then came the tell-tale hiss of the branding iron, a touch, the smell of burning flesh – clearly his own – and then…a delayed, but white-hot pain in the rear of his right shoulder.

Even though he had been determined not to, Draxaelen couldn't help but scream out in agony. Seconds later, with his scream dying on his lips, but still hyper-ventilating, Drax felt a breath against his right ear and then a sibilant whisper. "Your mine, now…slave."

Draxaelen was then roughly pulled to his feet, and chains were placed around his wrists and ankles by two Theran soldiers, while another two were now holding down poor Argaeus. Despite his own agony, Drax watched Zoninus pull the branding iron out of the brazier again and advance on Argaeus. "No, for pity's sake," cried Drax, as he watched in disbelief. "Not that shoulder."

Any illusions of humanity in the man were instantly banished, as Zoninus gleefully forced the branding iron into the back of Argaeus' injured shoulder. Argaeus shuddered on the floor in the grip of the two Theran soldiers, and then lay still – having mercifully passed out.

Drax hung his head in despair. The beginnings of an infinite hell were opening up beneath him. As if to confirm this, Macrinus strolled back up to him, wearing an evil smirk. "And now for your final lesson, slave." He paused and licked his dry lips. "Before you begin your new life – and the rest of your life – in the service of the Theran Empire."

Macrinus then turned to face the south harbour again, and Drax saw a new procession winding their way up the harbour road, albeit much slower, stuttering and stumbling. It was a familiar site to anyone who knew the ways of the Neo-Therans. There were around twenty prisoners – all men by the look of it. Men with their backs bent almost double by the crosses they were bearing upon their backs. A cold glove of fear encircled Drax's heart. He averted his eyes, refusing to look at the first face in the procession.

"What's the matter, Demon? Afraid to face the truth? Afraid to face the reality of *your* treachery?"

As the procession drew closer, Macrinus roughly grabbed Draxaelen's chin with one hand, and forced him to look up. "Your father, I believe?"

Draxaelen's eyes were already full of tears before he looked upon the face of the father he loved so dearly. The father who had taught him to be considerate and civil to everyone he met; who had taught him to hunt and to fish and to farm…and then they would return home to a meal lovingly prepared…by his mother. "*Oh, God, no!*" Drax looked into Macrinus' cold, merciless eyes. "What have you done with her?"

"Your mother? Your sisters? Oh, I think you know, my friend."

Draxaelen couldn't help himself. He threw his head back and issued a raw, primordial scream. When it was spent, he looked to his father who was now staggering alongside them. "Father, I'm so sorry," he sobbed. "I'm so sorry, I'm so sorry…"

He got the worst response imaginable. Nothing. His father's eyes were open – but they were empty, and they did not acknowledge him. What had they witnessed? The thought ripped Draxaelen apart and he began to sob – but Macrinus didn't even allow that. He grabbed Drax's chin roughly in his hand again and forced him to watch his father's cross being dropped carelessly into one of crucifixion slots along the seafront, his father's body jerking mercilessly and bringing on further oozings from his pinioned hands. His feet were then pinned to the cross with one huge nail and a savage blow of a lump hammer. Drax's father didn't even flinch.

Then, just when Drax thought that things couldn't get any worse, crosses two and three were mounted either side: his younger brothers aged just fourteen and eleven. Now totally numb, Drax felt that the only mercy was that both were barely alive – until his youngest brother issued an inhuman screech as his feet were pinioned with another enormous nail.

For several minutes, Draxaelen *yearned* for death, craving an end to it all. But then, very slowly, a new emotion was born. One he thought he had known before, but *never* with this intensity. He would *not* give in to that final release. He could not. Not now. As he watched the dying faces of his father and younger brothers, Draxaelen knew that with every fibre in his body, he must fight to stay alive. No matter where life was about to take him. It might take a year; it might take ten, maybe even twenty. But his family *would* be avenged.

With a certainty that was total, Draxaelen knew that he would be the man to kill first Maxi Zoninus and then General Macrinus Severus Vitellius. And then, if the Gods were good, he would send that scent-pampered, hair-oiled, deviant, the Emperor Vitasian Flavius Dominius to his maker; shortly followed by his evil son, the real orchestrator behind the throne and the true ice-cold heart of the Theran Empire: Calidius Antoninus Dominius.

CHAPTER 51   ARRAN
8th Tertiar, 1789   Day 99, 12:00

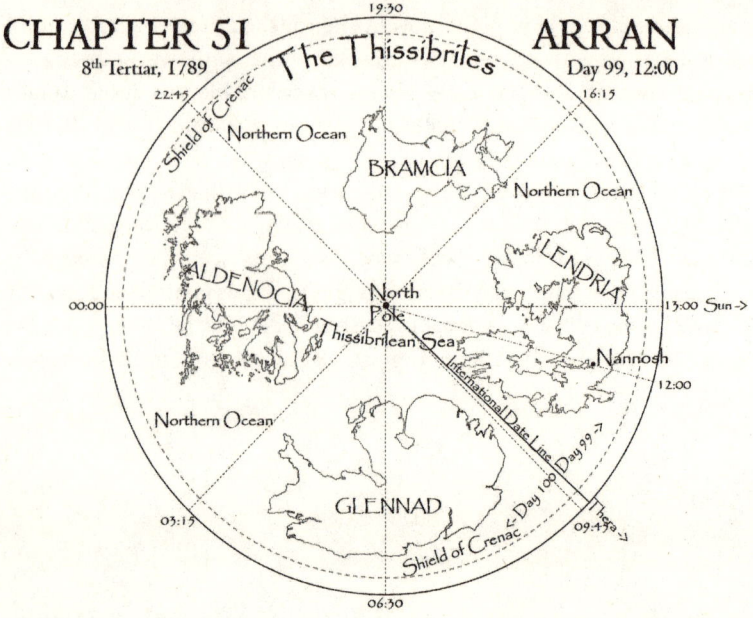

Arran Reed and Professor Doran were getting increasingly impatient as they were made to wait outside the private office of the Lendrian Prime Minister – or Ocateshia, to give the PM his proper title in Lendria. Lenahan Driscoll had been Ocateshia for the last four years but was currently lagging behind in the polls ahead of the national elections due in early Quarternar. He was therefore neck-deep in campaigning and putting the finishing touches to his manifesto.

Arran shook his head in frustration; Driscoll's manifesto would hold little sway with a half-league-wide asteroid. His look at Professor Doran said it all. Doran nodded, stood and walked over to the two security guards outside Driscoll's office. "Gentlemen, Mr Driscoll said he would see us at 10:30. It is a matter of great urgency."

"He's the Ocateshia, sir. He has an election to fight. Just be patient, please, sir, and sit down again."

Arran closed his eyes. The way things were shaping up, Driscoll would be off to Parliament before they'd get to see him, so Arran decided to move things along. He stood and walked purposefully towards the two security guards, who were already sensing trouble.

"Arran, leave it!" warned Doran.

One of the guards held up his hand. "Sir, if you don't sit down, I'm afraid we'll have to remove you from the building."

Arran was aware that kicking off outside the Ocateshia's private office was not the expected behaviour of the Astronomer Royal, but his frustration was about to veer beyond his control…just as the doors to the office opened inwards, and Driscoll – resplendent in his double-breasted dark green jacket and white stock – ushered out five members of his cabinet. No doubt they had been preparing their stance for this afternoon's parliamentary session. Arran almost felt sorry for Driscoll.

"Gentlemen," said Driscoll. "Please come in. As I'm sure you're aware," he said, closing the office doors, "I'm running rather late, and have a Parliament to attend shortly, so I can only spare you ten minutes." A tall and thin man, with dark hair and no hint of grey, despite being in his late forties, Driscoll stalked back to his desk and took his seat, a pair of intelligent blue eyes boring into them. "Now then, what is so urgent that I have to fit you in at the drop of a hat, eh?"

Arran and Professor Doran looked at each other, both unsure how to start the conversation. The Professor ventured first. "Last night, my esteemed successor here," he said indicating Arran, "quite rightly came to see me to seek a second opinion on a matter of grave importance."

Arran decided to grab the bull by the horns. "I'm afraid, Ocateshia, we are faced with an unparalleled catastrophe. A catastrophe that will render your parliamentary debate irrelevant."

"What the deuce are you saying, man?" said Driscoll, concerned and annoyed in equal measure. He was well aware that his two esteemed visitors weren't in the habit of playing practical jokes.

"I'm saying that twelve weeks ago, I spotted an asteroid heading for our inner solar system and which is around half a league wide. Since then, I have plotted its course, and I am now in no doubt that its trajectory will bring it straight towards our world. Last night, I asked the Professor to check, double-check and treble-check. He has. And he agrees with me. That asteroid *will* strike Thera."

Driscoll just looked at Arran, completely lost for words.

"I'm sorry to have to break it to you so bluntly, sir."

"Half a league wide?" asked Driscoll, the colour now draining slowly from his cheeks. "A mile-and-a-half?"

"It's an estimate, Ocateshia, but even at *half* that size, the ramifications for that asteroid hitting land on Thera are, as I said earlier, catastrophic. It may yet turn out to be larger than half a league."

"I'm sorry, gentlemen. I can't…" he turned to Professor Doran. "You do corroborate this?"

"I'm afraid I do, Ocateshia," responded Doran, gravely.

"And you have proof here, I take it?" asked Driscoll, indicating the rolled-up charts that Arran had brought with him and placed onto the Ocateshia's desk.

"Yes, I do," said Arran. "Now that the Professor has corroborated my charts, we should ask one or two other astronomers from the Royal Observatory to check – those who will treat this with discretion. We obviously don't want to go around shouting this from the rooftops."

"Absolutely not," agreed Driscoll. "So how many people know?"

"It's just the three of us, sir."

Driscoll sat back in his chair, put both hands up to his face and closed his eyes. "My daughter is only four years old," he said, in a lost voice. He then opened his eyes. "Do we have any chance?" he asked, now more focused, once more the professional politician.

"We have two chances, sir. In fact, you could almost say we have two chances out of three. Which sounds like good odds, I know."

"But?" asked Driscoll, knowing there was more to it than that.

Arran stood up and collected a convenient ornamental globe of Thera that was sat inside one of Driscoll's bookcases. He sat back down again and placed the globe on the desk in front of Driscoll. The Ocateshia's focus on his manifesto was now long forgotten.

Arran rotated the globe. It looked like all globes made in the northern hemisphere; populated with land and oceans around the northern half, and a blank white space for the bottom half. "Our best hope," began Arran, "is a strike in an ocean in the southern hemisphere," he said, still rotating the globe and dragging a finger all the way around the featureless white half. "Of course, there may not be such a thing, and it is all land – although that's highly unlikely. But if it is all land, and the asteroid hits there, then the strike could well be an extinction level event."

"Extinction level event?"

"Yes. A strike of that size, at the speed it will be travelling, would destroy everything within a five-hundred-mile radius. However, it will also likely destroy all animal life on Thera, too, within a matter of weeks – as the sheer volume of rock and earth displaced would go into orbit around Thera and block out the sun's rays. Without the sun's rays, all plant life dies. Without plant life, all animal life dies."

Driscoll leaned forward, his head in his hands again. He then rubbed his eyes and snapped back into focus once again. "Right. So, for a land-strike, it's irrelevant where it hits. It could hit the South Pole bang on the nose, and even we at the North Pole are finished?"

"Not necessarily," said Arran. "There are some long shots – but we'll come to those shortly.

"Well, I think I've got the measure of this, gentlemen. The best option is for a strike in the fabled Southern Ocean. The worst option is for it to strike land anywhere. Which means that the middle option is for the asteroid to strike the Northern Ocean, correct?"

"Yes, correct, sir. But the effects would be catastrophic."

"I can imagine. But not extinction-level?"

"Correct again, sir."

"Oh, to not be an island nation," said Driscoll, ruefully, sitting back in his chair.

"All four of our islands have high ground inland, sir. That's where we need to make for – assuming we calculate a Northern Ocean strike."

"And I take it you don't know *where* it will strike?"

"Not yet, sir."

"Not yet? This gives me hope that you *can* predict at some time in the future?"

"Yes, sir. We estimate that we'll be able to plot the point of impact, accurately, a few weeks before the strike."

"And exactly *when* are you estimating impact?"

"In around eighty four days' time, sir."

Driscoll sat forward again, ashen faced. "So, we have *some* time to prepare – but we don't know which eventuality to prepare for – yet?"

"That's about the size of it, sir."

"I need to get my cabinet back in here."

"Is that wise, sir?"

"What do you mean?"

"I would have thought that the priority is to keep this quiet for as long as we can – otherwise there will be mass panic and likely anarchy. And thanks to the Shield of Crenac, we can't head for Epanaga – where an ocean strike would mean *everyone* has a chance. So, at least for now, the less people who know in the Thissibriles, the better."

"Spoken like a politician, Mr Reed. You put me to shame."

"I've had longer to think about it than you, sir."

"But there are practicalities," went on Driscoll. "We have an election coming. I might not even *be* Ocateshia by the end of next month. What then? And how do I prepare for an election with this hanging over me?"

"So, realistically," said Professor Doran, "you need to dissolve Parliament and form a coalition government. Those people in that government would all need to know – but they can't tell anyone else – even their own families. Would you trust every member of such a coalition government to keep it secret?"

"It would be significantly less than a two in three chance," responded Driscoll, wryly. "Ye Gods, I'm not even sure I'm capable *myself* of keeping such a secret."

"As I keep saying," Arran began, "if it gets out, there will be chaos."

"Not if we move fast and impose Martial Law," said Driscoll. "Do you have any idea if any of the other islands are aware?"

"No idea, sir," said Arran. "It's possible they could even be ahead of us – but with all the same dilemmas around communication."

"Well, at the very least, I owe it to my Glennadian, Bramcian and Aldenocian counterparts to warn them. I think we're going to have to go for a combined Thissibrilean effort on this one. Can I count on your support for whichever route we decide to go down?"

"Of course, sir," said Arran.

"And I will make myself available in whatever capacity I'm needed," said Professor Doran.

"Thank you, Professor. Well, first things first. I need to make myself indisposed for this afternoon's Parliament. I think I will claim a migraine. Instead, I would like to spend the afternoon in conference with you two gentlemen, and one other colleague from the Royal Observatory for a third opinion – someone you can trust. I suggest that we meet back in my office at," he checked his pocket watch, "13:00, where we will also be joined by my deputy. I'll arrange to have some lunch brought in, and between the five of us, we will decide on next steps.

"Thank you, Ocateshia," said Arran, standing and shaking Driscoll's hand. "And keep hoping, sir. There are two scenarios that will leave our planet with a future."

"Thank you, Mr Reed," said Driscoll. He then blew out his cheeks and gave both astronomers a rueful smile. "I can't believe that only half an hour ago, I was worried sick about increasing the tax on fishing!"

CHAPTER 52 — EMILYA

9th Tertiar, 1789   Day 100, 10:00

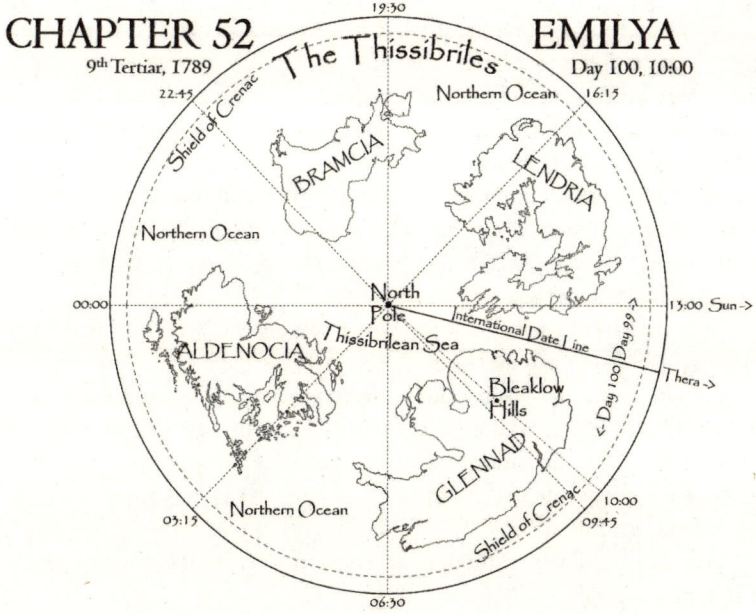

For the first time since riding up into the trees two days ago, Emilya spotted a break in the blanket foliage ahead. She had noticed the trees had started to become gradually smaller and less densely packed since they had left the tiny village of Ghannoots, earlier that morning. The gap in the path ahead was now affording Emilya a view of what looked like browny-green scrub, quite different from the rich green of the alpine trees she had become used to.

Five minutes later, the landscape opened up around them. The first thing Emilya noticed as they emerged above the treeline, was the buffeting wind. They had not been troubled by it previously, but now, Emilya's hair was whipping about and she was constantly, pulling it one way or another to keep it out of her eyes.

The path stretched out ahead of them, winding its way gently ever-upward through the barren moorland. There were clumps of heather and other hardy upland plants dotted about, but the only other features were rocky outcrops, and equally hardy sheep. When the sun came out, though, the whole landscape was transformed. As the sun was directly before them, to the south-east, Emilya forced herself to look left and right instead. She could see a steep corrie falling away a mile or so to her left, with the black shadow of clouds moving slowly across it, while another steep-sided corrie on the right looked considerably cheerier with just blue sky and sunshine directly above it.

Emilya also noticed that the smoother road surfaces that they'd traversed all the way to Ghannoots, had now been replaced by a rock-strewn path. The horses didn't seem to mind, but Emilya could imagine a great difference in comfort for those travelling by carriage. These thoughts inevitably made her think about Harry Black, again. The two soldiers had mentioned him back at the hostel in Ghintarton, two days earlier, and there'd been further talk of him at Ghannoots last night – giving Emilya something else to worry about. Later that night, Emilya had asked Jake to tell her what they knew about the highwayman.

"He was born the son of a lord, would you believe, who was also High Sheriff of Wrenko," Jake had said.

"Yes, but he was outlawed around fifteen years ago when he killed a man in a duel," said Elyse, taking up the story. "Accounts say that he shot the other fellow in the back after they'd only walked seven paces."

"Nice man," commented Emilya.

"Indeed," said Elyse.

"That story is disputed though," interceded Jake. "I take it with a pinch of salt, personally."

"Well, whatever happened," continued Elyse, "he was said to have lived in a cave on Bindom Moor for several years. The authorities eventually found it – empty, of course – and that cave has now become something of a tourist attraction."

"He then started robbing travellers in Wrenko," said Jake. "Mainly on the route from Sattellus to Dominniul. Rich pickings there, for sure. Unfortunately, the authorities never found where he was hiding out – leading them to believe he was being put up by accomplices."

"After a few years, he became a pest on the Dominniul to Ghantiss route – and there were even richer pickings on that route. There were a few casualties, too – where people were foolish enough to resist."

"And then he disappeared, about five years ago," said Jake. "Some folk said he'd been killed by a rival highwayman, others by government men. There's even one theory that the government caught him and sent him over the Shield of Crenac on the quiet!"

"And not forgetting those who said he'd left Glennad," added Elyse, "and now plagues travellers in the Nannosh area of Lendria. Others are convinced he just retired on his riches and is living it up somewhere in a remote part of Aldenocia."

"Meanwhile," said Emilya, "rumour is he's moved to Earl's Leet."

"As do rumours linking him from everywhere between Skeletofon and

Port Myra," said Jake, wryly. "As well as Undress to Yar on Aldenocia, Craffid to Vadstids on Bramcia, and Peregomat to Larresso on Lendria. So, who knows? But if he is up here, Emilya, we'll not miss him!"

"What do you mean?"

"He has, shall we say, a flamboyant and colourful dress-style. All part of his larger-than-life opinion of himself."

As Emilya mused on Harry Black, she noticed that the path had become grassier, whilst winding gently upwards to the right and left to avoid rocky outcrops. Emilya looked down to her right, where the terrain just fell away, with gulley's running in three different directions, each accommodating a narrow downward rush of a burn apiece. By this stage, all of the thorny and hardy bushes had disappeared and in their place was long hardy grass. Emilya then noticed the first barrow to their left – a large mound of grass about twenty feet long by ten feet wide by six feet high. Jake noticed her looking at it. "It's a Bronze Age burial chamber," he said. "At least two thousand five hundred years old. There are dozens of them up here. Some are even older."

"Why did they bury them up here."

"A lot of the tribes lived up here. It was easier to defend than the lowlands. But some think they were buried up here because it's closer to whichever Gods they worshipped."

"They should have buried them up near Kifsel Place then," said Emilya. "That's a few thousand feet nearer to the Gods."

Jake was impressed by her knowledge. "True. But you can't bury someone in solid rock. Here, the ground is diggable in places."

Shortly afterwards, they stopped beside a rocky outcrop for a drink, and Emilya looked back for the first time. The landscape descended towards the vast spread of trees, now almost a league behind them. Emilya then looked at the vistas to the left and right, while ahead was a vast, flat-topped plateau, constantly whipped by wind, and which was covered in dark peat, rusty-coloured scrub and clumps of grasses bleached a dull yellow – plus lots of shallow rocks, thrusting up from the ground. It looked like nowhere else on Glennad she had ever seen; they could quite easily have stepped out onto another world.

Emilya looked again at the ground. She'd seen the odd carriage pass them between Ghannoots and Ghintarton, two days back, but none on the moors, so far, and none visible ahead, either. She remained puzzled as to how carriages made their way across this hostile terrain. Jake noticed her looking in between watering the horses. "They have specially-made axles," he said. "Heavy duty, to withstand the constant buffeting from the uneven ground and the rocky outcrops."

Emilya was dubious. "But even so…"

"Oh yes, this route has brought a premature end to many-a-coach, I'm not denying that. That's why it's mostly for horses, and why most coaches go from Earl's Leet to Ghantiss via Kinnslyng or Bryde – and accept they'll have to do twice the distance than if they'd gone direct."

"And presumably also why the Independents selected their location for Earl's Leet."

"Exactly so, Emilya. Anyway," began Jake, pointing ahead. "We're going to cut across the centre of this plateau, and then at the far end, we'll double-back as we start to drop altitude a little and head north-west for a while. Then, there's a large arc that will bring us back on an easterly bearing to Ghintonoll – our last overnight stop before Earl's Leet."

After another thirty minutes, at around the centre of the plateau, they came upon a large cairn. "This marks the highest part of the Bleaklows," said Jake, dismounting. "It's customary to add a stone to the cairn," he added, casting about for an appropriate stone. He found a bit of loose rock at the base of one of the myriad outcrops, kicked it loose with his boots, picked it up and placed it towards the top of the large pyramidal mound of loose stone. Emilya and Elyse followed suit.

They took on water whilst beside the cairn and also watered their horses. Then, in the distance, to the north-east, Emilya spotted something she hadn't seen before: proper mountains – although the highest peaks were hidden amongst the clouds. "Is that the Umbricans?" she asked, pointing.

"Yes," confirmed Jake. "You should see them on a clear day from the seaboard side, though. They rise right up out of the ocean, most of them snow-topped throughout the winter months."

"Can you see Keplif Scale from here?" she asked, referring to Glennad's highest point.

"No," responded Jake. "It's off to the north from that lot," he said, pointing at the mountains.

"Have you ever climbed it, either of you?"

"No," said Jake.

"Yes," said Elyse.

Both Emilya and Jake raised their eyebrows.

"Don't do that, you two," reproved Elyse. "I've done a lot in my forty years. And I've climbed Keplif Scale twice."

"Twice!" chorused Emilya and Jake.

"Yes, twice. Once in my twenties and again eight years ago. There are organised climbs, run from the monastery at Kifsel Place. The whole area is magical. I will do it again, one day."

Emilya felt a terribly strong draw – almost a yearning – to experience the same thing. "Take me with you when you do, please," she begged.

"Absolutely I will," agreed Elyse with a wide and happy smile.

The penny then dropped for Emilya. "When you say 'magical' – is this one of your vortexes – where these energy lines cross?"

Elyse's smile remained and she nodded. "Almost certainly," she answered, very pleased with her student's insight. "No one is certain, but the power is strong, there. If we do go there, I promise you will be moved. You may even be able to see for the first time."

"To see?"

"It's difficult to explain, Emilya, and I don't want to because it should be experienced naturally."

"You mean, if you tell me what to expect, I might imagine it or even manufacture it?"

Elyse smiled proudly at her charge. "That is exactly what I mean."

"Hmm," said Jake, dubiously, breaking the slowly-building spell. "Well, I've been to the monastery," he announced, "and it was an interesting experience. An amazing feat of engineering and incredible architecture. But the monks there also import the finest wine, you know – made by their brothers at the twin monastery in the valley below. There's something about wine at altitude that…I don't know…"

"How could you climb to the monastery and not finish the job by summiting Keplif Scale?" accused Elyse.

"I'm a man of the sea, Elyse," responded Jake. "Heights like that are unnatural."

"You mean you just got blind drunk and couldn't be bothered."

"Aye, well, there was that as well," admitted Jake, wryly.

"Men!" exclaimed Elyse, rolling her eyes.

It took them another two hours to cross the plateau, and at the point that the track began to double back on itself, Emilya spied a shallow stream heading gently down towards a plunging gap to form a narrow waterfall. Even from a distance, she could see and hear the spray blowing noisily back on itself in the fierce westerly crosswinds, but by the time they were fifty paces away, she realised they were going to have to traverse some distance to the rear of it. It was either that or experience a total drenching. She started to veer off to the right when she realised that Elyse and Jake were making right for the edge. "Hey, you two," she shouted. "You'll get soaked."

"It's another of life's experiences, Emilya," shouted back Elyse, her voice being half-whipped away by the noise of the wind and the spray. "It's incredibly invigorating," she added.

Emilya paused for a second, very much doubting the wisdom of this, and feeling that she was quite the adult of the trio at this particular moment in time. Then she just shrugged her shoulders and directed her horse into a trot to catch them up.

As the trio approached the waterfall and its maelstrom-like shower, Emilya was astonished to spot a large number of sheep clinging to the ledges around the crevices that formed the tight U-shape through which the stream and waterfall dropped. By this stage, her hair and clothing were already soaking wet – but she really didn't care. It wasn't as icy as she'd been expecting, and it was making her smile…before her smile escalated into laughter.

By the time they'd passed through to the other side, both Emilya and Elyse were laughing hysterically. "That's one you can cross off your list, Emilya," said Elyse, once they had stopped laughing. "And you got it with a strong westerly, too – the best experience of all."

Now that the roar from the combined wind and spray was diminishing, Emilya asked the most pressing question on her mind. "Why are those sheep there, though?"

"Nobody knows," said Jake. "They've always been drawn to it."

"They make 'em hard up here, girl," said Elyse.

"Mad, more like," replied Emilya.

Elyse and Jake laughed at that.

"Well," said Emilya, looking first left at Elyse and then right at Jake. She then shook her curly dark-auburn locks from side to say, spraying the pair of them and forcing them to turn away. "What are the chances of us being dry before we get to Ghintonoll?"

CHAPTER 53   MAGNUS

9th Tertiar, 1789   Day 100, 16:00

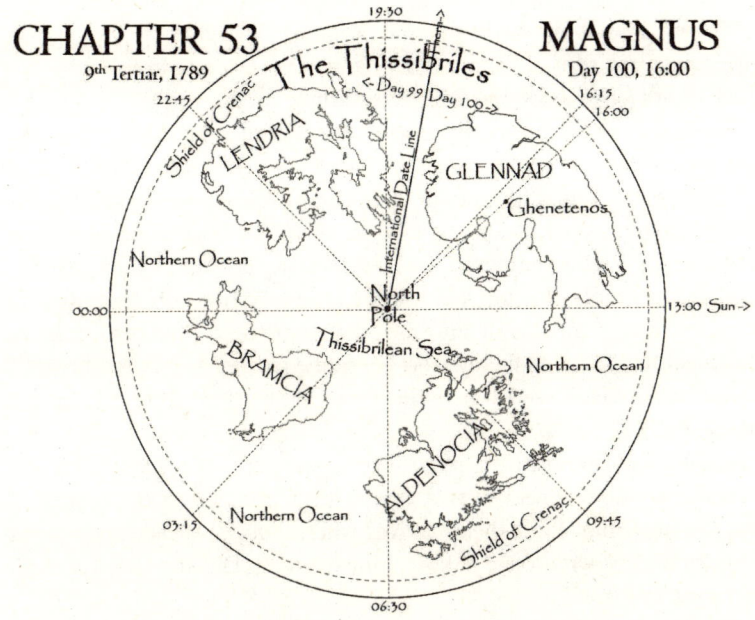

The stones were getting steadily larger as Magnus rode his troupe towards Ghenetenos. They'd had to send two of Hoskyns' men, Skinner and West, back to Ghantiss, as the fool had not thought to select men who could ride. The two hapless lackeys had been told to send two of John Russell's men in their place, once they got back to the palace; assuming they got to the palace before they passed their favourite tavern! The other ruffian, Gage, however, may well have spent much of his adult life in prison for various types of theft, but in between, or in his youth, he'd obviously learned how to ride a horse. Needless to say, the five soldiers selected were all expert riders and Magnus was soon leading them up to the former monastery that had been lovingly restored and fashioned into a large communal home for the druids who lived there. Word had obviously been passed on, as there was a reception committee waiting for them. Magnus jumped down off his horse and led his mare to the waiting robed druids. "A beautiful home you have here, my friends," said the Prince.

"We are honoured by your presence, Your Royal Highness," said a strange-looking man in his thirties. He was wearing a grey habit with the hood down – revealing long and curly black hair, and a long beard. Magnus was disgusted to see dreadlocks intermingled with beads in that beard. Just as repugnant was the black sun tattooed onto the man's forehead. This could only be the druid's leader, Emrys Dolmen.

"I won't beat about the bush," said Magnus. "We're here to have a chat with your sister. Elyse, I believe is her name."

"She's not here," answered Emrys, truthfully.

"I was told by her neighbour in Ghantiss that she was visiting you here for a few days."

"Forgive me, Your Highness. But why do you wish to see Elyse?"

"Ah, I forget myself," said Magnus, graciously. "My sister's horse has gone lame and she is rather desperate. Our stablemaster has been unable to help," he added, inwardly gloating that it was a little hard to tend a horse from a dungeon! "And I am reliably informed that your sister is the best healer in the kingdom. I was hoping to escort her to the palace."

"I'm afraid that Elyse left here three days ago for Kinnslyng, to visit my mother's sister."

Magnus didn't know whether to sneer openly or vent his anger. He was growing very tired of near-misses, and he was particularly growing tired of people lying to him about their relatives' whereabouts. Instead, he managed to shake his head and issue a disappointed smile. "Did she take the Earl's Leet road, perhaps?"

"Oh no, Your Royal Highness," responded Emrys. "You'd have to be rather naïve to visit Kinnslyng by that route. It's three times the distance and takes ten times as long."

Magnus issued another tight smile. "Quite so," he agreed. "Well, I'm very sorry to impose on you like this, but my troupe are a little weary, not to mention a little hungry. I will pay you handsomely," he said, taking out his drawstring purse, "if you would feed us and put us up for one night."

"There's no need to pay, Your Royal Highness," said Emrys. "It will be our pleasure to host such distinguished company."

"Ah, but I insist," said Magnus, counting out eight sovereigns, one for each member of his party and placing them into Emrys' hands. "All I ask in return, other than food and shelter, are directions to your aunt's house in Kinnslyng. We will ride there tomorrow, pick up your sister, and return to Ghantiss direct."

All the time he was talking, Magnus was watching Emrys' face like a hawk. To the head druid's credit, there was only the slightest movement of the pupils, and a slight tightening of his mouth.

"Of course, that will be no problem. Mario!" he called, gesturing to a giant of a man with a thick mop of black hair. "Please could you stable our guests' horses. Your Royal Highness," he said, turning to Magnus. "I will show you to our guest's quarters. Please excuse us if they are a little…basic."

"I'm no craver of opulence," said Magnus. "And I am very grateful for your hospitality."

"You're very welcome. I look forward with great anticipation to our communal evening meal. You will join us, won't you?"

"It will be our pleasure," responded Magnus, with a gracious smile. However, he was still watching Emrys Dolmen very closely. Anyone else would have missed it – but Magnus missed nothing. There was the slightest of commands issued by Emrys to a boy of around fifteen, standing alongside them – all conveyed with a subtle movement of the eyes. But it was a command, nonetheless.

As Emrys led them inside, Magnus noticed the boy didn't join them. With Emrys' back to him, Magnus quickly turned to Marler, and nodded his head in the direction the boy had taken. The ever-sharp Marler understood and peeled off from the back of the group.

Forty minutes later, Marler re-joined them in their quarters.

"Well?" asked Magnus, all hint of charm now extinguished.

"He went to the stables with the stablemaster. Ten minutes later, an old woman arrived with a back-pack. The boy took it, put it on, and then rode north."

"As I suspected, then. "He's going to warn them. Was there any way of telling which route he was taking?"

"I couldn't follow him, Sir. It would have been too obvious. But there are only two routes that way."

"Indeed. Kinnslyng or Earl's Leet. But which one?"

"My money is on Earl's Leet, Sir," said Marler.

"Mine too. Listen, Marler, do you think you could catch him?"

"I do, Sir, but begging your pardon. They'll notice I've gone. I'm a bit conspicuous," he said, pointing at his missing eye.

"I'll go," said Gage.

Magnus eyed the man. Thin as a rake and with a scruffy goatee beard that just added to his aura of shiftiness. Clearly a decent rider, though. But not yet in Magnus' league of trusted thugs.

"You're wondering if you can trust me," said Gage. "Well, you can't. I'm a habitual thief; a general wrong 'un. But I know which side me bread is buttered. I'll track him for you. I presume you want me to remain unseen, and not challenge the boy."

"Very good. Gage, isn't it?"

"Aye, that's right, Sir."

"Very well, Gage. And you are precisely right. I need you to track the boy all the way to Oscom, Elyse Dolmen, Emilya Luca and anyone else who is in their merry little band."

Magnus paused at that point, thinking their position through. "In fact, I'll need two of you to go." He turned around and eyed his five soldiers. He was certain he could trust all of them, but he needed the fastest. "Munton," he called. "Over here, please."

"Sir," said Munton, approaching and then standing to attention.

"You and Mr Gage here are going on an errand. There isn't a moment to lose, as you're already about an hour behind and it's getting late. Mr Gage will brief you on your way. Take your own horses. I'll say that I've sent you back to Ghantiss to fetch the two new recruits, seeing as Skinner and West have let me down."

"Understood, Sir."

"Excellent. And if you find the fugitives, Munton, you must come back to us immediately, as you're my fastest rider – you'll not miss us, as there's only one track between here and Earl's Leet. However, you, Mr Gage, will follow Oscom and his companions wherever they go. If that is Earl's Leet, then perfect. But do not get spotted. I don't want them alerted. Just keep them under observation. Can you do that?"

"It's what I was born for, Sir," said Gage. "They won't spot me."

"What if we don't find them in the next two days, Sir?" asked Munton. "Do you still want me to double back and brief you?"

Magnus paused and thought about the question. "That might make sense, Munton, yes – so that we're informed at the earliest opportunity. Your horse will be tired, though, after two days of hard riding, so you may need to hire a fresh mount." Magnus creased his brow as he analysed the likely timescales. His face then cleared as the logistics fell into place. "By my estimation, you should make Earl's Leet before nightfall, tomorrow. Assuming you've not already caught up with the boy, that will give you a night and most of the next day to try and turn them up. Meanwhile, our main party should be approaching Earl's Leet by late afternoon in two days' time. So, if you haven't located Oscom and his band by 16:00, I suggest you ride out to meet us, a league or two west of Earl's Leet."

"Understood, Sir."

Magnus turned to Gage. "And if you then go on to find them in Earl's Leet, you will need to hire an accomplice." He turned and rummaged in one of his saddle-bags, withdrawing a drawstring bag. "So, here's a bag of crowns to buy them with."

"An accomplice?" asked Gage, taking the bag with greedy eyes.

"Yes, Gage. You can't be in two places at once. When our main party arrives in Earl's Leet, you'll need an accomplice to keep an eye on wherever they are holed up, whilst you come and meet us half a league west of Earl's Leet. You will brief us, and then we can make plans for our quarries."

"A nice little tragedy, no doubt," said Gage, his thin smile revealing his yellow teeth.

"Quite so," agreed Magnus. "But only after they have revealed the location of my sister," he added, his eyes flashing a warning at Gage – who instantly glanced shiftily at Munton, realising his faux-pas.

Marler nodded his approval of Magnus' plan. "Very thorough, Sir. This ends in two days' time."

"Indeed," agreed Magnus. "Now, cut along you two. The Princess Alicya's life may depend on your errand."

As Magnus watched Gage and Munton depart, he felt a swell of satisfaction. They were closing in. Even allowing for tonight, if they left early the next morning, Magnus was confident they would reach Earl's Leet inside two days. Despite his desire to close this little episode down as soon as possible, there was no real hurry. And for now, he and his remaining troupe needed to freshen up and put on their false façades, ready for their evening meal.

Two hours later, Magnus was enjoying a delicious communal meal with the druids of Ghenetenos. The wine was flowing, and he was expectant of loosening tongues. He had even allowed the conversation to turn moderately personal, as Emrys Dolmen's mother, Martha, had quizzed him about his expectations for future marriage. There was something unnerving about the way Martha Dolmen looked at him, though. She was totally unafraid and not remotely overawed to have the heir to the Glennadian throne in her dining room.

"And what about your grandchildren, Mrs Dolmen?" asked Magnus trying to gauge how adaptive she was.

"My grandchildren?"

"Yes, I saw children with Emrys and Lyanna earlier, although one of them looked to be in his mid-teens."

"Oh, that would have been young Owen, the farrier's son. He's teaching the little ones about all things horse at the moment."

"Yes, but I'm sure I heard someone mention an 'Edwyn', earlier."

"Yes, that's Emrys' eldest," said Martha, with a sweet smile. "He went north to Kinnslyng with Elyse, three days ago. Any excuse to go to the seaside, that one."

"I thought you said two days ago, earlier," responded Magnus.

"No" said Martha, shaking her head, unperturbed. "It was definitely three days ago."

Magnus nodded back, impressed with Martha's cool reaction; not the slightest bit intimidated.

"Would you mind if I dealt the cards for you, Your Royal Highness?" Martha asked, right out of the blue.

Magnus was quite off-balanced by that and, as the room had gone quiet at that point, he was somewhat backed into a corner. The infernal woman had turned defence into attack. He laughed nervously. "Oh, come now," he said, hoping his dripping scepticism would see Martha back off.

He was mistaken. The woman's eyes flashed with the scent of victory. "There's no need to be afraid," she cooed.

"Afraid!" exclaimed Magnus, his accompanying laugh sounding distinctly nervous. "Of some random cards!"

His men all laughed at that.

"Go on, Your Royal Highness," encouraged Emrys. "It's only a bit of fun."

They'd got him, damn them both. He could hardly back down now. "Oh, go on then," he said, with forced resignation, shaking his head at the same time. "But you'll have to explain this mumbo-jumbo to me first, as I've no idea what takes place at a card reading."

"It's very simple, Your Royal Highness," said Martha. "There are exactly one hundred cards in the deck. Lyanna, would you mind fetching my special deck, please?"

"Special?" queried Magnus.

"You are the Prince of Glennad, Your Royal Highness."

Damn it, why did he feel so uncomfortable?

As the pack of cards arrived, Martha dropped the set of one hundred into her hand, and then spread them expertly across the table in a wide arc. The colours on the back were a spooky dark blue with black silhouettes. The room was now completely silent, everyone's attention drawn to Martha's cards. The wind rattled slightly at the dining room windows. Magnus half-expected the hoot of an owl to follow or the howl of a wolf, but the only sound which followed was the soft guttering of the candles and the asynchronous respiration of around thirty very expectant people who had crowded around them.

"Each card depicts an event," Martha began, drawing his attention back down to the table and the cards in front of them. "The player selects just three. The first card will depict a major or pivotal event in that person's past.

The second will depict a major current event." At that point, Martha looked Magnus right in the eye, and the Prince cursed himself for widening his gaze. "And the third card," continued Martha, with a suitable pause, "depicts a pivotal event in the person's future. This can represent a major triumph… although it can, on occasion…interpret their mode of death."

Magnus let out a long breath. "Mrs Dolmen…"

"Don't you want to know?" she teased.

"But they're only cards."

"Are they?" she questioned, mockingly. Martha then flipped all of the cards onto their fronts, gathered them up, shuffled them, and then fanned them out again, this time face-down."

"The card of your past, Your Royal Highness. Choose."

Magnus instinctively reached out and then withdrew his hand immediately. *What was the matter with him?* His stupid hand was *shaking* slightly, too, so, he darted it out to hide the fact, and pulled out a card from two thirds of the way to the right. It now lay isolated from the rest, still face down.

Martha calmly reached out and turned the card over.

It was a picture of a shark.

All the colour drained from Magnus' face and he remained silent.

"This is of significance to you?" asked Martha, quietly.

Magnus still didn't answer. He was dumbstruck.

"Sir?" asked Marler, from his right-hand side.

"I was six years old," said Magnus, in a small voice.

Marler and Hoskyns exchanged glances. This wasn't the prince that they knew.

"You were attacked by a shark?" asked Martha.

Magnus raised his eyes, slowly coming out of his shock, and a typical Magnus-like smirk began to unfurl. "How did you do that?"

"I did nothing. The choice was yours, and yours alone."

"You knew about the shark attack. I bet they're all sharks," he said, flipping over a range of twenty-or-so cards. They were all different. They were also very diverse: objects, animals, buildings, landscapes, symbology, abstracts. But only one shark.

Magnus' own blue eyes locked onto Martha's penetrating azure pair – but he soon realised he wasn't going to win this psychological battle. He therefore looked away but laughed at the same time. "Well, I'll be…"

Martha finally looked away, the ghost of a smile on her face. She then picked up the deck of cards, shuffled them again, and then spread them out in another large arc, again all face-down. "The card of your present, Your Royal Highness."

Once again, you could hear a pin drop. Once again, Magnus could feel his hands shaking, which was why he was keeping them tucked away under his folded arms. This time he went for a card towards the left-hand end of the arc, quickly pulled it out and left it face-down on the table.

Once again, Martha reached out and turned the card over.

Magnus actually laughed out loud at what he saw. It was a picture of a naval captain.

Neither Marler nor Hoskyns were laughing though. Both of them were now quite tense, so Magnus leant back in his chair, still smiling, and patted both henchmen on the back. "Come along, men, loosen up. That card is irrelevant. I don't know any ship's captains, so this is clearly a load of old nonsense."

Martha nailed him again. "Well in that case, Your Royal Highness, you won't mind picking your future card then." She smiled at him. "Will you?"

This time, Magnus couldn't hide his scowl. He wasn't used to being given the psychological run-around by anyone else; that was his domain. And from a sixty-year-old woman, too. Well, he thought, let's see what the old witch has in store for me. He didn't know how she had fixed the cards, but he knew that she had.

"The card of your future, Your Royal Highness," prompted Martha, her voice as soft as a kiss, but her eyes as sharp as pins.

"Very well," he said, swallowing once. "A major triumph, you say?"

"Or your mode of death."

Martha was a whisker away from being treasonous, and every person present knew it. Nevertheless, the tension in the room was on a knife-edge, while Magnus' curiosity was beginning to overtake his fear. His hand had also stopped shaking. This time, he deliberately added to the drama himself, and his hand went slowly and surely to a card almost dead-centre – maybe one notch to the right. He pulled the card out slowly and left it face down.

For a third and final time Martha calmly reached out to the selected card and turned it over.

It was fire.

CHAPTER 54 — WILL

9th Tertiar, 1789   Day 100, 13:00

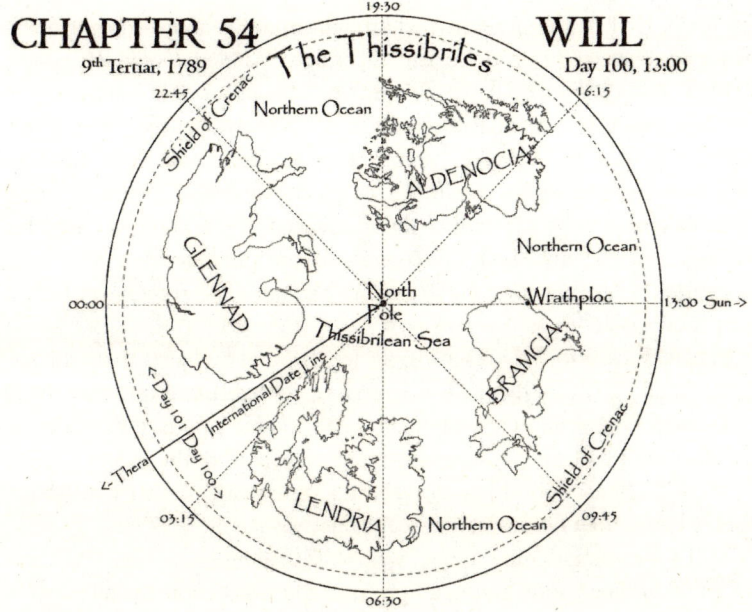

Will was concentrating hard on the little circle of light that had appeared at the centre of his vision. There had been times over the last two days, since Nate Turner had seen him safely out of the mine, that he'd thought he would never see again – but he had largely remained positive.

"*You were looking right at Dylan's candle when the gas ignited,*" Robbie had said. "*It will only be temporary.*"

"*It'll come back, young Will,*" Nate Turner had told him. "*The same thing happened to Alf Lynn way back in '54. He was blind for three days before his sight returned.*"

It had rained for the majority of their journey on the horse that Will was sharing with Turner, and Will was soaked to the skin. Given his lack of sight, the presence of Turner behind him was vaguely reassuring – although Will wasn't ready to relax yet, and he was still fairly sure that Turner had been the trigger for the explosion at Cabrenar, and the likely deaths of Dylan and Robbie. He'd thought so much about Robbie throughout this journey. Blindness had probably been a blessing back in the mine, as the agony that his mentor had been in had been evident in every whispered word. Will felt that pain almost physically, not just through the minor burns of his own, but right through his core.

Turner had burns, too, and Will suspected they were worse than he was letting on. He'd shared the salve he'd brought from his home, treating Will's own lesser burns to his face and arm as gently as his Mam would have done. Blinded, Will could actually *feel* Turner's emotional turmoil – although he hadn't forgotten how hard Turner had struck him back in the mine. It was only the second time in his life that he'd been knocked senseless; the first had been after running into a cast-iron wall-bracket outside Cabrenar Smithy. Dylan had been chasing him when the accident occurred. The concern on his Mam's face was so vivid, he felt he could reach out and touch it -.

Turner's wheezing voice cut across his thoughts. "We're approaching a port, young Will," he said.

Hauled back into the present, Will decided that he hated that address. Turner made it sound like he was special or related. Either thought made Will's skin crawl. And in any case, Davy and Robbie had used that address as well – but it had sounded very different coming from them.

"It's at the bottom of this valley, about a mile away," Turner was saying. "Please don't shout out or make a scene once we arrive?"

"What are you planning to do?" was Will's response.

"You'll find out, soon enough. I promise you won't come to any harm."

"Which port is it? Craffid, Phanter, Rybar?"

The only response was silence.

"Or have you gone south-east – to Wrathploc?"

"You're certainly a smart one, young Will."

"What are you going to do with me?" he asked, yet again.

"Like I've told you every time before. I don't really know. But I'm not going to hurt you."

"But you must have a plan."

"A vague one."

"Which is?"

Silence again.

"Well," began Will. "If we're making for a port, chances are you're looking to take a boat somewhere."

More silence.

"All I need to do is shout out before we get on that boat."

"In which case, we'll have to do this the hard way, then."

Will didn't like the sound of that. "What do you mean?"

Turner didn't respond. They trooped on in silence for another two minutes before Turner brought their horse to a stop. Will had no idea where they were, and he could only hear the vaguest echoes of habitation – which may well have been a trick of the wind or his imagination, anyway. Turner dismounted behind him, before strong arms hoisted him out of the saddle. Once again, Turner was nothing but gentle with him. "I'm sorry, young Will, but I have no choice. Hold out your hands."

Will briefly considered struggling, but decided it wasn't worth another knockout blow. He complied, let Turner tie his hands and feet and then lie him on his side in what felt and smelt like long grass. Long wet grass. That was followed by the application of a rag across his mouth, tied tight enough to stop him from calling out, but not tight enough to hurt. Finally, Turner laid either his coat or a blanket around Will to keep him warm. He then appeared to have second thoughts about the gag, and eased it loose. "I'll be totally honest with you, young man. Yes, we're half a mile from Wrathploc. Yes, I've enough money to buy a boat – although I'll gladly steal one if opportunity presents. But no, I don't know where we're going – other than down the east coast towards the estuary."

"The estuary."

"Aye – with Perebkom on one side and Hardilfvenom on the other. I've half a mind to pitch us as fishermen. Father and son. Is that so daft?"

"What about me Mam?"

There was a long pause. When Turner next spoke, his voice was heavy with grief. "She won't -. She might…"

There was another pause. Turner then blew his nose. "I'm sorry, Will, lad," he said, finally. "Truly I am." And then he was applying the gag again. "I'll take you back to her, one day. I just can't do it now."

Will wasn't sure how long he'd been left for because he had fallen asleep, despite being cold and wet. He soon forgot his discomfort, though, when he opened his eyes. It was dark, yes, but he could see movement, too. As the movement was close-up, Will surmised it was the grass wafting back and forth in the wind. He waved his bound hands in front of his face – and the shadows immediately darkened.

Given it was likely now night-time, Will was unable to judge the extent to which his eyesight had returned. But the fact that it had brought him great joy and relief. So long as he kept the fact from Turner, he would have every chance of getting away – preferably before Turner got him on this boat. Will didn't know his geography beyond northern Bramcia, but he was certain that Wrathploc was considerably nearer to Cabrenar than this estuary place that Turner had mentioned earlier.

It was another hour before Turner finally returned. The first thing that Will noticed, as Turner bent down to help him to his feet, was the smell of ale on his breath. "I've found a boat," was all he said.

He said little more until the boat was out on the Northern Ocean and heading southwards. In between, a bound and gagged Will could only rejoice in the fact that he could now see what was happening thanks to the moonlight and a few lighted torches on the outskirts of Wrathploc. He certainly saw Turner leave his horse in a stable – which again, suggested someone with a heart – before he led Will down towards a deserted quayside where half a dozen boats were bobbing about on the now-calm midnight tide. Turner selected a wooden rower, slipped the moorings, and was soon rowing backwards, fairly expertly, out of the harbour.

And that was that. There was no opportunity for Will to call out because he still had his gag in place, and in any case, there wasn't anyone about. Oddly, Will wasn't too panicked. He wouldn't ever relax in Turner's presence, but Turner genuinely didn't appear to wish him any harm, either. This left Will confused as to why Dylan had been so spooked by Turner. Nevertheless, with Will's sight having returned and figuring that Turner would have to release his bonds and gag once they reached their next destination, his chances of escape had definitely improved.

CHAPTER 55   ARRAN
9th Tertiar, 1789   Day 100, 11:00

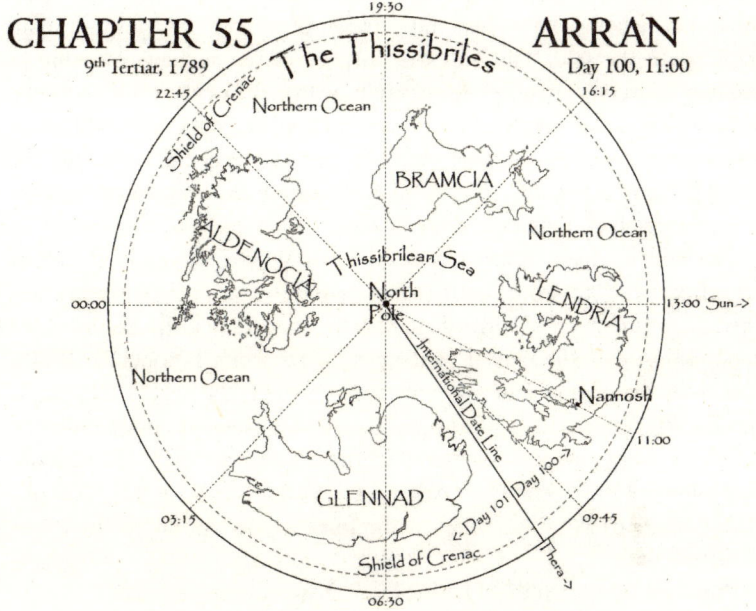

As requested, Arran and Professor Doran had taken a third astronomer into their confidence. Jim Geraghty had never aspired to be Astronomer Royal in his twenty-five years of service, always happy just to learn. This meant that his astronomical knowledge was extensive. He knew the name and position of every star, nebula and galaxy in the cosmos; more particularly, his knowledge of alignment and movement of celestial bodies was the best in the kingdom. That said, poor Jim had regularly expressed since they'd brought him on board that he wished they hadn't bothered, and left him blissfully unaware – this after he had confirmed the theory: *Yes, the asteroid will strike Thera.*

Arran still remembered the look on Lenahan Driscoll's face. The Ocateshia had been hoping his current and previous Astronomer Royals were wrong. Jim Geraghty's diagnosis meant there was little chance of that now and Driscoll was fully reconciled with the fact that Planet Thera was facing a global catastrophe. During the course of the night, Driscoll had brought six of his most-trusted members of the cabinet into the fold – each of whom now carried the same burdened look in their eyes. The ten of them had agreed unanimously that today's session of Parliament, like yesterday's, would have to be abandoned; their dilemma was what to tell the other two hundred members of the house. In the end, they'd had little choice but to bring the leaders and deputies of each of Lendria's four main parties into the fold. This was the purpose of the current gathering in Lenahan Driscoll's office, while hopefully, within the week, would come the formation of a four-party coalition and an explanation to the public that they were experimenting, attempting to find a balanced government and the right blend across all parties, with compromise ensuring that all policies would be partly or fully represented.

The first of them to arrive was Aloysius Whyte, a pompous, former magistrate, who still wore his official wig to hide his lack of hair. Meanwhile, the tight cream breeches did little to hide his expanding girth. Leader of the Republicans, and the closest challenger to Driscoll's Democrats, Whyte knew very well that he had a decent chance of being the next Ocateshia. As far as he was concerned, failure to attend yesterday's session, and cancellation of today's, were just desperate tactics from a desperate man. His face was like thunder. "You'd better have a damn good explanation for this, Driscoll," he had snarled, as he took one of the fifteen seats that faced the Prime Minister's desk.

"You will soon wish that I hadn't," was Driscoll's curt response.

"What? What's that supposed to mean?"

"Yes, you don't fool us, Driscoll," said Whyte's deputy, as he sat down beside his leader. Gerry Phelan's distinctive feature was his crooked mouth, which only opened on the right-hand side when he spoke. It made all his words appear to be snide ones. "But cancelling Parliament is a little extreme. Even for a desperate man like you."

Driscoll chose to ignore that comment and waited patiently as the other leaders and deputies filed in, one-by-one. Much as he disliked both Whyte and Phelan, Arran actually felt sorry for them for what they were about to hear. He felt sorry for all of them. They all had wives, children, grandchildren.

Thirty minutes later, after Arran, Professor Doran and Jim Geraghty had delivered their hastily prepared presentation, Whyte shook his head in disbelief. "So, you're proposing that we suspend Parliament for two months and rule as a coalition – to see if this fallacy comes true. And when it doesn't, what then? A quick coup? Or do I wake up in the middle of the night to find an assassin with his knife at my throat?"

"Damn it, Whyte!" said Driscoll, leaning forwards. "I'm a man of peace, a man who strives to deliver the best to his people. A man who believes fervently in democracy. And you know that very well."

"I know nothing of the sort," snarled Whyte, jumping to his feet. "Come on Gerry. We're leaving now."

Whyte and Phelan weren't the first two to leave their seats though. The burly Ged Brady, deputy of the Libertarian Party, beat them to it, and stood directly in front of the closed doors, his arms folded. He was joined shortly afterwards by his leader, Donny Whelan. "You're going nowhere, Aloysius Whyte," said Brady, placing a huge hand on Whyte's chest to stop his forward advance.

"You dare to -."

"Oh, grow up, Whyte!" demanded a commanding voice, which cut through the building confrontation. Arran was astonished to see that the statement had been issued by Professor Doran. "You were a trouble-maker at school, and you're still a trouble-maker now. Do you really think that the Prime Minister of Lendria would dream up a story like this?"

Whyte turned around and jabbed a finger in the Professor's direction. "You are not my teacher now, Doran," he snapped, through gritted teeth and putting great venom into the Professor's surname. "And I was *not* the only trouble-maker, either."

"True," admitted the professor. "But you were comfortably the worst."

Arran could feel events starting to spiral out of control, so he stepped across the eyeline of both men. "Mr Whyte," he said calmly. "You have a family, yes? A wife and three children?"

"Are you threatening me?"

Arran closed his eyes but kept his cool. This man would try the patience of a Saint. When he opened them, he looked Whyte in the eye. "I saw your boy got a First at Iblund. You must have been proud."

"What? What's that got to do with anything?"

"You want him to go into Law – as you once did, am I right?"

Whyte didn't respond. He just stared at Arran, unable to comprehend where this was going.

"Well, that's probably not going to happen, Mr Whyte," continued Arran. "Depending upon where the asteroid hits, there may be no more Iblund University, or a Lendrian Parliament. And there may not be an Ocateshia for a very long time – if ever again."

"The prime motive for this meeting," said Driscoll, smoothly taking over, "was to suggest that we suspend Parliament, and elect ourselves as a coalition party – all four of us – Republicans, Democrats, Libertarians and Constitutionalists. We have a massive collective responsibility. The greatest responsibility anyone has ever had in the history of our nation. As do the leaders of all other nations. And I'm inviting you to be part of that, Aloysius. We must set aside our differences, and work out what is best for every last man, woman and child in our country. Once we've done that, we will talk to our three sister nations, and we will attempt to assemble an even larger coalition. Now, does that make sense to you?"

Whyte continued to look at Driscoll but remained silent. Eventually, his shoulders slumped, arms by his sides. He looked at the floor – and maybe for the first time in his life, Aloysius Whyte apologised.

"Apology accepted," said Driscoll, without hesitation. "Please, gentlemen," he said. "Please re-take your seats. We have much to discuss, and so much more to prepare."

CHAPTER 56   CALIDIUS
10th Tertiar, 1789   Day 101, 13:30

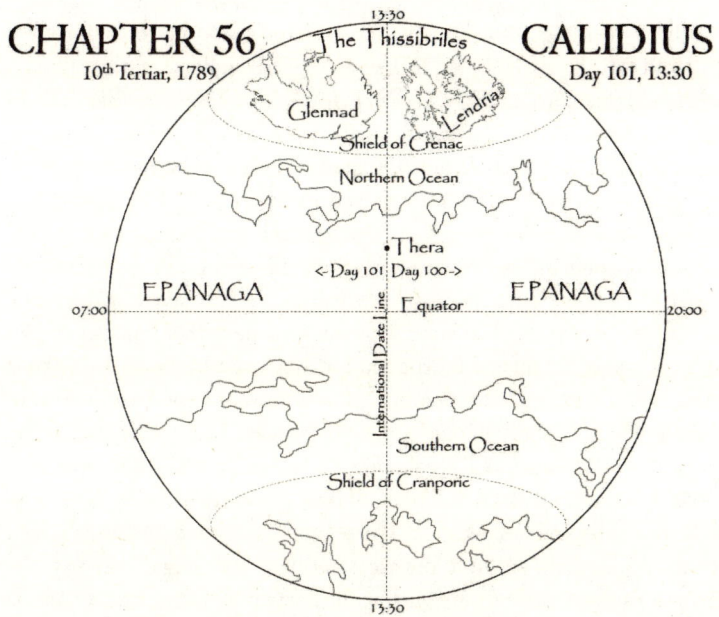

Calidius closed his eyes to calm his nerves. It was less than three days since Emperor Vitasian Flavius Dominius had been found, murdered in his bed beside his two dead lovers. Vitasian's state funeral had taken place yesterday. Today, he, Calidius Antoninus Dominius, would be crowned the 316th Emperor of Thera. Therans did not tarry. Tarrying in Thera offered opportunity, and there were always predators with eyes on the throne – although competition today was not as it had been in times of antiquity.

Calidius almost smiled. Back then, it wasn't considered a good coronation unless half a dozen pretenders had been slain in the days leading up to the event. Had it still been a fight of the fittest, though, Calidius would have backed himself to triumph. But thanks to a millennium of progress, here he was, standing unopposed before the massive gilded doors of the Grand Basilica of Thera, dressed in the finest golden robe in the world, and draped with the richest cloak of dark red exquisitely embroidered with gold. Here he was, backed by his retinue of personal guard, also resplendent in the red and gold of *Legio 1 Victrix*, followed by high-ranking senators and Theran officials who vied to outdo each other with opulent garb and adornments, followed by the even more resplendent primates and high-ranking priests.

Calidius could hear the excited murmur beyond the closed twelve foot-high Basilica doors. He had been a child when his father had been crowned, twenty-three years ago, but he still remembered the occasion with great clarity. He certainly remembered the longing of his eight-year-old self to be the subject of this coronation, one day. Knowledge of Nessemi did take an edge off the occasion, but the future wasn't fully known, and they may yet all be spared. His biggest issue, short-term, was keeping the secret – having already sent assassins to silence two senators suspected of whispering to their wives. Naturally, the wives had been silenced, too.

Calidius' thoughts were brought back to the present, as the huge basilica doors began to open inwards, slowly revealing the vast space within. The ancient church was packed; anyone who was anyone in Theran society had secured their seat, by means fair or foul. It may even be, mused Calidius, that 'means foul' had created more vacancies for the privileged ten thousand!

Looking ahead, Calidius could see arch-primate Didius Severus in the distance, at the high altar. Tall, erect and splendid in his robes and mitre, his hawk-like face lasered in on Calidius. Didius gestured with his hand that Calidius should begin his slow walk. The second he stepped forward a dozen musicians lifted their six-foot bronze trumpets and began to play the Coronation Fanfare. Others were playing the deeper-sounding bronze *cornus* which curled around their bodies in a vague G shape. The combined sound was magnificent, triumphal.

As Calidius entered the basilica, the congregation were on their feet, turning to behold their new emperor, many saluting with their right arm across their chests as he passed them, while others were offering him their personal blessings and affection. In front of him, children in flowing white robes were scattering petals of blue, red, yellow and purple, and to the front, in the stalls, the choir had taken up their melodious chant which perfectly complimented the harmonic swell of the brass orchestra. Everything was perfect.

Except they may all be dead in just over eighty days.

Calidius eventually reached the three steps to the high altar and ascended them, sedately. He then stopped and knelt on the burgundy cushion at the feet of the arch-primate. Calidius rather resented the deference, but it was a necessary gesture. It was tradition, after all. As was the magnificence of the Imperial Regalia behind the arch-primate.

The horns and the choir had now fallen silent, replaced by a tangible air of expectancy. Calidius heard the congregation take their seats behind him. Didius Severus waited a few seconds, building the moment…and then he began his sermon. Calidius heard none of it. Despite the threat of world's end, despite the moment of his fast-approaching annunciation, try as he might, Calidius could not take his eyes from the spectacular crown, sat on another burgundy cushion, some four feet from where he was kneeling. Eight-sided and made of solid gold, the Imperial Crown was inlaid with the most priceless collection of rubies, emeralds, sapphires and garnet, and was widely-known as the most valuable artefact in northern Epanaga and almost certainly in the entire world. Close-up, Calidius could see why.

To the left, on another burgundy cushion, rested the Imperial Orb, its spherical golden base the perfect size to fit in the palm of his hand, and the golden cross that rose above it also inlaid with spectacular gemstones. To the right was the forty-five-inch Imperial Sword, currently in its breathtaking golden scabbard, but with the legendary sharkskin hilt and its stupendous, enormous ruby pommel both visible. This Imperial Regalia symbolised both the arch-primate's right to crown, and also the emperor's role as the protector of the Theran Church. A coronation by any other than the arch-primate, would render the imperial title of *Imperator Electus Theraeon* null and void.

As would a half a league-wide asteroid.

And yet, Calidius remained mesmerised by the regalia, and deaf to the Coronation Prayer, currently being offered up by the arch-primate and responded to by the congregation. Then, with a shock, Calidius realised that it was almost through as he tuned in to the final words.

"…look, Almighty God, with a serene gaze on this, upon your glorious servant." The arch-primate then stepped forward and lifted the heavy crown from its cushion before turning and stopping in front of Calidius. He then slowly, reverently, lowered it on to his head.

It felt like the world.

Minutes passed. Calidius eventually tuned back in to the arch-primate: "…honour and glory are yours, through the infinite ages of ages. Amen." Didius Severus then reverently, placed the Imperial Orb in Calidius' outstretched left hand, and the Imperial Sword, now drawn, into his proffered right. "Receive this sword by the hands of primates, who are consecrated to deliver it to you, with our blessing, to serve for the defence of the Holy Church, divinely ordained."

The congregation then took their cue and began to chant a series of formal acclamations which affirmed that Calidius was now recognised as the 316th Emperor of Thera.

It should have been the moment of his lifetime, but Calidius could not banish the terrible burden of responsibility that he now carried; a burden a thousand times more significant than that held by any of his three hundred and fifteen predecessors. Nevertheless, despite the pending peril, despite the possible end of all life on Thera...he was still emperor. And should this world survive, Calidius was determined that he would be remembered as the greatest emperor of all time...and certainly the most feared. He had much work to do. But first, he would have to receive the acclaim of his people.

Calidius rose and turned to face the congregation.

"Hail Calidius, 316th Emperor of Thera," acclaimed Didius Severus.

"Hail Calidius!" went up the chant. "Hail Calidius! Hail Calidius!"

CHAPTER 57 — EMILYA
10th Tertiar, 1789 — Day 101, 15:30

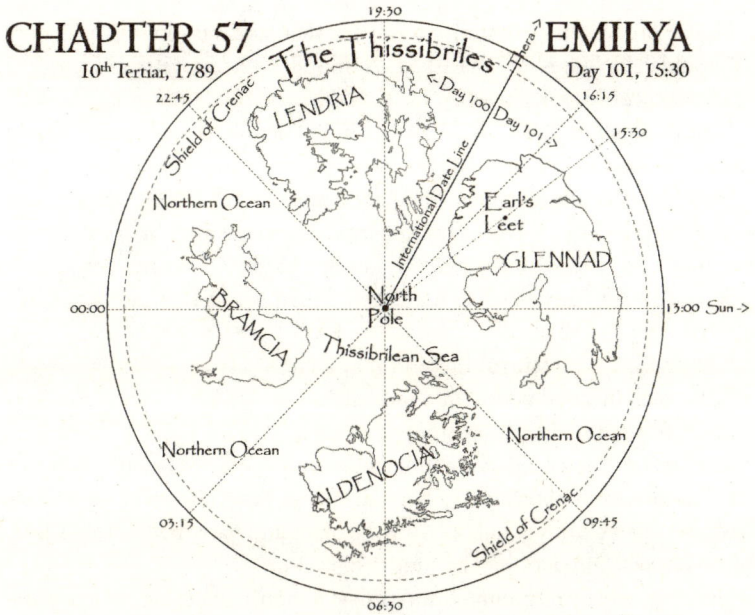

Although they had been heading gradually downwards from the plateau for the last four hours, the landscape around them was still bleak, yet it undeniably had beauty, too. Outcrops of rock still appeared on all sides, amid long grasses and heathers, and Emilya could see a great arc of sheer gritstone edge circling around to her left. Beyond that was a valley and the first glimpse of lower ground that she had seen in the last three days. Emilya figured that Earl's Leet would be somewhere down there; not in the valley, but half-way up on a large shelf of land, which was how Jake had described it to her.

"Another two hours, you reckon?" asked Emilya.

"About that," confirmed Jake.

Emilya had mixed feelings about reaching their destination. It would be nice to settle down in one place for a while, and she was excited to see what Earl's Leet looked like, given it was relatively modern. On the other hand, she would miss the travel, seeing something different around each corner, constantly feeling the wind in her hair; not to mention the odd blowback waterfall!

Emilya smiled at the memory of the three of them at Bleaklow Downfall; just like kids in a fountain. It perfectly encapsulated the magic of these last few days, and the wonderful sense of freedom.

Emilya broke off her reminiscing, aware that Jake was looking back over his shoulder. "What is it?" she asked, as they all turned together.

"Rider coming in. Fast, too."

"Just the one, though," said Elyse, using a hand over her eyes to shield against the sun.

Emilya's heart missed a beat. She'd done much daydreaming during their journey, much about Edwyn and implausible reasons why he would come after them. So, although the rider did look just like Elyse's nephew at this distance, Emilya suspected it was her yearned-for fiction playing tricks with her eyes. But then…

"Oh my God!" exclaimed Elyse. "It's Edwyn!"

"This can't be good news," said Jake, grimly.

Emilya's heart had nigh-on stopped beating.

Sixty seconds later, Edwyn approached, having eased his bay down to a trot. The horse was absolutely lathered in sweat. Edwyn wasn't much better off: dishevelled clothing, hair all over the place and part-matted to his face, hollow cheeks, and dark patches under his eyes.

Elyse had already dismounted and rushed to him, helping her tired nephew out of the saddle. "It's Magnus, isn't it?" she asked, voicing the fears of all three of them.

"Yes," gasped Edwyn, breathing heavily. "He turned up at about four o'clock yesterday afternoon."

"What!" exclaimed Elyse. "And you made it here since late yesterday afternoon?"

"Yeah," said Edwyn, flashing a smile for the first time. "I stopped at the hostel in Ghintarton last night – got there about midnight – uphill, most of that section, so Garresh needed a rest," he said, patting the neck of his bay, whom Emilya noticed had four characterful white socks. "I figured I could get to Earl's Leet in one day from Ghintarton. Seems I was right. Although I did get up at four!"

"What can you tell us?" asked Jake, ever the practical one.

"He had eight men with him. I counted five soldiers; didn't like the look of the other three."

"What did they look like?" asked Jake.

"One of them was missing an eye."

"Marler!" said Jake, with great distaste.

"Another had heavy, jutting eyebrows, dark hair -."

"And Hoskyns!"

"And the other was a younger bloke, thin, shifty-looking."

"Just the type of cut-throat that Magnus likes to employ, then."

"And did they say why they were there?" asked Elyse.

"Yeah, some tosh about needing you, Auntie."

"Me?"

"Yeah. Apparently, the Princess Alicya's horse went lame, and you're the only person in the whole kingdom who can sort it out."

"What did Emrys say?"

"Told him you'd left for Kinnslyng three days earlier."

"And did he believe him?"

"Probably not. Dad gave me the nod when Magnus wasn't looking. Problem is, I think One-Eye saw him – ironically!"

Emilya smirked at Edwyn's little quip.

"Were you followed?"

"Not immediately, but I wouldn't rule it out. I had a good start on them. I've been worried sick they *were* following me, but had skipped an overnight stop at Ghintarton and had got to you first."

"Well," said Jake, clapping Edwyn on the shoulder, "if they did follow you, they haven't got your tenacity, young man. Thank you."

Elyse's response was to embrace her tall and slender nephew and kiss him on the cheek. Edwyn smiled and then smiled at Emilya. "Hi," he said, raising his hand.

"Hi," responded Emilya, with a shy smile, also raising her hand.

They both laughed. Then Emilya said: "I don't know why we're laughing, though."

"No," agreed Edwyn. He turned to Jake. "What are you going to do?"

Jake gave a big sigh. "I'm afraid this changes our plans. I mean, we're assuming that it's you he wants, Emilya, after that business at your father's bakery. But if he knows that I'm with you too – which he likely does, given he's tracked us to Ghenetenos – then it makes more sense that *I* would become the main target. I mean, your 'crime' is lame. But mine, I held a cutlass to his neck, nicked him and then humiliated him by exposing his privates."

"Truth be told," said Elyse, "he's more likely to see an opportunity for killing two birds with one stone."

"Indeed," agreed Jake. "Which is why I think we need to split up. Give him two targets instead of one. If we hide you two away, I'll do my best to lead them away from you."

"Oh no! exclaimed Emilya. "We can't break up."

Jake put his hand on Emilya's shoulder. "We need to, Emilya. For your sake. And I'm sure I don't need to ask…" he said, turning to look at Elyse.

"Of course not," confirmed Elyse. "I'll do whatever is necessary to protect and support you, Emilya."

Emilya suddenly felt her mere fifteen years and could do nothing to stop the tears from welling up. "That horrible man!" she said, and actually stamped her foot, in time.

"I'll come with you as well, if you like?" offered Edwyn.

Emilya's immediate response was an overwhelming desire to agree. But then she stifled that thought. Edwyn deserved no further risk in this; it was enough that they'd put his wonderful aunt at risk.

"I don't think that would be wise, Edwyn," said Elyse, perhaps in a bid to protect her nephew. "The authorities are likely looking for two females and one male. But thank you for offering, and I know you meant it," she said, briefly flicking a glance at Emilya's unhappy face.

"You should make for Kifsel Place," said Jake. "The monks will take you in at the monastery there. With a bit of luck, climbing mountains will be too much trouble for Magnus. Or maybe he won't be interested in you, anyway, and he'll chase me down the River Esou – which is where I intend to make for, making a lot of noise as I go. From there, I'll lead him a merry dance across southern Glennad."

There was silence for a few seconds, then Jake continued. "I'll get word to you at Kifsel, somehow. I'll also assess the danger. If Magnus is unbothered by you, you can just stick it out at the monastery for a few months and then maybe even go home to Ghantiss later this year."

Emilya and Edwyn briefly caught each other's eyes.

"On the other hand," continued Jake. "If he *is* still bothered by you, he'll likely disregard sanctuary – so I'll send warning to you and you could perhaps make for the coast, maybe disguised as monks, and then take a boat to Lendria. He definitely won't be able to touch you there."

Emilya was watching Edwyn's face all the time and felt a little surge of hope at how his features fell when Jake mentioned Lendria.

Elyse turned to her nephew. "Edwyn," she said, taking both of his hands in hers. "You need to make your way back to Ghenetenos now. Your Mam will be worried sick."

"You can ride with us for a bit, son," said Jake, "as I would suggest going back to Ghenetenos via Kinnslyng. You don't want to be bumping in to Magnus and company coming in from the Bleaklows."

"Absolutely not!" exclaimed a worried Elyse.

"Fortunately, we're close to the junction of the Ghenetenos and Kinnslyng roads. You can double-back north-west down the valley. Although it's quite a bit further around, it's a lot easier, terrain-wise. Your horse will certainly thank you for it, anyway."

Edwyn patted his bay on the neck again. "Yes, poor Garresh. I'm so sorry, girl."

Jake was now looking back along the road that eventually double-horseshoed back to Ghintonoll. You could see a long way back, and there was no evidence of a posse heading their way: just a couple of pairs of ordinary travellers. "Did you get any indication of whether they were staying at Ghenetenos last night?"

"Definitely staying at our place, last night," confirmed Edwyn. "Prince Magnus asked, and father agreed to put them all up and provide them with dinner."

Emilya felt a pang of yearning at that, vividly remembering how wonderful that evening meal had been four nights ago; the pale-blue dress, the convivial atmosphere, talking to Edwyn on the veranda. It was hard to imagine someone as noxious as Prince Magnus being waited on in the same fashion. It almost spoiled the memory.

"Good," Jake was saying. "That suggests that he isn't in a tearing hurry – which means he and his men are probably stopping in Ghannoots tonight. They certainly won't have got further than Ghintonoll, but my money's on Ghannoots – meaning they're travelling twice as fast as we were. This means they'll likely arrive in Earl's Leet tomorrow afternoon or tomorrow evening."

"I'm inclined to agree with you," said Elyse. "But it doesn't give us much leeway, does it?"

"Agreed," said Jake, jumping up onto his horse. "There's no time to waste. So, Edwyn, I suggest we walk you and Garresh to the junction on the outskirts of Earl's Leet, say our goodbyes, and then we three will lose ourselves in the town. We then go our separate ways early tomorrow morning."

As they set off, Jake and Elyse rode side-by-side up-front, and Edwyn pulled in alongside Emilya. "I'm glad you're all right," he said.

Emilya gave him a sad smile and instinctively held out her left hand, as was Elyse's habit towards her. Edwyn immediately held out his right hand, and their fingers briefly entwined before they let go, both overly self-conscious. Then their eyes met. Emilya looked down, immediately, but then bravely looked back up again. "You've just done an amazing thing, Edwyn. Thank you so much."

"I wish things were different," said Edwyn, simply.

Emilya closed her eyes. "Me too," she whispered.

They carried on in silence for a minute, Emilya racking her brains for something to say. Then it came to her. "Oh," she began. Edwyn looked up, expectantly. "I got it out of Elyse what Earth Studies are."

Edwyn briefly blushed. "Not everything, I hope."

"What do you mean by that?"

"Oh, nothing," said Edwyn, innocently.

"Oh, come on, Edwyn," said Emilya, once again feeling that tiny flutter in her stomach at speaking his name. "What did Elyse say to me?" she said, recollecting. "'The human body is a powerful thing, Emilya.'"

Edwyn couldn't help but smirk, despite his discomfort. "It's not what you think," he said.

"I should hope not," responded Emilya, wryly.

Edwyn didn't respond to that, so Emilya probed a little more. "Have you ever felt this 'power' that she talks about? From the earth? From the stones? From the trees?"

"Some people feel it more than others. Like Aunt Elyse does. And particularly my grandmother. I'm not tuned in the same way," he said, sounding disappointed.

"Well, I'm glad you're not," said Emilya. "It sounds scary."

Edwyn looked up at her. "It can be very scary," he said. "I've seen it. I've *felt* it."

Emilya's whole body shuddered at that. "Elyse said she wanted to show me, one day."

"Well," said Edwyn, flashing her a shy smile. "If she does, I will gladly hold your hand if you feel scared."

"Aw, thank you Edwyn," said Emilya with a warm smile. "That's a lovely thing to say."

"I wish things were different," said Edwyn again. This time he qualified why. "I've never met anyone before like you. I mean, you're different. But in a good way. I feel…comfortable with you…" he tailed off, clearly feeling terribly self-conscious.

"Well," said Emilya, a slight smile playing about her lips. "The feeling's mutual, Edwyn."

Edwyn issued a little smile of contentment at that but carried on looking straight ahead.

A silence then fell as they began to descend around a large arcing ledge of land – and Earl's Leet gradually appeared before them, spread out across a level plateau half a league ahead, wedged between hills to the north, west and south. The valley then continued to descend at the other side to the east of Earl's Leet. And somewhere to the south, thought Emilya, was the remains of her grandfather's aqueduct. Given it sounded as if she and Elyse were off north-east to Kifsel Place, it was now unlikely she would get to see it. At least not this time, anyway.

As for Earl's Leet, it was not so very different to how she had imagined it. There weren't any high towers or steeples, no golden palaces or opulent buildings, but there were hundreds of precisely-constructed stone and red-brick buildings packed in around the centre of the town, while towards the outskirts, there were more functional wooden buildings for the workers and their families, but which mostly looked very neat and presentable.

Emilya then looked to her left, where she could see another road coming up out of the valley and rising towards an intersection with their own road. With a surge of regret, Emilya realised that this must be the road from Earl's Leet to Kinnslyng. "Oh no," she said, quietly.

Shortly afterwards, they all dismounted. Elyse came straight over to Edwyn and embraced him again. She then held his face with both of her hands and kissed him on the forehead. "You are a wonderful young man, Edwyn, and I am so proud of you. But you must go now." Elyse nodded down the other road. "That road will take you all the way to Kinnslyng."

"Isn't it a bit too late for getting to Kinnslyng tonight?" asked Emilya, suddenly worried.

Jake considered. "You have a point, Emilya. Riding hard without stopping, Edwyn wouldn't make Kinnslyng before midday tomorrow. But given Garresh isn't fresh, that's not likely, either."

"What if we all go down the route to Kinnslyng?" asked Emilya, hopefully. "Prince Magnus won't be expecting that, will he?"

Jake and Elyse looked at each other. "We could find a hostel on the Kinnslyng road for tonight," said Elyse. "Then tomorrow morning, first thing, we all go our separate ways. Edwyn to Kinnslyng, you back to Earl's Leet, and me and Emilya on the path to Kifsel Place."

"Hmm," mused Jake. "Not in a hostel, though. I know we're not expecting Magnus and his crew to turn up until tomorrow, but if they did turn up tonight, and started looking along the Kinnslyng route, hostels are the first places they'll go. As it happens, though, I do know a dairy farmer three leagues north-west of Earl's Leet, off the Kinnslyng road. We can make it there in two hours at a gentle trot. And I agree, it won't do us any harm keeping out of Earl's Leet, tonight. The fewer people who see us, the less information Magnus will get."

"We're all agreed then?" asked Emilya, her face lighting up.

"Agreed," said Elyse.

"Agreed," added Edwyn, also with a happy smile.

Emilya saw Jake and Elyse look at each other and briefly smile.

"Right, let's get a move on," said Jake. "Are you up to a trot, Emilya."

"I'll try my best," she said, and tapped her heels to the flanks of her horse who immediately broke into a credible trot. True, Emilya nearly lost her balance in the first second, but she had been prepared for the movement and soon compensated, finding herself rising and falling in the saddle as Elyse had taught her. "Come on then, slow-coaches," she called over her shoulder.

Suddenly, the world was a wonderful place again. At least for the next few hours, anyway.

CHAPTER 58 — ALICYA

10th Tertiar, 1789 · Day 101, 16:00

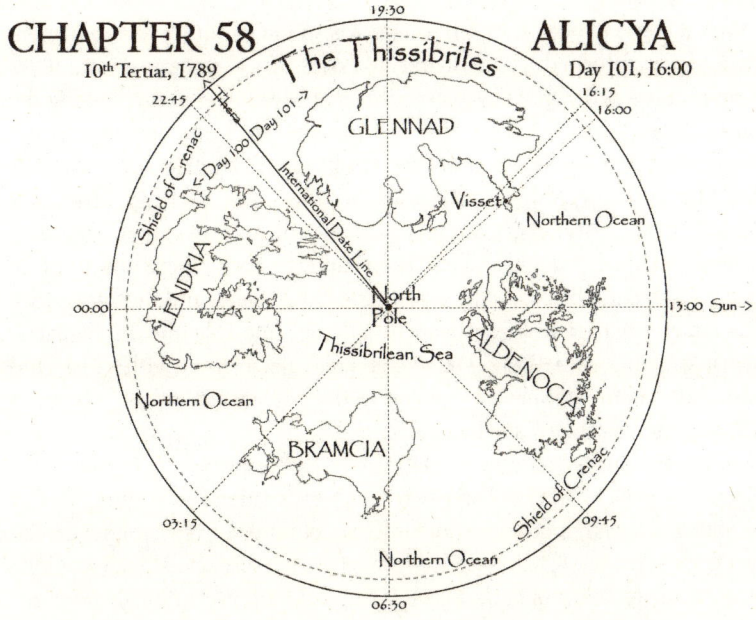

Alicya had picked up Dobbig's 1781 version of *Thera: Our World, Not an Empire* again. Vixey wasn't on her mat, though: the last two nights she had reverted to nature and taken to prowling the forested area to the rear of Gawain's apartments, something which Alicya had mixed feelings about. Alicya herself had spent most of the last three days exploring the beautiful and quaint fishing port of Visset – and in appropriate lady's attire, too, after Gawain had asked Mrs Baker to purchase a full-length, russet-coloured dress with matching shawl; nothing too glamorous, but ideal for blending in with other wealthier townsfolk. Alicya was already on speaking terms with grocers, bakers, tailors and furniture-makers, while her favourite pastime was sitting outside harbour tearooms, watching the comings and goings in the harbour; mainly fishing vessels, but with the highlights being the twice-daily ferries from Visset to Port St Humo and Ghantiss, and the two pleasure cruisers which traversed the eastern Wrenko coastline with its wealthy, well-dressed passengers.

Today, though, the weather had turned inclement two hours ago, so she had hurried 'home', shed the cloak she had rather fortuitously purchased yesterday, and taken a bath. Of course, Mrs Baker was still home, putting the finishing touches to a delicious-smelling fish pie. The woman was an absolute wizard with food; she could certainly understand why Gawain paid her twice the going rate.

Mrs Baker had been shocked to find Alicya in Gawain's guest apartment when she had turned up for work, two days ago, despite Gawain's letter explaining everything. Alicya suspected that Mrs Baker wasn't buying the 'cousin from Ghantiss' story and had initially not quite covered up her disapproval. But she was a sweet old soul, and Alicya had soon won her over. She had even offered to help with the housework, although Mrs Baker wouldn't hear anything of it. She had welcomed an audience when preparing the evening meal, though, and had been happy to teach Alicya how to make pastry, slow-cook beef, rapidly dice carrots and celery, and de-fillet a fish, plus many other tricks of her trade – although the fish-filleting had seen Alicya gagging; something Mrs Baker had seized upon with relish and teased her about. "I'll have to tie you to the kitchen table then, when I'm next skinning a rabbit!" she had joked.

Alicya had just shuddered at that. She loved bunnies.

Earlier today, Mrs Baker had given Alicya instructions on keeping the fish pie warm; likewise, a delicious-looking dish of buttered vegetables. She had then gone to make Mr Baker's evening meal. Alicya suspected that it wouldn't be quite up to the standards that Gawain enjoyed, even though poor Mr Baker would have been out all day in Port St Humo Bay catching crab, lobster and shellfish.

To pass the next hour until Gawain returned, Alicya opened Dobbig's book where she had left it three days ago: the late 10th century. This was the point at which conflict began between the four nation islands of the Thissibriles, and which lasted, on and off, for some five hundred years. Before delving into the history, though, Dobbig digressed, stating that it was also during the late 10th century when romantic theories began to circulate about lands at the opposite end of the world, which were similar to the Thissibriles, and perhaps also protected by a magnetic shield. Dobbig explained how various medieval story-tellers began writing of heroes and great explorers who would discover a route through the Shield of Crenac, through blistering central Epanaga, into the southern hemisphere, and then beyond southern Epanaga to the lands at the other end of the world – this despite Neo-Theran claims that they were still yet to cross *The Desolation* themselves. Alicya was open-minded about that one – although she didn't feel this made her a Conspiracist, either!

Dobbig's book then returned to Thissibrilean history. Alicya began to skim-read, covering how Glennad began to rule parts of western Lendria and eastern Aldenocia in the 11th century, which led to a major rebellion in Lendria in the early 12th century. This led to a brutal invasion of Lendria in

1113, but whilst the Glennadians were busy with Lendria, the Aldenocians rebelled and ousted the Glennadians from their island.

Alicya knew the rest by heart. The Glennadians avoided dividing their forces and pressed on with their subjugation of Lendria, forcing them to submit to Glennadian rule in 1117. Glennad then attempted to regain their foothold in eastern Aldenocia in 1118, but found their second attempt much harder than the first. The Aldenocians were better prepared, had better defensive positions and had signed an alliance with Bramcia. The Bramcian navy then came up behind the invading Glennadian fleet and, between the two of them, the Aldenocians and Bramcians smashed the Glennadian fleet to pieces.

With Aldenocia and Bramcia free of Glennadian rule, the rest of the 12th century saw Lendria constantly rebelling, while in 1201, Aldenocian and Bramcian forces landed in eastern Lendria and began to sweep across the island, freeing the Lendrians from Glennadian rule as they went. The Glennadians were left with no choice but to retreat to Glennad, but the alliance of Lendria, Aldenocia and Bramcia didn't leave it there. They invaded Glennad in 1202, forced the Glennadians to surrender, and a major peace treaty, the Treaty of Ghantiss, was signed in 1203. The lesson appeared to be learned by all and war, such that it had been, was consigned to the past. The rest of the 13th century, along with the 14th, saw the four nations self-rule, and by the 15th century, commerce was booming and a four-nation trade agreement forged, uniting all four islands for the first time. The first Parliaments were formed in the 16th century, while the 17th saw a brief experiment with a United Parliament across all four islands. This lasted for twenty-four years, before it was decided in 1678 to go back to Home Rule for each nation, lest the increasing tensions – particularly on fishing rights in the Thissibrilean Sea – escalated into something worse.

The Act of Union followed in 1707, whereby the four Parliaments united in the passage of general Thissibrilean law; in other words, major Acts of Parliament could only be passed following agreement by all four countries, the intention being to synergise general law and commercial development across the Thissibriles. The move proved a great success, with common sense-based decision-making largely outweighing personal and national interest. Indeed, shared passage of law and the resulting shared progress had become an important factor for the united Parliaments, although it was rare for anything controversial to be offered up for debate. Most policies were accepted by all, and the Thissibriles, as a whole, had accelerated their progress thanks to this collaboration. The timing was ideal, too, with the onset of the Industrial

Revolution just around the corner, and the ensuing eighty years or so saw equal industrial development in each country.

Also, in 1707, the concept of a Grand Sovereign had been introduced, and succession agreed via rotation amongst the four countries, as opposed to by inheritance. In 1707, the first Grand Sovereign was Queen Layla II of Aldenocia, who was succeeded by King Gwyn XII of Bramcia in 1729, who was succeeded by King Wilfred II of Glennad in 1753. The fourth Grand Sovereign was the current incumbent: King Cillian III of Lendria who had acceded in 1777.

Around fifteen minutes before Alicya was expecting Gawain to return, she began preparing the dinner. She started by warming up a couple of plates on the stove, then poured two glasses of white wine and set them down on the dining room table. She then laid the table with cutlery and condiments, before returning to the cooker and taking out the fish pie. It had a lovely brown crust on top and smelt divine. Alicya placed the bowl containing the pie on a mat in the centre of the table and then placed the buttered vegetables alongside. She was just placing two large serving spoons alongside each dish when Gawain came through the front door.

"Oh, my," he said. "That smells like a Mrs Baker fish-pie special."

"Your seat awaits, my Lord," responded Alicya, gesturing towards the fully laid table. Gawain hung up his cloak and then took his seat, with Alicya taking the seat opposite. "Shall I be mother?" she asked.

"Of course," indicated Gawain.

"I have to say," said Alicya, plunging the spoon into the fish pie and depositing a large steaming portion onto Gawain's plate, "that your Mrs Baker may even be a superior cook to our own Mrs Alsnow."

The words were out before she realised what she'd said. "Vegetables?" she asked, trying to distract Gawain.

"Most definitely," agreed Gawain. "Mrs Alsnow, eh? So, you came from a family wealthy enough to have their own cook?"

"Yes, and no doubt she's still feeding my darling brother this very evening," responded Alicya, loading up her own plate. She then picked up her glass of white wine. "Here's to freedom from tyrannical brothers."

"To freedom," said Gawain, touching his glass gently to Alicya's.

"So, I would ask you about work today, Gawain, but perhaps we should park that conversation until after we've finished eating?"

"Mmm," agreed Gawain. And then "Oh," he added, an exclamation of ecstasy as he tasted the fish pie. "Oh," he repeated. He then swallowed his first mouthful. "Mrs Alsnow can top this?" he asked.

Alicya was enjoying her first mouthful, with eyes closed. She then opened them and looked at Gawain. "She was…is…a heavenly cook. I think there is little to separate them. But you're right: this fish pie is divine. And the vegetables, too. Cooked to perfection."

"Agreed about deferring talk of shop, by the way. But it has been a most interesting day. More about that after dinner." Gawain paused as he ate another mouthful of fish pie, although his face had a frown on it. "Mrs Alsnow," he said. "Why does that name sound familiar to me?"

"I've no idea," replied Alicya, innocently. "There are probably lots of them."

"I'd say not," said Gawain. "It is a most unusual name. How do you spell it?"

"Well, as far as I know it was A-l-s-n-o-w."

"I'm sure I've read about an Alsnow in the Ghantiss Times. "Yes, hang on, it's coming back to me now. There was an Alsnow from Ghantiss who was convicted of bigamy. Edward Alsnow was his name. Ha!" exclaimed Gawain, pleased to have solved his little riddle. "I do hope your Mrs Alsnow wasn't *his* Mrs Alsnow."

"I'm sure she wasn't," replied Alicya, trying to sound casual.

"Yes," said Gawain, his eyes distant as he struggled to remember the detail. "He was a merchant who alternated between Ghantiss and Dominniul. That's right. He had a wife in Dominniul who was a seamstress, but the most unfortunate was his other wife in Ghantiss, as she was…"

Gawain dropped his knife, then dropped his jaw.

Alicya's hands flew to her face, and a second later, she felt the hot sting of tears. "Now I've gone and ruined everything," she sobbed.

Gawain was still in total shock, unable to speak.

Alicya pushed her chair back, threw down her napkin and turned to make a dash for her apartment.

However, the gentleman in Gawain overcame his shock and he rose and stopped her, gently putting his hands on her shoulders. Alicya couldn't look at him and kept her head bowed.

"It all makes sense now," said Gawain in a quiet, awed voice. "Your manner, your knowledge, your intelligence. Your name. Al?"

Alicya kept her head bowed. "I'm so sorry to have troubled you."

Gawain gently put his hand under Alicya's chin and encouraged her to look up. His face was a blur through her tears, so she wiped them away – to see Gawain looking at her in a new light. "I saw you once. About four years ago. My parents and I took a boat to Ghantiss to see the celebrations for the

King's Silver Jubilee. I can see the same girl looking back at me now. My God! Your brother…is *Prince Magnus*?"

"He had raped and killed a poor fifteen-year-old."

"Freya?"

"Yes, Freya. Freya Colin. A baker's daughter. I found him with her. I refused to keep quiet. It was a fatal mistake."

Alicya saw Gawain's eyes go hard – the first time she had seen anything but kindness and innocence in them. "He left you for dead? On Cemetery Island?"

Alicya then poured out her story, all the time stood there, very conscious of Gawain's supporting hands on her shoulders. Gawain was the stellar opposite of her brother, but at present, he was oscillating between shock, anger and bewilderment. He didn't once show any concern for his own predicament. Alicya was very aware how things could turn out for Gawain if he was caught harbouring a princess who must by now be presumed either a hostage or dead. What he did say, when she had finished, made her cry. "I'm very proud of you, Alicya. What you did to survive is beyond imagining."

Alicya let herself go and sobbed openly. She also made damn sure she had forward momentum. Being the consummate gentleman, she knew that Gawain would comfort her and so she let herself fall into his embrace. Of medium height, Alicya's head rested perfectly on the tall doctor's shoulder, but the thrill of that was nothing compared to when he placed a hand behind the back of her head and tenderly stroked her hair.

Neither of them spoke, although Alicya imagined that poor Gawain's head must be in overdrive. They stood there in silence for a full five minutes, before Alicya drew back and wiped her eyes. "I'll pack my things – such that they are – and leave first thing in the morning. That is, if you will allow me to stay one more night."

Gawain didn't answer back. Instead, he kissed her, briefly. Once. Then twice. The third kiss lingered and Alicya responded immediately. She had never been kissed before but had often talked about it with her ladies in waiting. It wasn't difficult. It was wonderfully natural. Her heart went from fluttering one second, to fit to burst the next.

The kiss lasted for a full minute. When they stopped, Alicya's head was back on Gawain's shoulder and his hand was at the back of her head again, while her face was flushed, and her heart was thumping in her chest. This was clearly what heaven felt like.

"I had hoped you might stay a little longer than one more night. Al."

Alicya just smiled, determined to enjoy the moment, determined to ignore the ramifications of their absurd position. At least for now.

"I do hope I haven't just committed treason, though."

Alicya loved the sound and reverberation of his voice-box so close to her head, but she still pulled back to look Gawain in the eye. "No one has to know," she said, in a hushed voice. "I can be anyone. Anyone you want me to be."

They held each other close for another minute, in wonderful silence, before Alicya spoke again with her head back on Gawain's shoulder. "I understand how desperately odd this must be for you. I wouldn't blame you for being scared off; scared of the possible ramifications if -."

"I couldn't live with myself if I let you go."

Alicya pulled back to look at him. "Why ever not?" she asked, quietly, hoping.

"Because," began Gawain, pausing, looking down, then up again. "Because I loved you from the first moment that I saw you come out of that cupboard. In a ridiculously large greatcoat and mismatched boots, holding a baby fox."

Alicya's head was a whirl and she did something terrible. She laughed. But Gawain laughed too. Their understanding was a natural one. "That's double-treason," she said.

"I mean, I know I'm not the Prince of Lendria or the Duke of Dominniul, but I swear from the bottom of my heart, that I would never stop loving you."

"Well, the Prince of Lendria is fifty-five, and the Duke of Dominniul is a hunchback. So, I guess you'll have to do!"

"So, you will stay one more night then?"

"I had hoped you might want me to stay a little longer," said Alicya, mimicking Gawain's earlier line.

"Well, this is totally insane. I can't believe I'm saying this. You're the Princess Alicya of House Havreno. But if you want to, you can stay with me for the rest of your life."

"That's treble-treason, now."

"I'm a dead man."

Alicya put her forefinger on Gawain's lips. "It was a few hours later for me," she said.

"Later? What do you mean?"

"It was when you laughed at my triple turn-ups. Well, *your* triple turn-ups, as it happened.

"You mean?"

"Yes. That's when I first knew that I loved you, too."

CHAPTER 59 — EMILYA

10th Tertiar, 1789 — Day 101, 17:30

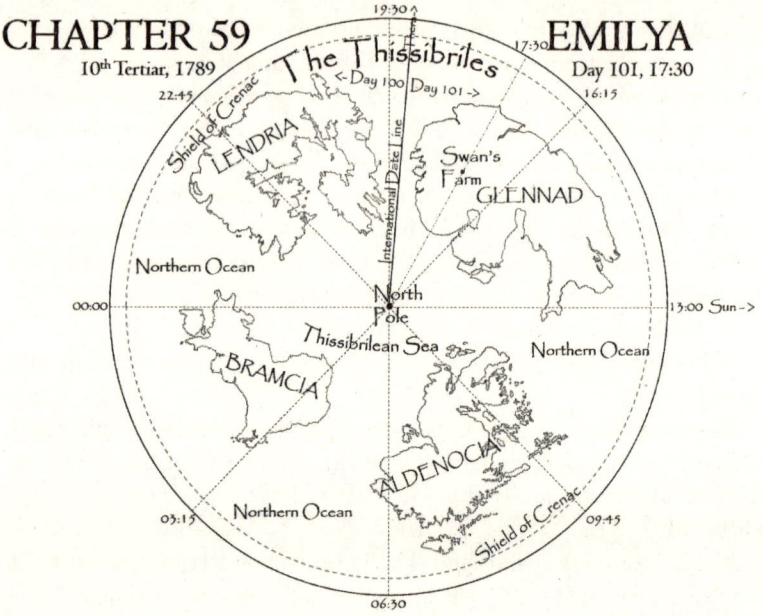

The road from Earl's Leet to Kinnslyng continued to head gently downhill, while the landscape started to open up, with fields, trees and meadows appearing on either side along with an increasing array of bird-life and insects. There were also tantalising glimpses of the northern lakes in the distance. Having slowed down from a trot to a walk, though, neither Emilya nor Edwyn had noticed much of their surroundings, having eyes only for each other. Edwyn had been opening up about his upbringing and studies, while Emilya had shared a detailed account of her childhood, including losing her mother when she was six years old. Both had listened avidly to each other's stories and asked many questions in return.

They had now lightened up and were talking about travel, with Emilya confessing to only having been on a small boat in Ghantiss Bay, and on a barge once for three miles up the Ghantiss Canal. In return, Edwyn was telling how he had once travelled by stagecoach from Ghenetenos to Kinnslyng to visit his Aunt Maud and Uncle Alec.

"Ooh!" exclaimed Emilya, pushing her nose up with her forefinger. "Who's the posh one then."

"That's not a flattering look, Emilya," joked Edwyn.

Emilya did the gesture again, but this time accompanied by three oinks. Edwyn repeated the gesture and gave her three oinks back – at which point, they both burst out laughing.

Emilya spotted Jake and Elyse up ahead share a smile, before Elyse turned around in her saddle, all smiles. "Now children. Behave please."

Emilya was about to respond when movement up ahead caught her eye. They were about to enter a stretch of road which cut through woodland, and there were three riders approaching. The two on the outside were dressed in grubby brown and grey roughspun clothing, but the man in the centre was ludicrously over-dressed. His scarlet coat was exquisitely embroidered in gold up the centre and around the huge turned-up cuffs, from which appeared the extravagantly frilled cuffs of his pristine white shirt which matched his white-frilled stock. Topping it all off was a luxurious tricorn hat, while his long and sleek dark hair was neatly tied with a large black velvet ribbon. The most noticeable accoutrement, though, was the pistol he was brandishing in his right hand, with his left hand holding the reins and steering his jet-black stallion.

Emilya immediately knew who the man in the middle was. *We were dispatched up here to confirm reports that Harry Black is on the prowl.*

"I think we'd best stand still," said Jake, encouraging his horse to stop as the three men pulled up sharply in front of them, skittering stones in different directions. Harry Black then dismounted in one fluid movement and swaggered up to them, gun pointing straight at Jake's forehead, having singled him out as the main opposition. "Dismount, my good man," he requested, in a ludicrously plummy tone.

Jake did as he was told, keeping his eyes focused on Black's all the time.

"Well," said Black, encircling Jake. "What have we here?"

Jake kept silent.

"A man, and his family, perhaps? Either that or a very lucky punter who likes his lady's young. Ah, I reassess," said Black, throwing a disparaging glance towards Elyse. "There's mutton afoot."

Elyse's eyes flashed. Jake remained silent.

"So, nothing to say for yourself then?" said Black, who was now stood in front of Jake. He then narrowed his eyes. "Do I know you?"

"What are you doing up here?" asked Jake, never once looking away from Black's eyes.

Black raised his pistol, walked forwards two paces, and placed the muzzle right in the middle of Jake's forehead. "I think you'll find that I'm the one asking the questions, sir."

"Only you're a long way from your usual manor," said Jake, as if Black hadn't even spoken.

Black was staring at Jake's face. "I do know you, don't I?"

"And on the low road through the Bleaklow Hills – must be some of the most miserable pickings in Glennad, I'd have thought."

"Not as miserable as you might think," responded Black, having been drawn into the conversation. His pistol was still placed in the middle of Jake's forehead, though. "The odd rich merchant passing between Earl's Leet, Ghantiss and Kinnslyng, tend to carry much loot. Longer trips, you see. And in the Bleaklow Hills, there's less chance of being caught by the King's men."

"Well, as you can see, we're not rich merchants."

"No," said Black, now pulling back the safety-catch on his pistol. "But I do know you from somewhere."

"Troubling, isn't it?"

"Well, I'm going to count to three, and in that time, you will tell me who you are – before I rob you and your two ladies here of every last valuable that you have. One."

Jake deliberately looked sideways at Elyse. As he had anticipated, Black did the same. That was why Black never got to "two".

In one fluid movement, Jake back-fisted the pistol to the right, which promptly went off with the bullet missing Jake's ear by a whisker. Before Black could comprehend what was happening, Jake had head-butted him squarely on his nose, Emilya actually *hearing* the crack of bone. As Black fell backwards, Jake also wrenched the pistol from his grasp and tossed it to Elyse, who promptly caught it, and pointed it at the two stunned lackeys. "Get on the ground now, face down, hands on your head," said Elyse. The two lackeys complied without question.

Meanwhile, Jake's trusty cutlass was already at the sprawled Black's throat. "Carofimbel, Septenar 1785," said Jake. "The Black Pig."

But Harry Black wasn't really in a state to comprehend, as he was gingerly holding his shattered nose with his right hand.

"You fell for the same ruse, back then," said Jake, with disdain.

Realisation dawned on Black, despite his discomfort. "The captain of the frigate," he said nasally.

"You pick-pocketed my first officer. You were good – but I never miss a trick."

"I owe you twice over then."

"I think you'll find that I'm the one asking the questions, sir," said Jake, repeating Black's line from earlier.

"Very droll, Captain," responded Black from his prone position. "So, what are you going to do with us?"

Jake kept silent, thinking.

"I can't believe my career is going to end here, inland, at the end of a good captain's cutlass!" moaned Black "I don't suppose I can talk you into coming into business with me?"

"Well, ironically, right now, I'm probably a more wanted man than you are, Black."

A flicker of hope stirred in Harry Black's eyes. "I can make it worth your while. I'm the richest man in Glennad after the King. Oh, and that oaf, Prince Magnus, of course."

Once again, Jake said nothing. Elyse piped up instead. "Jake, you can't be seriously thinking of teaming up with Harry Black, can you?"

"Teaming up isn't quite the phrase I would have used."

"Jake!" exclaimed Emilya, now also alarmed by her companion's apparent line of thought.

"I'll need you to lose your two lackeys."

Harry Black could hardly believe what he was hearing. "Done. I'll pay them double what I promised and tell them to double back to Kinnslyng. If they return, I shall flay them myself."

"Jake!" exclaimed Emilya and Elyse in unison.

"I'll also need you to lose that ridiculous clothing."

"What, you can't be serious?" spluttered Black. "What about my reputation?"

Jake just gave him a cock-eyed look.

"Oh, very well," said Black, struggling to his feet. "I'll swap with Turnip there, if you like?" he said, indicating the prone thug on the right.

"Perfect," agreed Jake. "If you don't mind, I'll supervise this little swapping of attire, gentlemen."

For the last twenty seconds, Elyse had been observing the conversation open-mouthed. She now jumped down off her horse and waved the pistol in Jake's face. "Just what the hell do you think you're doing, mister? You can't trust him. He's robbed *hundreds* of people."

"I'm cut to the quick, my lady," said Black with mock hurt.

"Number one," said Jake. "My way, we don't have to kill him or his lackeys."

"I very much like 'number one,'" said Black.

"So! Instead, we just tie them up and leave," said Elyse.

"I like that even better," agreed Black.

"And if they manage to break free, they might come after us," said Jake.

"Sir, you have my sincerest promise that I will not come after you."

"Shut up, Black!" chorused Jake and Elyse.

"Charming!" said Black, still tenderly holding his nose.

"We tie them up and hand them in at Earl's Leet, then," said Elyse.

"You're not going to Earl's Leet, Elyse. We've already established that."

Throughout the entire exchange, Black's head was moving back and forth from Jake to Elyse. Emilya, meanwhile, was starting to understand where Jake was going with this. "Oh, very clever," she said, quietly.

Elyse looked at Emilya as if she were mad. "Emilya?"

"Think about it, Elyse," said Emilya. "Who would Magnus want more than me or Jake? Who else is he most likely to go after and forget about us?"

"Ah," said Elyse, now looking at Jake with more favour. "Ah," she repeated, now with the ghost of a smile.

"I don't suppose you'd care to tell me why you brigands are so obviously on the run from the Crown, would you?" asked Black.

"Stay where you are!" commanded Jake, spotting one of the lackeys moving. The lackey froze.

"We're no brigands, Mr Black," said Elyse, as she walked towards the two lackeys, pointing the pistol at them. Both now had their hands against the back of their heads again.

"Well, it doesn't sound like it to me, madam."

"Erm, could someone explain to me what's happening, please," piped up Edwyn for the first time.

"Our plans are still largely the same," said Jake. "It's just that I will be taking on a new recruit, and I won't be stopping the night with you. My only dilemma now, is what to do with those two," he said, indicating the two lackeys who were still sprawled on the floor, face-down.

"We won't do nothing," said one of them.

"We won't say nothing neither," said the other.

"Yes, very convincing," said Jake, in a wholly dubious tone.

"I don't suppose it will help if I say that I can vouch for their good character?" asked Black.

"Not on any level," was Jake's response, with the vaguest of a smile. Then it came to him. "Right, gentlemen. On your feet please." The two lackeys stood up. "Stand with your men, Black."

"What about my attire."

"You can keep it on. I've a new use for that. Now, turn around, and start leading your mounts towards Kinnslyng."

"We're going to walk all the way to Kinnslyng?"

"No, you're going to walk for another half a league. I am then going to have a lot of explaining to do."

Half an hour later, Jake was marching his three captives at gunpoint up a long path to a farm, whilst a mounted Emilya, Elyse and Edwyn were leading the other four riderless horses between them. Before them was a large brick farmhouse, a smithy and lots of sprawling farm buildings, including barns, hen-roosts and sheds. The path was unobscured, so it was no surprise when two men came out of the front door and walked cautiously up the path towards them. One was a grizzled man in his fifties with frizzy grey hair and a bushy grey beard. The other was much younger, maybe in his mid-twenties, of average height, light-brown hair, of stocky build, and wearing a blacksmith's apron.

When they got within a few yards, the old farmer's face broke out into a huge grin. "Well, I never! If it aint me old captain. What the blazes are you doing here, skipper? And who's this?" he asked, looking aghast at the character in the flashy red and gold garb. "You surely aren't bringing me…"

"He surely is," said Harry Black. "Sir Harold Horatio Black, at your service, sir."

The farmer didn't say anything for a while, but just stood there with his mouth open. Eventually he found his voice and turned to Jake. "Erm, an explanation would be appreciated, Captain."

"Of course, Clyve. First of all, everyone," said Jake, turning to his crew. "This is Clyve Swan. He was my lieutenant for six years on the Thissibrilean Sea – Bramcian Navy – before he retired a few years ago and took up farming."

He wasn't in the Black Pig, four years ago, was he?" asked Black, his hand automatically rising to his aching nose.

"And this must be Clyve's son, Jared," said Jake, completely ignoring Black.

Jared Swan put out his hand. "It's been a long time, Captain Oscom."

Jake took his hand and exchanged the firmest of handshakes. "You were still a boy," said Jake. "But look at you now: a fine figure of a man. How old are you now, Jared?"

"Twenty-four," replied Jared.

Clyve interrupted by clearing his throat. "And your, erm, companions?

"Yes, the lady with the two pistols is Elyse Dolmen from Ghantiss. The young lady on the horse is Emilya Luca, also from Ghantiss, and the young man is Elyse's nephew, Edwyn, who lives in Ghenetenos."

Clyve and Jared waved at all three as they were introduced. Brief smiles and waves were returned. "Welcome all," said Clyve, although he was still clearly unsettled. "Now, erm, no offence ladies and gentlemen, but if it's all right with you, I'm rather more interested in understanding why you're bringing the most-wanted man in Glennad onto my premises?"

"Now that," began Jake, "is a very long story. I was rather hoping I'd be able to tell it to you over a tankard or two of your famous cider."

Clyve eyed his former captain, shrewdly. "Why do I have the feeling I'm going to regret this?"

"Oh, you have nothing to fear, old friend. Mr Black and I will be on our way to Earl's Leet shortly. I am looking to impose on you with the others – although only for one night, I can promise you that.

"Well, as ever Captain, I trust you implicitly. And I really can't wait to hear this story. I'll have Meg prepare extra for dinner, and Jared will show you where you can sleep – although there won't be beds for everyone, but the straw in my barns is dry and soft enough for most. And then you can regale us after dinner."

"I look forward to it, Clyve. And thank you," he said, putting his arm around his former lieutenant and patting his shoulder. "I knew I could rely on you, my friend."

CHAPTER 60   JAKE
10th Tertiar, 1789   Day 101, 20:00

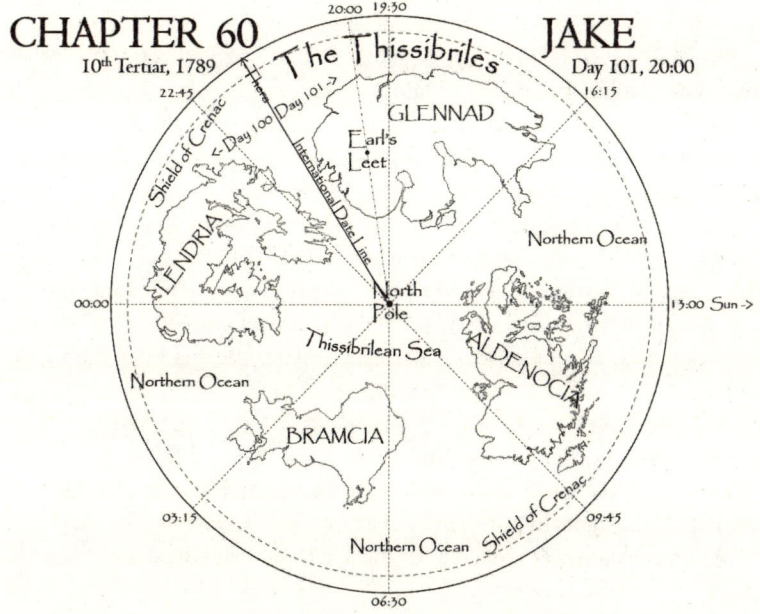

Harry Black was no longer in his normal flamboyant attire. He had been forced to change into brown and grey roughspun farmers clothes and black leather boots, and his brash attitude had disappeared along with his attire. Jake had just finished their collective tale of woe, which had begun with a fifteen-year-old girl trying to save a tiny terrier from a brutal death.

Jake had had all on not to laugh earlier that evening, when Emilya had put down little Theo amongst Clyve and Meg's farm dogs. Black had gone down on both knees, talking to the little terrier like you would to a baby. Even more bizarrely, little Theo had responded to the rogue's cooings, actually rolling over on to his back so that Black could tickle his tummy.

Despite her open hostility to Black, Elyse – along with Emilya – had actually smiled at the surreal scene. "So, Harry Black's got a heart then," she'd said. "Who'd have thought it?"

Black had hauled himself back to his feet, rather self-consciously. "Yes, well don't you go telling anyone, madam, otherwise you'll destroy my reputation."

"There he goes again," Elyse had said to Jake and Emilya. "Banging on about his precious reputation again."

Jake was drawn out of his reverie as he became aware that Clyve was talking. "You're all welcome here any time. Well," he corrected himself.

"Except for Mr Black and his two associates, that is."

"We shall not be troubling you again, sir," Black had replied. "We are all three very grateful for your hospitality."

"And we should be even more grateful," said the one Black had called Turnip, a wiry, dark-haired fellow who was missing one of his front teeth, "if you would allow Swede and me to leave with Mr Black."

"Swede!" exclaimed Elyse. "He's called Swede?" she asked, nodding at Turnip's ginger-haired companion who sported two crooked front teeth with a large gap between them. He also had two golden earring loops which jiggled whenever he talked. "You're called Turnip and Swede?"

"Nicknames, of course," confirmed Black. "After the quality of their grey matter!"

"It's a good job you pay us well," said the dark-haired one, sourly.

"I'm sure you call me worse, Turnip."

"I'm afraid that Clyve will not be allowing you to leave for another two days," said Jake, ignoring the banter. "But you will be well looked after."

"We'll be even better looked after if you cut these ankle bonds," growled Swede.

"They will be cut in two days' time – when the rest of us have safely gone our separate ways."

"I don't suppose you'll take my word of honour that we won't follow none of you," said Turnip.

"I don't suppose I will, no," confirmed Jake.

Harry Black laughed at that. "It seems as if you gentlemen will have to remain hopping mad for two days."

"Very funny, Black," said Swede, sourly.

"Yeah," agreed Turnip, sourly, looking at the thick rope that bound his hands. "We'll not be escaping, neither. Of all the blokes to run into in the hills, we run into a couple of bleedin' knot-expert sailors! Inland, too! Just my bleedin' luck, that is!"

Turnip's downbeat diatribe and forlorn look tickled everyone around the table, and before they knew it, the laughter began to escalate. Turnip and Swede initially took offence at the laughter, but eventually saw the funny side of it and joined in. In between the bouts of laughter, Turnip managed to blurt out, "Couple of bleedin' sailors", and they all set off rocking again.

Having begun to relax after their delicious meal of vegetable and mutton broth followed up with honey-cakes and oaten biscuits, Harry Black brought them back to Jake and Emilya's plight. "Well, as you can probably imagine, I'm not the most sympathetic of men. But I do take umbrage with a full-grown prince threatening a fifteen-year-old girl. So, old man," he said, addressing Jake. "I'll gladly help with whatever ruse you've got planned, and I'll make no attempt to leave you in the lurch, either. I assume you'll be looking to use me to help draw the Prince off young Emilya's trail?"

"That's the plan," replied Jake. "Old man," he added.

"Well, if you want my vastly-experienced opinion, old chap, the best way to get Prince Magnus' attention is by holding him and his posse up on the approach to Earl's Leet."

"What, just the two of us?"

"Ah, well there you have it, sir. We would be infinitely more capable of pulling it off if we were a quad squad."

"And I suppose you expect me to arm you as well?"

"Well, there's no point bothering if we're not armed."

"You must think I was born yesterday, Black. The second I turn my back -."

"I give you my word that we will not betray you. I live for the excitement of the challenge, Mr Oscom. And the richer they are, the less my conscience bleeds."

"Conscience! Pah!" exclaimed Elyse.

"You really do misunderstand me, madam," responded Black, looking quite hurt. "This is a challenge that I would relish – and I'm sure my erstwhile colleagues would, too."

Turnip and Swede uttered various approvals and nods to this suggestion, which set Swede's earrings jiggling again.

Jake considered the proposal. "I'll need you for several days beyond tomorrow. And I don't deny that I could happily use all three of you."

"Jake!" said Elyse, warningly.

"Think about it, Elyse. If they're as good as their word -."

"Pah!" echoed Elyse and Emilya.

"If they're as good as their word, we won't need to worry about these two," said Jake, nodding at Turnip and Swede, "pursuing young Edwyn."

"And why would we do that, anyway?" asked Swede, exasperatedly. "I mean, we know you now. It'd be like doing the dirty on family."

"Oh, I've heard it all now!" scoffed Elyse.

"All right then. Why would we hold up a boy who isn't carrying any valuables – if you want to look at this from a purely economic viewpoint?"

Jake was eyeing Elyse. "He's got a very good point."

"I'll tell you what," said Black. "As a mark of my newly turned-over leaf, I will gladly donate our takings to the good Clyve and Meg, how's that?"

"I can't believe what I'm hearing," scoffed Elyse.

"I'm happy with that," agreed Turnip. "As a reward for the tastiest broth I've ever had."

"And the most scrumptious honey-cakes, too," added Swede.

Despite the farcical situation, Meg was positively beaming at the flattery. "Oh, give over," she said, wafting a plump hand at Black's lackeys.

"Do you make a habit of disarming those around you?" asked Elyse, still far-from convinced.

"I can see that it will only be deed that will convince this ice maiden."

"Right, you've got me," said Jake. "The four of us will sleep in Clyve and Meg's barn tonight. I'm afraid I will have to insist on the ankle restraints gentlemen. But first thing tomorrow morning, I'll cut you free and we'll go and get ourselves dug in somewhere on the Ghintonoll road. But I'll be taking care of the pistols right up to the point that we see His Royal Highness and posse."

"Well, I'll drink to that," said Black, raising his tankard. "To new partnerships," he announced, and didn't bother to wait for the others to join him in draining his cider.

CHAPTER 61 — MADELEINA

10th Tertiar, 1789 — Day 101, 19:15

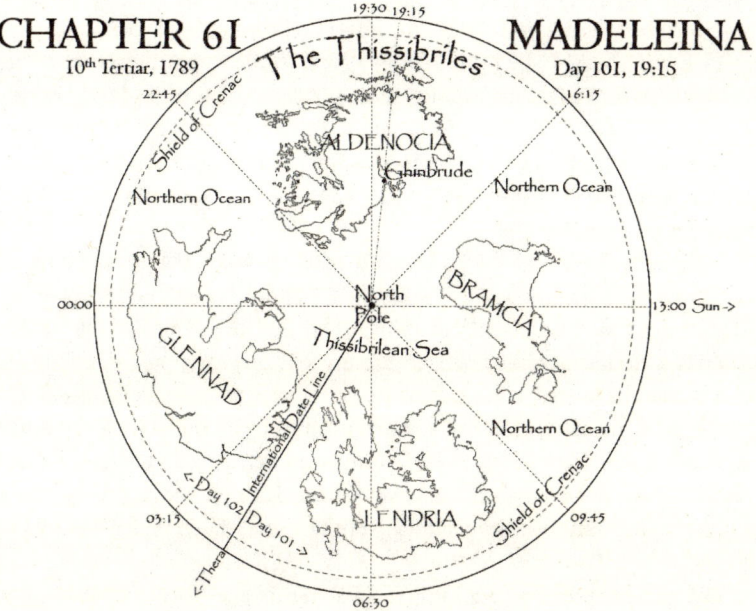

Princess Madeleina of Aldenocia had just been sick. For the third time. Worse still, her mind now seemed to be impaired. Earlier that morning, she had been capable of visualising every single note of all four movements of her concerto, with not even the vaguest need for a piano in front of her. Ten hours later, her mind had turned to mush and her fingers to jelly.

Why was she doing this? She was a princess, betrothed to Prince Bernard of Lendria, and destined to one day become his queen. She didn't need to impress anyone.

Oh, but you do, said her inner voice. *This is exactly why you are doing this.*

She knew it, too. At only eighteen years of age, this was all about showing the world that she was far too young and talented to be forced into marriage with a balding, rotund, twice-widowed fifty-five-year-old.

Madeleina closed her eyes in misery at the unfairness of it all. Maybe one day, soon, someone in government or the royal family would demand a change to such outdated tradition.

Her shoulders slumped. "Aye, and pigs might fly, too," she said in her lilting brogue, whilst looking at her mournful reflection in the large and ornate dressing-room mirror.

"Your Highness?" asked a very similar brogue.

"Oh, it's nothing, Aggie. And don't call me that."

"Sorry, Your -. Are you still feeling unwell...Princess?"

"I've been better," she said, issuing a weak smile to the reflection of her youngest and most-recent lady-in-waiting. Pale, red-haired and only fifteen, Aggie still looked very girlish. But then Madeleina examined her own face in the mirror, and her shoulders slumped again. Aggie wasn't the only pasty-face around here. She turned to address her oldest friend and confidant. "Perhaps some more rouge, Charlotte?"

"Of course, Your High-." Charlotte stopped herself and put up an apologetic hand. All three girls laughed – and then Charlotte gently set to work on Madeleina's pale cheeks. Madeleina watched her in the mirror. She envied Charlotte. No responsibility of birth and unlikely to have a man old enough to be her grandpa foisted onto her. And beautiful too – raven-haired, rosy cheeks (no need for any fake rouge there), full lips, and a figure both bursting out and pinched in the right places. Such a contrast to herself – and Aggie, for that matter. Men went overboard about Madeleina's fair hair and fair complexion, and her apparently 'delicate' features, but she would much prefer to look like Charlotte.

Just as Charlotte was putting the finishing touches to her cheeks – and which were indeed looking better – there was a knock on the dressing room door. "We're ready for you, Your Royal Highness," came the tones of Fraser Cameron, the concert hall owner.

"Oh, Lord!" exclaimed Madeleina.

"Your Highness?" asked Cameron, sounding concerned.

"I'll be out in one minute," she responded.

As Madeleina stood, somewhat shakily, Charlotte took hold of both of her hands and looked her in the eye. "Just take some deep breaths, Maddie." Madeleina nodded, and did as she was told. "That's right," approved Charlotte. "Now, listen to me. You are the most talented piano player in the Thissibriles. You are playing your own composition. So, the moment you sit on that stool and play your first notes, everything will come back to you...and you will be filled with joy as you show the world what you can do. You will feel every nuance, you will emote every note – just as you always do when you are practising."

Madeleina lifted her head and stuck her chin out. "Thank you, Charlotte!" She gripped her friend's hands tighter. "What would I do without you?"

"Find someone else to drop spiders on, no doubt!"

That broke the mood, and both girls collapsed in a fit of giggles – whilst Aggie looked alarmed. "Spiders?" she asked.

"Your time will come," responded Charlotte. Aggie looked even more alarmed at that.

Meanwhile, Madeleina had straightened up and put her shoulders back. "Thank you, Charlotte," she repeated, with a little more confidence. She then took another deep breath and gave her friend a nervous smile. "Why do I feel like I'm about to go into battle?"

Both girls laughed briefly, before Madeleina turned around and gracefully exited the dressing room, her head held high. She then took the arm of Fraser Cameron, who proceeded to walk her to the back of the stage, beyond which she could hear the excited hubbub of the audience. Her heart began to flutter again.

Seconds later, Fraser Cameron led her up the steps and on to the stage, where her orchestra were already assembled. As her magnificent ivory-coloured dress swished across the stage floor, the chatter died down, and an expression of marvel passed around the concert hall.

The dress had been especially made for the occasion. Made of the finest silk, by the finest dressmaker in the land, the segments of the skirts were alternated in subtle lighter and darker shades of ivory, giving the illusion of a shimmer. Two exquisitely-embroidered ivory bows appeared in the middle of the two front panels, a lighter ivory bow in the darker panel and vice-versa, while the bodice continued the same ivory contrast with one central bow just below the neckline – the latter being suitably high enough to offer only the merest hint of the Princess' modest cleavage and the waist suitably pinched to show off her slim figure to the full. The sleeves were a combination of silk and lace, this time embroidered with tiny bows, but cropped between the elbow and the wrist so as not to hide or inhibit her piano-playing. The Princess' glittering diamond tiara completed the stunning ensemble, nestling in her fair hair that had been classically swept back and beautifully gathered at the back.

As Madeleina took a seat at her priceless mahogany grand piano, and arranged her dress around her, Fraser Cameron walked out to the front of the stage. "Ladies and gentlemen," he announced, after the expressions of wonder at Madeleina's appearance had died down. "I give you the Princess Madeleina of Aldenocia, who will now play for you her very own concerto, in public, for the first time. This is not a standard concerto – for it has four movements instead of the usual three. However, this is necessitated by the fact that the overall title is: *The Thissibriles*."

An expectant series of 'oohs' and 'aahs' circulated around the auditorium. Meanwhile, Cameron had paused and appeared to be briefly considering something. His monologue continued, in his clipped Aldenocian brogue, with great emphasis on his rolled R's. "I mean, Her Royal Highness could have left it at just three movements…but who should she have left out?"

A murmur of mirth passed around the hall, this time.

"Not Aldenocia, for sure," continued Cameron.

"Leave the Glennies out," suggested one voice from the stalls.

"Yeah, sack the Glennies," came another from the circle.

A huge round of laughter and a few rounds of applause greeted this banter, along with various shouts of "Down with the Glennies" – and a few more forthright opinions, too!

Cameron was milking his audience now, raising his hands to quieten things down, albeit with a mild smile on his face. "Ladies and gentlemen, please!" he exclaimed, in mock outrage. "Of course, I do understand that you mean no offence and that, actually, your collective outbursts are merely a mark of your…deep *affection* for our cousins across the water."

This latest statement evoked the hoped-for swathes of belly-laughter from all quarters of the audience, along with both cheering and jeering.

"Anyway," said Cameron, raising his hands again to bring some order to proceedings. "We must now be very serious. We all love and know our princess as the finest pianist in the four kingdoms. And I also know that the Princess is an avid student of the geography of all four lands, too – each of which is filled with its very own characteristic beauty. From the magnificent architecture of Ghantiss and Dominniul in Glennad, to the rugged coastlines of Emerald Lendria, to the valleys and vast sandy beaches of Bramcia – and finally – to the indescribable beauty of the glens and bens and lochs and islands of our very own dear Aldenocia."

Cameron paused. You could now hear a pin drop. "The Princess has captured all of this in her concerto, and so much more. Each country will appear in the order just mentioned, and her Grace will transport you to each country, for all the world as if you were setting foot there yourself. I would encourage you to close your eyes, and imagine you are there, that you can see the sights, hear the sounds, smell the smells.

"The first movement, 'Glennad', will feature the Princess as soloist on the grand piano. The second movement, 'Lendria', will feature joint soloists on the violin and the flute. The third movement, 'Bramcia', will feature joint soloists on the harp and the cello. And the final movement, which is called 'Aldenocia', will see her Royal Highness take the lead again on the piano."

As Cameron paused again, a total hush remained throughout the auditorium. "We are all very privileged to be here on this day, and in the decades to come, you will be able to tell your children and your grandchildren that you were there. You were there when *The Thissibriles* debuted in Ghinbrude. You were there, when what I believe will become the most important musical works in the history of our nations was first played, by the very person – the very brilliant person – who composed them.

"Ladies and gentlemen, I give you Her Royal Highness, Princess Madeleina of Aldenocia."

This time there weren't any hoots, jibes or whistles; just an enthusiastic swell of applause, from a now-very expectant audience. Then, the applause died away, and for several seconds, there was total silence again.

Madeleina composed herself, placed her delicate hands above the keys and nodded once to the conductor. He, in turn, turned to the violin section and prompted them into the gentlest and sweetest of introductions. As the melody gently switched between harmonic and melodic, from major keys to minor, Madeleina began to intertwine her own solo. Gently at first, like the light mist which sometimes shrouds the ancient stones at Ghenetenos. Then at other times, there were swelling crescendos where the horns delivered depth and, at times, menace – sometimes accompanied by the drama of a sequence of rolls on the bass drum. This section encapsulated the majesty of the rocky western peninsula of Wrenko. And then at other times, Madeleina's piano would weave gently in and out with the woodwind section, imparting perhaps a vivid image of the depths of summer: maybe a weeping willow in a green meadow beside a sparkling river, or little ponds glittering softly in secluded dales. On other occasions, a flute and oboe evoked images of crystalline winters in the hills and mountains, with hoar frost on the trees and lakes and juvenile rivers frozen for weeks on end.

Throughout, and as Charlotte had predicted, Madeleina lost herself in her performance, remembering every nuance, living every note. She breezed through the pipes and fiddle accompaniment of Lendria, evoking a sense of ethereal magic, followed by the swelling majesty of Bramcia, which was powerfully assisted by the sublime voices of an all-male choir. And then she lovingly crafted her own country. The ruggedness of Aldenocia's myriad islands and coastline was captured by fingers moving so fast they appeared to blur, and then the tranquillity of the glens was encapsulated by a total contrast of gentle chord-play, each exquisite chord allowed to sustain for several seconds before melding into the next.

And then, the grand finale. The majestic bens brought about a reintroduction of those horns and the bass drum, building up and up and up into a final crescendo. And then, as the last collective and titanic note of the orchestra gradually died away, Madeleina wove a simple refrain of seven notes, over and over, gradually fading away to nothing. As she played her last note, she kept her head bowed; she didn't look at the audience. A deathly silence fell around the auditorium. Madeleina then slowly raised her head, coming out of her trance, turned to her bewitched audience – and smiled.

The applause built slowly, the awestruck audience also coming out of a collective trance. And then the spell was broken, and everyone was on their feet. The appreciation was rapturous, tumultuous, and went on for a full five minutes.

Madeleina turned to look for Charlotte in the wings. And there she was, clasping her hands together in great pride, lines of tears glistening on her cheeks.

CHAPTER 62   ARRAN
10th Tertiar, 1789   Day 101, 20:45

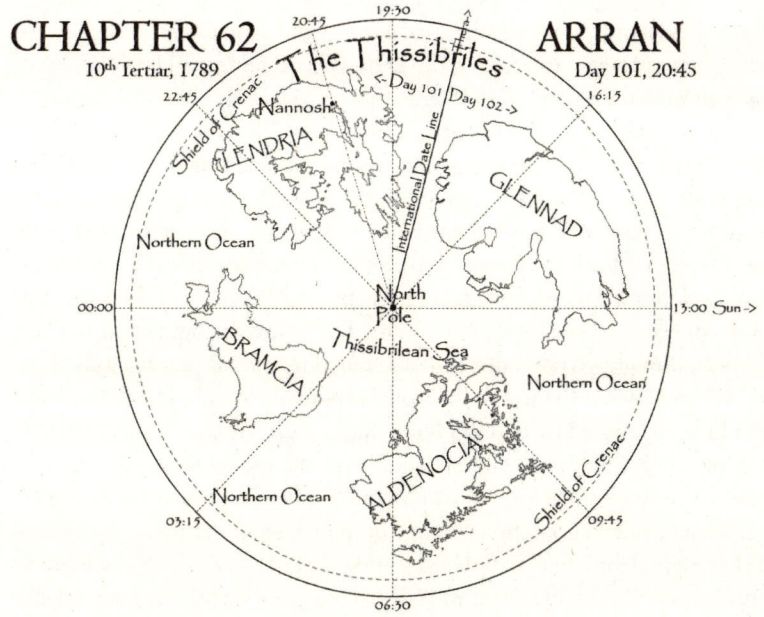

Arran Reed still hadn't written back to Ella, but he knew that he had to, tonight. Her last letter had remained unflinching in her claim that she still loved him and always had. She had also reiterated that line about 'not knowing how to take their relationship to the next level', which he took to mean a more physical plane. If Ella had sat down with her parents to discuss that, back in 1771, it would have spelt the end for their relationship, as a physical relationship was frowned upon outside of marriage. It certainly made Arran understand the responsibility parents have in advising their children. One fervently-held opinion at a certain point in their lives – whether right or wrong, and indeed an opinion which may even *change* with age – could lead to advice which would change the course of a son or daughter's life forever.

The other aspect of the last letter that had hurt was how she had described Mal, back in 1771. *"He was rich, he owned and bred horses, had his own coach, regularly took me out for meals, took me for splendid days out in the countryside, for expensive holidays abroad."*

In other words, he had swept Ella off her feet. The contrast between Arran and Mal, in 1771, must have been very stark: boy versus man. All Arran had offered, by comparison, were walks in the park, holding hands, and promises of forever. Arran sighed at the memories that this stirred. He and Ella had always held hands, wherever they had gone – right up to the very last moment when one of them departed on the end-of-weekend ferry. How could they have given that up?

Alas, perhaps materialism had followed for Ella at the expense of true love. If so, the gradual realisation would have brought an increasing emptiness that would have blighted Ella and Mal's marriage. Ella's anguish would have become more acute with every passing year – along with resentment on both sides; one for being locked out and the other for a love lost. Inevitably, Ella had eventually reached out to the one who she now understood loved her the way she wanted to be loved…but far, far too late.

Well, thought Arran, bitterly. If she only knew what was awaiting them *all*. When Ella and the rest of the world eventually found out, such anguish would be magnified tenfold. *All those wasted years*. Which is why he *had* to see her again. He was certain he would still feel the same way about her – but he had to be sure. And he also had to decide on whether he should tell her what he knew about the asteroid – despite the non-disclosure agreement he had signed for Lenahan Driscoll, earlier that day, and which would mean imprisonment if he breached it. He'd likely not be seeing her ever again if that happened.

Arran sighed. He'd been around these houses so many times before. It really depended upon where the asteroid was going to hit. If it was to be a Northern Ocean impact, they would likely all survive sheltering in the hills and mountains. Was it possible that they could start a new life together after the event and during the rebuild of their islands? There would be unparalleled devastation, but life would be wonderful – as it would go on; although probably not wonderful for Mal and the boys. But if the impact were to be on land, well, didn't that strengthen the case to see Ella even more? But where could things possibly go after that? Ella had two children. And a husband.

Arran shook his head in despair. He was damned either way, although a selfish part of him wanted to run to Ella regardless, and spend whatever time was left with the woman he had loved all his adult life. Alas, he had additional responsibilities, now, and important work coming up. Perhaps they could meet after that?

Sighing again, Arran picked up his pen and began to write.

CHAPTER 63   EMILYA
11th Tertiar, 1789   Day 102, 09:00

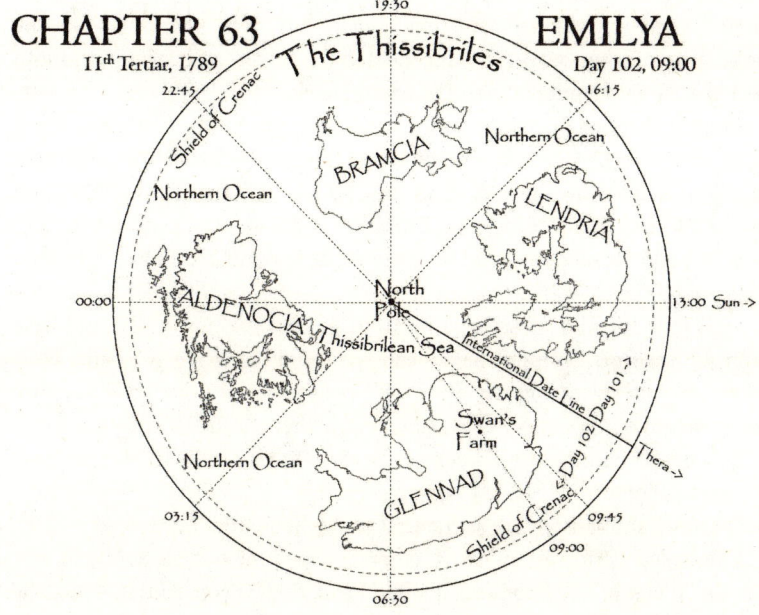

It was the moment she had been dreading. For Jake, Harry Black and his two lackeys, horses had been saddled. For herself, Elyse and Jared, backpacks had been made up, including clothing for the mountains. And for Edwyn, Garresh was rested, refreshed and now in a fit state to take him to Kinnslyng and then home to Ghenetenos. She really didn't know when she would see him again – if ever.

This awful moment was in complete contrast to last night, when they had talked until two in the morning; when they had held hands all night and not let go; when they had used fingers and thumbs to gently caress each other's hands. It had been so beautiful. Eventually, Jake and Elyse had gently separated them and escorted them to their respective beds. But at least if the worst happened and she never saw Edwyn again, she would always have memories of those few precious hours.

"You *will* see each other again," Elyse had coaxed. "This separation will only be for a few months. Magnus will lose interest, you'll see. And then you and Edwyn will have the rest of your lives ahead of you."

Those words had warmed her, but they did nothing for the ache in her heart as they now faced each other in the stables. Emilya was aware that everyone else had melted away, and she felt a moment of warm appreciation for that. Edwyn put up his left hand and she put up her right to meet it.

Their fingers intertwined. He then put up his right hand, all the time looking her in the eye. As she intertwined the fingers of her left hand into his right, Edwyn smiled at her. She smiled back.

They stood like that for a while, without words. And then Edwyn did what she was desperate for him to do. He released her hands and then slowly moved his own up her arms to her shoulders and gently pulled her towards him. Just to be held by Edwyn was off-the-scale wonderful, but then he gently leaned his head down towards her and kissed her lightly on the lips.

How long the kiss lasted for, Emilya would not remember. It could have been ten seconds; it might have been ten minutes. When she came back down again, she was vaguely aware of her arms around Edwyn but could not remember the action of putting them there. And then it was over. Edwyn gently eased himself backwards, although he still had his hands on the tops of her arms. "I have to go now, Emilya."

"I know," she responded, as the first tear rolled out of her eye.

Edwyn leaned forward again and gently wiped the tear away. "I will wait for you," he said. "However long it takes. I *will* wait for you. And there will be no one else."

That broke Emilya. She began to cry and there was nothing she could do to stop herself. Edwyn pulled her towards him, and she rested her head on his shoulder, her sobbing eventually subsiding, while Edwyn gently ran his fingers through her thick dark-auburn hair. The sensation was heavenly.

Eventually, they parted again. There were no words to describe the levels of unfairness. "I'll write to you," she said.

"That would be wonderful," said Edwyn. "But I don't think it would be wise. At least not at first. Until we know he's lost interest, you shouldn't do anything that might reveal your location."

Emilya was too emotionally exhausted to be angry at that. And in any case, she knew that Edwyn was right.

"In time, we'll get messages back and forth one way or another," said Edwyn. "I'm sure that Clyve, Meg and Jarred will know people who travel back and forth between Earl's Leet and Kifsel Place."

Emilya could only offer a watery smile to that.

"I'm going to go now, Emilya. You need to go and say goodbye to Theo."

And that was it. Edwyn kissed her once on the forehead and turned around to lead Garresh from the stable. He turned around twice as he went, smiling both times. Then Emilya saw Elyse trot up to him and throw her arms around her slender nephew, kissing him three times in the process. Edwyn then mounted Garresh, turned one more time to Emilya, smiled and waved…and then tapped his heels to Garresh's flanks and cantered up the farm drive towards the road to Kinnslyng.

"I love you, Edwyn," whispered Emilya, tearfully. "I really do."

And then Elyse was hurrying towards her, and she broke down all over again as Elyse enfolded her in a motherly embrace. "I know, I know," she said, also stroking Emilya's hair. "I swear to you, Emilya, I will bring you safely home to him within a year. And then everything that you've gone through will have been worthwhile."

When Emilya's tears had dried, Elyse addressed the next obstacle. "So," she began, gently. "We now need to say goodbye to Theo. Are you ready for this?"

Emilya nodded and even managed to find words. "It won't be so hard. Because I'll know that Theo is in a much better place than he would be in my harness."

"That's the spirit," said Elyse.

As it turned out, saying goodbye to Theo was hugely emotional, too. Those big eyes had turned all sad, as if he knew that this was a parting with someone who loved him dearly. "You'll be fine here, Theo," she'd coaxed, her voice catching. "Clyve and Meg will look after you. You've got Mitzy, Rollo and Luther to play with, and a farm is a wonderful environment for a little doggy to grow up in. And I will come and see you as often as I can."

She'd been stroking his head as she'd said that, but still Theo looked sad – and so she'd gathered him to her chest and let him lick her face one last time. Could life really get any crueller? In the last week, she'd had to say goodbye to her father, her brother and sister by proxy, dear old Albert, Edwyn and now Theo. And all because of one vain, cruel, spoilt, *ridiculous* man. Much as Emilya had found love in the last week, she feared that she had also learned to hate, too.

That left one final goodbye – for the man who had saved her life eleven days ago. Emilya didn't hold back. She walked assuredly towards Jake without breaking her stride, throwing her arms around his neck. Jake picked her up so that her feet left the ground and swung her round once before putting her down. Despite their situation, both were smiling. Emilya thought that Jake didn't smile half enough.

"I can't thank you enough," said Emilya. "Yet I've ruined your life."

"You have not, Emilya Luca," responded Jake Oscom. "I'd do the same a million times out of a million. And in any case, this is an adventure I'll never forget."

"Aye, and it's not over yet," interceded Harry Black.

"There you are," said Jake, nodding at Black and his two lackeys. "Myself and my new associates here are about to have a whale of a time – and that's all thanks to you!"

Emilya looked dubious but managed to force a smile. She poked Jake in the chest with a forefinger. "You're just trying to make me feel better."

"I?" asked Jake, all innocence.

"You," confirmed Emilya. She then turned to Harry Black, conscious of the fact he had also joined with Jake in trying to make her feel better. That didn't change who and what he was, though. Despite her mere fifteen years, she decided to read the Riot Act to the legendary Harry Black. "And as for you," she began. "I expect you to look out for my friend. If I hear that you," she paused, and then looked at Turnip and then Swede, "or you, or you have betrayed him, I will hunt you down and make you pay."

For once, Harry Black didn't joke. "I promise you, here and now, that we three will do everything we can to help your friend lead the foul prince a merry dance across Glennad. We will also do our level best to protect Mr Oscom from harm. But above all, I do not want to let *you* down, Emilya Luca. You are a remarkable young lady."

Emilya was quite taken aback at that, finding herself lost for words.

"And one day, I will tell you the story about how I came to embark on such a vile path of felony. I suspect that you will be rather surprised, and maybe even a little bit understanding."

Emilya saw Elyse's eyes roll at that, but Emilya was intrigued. "I hope that we *will* have that conversation one day soon, Mr Black."

Harry Black nodded at Emilya, and then nodded at Jake. "I believe it is time we began setting our trap, my friend."

"Indeed," agreed Jake. "But first, let me say goodbye to our hosts." He then strode over to Clyve, Meg and Jared, shaking hands, kissing Meg on both cheeks and thanking Jared and telling him that he knew he could rely on him to look after Elyse and Emilya.

He left his last goodbye for Elyse. "And as for you, my lady," he said, taking her hand.

Emilya watched as Elyse's gold bracelet slid gracefully down her tanned forearm, before she fake-curtsied in response.

"As for you Elyse, I cannot imagine a life without you," added Jake, solemnly.

For once, Elyse was taken aback. Emilya knew very well that Jake wasn't the kind of person to show emotion or affection in public, so those words must have taken an enormous amount of courage. Elyse eventually found her voice. "And neither I without you," she replied, perfectly straight-faced, her eyes speaking the same words.

Jake continued to look at Elyse, and then bent over and kissed her hand once. "Till we meet again then, my dearest Elyse."

This time Elyse could find no words.

CHAPTER 64   JAKE
11ᵗʰ Tertiar, 1789   Day 102, 10:05

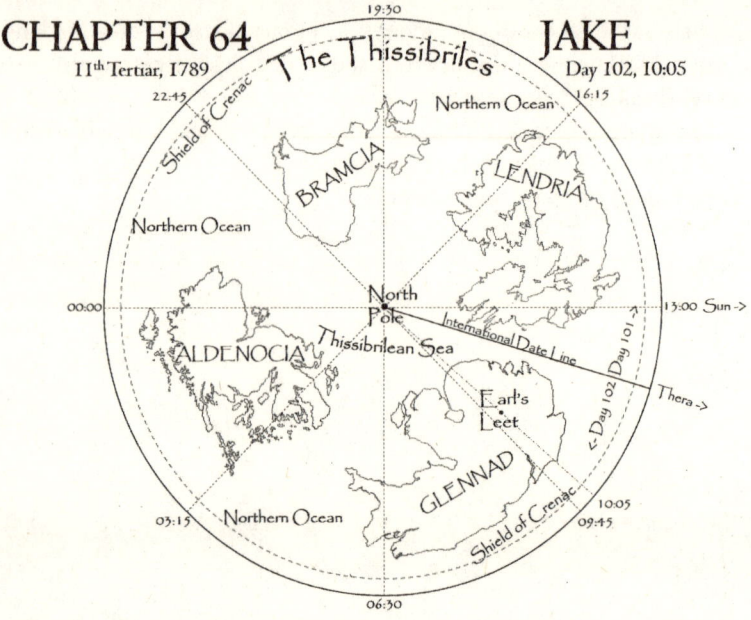

"That was very difficult for you, sir, was it not?"

Jake looked across at Harry Black as they rode side-by-side up the driveway from Clyve's farm. "Aye," was all he could manage.

"If it's any consolation, she loves you back."

Jake kept his eyes pinned forwards. "Aye," he said quietly.

After that, they turned left onto the road bound for Earl's Leet at a canter, each armed with a single holstered pistol – Jake having relented on arming his new companions due to a cautious improvement in trust between them all. During their short journey, words were few and far between in respect of Jake's recent sacrifice. Even Turnip and Swede, riding behind them, had little to say in the hour it took them to reach the junction with the higher route which doubled-back to Ghintonoll, Ghenetenos and ultimately Ghantiss.

Jake reined in, and his three companions followed suit. "We're not expecting His Royal Highness for another seven or eight hours. But just in case, I'll go and have a scout ahead." And with that, Jake touched his heels to his horse and scooted up the rise, doubling back above the three outlaws. He soon tucked himself in to the side of the road where he could see west for a league or so. There were several riders heading from Earl's Leet towards the Bleaklow Plateau, but no one coming in the opposite direction – which made sense, as most inbound travellers had usually travelled for the entire day before they got this far.

Satisfied that Magnus and his posse weren't anywhere near, Jake scanned the terrain on both sides of the road. Unfortunately, trees were less populous the further away from Earl's Leet you headed, which meant the ambush would need to be closer to the town than he would have liked, but it would have to do.

Half an hour later, the four outlaws were hidden in a large copse of chestnut trees and bushes on the south side of the eastbound road into Earl's Leet. "Ah, an old haunt of mine," Harry Black had said, as Jake had slowed them down on approach. Black was now looking around with satisfaction as if he genuinely *had* been re-acquainted with an old friend. Meanwhile, the dark-haired Turnip was dutifully tying their horses to trees, after which he moved from one to the other diligently feeding and watering them, while the ginger-haired Swede was acting as lookout for a posse of men protecting a central rider coming in from the west.

Jake and Black were soon discussing how best to approach the ambush. "Young Edwyn said he had eight men with him," said Jake.

"Well, if it were me, I'd have sent a fast rider on ahead to locate us," said Black.

"As would I," agreed Jake, on reflection.

"Maybe two," said Black. "So that one could report back and the other could keep an eye on us."

"Agreed – although I think it fair to assume they failed in that task."

"Hmm," said Black. "You have to assume all outcomes in this game."

"I can imagine," responded Jake, wryly. "You think we might have been compromised?"

"It's just a possibility, that's all. But if we are being watched, the watcher isn't going to get to Magnus and his men without us seeing him first, is he?"

"And if they are still looking for us in Earl's Leet, that means our prince's posse, including himself, is down to eight, maybe even seven."

"So," began Black. "I propose that we plan our attack on the basis of eight men."

"Agreed. So, how do we play this?" asked Jake, rubbing his chin.

"I suspect you already know the answer to that one, Jake."

Jake looked at him. It was the first time that Harry Black has addressed him by his first name. Black raised his right eyebrow, questioningly.

"I'd rather not," he responded.

"If we don't take men out of the equation, they will overrun us."

"How many do we take out?"

"Four, sir. We have four pistols and four sets of hands."

"I don't like it," began Jake.

"What do you think he plans to do with you, if he catches you?"

Jake looked at Black again. "Nothing good," he replied.

"He will put you to death, sir. And his method may not be pleasant."

"But his men have never done me any harm. Why should I hurt, or worse, kill them?"

"Dear oh dear," began Black. "I'm afraid you wouldn't last five minutes in my trade, Jake. Look!" he began, changing tack slightly. "I'm willing to admit that it isn't entirely necessary to *kill* four of his men. But I'd rather have just four men on my tail than eight."

"So, we just incapacitate four of them instead."

"Pah!" scoffed Black. "If you're hoping that all four of us can put a bullet through the legs or shoulders of four men, riding hard…" he tailed off, meaningfully.

Jake didn't respond immediately.

"And in any case," continued Black. "Do you really think your sentence will be lightened just because you shot to incapacitate and not to kill? Not that you'd ever convince any royal Ghantissian magistrate of that argument, anyway."

"Yes, but *I* will know that I only shot to injure."

Harry Black just smiled at that. "Very well," he agreed. "You're the boss. Four shoulder shots it is, then."

Jake was shaking his head, not entirely happy with the agreement, but glad they at least had the beginnings of a plan.

"So, assuming they are eight," said Black, "and we succeed in taking out four, we must then quickly ride out to the other four and aim our pistols before they can draw their muskets."

"The question is, do we all four point our pistols at Magnus? Or do we individually pick each of the four?

"So long as we're pointing before they're drawing, it won't matter. The next thing is to force them to throw their weapons to the floor. If they do not, I will shoot one of them dead, Jake."

Jake just looked at him.

"If it's me or them, I choose them."

Reluctantly, Jake nodded. He then closed his eyes. "Heaven help us. He is going to be one apoplectic little psychopath!"

"Well, that's what you want, isn't it?"

"Hmm," responded Jake. "It's a little different when you get down to the nitty-gritty."

"And are you still wanting me to change into my flamboyant apparel?"

"Oh yes," agreed Jake. "We need to make sure he knows that Jake Oscom has teamed up with Harry Black."

"Splendid," said Black, moving over to his horse and opening one of his saddlebags.

"I'll be with your lookout colleague when you're done," said Jake.

For the next eight hours, Jake and his party rotated watch. The only significant event had been a single soldier riding fast, west-bound, about half an hour ago. "That'll be Magnus' scout from Earl's Leet," Harry had said, confidently.

"Aye," Jake had agreed. "A very disappointed scout, I am hoping."

"They'll be in the foothills of the Umbricans by now, my friend," responded Harry, patting Jake on the back, knowing that Jake was still worrying about Emilya and Elyse. "And that Jared Swan seemed a very capable young man, to me."

"Aye," Jake had agreed, quietly.

Jake was still on watch when he saw the posse of eight men cantering down from the plateau. Even from this distance, it was clear that Prince Magnus rode in the middle of them; the man even rode a horse arrogantly, mused Jake. He then raised his fingers to his lips and issued a shrill whistle. Within seconds, his three accomplices were beside him.

"I see him," said Black from over Jake's right shoulder. Black was back in his red and gold apparel, white frilled shirt and cuffs and his jaunty tricorn. Jake's mouth twitched into the vaguest of smiles as he briefly took in the ensemble. "If they stay in that formation," Black was saying, "the four we take out are the front two, the man this side of Magnus, and the one at the back on our side."

"So, a two-phased attack," responded Jake, immediately seeing how it would play out.

"Not necessarily," said Black. "Given the angle of approach, we can do this more-or-less simultaneously if we spread out. I suggest you and I get entrenched at the eastern end of this copse, and we take out the front two when they are still approaching us. Turnip and Swede hide at the western end of our cover, and they can take out the other two when they're more-or-less level. I suggest that they fire first, and we fire a split-second later."

"Well," mused Jake. "That looks like a workable plan to me. I reckon we've got about five minutes until they're here, so I suggest you two go and find your cover, sharpish," said Jake, pointing to the western end of the copse. "And don't kill anyone, please."

Jake saw a look of amusement pass between Turnip and Swede, before Harry Black gave them his look. "Shoulders, please, gentlemen." The smirks disappeared, they both nodded and then made their way to their position. Jake and Black made off in the opposite direction, finding a suitable thicket beneath some stout chestnut boughs.

"What do we do if there's a party coming from the opposite direction?" asked Jake, as they knelt amongst the thickets.

"They'll be more worried about us than we will of them – especially once they hear pistols going off. They'll likely turn and flee – conveniently reporting to everyone in Earl's Leet that Harry Black has just held up Prince Magnus. You won't get much better publicity than that, my friend!"

Jake actually found himself smirking at that. He then turned his head to look at Harry Black for one last time before they instigated their attack. "You really do enjoy this, don't you?"

"I will enjoy bringing the Prince down a few notches, that's for sure."

"Me too," agreed Jake. He then released the safety catch on his pistol. Harry Black did the same. "Good luck, Harry," he said. Using the notorious highwayman's first name felt odd.

"Good luck to you, too, Jake.

Jake nodded once and then switched his attention to his left. He could hear the posse approaching as well as see them, and they were coming at some pace, too. This clearly wasn't going to be easy. In tandem with Harry Black, he double-checked his safety catch was off and took a steady aim. In his mind's eye, he could see Turnip and Swede doing the same, albeit from a slightly different angle.

The eight pairs of hooves came closer and louder, and closer and louder. Jake became increasingly tense, but his trigger-finger remained rock-steady, poised for action. No matter where Turnip and Swede hit, Jake was determined not to be distracted; he *would* take his man through the shoulder. To be fair to Turnip and Swede, though, he and Black would have wider targets to aim at – but it was too late to change positions now.

The posse were almost upon them now, closer and louder, closer and louder…and then *bang-bang*.

Jake's pistol kicked immediately, totally synchronous with Harry Black's. *Bang!*

Four puffs of smoke drifted out of the chestnut copse. Despite being knocked backwards, the two front-riders somehow managed to hang onto their reins and remain mounted, despite the lead-shot in their respective shoulders. The other two, further back on the copse side of the track, were thrown from their saddles.

Jake didn't have time to check if Turnip and Swede's targets were alive or dead, although he was aware of one of them moving and moaning. The Prince and the other two riders immediately reined in, their faces a combined tableau of panic and confusion. Jake and Black came out to meet them, with Turnip and Swede running fast to catch up from behind.

"Keep your hands in the air, gentlemen," ordered Black, in a commanding tone. His order was mainly directed at Magnus and the three uninjured men, one of whom Jake recognised as the one-eyed Marler. "Throw your pistols and muskets to the ground. Now."

Harry Black was very much the man in charge.

With his face beginning to transition from shock to anger, Magnus unholstered his pistol and threw it to the ground. He nodded at Marler who did the same. The two remaining soldiers also threw their muskets to the ground.

Jake then spotted one of the injured vanguard riders attempting to unshoulder his musket. "Drop it, sir," he commanded, his own pistol levelled at the soldier's head.

Knowing he was beaten, the soldier did as he was told, also wincing with pain from the wound in his shoulder which was already weeping red on red.

Turnip and Swede joined Jake and Black, having collected muskets from the other two fallen riders – both soldiers – and now picking up weapons three, four, five and six from the Prince and the uninjured men. Jake noticed that one of the fallen riders behind them wasn't moving.

"Do you ruffians not know whom you have attacked!" demanded one of the mounted soldiers.

Harry Black ignored him and indicated with his head that Turnip and Swede should collect weapons seven and eight from the two front men – one of whom Jake could now see was the heavily-moustached Hoskyns. Foolishly, Hoskyns attempted to draw his pistol. Turnip shot him right between the eyes.

Hoskyns' eyes glazed over, and he toppled backwards off his horse, hitting the ground like a sack of potatoes.

Jake shut his eyes for a second. His days in Glennad had just ended with that action. Although, to be fair, they had ended the second he had fired his pistol into Hoskyns' shoulder…and probably ten days earlier in an alley in Ghantiss.

"Please remain very still, all of you," commanded Black. "That should *not* have been necessary."

Magnus gritted his teeth. "We have nothing of value, you imbecile."

"It's not *value* that we seek, Your Royal Highness," said Jake, stepping forward. "It's sport."

Prince Magnus' face went white in an instant. Firstly because of the implications, but secondly because he now realised that he had been held up by his very own quarry. He soon recovered his composure, though. "Oscom!" he hissed. "What have you done with my sister?"

"Your sister?" responded Jake, confused.

"You have kidnapped my sister, you blackguard. And you intend to ransom her."

Jake was profoundly lost for words.

"He is trying to get inside your head, Jake," announced Harry Black. "Allow me to take over." He turned to face the Prince of Glennad, gave him a large icy smile and then pointed his pistol at his forehead. "Get down from your horse, Your Royal Highness."

"How dare you command me, Black."

Harry Black merely released the safety catch on his pistol. Jake felt himself tense as much as Prince Magnus did. Fortunately, the Prince recognised that he had no choice and dismounted. "I will have all of your heads for this.".

"That is highly unlikely, Sir," responded Black, "if the evidence of the last twelve years is anything to go by."

Whilst this exchange was going on, Turnip and Swede had returned with all eight weapons: five muskets and three pistols. In true highwayman fashion, Black, Turnip and Swede were soon holding a pistol apiece in each hand, while the five spare muskets had been stashed a safe distance away from their prisoners.

As he had throughout the exchange, Jake was looking east and west along the roadway. He now spotted a couple of riders heading in from the west, and a damn coach with large reinforced wheels and axels approaching from the east. "We've got company," he said to Black.

Harry Black took charge again. Inside thirty seconds, he had the four uninjured men – including Magnus – lying face-down on the road with their hands behind the back of their heads. The vanguard soldier with the injured shoulder was allowed to sit by the roadside, albeit with his hands tied. Hoskyns was dead, and of the other two – who had been shot by Turnip and Swede at the start of the ambush – one was clearly dead and the other in a bad way. Black then ordered Turnip west, on foot, and Swede east. "You know what to do gentlemen."

"Please try not to kill anyone else," implored Jake.

Both lackeys nodded and set off in opposite directions, holding two pistols in the air. The pair of riders approaching from the west were soon riding back from where they had come – towards nothing but bleak, open hills and moorland. It was also doubtful that any other travellers they encountered would continue to Earl's Leet, either – at least not for some time – meaning a rescue for the Prince wouldn't be coming from that direction any time soon. As for the coach, its occupants were already lying face-down on the floor, and Swede was relieving them of their possessions.

Jake briefly closed his eyes again. They weren't supposed to be robbing anyone. Then again, these leopards not changing their spots would certainly add to the furore, which was the whole purpose of the exercise. And now, Swede was ordering the single coachman and the protesting passengers – a middle-aged man and woman – to strip down to their birthday suits, revealing white and saggy flesh on both passengers contrasting with that of the toned and tanned coachman. The levelling of Swede's pistols had dealt swiftly with any thoughts of non-compliance, though.

Once Turnip and Swede re-joined them, they set to work making a small fire using brushwood and Harry Black's flint-striking device and began burning the clothes of the coach party.

"What the devil are you doing?" came Magnus' muffled voice, from his prone position, having heard the crackling of fire and smelt the smoke from the burning clothes. He craned his neck to try and see.

"Keep very still," demanded Black, now with his pistols holstered and a wickedly sharp rapier drawn and pointing at Magnus' back. He moved the point down to Magnus' waist, and expertly flicked it upwards, ripping open Magnus' glorious blue tunic and opening up his shirt beneath, too. Such was Black's expertise, that no tell-tale red lines appeared.

"Hell's teeth, what are you doing, man?" demanded Magnus, still sounding more angry than afraid.

Black ignored him and opened up his breeches instead.

"You cannot -."

"I'd advise you to keep quiet and not move, my friend," was Black's response.

"Friend!" screeched Magnus.

The next second, Turnip and Swede grabbed a boot each and hauled them off.

Five minutes later, all members of the Prince's party – whether alive or dead – had been relieved of their clothing, all of which was now blazing away on an increasingly blackening pile to one side of the road.

Jake approached Prince Magnus, who was back lying face down beside the road – albeit now naked and with his hands tied behind his back. "Your Royal Highness," he began.

"You're a dead man walking, Oscom."

"You aren't likely to appreciate me sparing your life then?"

"You clearly haven't got the guts to take it."

"What did you mean about the Princess Alicya?"

"Ha! That's for me to know and for you to worry out."

Jake nodded twice. He wasn't going to get anything from the Prince.

"You've only got yourself to blame for this," said Jake.

"Really!" responded Magnus, his tone laced with scorn. "And where is Emilya Luca, pray tell?"

"I've never heard of an Emilya Luca. Was she the girl in the alley?"

"You know damn well that she was."

"I know nothing of the sort."

"Oh, so you just happened to be out here on the same route that she and Elyse Dolmen were travelling, were you?"

Jake had no immediate answer to that. After a few seconds, he changed his tack. "I am quite happy for you to come after me and my new companions." Jake paused briefly. "If you think you have the intelligence and the courage, that is. But having spent a few minutes in your vile and cowardly presence – twice, now – I have no doubt that you will stick to hunting down little girls, instead."

The noises that began to come out of Prince Magnus' mouth were like nothing Jake had heard before. For Jake, it was no laughing matter, but when he turned around, he saw Harry Black with a wide grin on his face, silently applauding him, whilst Turnip and Swede were sniggering like a couple of schoolboys. Nevertheless, despite the threats and demands from the prone and naked Prince Magnus, neither Jake nor Harry Black spoke to him again. Turnip and Swede quickly went to retrieve their horses, and they all left the scene at a gallop in the direction of Earl's Leet, passing the middle-aged couple who now huddled naked and bound in their coach along with their bewildered coach-driver.

CHAPTER 65 — MADELEINA

11th Tertiar, 1789 — Day 102, 13:15

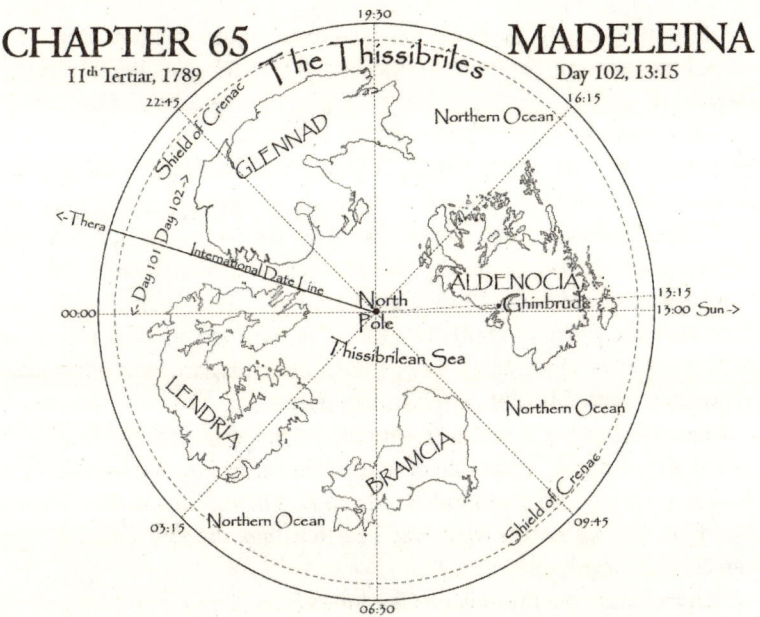

Princess Madeleina was alone in her drawing room and quite miserable. Her betrothed, Prince Bernard of Lendria had arrived at the palace in Ghinbrude earlier in the day, and she was expected to receive him shortly and be his hostess for the rest of the day and evening.

There was a sudden knock at the door which made Madeleina jump, followed by an "it's only me" from Charlotte, her lady-in-waiting.

"Come in, Lottie," said the Princess.

The raven-haired Charlotte entered, unable to hide a mischievous grin across her rosy cheeks.

"Well, I'm glad you're happy," said Madeleina, all sour-faced.

"He's in the Great Hall with the King and Queen," said Charlotte.

"And how are mother and father performing their hosting duties?"

"As regally as anyone who knows them would expect, Princess."

Madeleina issued a big sigh, and her shoulders sagged. "And how does Prince Bernard look?"

Charlotte stifled a grimace and then nodded her head. "He looks…well, Your Royal Highness."

"Don't call me that!" snapped Madeleina. "He looks well?"

"Yes. Well."

"What do you mean by 'well'?"

Charlotte paused. "He has a…a high colour, Your – I mean, Maddie."

"A high colour? That will be the blood pressure, no doubt," opined Madeleina.

"That's rather unkind if you don't my me saying."

Madeleina glared at her friend. "Unkind!" she exclaimed. "I'll tell you what's 'unkind', shall I? 'Unkind' is expecting an eighteen-year-old to…to. Oh!" she exclaimed, throwing her hands in the air before standing and pacing about her bedroom. "I'll tell you something, Charlotte."

Charlotte raised her eyebrows, questioningly. "Your Highness?".

Madeleina ignored the title this time. "When I am queen, I will *never* subject my own children to this archaic, outdated, ancient, outmoded, antiquated…antediluvian…prehistoric…farce!"

Charlotte put her hand to her mouth at the Princess' building-to-a-crescendo outburst. It was one of Madeleina's affectations and was often done for comic effect around her friends. On this occasion, though, Charlotte knew that the vent was heartfelt, but she still couldn't stop herself from smirking.

Madeleina caught the look on Charlotte's face. "This isn't funny, Lottie," she said, now deadly serious. "This is my life!"

"I'm sorry, Your Royal Highness."

Madeleina looked at Charlotte and cast her eyes heavenwards but let the use of her formal title pass again. "In exactly forty-five minutes' time, I'm supposed to present myself to the Great Hall."

"I know, and hence I was wondering if you wanted to wear anything more spectacular?" suggested Charlotte.

Madeleina looked down at her beige dress with its embroidered, full-length sleeves, having earlier thought that this would be perfectly *un*spectacular. A new thought struck her. "I'm wondering," she began, with narrowed eyes, "if perhaps we should go the other way."

"The other way?"

"Yes, why not. Oh Charlotte!" she said, suddenly becoming more animated. "What sort of a message would that send out if I did go the other way? If I turned up in rags?"

"It would send out the sort of message that would get you carpeted by your parents, for starters – not to mention cause humiliation to the Aldenocian royal family, and insult to the Lendrian royal family," counselled Charlotte. "And, quite frankly, it would make you look like some kind of a raving lunatic, too!"

Madeleina just stared hard at Charlotte. "Remind me, Charlotte," she began. "Why are you my friend?"

"I *am* your friend, Madeleina," said Charlotte. "And if you really were serious about doing something like that – and I think you were, just for a moment – it is my duty to counsel you otherwise."

Madeleina continued to stare hard at Charlotte – and then suddenly, she burst out into hysterics. "Your face!" she said.

"You were serious!" accused Charlotte. "I know it! You were truly considering rags."

"Oh God, I was," admitted Madeleina, her mood taking a downswing. She threw herself onto her chaise-longue, feet up over one end, arm draped over the top. "Oh, what am I going to do, Charlotte? I can't marry him."

"Have you ever spoken to him?"

"To whom?"

"To Prince Bernard."

"Yes. Twice. Once at father's sixtieth birthday, and again, last year, at the Union Celebration," she said, her latter reference being the 81st celebration of the Act of Union of the Thissibriles.

"And?"

"And what?"

"What did you talk about?"

"Oh, I don't know. The food, the weather, the band. What does it matter?"

"Well, how did he seem?"

"Fat!"

"Maddie!"

"Oh, he was perfectly polite. Although I did catch him looking at my cleavage once."

"Hmm," mused Charlotte. "That's not a good sign then."

"Why not?" demanded Madeleina, testily. "What's wrong with my cleavage?"

"Nothing, nothing," responded Charlotte, hurriedly.

"We can't all have it bursting out of our bodices, can we?" said the sullen princess.

Charlotte couldn't help but glance down at her own endowment. She looked back up again. "I meant it's not a good sign if he's looking at you… like that. Sizing you up."

"Oh Charlotte, don't!" said Madeleina now standing up and actually gagging. "Oh my God! I cannot…" she tailed off. She had her hand raised towards Charlotte, and her head was turned away. She then recovered and turned back to face her friend. "I always thought that dear Henry would be…"

"He's your cousin, Princess."

"He loves me."

"And do you love him?"

"Yes. No. Yes, but not in that way. Oh, I don't know."

Charlotte waited a moment and then pressed on with her thoughts. "When I asked if you'd spoken to him, I was trying to understand if he was, well, reasonable…thoughtful…nice."

Madeleina issued another big sigh. "Yes, he was all of those things." She flopped back down onto the chaise-longue. "I can't accuse him of being a monster."

"So, this is good," said Charlotte.

"Good!" exclaimed Madeleina, her face screwed up in astonishment. "There is nothing remotely 'good' about any of this. Once again, Charlotte, I find myself questioning your counsel."

"What I meant, was that if he is nice and thoughtful and kind…you might be able to reason with him."

"In what way?"

"Tell him…tell him that you never expected to marry -. No, that won't do," said Charlotte, creasing her brow in concentration. "Ask him…yes, ask him if he is comfortable marrying someone so young."

"What good will that do?"

"You might find out if he is uncomfortable marrying someone thirty-seven years his junior; marrying someone who is barely out of childhood."

"And I also might find out that he is *very* comfortable marrying someone thirty-seven years his junior," objected Madeleina. "Even if she does have rubbish cleavage!"

"Well at least you'll know."

"I already know. He's a man!"

"Forgive me, Your Highness, but what do you really know of men?"

"Enough!"

"Look, what I'm getting at is, that if you can establish any level of discomfort on his part, you can eat away at it. Make him see that this isn't a suitable marriage at all. Talk to him as an adult, in an adult way."

"He's destined to be King of Lendria, and he wants a son!" exclaimed Madeleina. "A son which neither of his first two wives could give him. He stands a far better chance of achieving that with someone like me…"

Madeleina tailed off, putting her hand at the top of her chest to prevent herself gagging again.

"You could always tell him that he can't have his way."

Poor Madeleina just put her head in her hands at that thought.

"Seriously, Princess. You could tell him it's just not right. Women can still bear children in their thirties and forties. Such a woman would be a much more sensible match for a fifty-five-year-old man."

Madeleina just looked at Charlotte, but said nothing.

"I'm not putting this very well, I know," admitted Charlotte. "But what I'm driving at is…is –."

"To shame him," completed Madeleina. "Not in public, but in private – between just the two of us."

"Yes, sort of," agreed Charlotte.

"Well," began Madeleina. "He really is my only hope, so it's not such a daft idea. Because all mother and father can think about is strengthening the bond between Aldenocia and Lendria. Politics and history is everything to them. Particularly with the Abolitionists ramping up their opposition. Me, I'm nothing."

"Well, at least they're not looking to strengthen bonds between Aldenocia and Glennad. Otherwise, you'd be marrying a psychopath."

"A very handsome psychopath, though. And we don't know if the rumours are true."

"He raped Lady Shona on his last visit here, Maddie!"

"We've only got Shona's word for that –." Madeleina broke off when she saw Charlotte's horrified face. "I'm sorry, Lottie, that was awful of me."

Charlotte wasn't so easily placated. "Yes, it was. And what about Nibbles?"

"Yes, Nibbles. I'd forgotten about him," said Madeleina, her eyes now misty at the thought of her former pet rabbit. Nothing had been proven, but the day Prince Magnus had gone out hunting with her father and uncles, her poor snowy rabbit had been found dead and full of buckshot. Nothing like that had ever happened before or since. But no one was allowed to press the matter; it was all swept neatly under the palace carpet.

Madeleina then shuddered as she remembered Magnus' cold eyes. He had undressed her with them – and then smiled full in her face. But there was no warmth in that smile. "You make a valid point," said Madeleina, quietly. "Maybe I am better off with a kindly old man. And at least I'll still likely be young when widowed!"

Charlotte bent down on her haunches and took Madeleina's hands. "But you can still work on his conscience, yes?"

"I can," agreed Madeleina.

"So, you never know. You might yet come out of this unscathed."

Madeleina gave her head lady-in-waiting a wistful smile. "Thank you for your counsel, Charlotte. You have, at the very least, made me see that there are worse things in life. And yes, there is still hope, too."

CHAPTER 66 — DAVY
11th Tertiar, 1789 — Day 102, 12:30

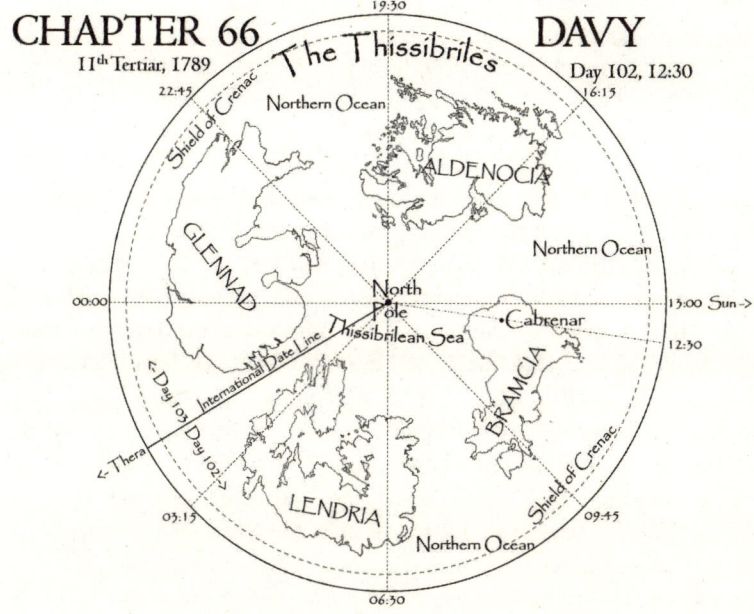

It was Davy's eighth funeral of the week, but this one would be by-far the hardest.

Davy looked across at Carys as they prepared to enter the small church. He was determined to keep her at the forefront of his thoughts. True, he had lost an ever-present in his life. *You're my best friend, Davy*. Those words still cut him to the core. As did the words which had followed. Those three little words. But Carys had lost her husband and soul mate. She was a widow at only twenty-one years of age.

Daisy sensed what he was thinking and clasped his hand tighter. He bent over to kiss her on the top of her head – and immediately regretted it, for Carys had seen. He saw Carys stifle a sob and felt an enormous stab of guilt. Both for that action, and because he was still alive. It should have been he who was reprimanded by Stan Eckersley, eight days ago. It should have been he who was working double shifts.

Davy then felt a pang of compassion for Stan Eckersley. Had he reasoned the same way – that if he hadn't been so hard on Robbie, over something that was essentially so trivial, then Carys wouldn't be standing here a widow today? Then again, as the off-shift pit foreman, Stan Eckersley had plenty of other things to worry and grieve about – not least the loss of many of his life-long colleagues, including his co-foreman, Dai Morgan. Poor Dai had been buried yesterday.

Also buried yesterday had been Dylan Lowe. It was one long nightmare. Poor Edyth Lowe had buried one son and had given up hope of finding the other after the mine had been flooded yesterday. Neither he, nor Stan Eckersley, nor any of the JPs or officials involved in the search for Will had had the heart to tell her – about the likely cause of the blast, or the suspected abduction by Turner. The poor woman had suffered enough.

Of course, someone would eventually tell her, or she would see the posters advertising Will's disappearance when she eventually steeled herself to go out – and the truth would certainly come out at the disaster inquest. How could he ever look her in the eye again? He had been so close to visiting Edyth and telling her what he knew on many occasions. Every time, he had either heeded the warnings of others, or he'd simply lacked the courage to do it. Everyone's hope – his own included – was that the authorities would track down Turner and Will before Edyth learned the truth, and Edyth Lowe would then rejoice at the return of a surviving son. But the longer the search went on, the more Davy believed that he would have to be the one to tell Edyth the truth. *Perhaps tomorrow?* Yes, he resolved. He *must* tell her tomorrow.

As for today, it was all about Robbie Russell. Today was also slightly different to the previous two days of funerals, as the Prime Minister, David Grey-Doogell was amongst the mourners. They ought to be feeling honoured – but it really didn't help much at all. Robbie was still dead and Carys was still a widow.

Davy looked across at the PM, standing with his hands clasped and his head bowed. The stories were that the PM had taken the disaster badly; personally. Davy knew David Grey-Doogell's story well. It was one which all working-class men aspired to, as it was well-documented that his grandfather had been a Bramcian coal miner who had risen to be a foreman, thus earning enough money to send his son – David's father – to a state school. David Grey Senior had become a prominent and respected parish councillor, which had enabled him to send his own son to Craffid University where he had studied law. Following graduation with honours, David Grey-Doogell (Doogell courtesy of his mother) had soon set up his own law practice in the back parlour of an uncle's house in Whelplil. The practice flourished, and his standing in society had enabled him to become involved in politics, eventually joining the Liberal party with whom he would eventually rise to the position of leader and Prime Minister, elected off the back of his popular manifesto for reform – including reform in the mines and the way in which they were run. He had largely delivered, too, and was a hugely popular Bramcian Prime Minister.

Davy switched his attention to Carys, standing by the open church doors with her head on her father's shoulder and her mother's arm also around her. Her mother then led her slowly into the church, and the mournful congregation began to follow. Davy then heard the horses pulling the carriage bearing the coffin up the steep hill to the church. When the heads of the horses appeared, he could see the tremendous amount of strain that it put on their valiant bodies to pull the carriage.

As the coffin approached the church, Davy squeezed Daisy's hand. Daisy gave him a watery smile and then also went into the church, while Davy moved to take up his position at the head of the carriage alongside Robbie's father. Eric Russell leaned across and shook Davy's hand. "I'm sorry for your loss, son," he said.

Davy blinked back the tears. This was Robbie's father, who had lost his youngest son, but he was actually seeing the grief of others. Perhaps it gave him a kind of comfort to see how much his son had been loved. "I'm dreadfully sorry for your loss, too, Mr Russell."

Eric Russell gave Davy a sorrowful smile and nodded once. "I know you are, son."

Davy then turned to face the front and did his best to keep a grip. He had a reading to do shortly, for which he was deeply honoured, and there was no way he was going to let anyone down.

As the last of the congregation filed slowly into the church, the six pallbearers moved side-by-side and put their arms around their partners' shoulders. Robbie's coffin was then lifted and smoothly rolled out onto their collective shoulders. Davy had tensed his body to take the weight, but even so, the coffin was heavier than he had been expecting. Nevertheless, he remained upright and strong. Seconds later, the funeral director began his stately march into the church, and the six pallbearers followed, bearing the body of their beloved son, brother, cousin, nephew and friend.

As they walked sedately up the central aisle of the church, Davy was aware of people sobbing and blowing noses. He then heard a cry of grief that could only have come from Carys as she saw the coffin approach. It must have felt very final for her. This really was the most awful of places in the human journey.

Once they had laid Robbie's coffin on the bier in front of the priest, Davy took to his seat on the second row behind the distraught Carys and her mother. Daisy's hand was instantly in his and her face was wet with tears.

Oh, I am so going to look after you, my love.

The rest of the ceremony was a blur. He delivered his reading in a kind of detached haze, but he knew well enough that he had read loud and well-paced and very clear. That was the only help he could give to Carys and to Robbie's mother and father and family on this dreadful occasion.

The burial had followed, and now the mourners were mingling and perhaps sharing a solemn anecdote or two. "I thought you read splendidly, young man," said a voice beside him.

Davy clicked out of his trance and turned to thank the man – and was astonished to see that David Grey-Doogell was holding out his hand to him. Davy took the Prime Minister's hand, and the handshake was warm and firm. "Thank you, Prime Minister. It was a great honour for me."

"You were obviously a very dear friend to Robbie, elsewise…" he left the rest unsaid.

"The world is a lesser place than it was four days ago, Mr Grey-Doogell."

"It certainly is, young man. And I will personally see to it that the families are properly looked after, and suitable memorials are raised. I have already started the Cabrenar Bereavement Fund to this end."

"That's wonderful, Mr Grey-Doogell," said Davy, genuinely relieved, his thoughts flicking immediately to poor Edyth Lowe. "There are people here whose needs are desperate."

"We will help them as much as we can. But of course, nothing can bring back their loved ones."

"I held his hand whilst he died," said Davy. He had no idea why he had offered that information to his country's Prime Minister. "He told me to tell Carys that he loved her. And his Mam." Davy paused. "And then he told me that he loved me, too. And I never told him back."

David Grey-Doogell, Prime Minister of Bramcia then did a remarkable thing. He wept.

"Oh, I'm sorry, Prime Minister, I shouldn't have…"

"Nonsense, dear boy," said Grey-Doogell, now drying his eyes with his handkerchief and trying to laugh at himself. "What am I like?"

As the Prime Minister attempted to recover himself, Daisy joined them and put her arms around Davy and also told him that she loved him too. "Well, well, well," muttered the PM. "Mercy me. What wonderful people you are. Might I know your name, young man?"

"Davy Sheerin, Mr Grey-Doogell."

"Ah! So, you're the star rescuer as well! Rescued more miners than anyone else. You must be mighty proud of your husband, madam," he said to Daisy. "I can promise you, young Davy. You and your fellow rescuers will be honoured and rewarded for your actions."

"I don't want any fuss, Prime Minister."

"Nonsense, my boy. There will be fuss. I shall see to it, personally."

"Thank you, sir," was all that Davy could muster.

"Well, I really must be going. My carriage awaits," he said, gesturing towards an impeccable black carriage which had the red Bramcian dragon emblazoned on the side. "But if there is anything that I can ever do for you, please don't hesitate to ask. Here is my card. Please feel free to write to me at this address, at any time."

"Thank you, Prime Minister. And thank you for coming."

"It was my honour, Davy Sheerin."

CHAPTER 67 DRAXAELEN

11th Tertiar, 1789 Day 102, 11:00

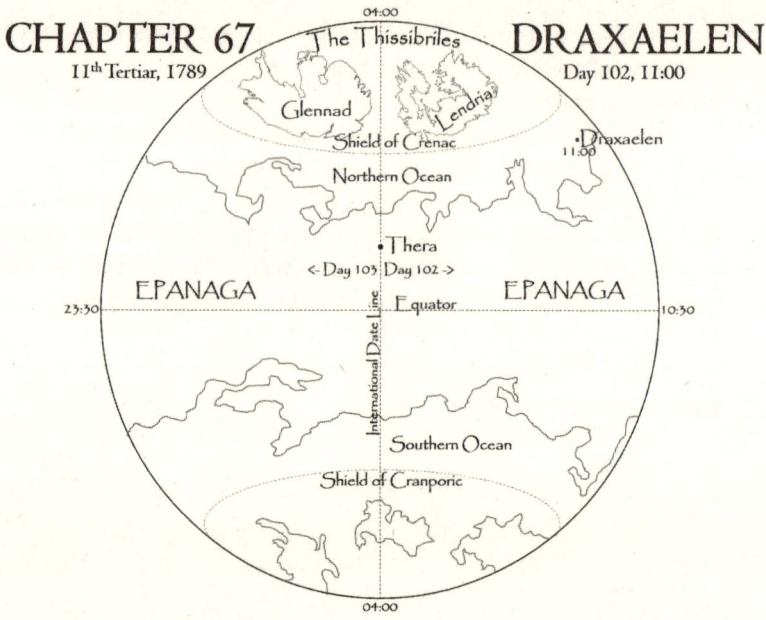

For the fourth day running, Draxaelen's world was limited to the elbows of the men on either side of him, and the bunched muscles in the shoulders of those in front – each of them sporting an 'MZ' brand on the rear of their right shoulders. His own branding still felt raw with each draw on the oar; draws which also incurred a constant aching in his shoulders, back, neck and arms, and offered no chance for the raw, weeping calluses on his hands to heal, either. His mini-world was completed by the vomit, excrement and urine sloshing around his ankles and beneath the raised bench upon which he sat.

Like his one hundred and seventy nine fellow-slaves, Drax had quickly learned to coordinate his efforts with theirs, rowing to the beat of a monotonous drum, lest they lose more skin from their backs. And like one hundred and seventy fellow-slaves, he had also learned to keep his mouth shut; the other nine were now at the bottom of the Northern Ocean and their surviving colleagues were having to work that little bit harder without them. But worst of all, due to the repetitive nature of the draw, each hour felt like a day, and each day like a year. And with how many more days to come just like this? Hundreds? Thousands, perhaps? Or maybe only tens, given these inhuman conditions.

Drax gritted his teeth in defiance. *He would not die*. Death would not rob him of his revenge. Revenge on Maxi Zoninus, the slave-master with the mismatched eyes who had cruelly branded him, and then demonstrated the extent of his malice by branding Argaeus on his wounded shoulder. Revenge on Macrinus, the dead-eyed Theran General who had crucified his father and younger brothers in front of him. And revenge that would seem laughable to any Theran: to kill Vitasian, the elder, ordering a multitude of atrocities from the safety of his opulent palace in Thera, amidst oils, incense and pretty-looking boys and girls, and Calidius, the younger, more active, crueller, the driving force behind conquest and all the devilry that went with it.

For now, though, he just had to survive.

As he pulled relentlessly on his oar, Draxaelen's thoughts drifted to Leonnatus, his former close friend. Leonnatus would only have betrayed Drax under extreme duress – perhaps to prevent *his* father and brothers from being crucified, or *his* mother and sister from being raped and murdered. That was the way this inhuman empire worked. It fed men like Macrinus, enabling them to do anything they pleased. Nevertheless, Leonnatus' betrayal had still decimated his *Demonata*. Over two hundred had died in the attack by musket-armed Theran legions in Alsethonisca's market square. However, crucifying young and strong warriors was largely a waste of manpower, hence the surviving *Demonata* were now manning five of the galley ships destined for Eastern Epanaga and the further expansion of the Neo-Theran Empire – as were many innocent citizens of Alsethonisca. Rounded up and divided into chain gangs, Drax had found himself one of a galley-slave crew of one hundred and eighty oarsmen that had left the harbour of Alsethonisca later that afternoon on the 8th Tertiar.

Draxaelen tried to blot out the face of the wife of one of the civilian Alsethoniscan's whose husband – a mere cobbler – had been roughly seized from the watching crowds and assigned to Maxi Zoninus and his sizzling branding iron. His wife had managed to break through the cordon of Theran soldiers, wailing at them to release him. General Macrinus had thrust his sword straight through her face. Drax had watched as the sword had punched out the back of her skull, bits of cranium and brain spraying everywhere. He had seen such sights before, but always on the field of battle; never before an innocent, and certainly not a defenceless civilian woman.

After that, there had been no resistance. Despite their fierce reputation, the overwhelming opposition numbers had presented Drax and his men with a stark choice. Surrender, or be responsible for soaking the streets of

Alsethonisca with the blood of innocent men, women, and children. Either way, Demonacia was crushed. Again. But at least surrender meant that most Alsethoniscans still lived, and he did not have widescale civilian deaths on his conscience, while his men still had a small chance of fighting another day.

His family did not have that chance, though. For a split-second, the grief became overwhelming and he let out a muted sound of despair. The ever-attentive whip-master heard it, and the whip cracked once. Draxaelen roared with pain but didn't let up his grip on the oar. In fact, he pulled even harder. Within seconds, though, he knew that the latest lash had cracked right across an open wound. Yet still he pulled on his oar…on and on, opening it up still further. *Just focus on the oar*. Focusing on the oar helped to deal with the pain.

After half an hour, the intensity of the pain from the wound began to subside. Drax was cross with himself. It would serve no purpose objecting, railing or showing any evidence of dissent or grief. That would only leave him further away from his goals of revenge. He *must* always show supplication; keep his wits about him and observe – although, in truth, he was already familiar with every detail of his surrounds; they would remain branded upon his memory for as long as Maxi Zoninus' iron-brand mark would remain on his back.

Nevertheless, Draxaelen began again to scrutinise the galley-ship with each backward pull on the oar. Despite great advancements in shipbuilding, galley-ship design hadn't changed in over a thousand years, and they were still largely propelled by humans. It was a perfect way to keep convicts, criminals and enemies of the Empire employed and away from mischief-making, and it was also a very cheap way to build and then propel a ship half-way around the globe on military missions. The rights of human beings did not come into it.

Draxaelen's galley was identical to the four others that had set sail from Alsethonisca harbour, three days ago: a long and slender hull, a shallow draft, a low freeboard, and composed of two levels. The slave level, below decks, was hot and sweaty and permanently besieged by foetid air. It was comprised of thirty bays for the one hundred and eighty rowers arranged in rows of six berths, three on either side of the gangway. Each trio were arranged in tiers: the rower on the outside against the inner hull of the ship, standing and the highest, and hence his oar dipped into the water at the steepest angle; the rower on the inside and against the gangway, the lowest and seated, with his oar entering the water at the shallowest angle. An ingenious arrangement to exact optimum speed which had served the Theran Empire for nearly two thousand years. Draxaelen was in the central position of his trio. Meanwhile, up and down the gangway, three whipmasters stalked back and forth, looking for the slightest excuse to engage their equipment.

Drax had memorised every detail of those three whipmasters. One of them was missing the lower half of his left ear, another had large warts on his back, and the third sported a totally shaven head with a strawberry-coloured birth-mark at the base of his neck. Drax had worked out their height and weight; he knew intimately the way they walked, the way they looked at you, their facial mannerisms. He knew he would dream of these men, many times. And, perhaps one day, he would kill them, too.

Above the whipmasters and the central gangway, were iron chandeliers each housing a dozen candles, thus enabling Draxaelen to view all his fellow sweat-drenched *Demonata* in front of him, both night and day. He knew many of them by name. Poor Argaeus wasn't amongst them, though, and neither was Crateuas. Drax could only pray for them, particularly Argaeus, whose chances of having survived this long were not good, given a likely untreated shoulder full of lead.

The only other constant was the drum-master, repeatedly beating out his rhythm, all day and for half of the night, too. Thankfully, today had been normal pace, throughout – given they had been forced to practice battle speed, attack speed and ramming speed twice apiece on day's two and three. A small number of the less-robust amongst them had collapsed during ramming speed practice.

To keep his mind focused, Drax ran through what he had memorised of the top deck. A large central main sail in dark red, embossed in gold with the imperial eagle, and a smaller fore-sail, while either side of the main sail was a forecastle and aftcastle for observation. Of course, those sails were only of use when the wind was behind them. The advantage of having a *human* propulsion system, was that the galley could be navigated independently of winds and currents, and it wasn't unusual for chain-gangs of one hundred and eighty oarsmen having to row directly into the teeth of a roaring maelstrom. As for their cargo, this was mainly weaponry – guns catapults and cannons for the legions travelling on other ships – including those bogus Adcian warships that had docked at Alsethonisca, three days ago.

Drax kept pulling on his oar, despite the constant blood that oozed from the sores on the palms of his hands. Never once did his rhythm falter. All he could do was row, until the beat-master finally called a stop, after which the galley would sail or drift for a handful of hours.

In between stopping rowing and falling into an exhausted sleep, Drax would fight to stay awake for a fourth night running, to receive his allocation of rancid gruel. The first night, he had nigh-on spat it out – but had forced himself to keep working it around his mouth before he felt ready to swallow. Then he had repeated the action – until the gruel had all gone. The second night, he had eaten it faster. Last night, he had wolfed it down.

Suddenly, Draxaelen's concentration was broken by movement at the front of the deck – although he made sure his rhythm remained uninterrupted. A shadowy presence was slowly moving down the gangway, inspecting the men on each side, whilst nodding his head in approval. As the man moved underneath the nearest iron chandelier, Drax saw that it was Maxi Zoninus – clearly inspecting the condition of his property. Despite the subdued light, gemstones glittered on every finger and gold ornaments sparkled on his wrists and around his neck, whilst Drax's eyes almost watered at the overwhelming scent of rose and saffron as he approached. Their eyes met. Maxi Zoninus came to a standstill. "You look fit," he stated.

Drax just snorted but didn't reply.

"Keep it that way, my friend," said the swarthy Zoninus. "Survive…and you will be rewarded."

"Pah!" Draxaelen couldn't help himself.

The nearest whipmaster moved in, but Zoninus stayed him with a raised hand. "I mean it, so mark my words, slave. I see fire and potential in you."

Zoninus then moved on further down the gangway beyond his vision, leaving Drax to puzzle over the slavemaster's plans for him.

CHAPTER 68   CALIDIUS
12th Tertiar, 1789   Day 103, 11:00

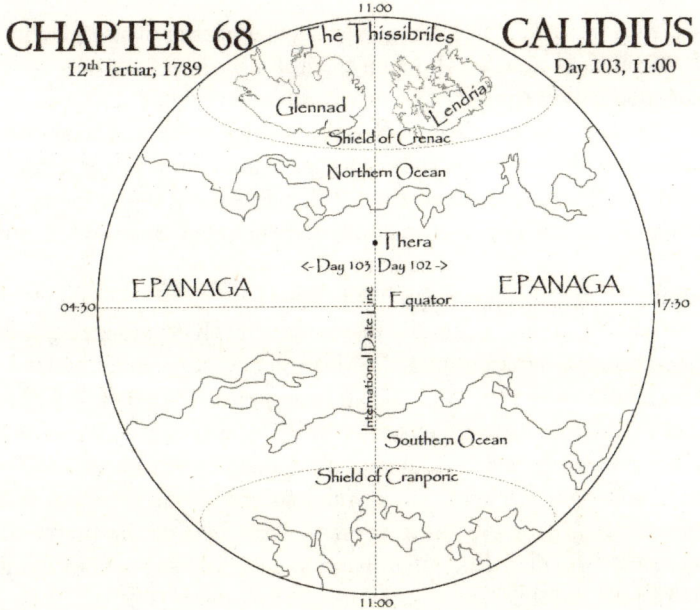

Emperor Calidius Antoninus Dominius, the 316th Emperor of Thera, did his usual thing: circling slowly, anti-clockwise, on the central dais of the *Curia*, making eye contact with every senator in the five stacked levels of wooden benches around him. After a full revolution, he stopped and addressed the half he could see. "Honoured members of the Senate of Thera," he began. "I can only apologise for the burden that I have bestowed upon you."

Calidius moved slowly a quarter to his right, now moving in a clockwise direction. "Of course, you will by now have acknowledged," he paused, "that I had little choice."

A low level of mumbled agreement greeted his words.

"It is now five days since I broke the catastrophic news to you. I am beyond pleased with you all," he said, pausing and moving another quarter to his right, "that I hear no word of our pending catastrophe on the streets of Thera. Thank you for your loyalty, senators."

Nodding sage heads greeted this last statement. Of course, he had made it perfectly clear last time what would happen to those who talked. And yet, it had still been necessary to take action. No doubt the handful of empty seats would hone his senators' loyalty further.

"However," said Calidius, moving another quarter to his right. "We must now, more than any other time in the past, sculpt our empire into one which is lean," he paused, and then moved another quarter to his right, now back facing his first audience. "And mean," he finished.

Again, nodded agreement and murmurs of assent greeted his words.

"We must also give the Theran public something to distract them over the next seventy days or so. Something bigger than we've ever done before." He moved another quarter to his right. "Therefore, we will give them," he paused for effect, "the largest gladiatorial tournament in the history of our empire."

Murmurs of agreement came from all sides now.

As he spoke, Calidius made sure that he kept revolving every couple of sentences to keep everyone engaged. "This will be a national tournament. Every town and city in Liatia will hold its own games. Every fight will be to the death. Only the most-skilled will survive in each city – and we will then pit them against the most-skilled from another city. Eventually, we will have our eight strongest cities still standing – one of which will undoubtedly be Thera. All those winners – the best of the best from around Liatia – will then descend on Thera and the Mesocluso towards the middle of next month. They will be joined by hundreds of established gladiators from around the empire. The main competition will then commence, lasting for four days, and the Grand Finale will be on 37th of Quarternar – Day 173 of our year – a day which we believe will be around ten days before Nessemi strikes.

"If our plan works, then up until Day 173, the people of Thera will have been so distracted with our Games and our other measures – I will come to those, shortly – that they will only be seeing the new star in our sky as a sign of future blessing."

Calidius paused, assessing the mood. As expected, every single senator was hanging on his every word and so he continued. "By Day 173, we will also know *where* the asteroid will strike our planet. We will therefore know which measures we will be taking to attempt to survive this kiss of Nessemi. Clearly, our hope is for an ocean strike. If that is the case, we will simply tell the people of Thera the truth, and let common-sense prevail if a *Northern* Ocean strike is expected; anyone who chooses to remain within thirty leagues of the coast deserves no place in my empire. However, if the news is dire, I have no shame in announcing how we will react."

This time, Calidius rotated slowly through three hundred and sixty degrees, ensuring he had everyone's undivided attention. "The chosen ten thousand will very unobtrusively migrate southwards to their designated shelters, commencing the evening of Day 173. You tell no one. If you do, we will have an uprising on our hands. An uprising like no other before – because these rebels would have *nothing* to lose."

Calidius paused before continuing. "So, these Games constitute one of our major distractions from this crisis. The other, we have already christened…as *Expurgatio*."

Calidius slowly rotated again, assessing the mood all the time. The Senate was still compliant – despite the obvious connotations of what he had just said. "Yes," he began. "I am talking about being lean and mean again. To see our way through this crisis – however it pans out – we need to be rid of our dead wood. We need contributors, not takers; everyone pulling in the same direction. For in unity, there is strength. As for *Expurgatio*, I have been locked away either side of my coronation, with three of my most trusted senators. I would now like to invite up onto the dais, Senators Valerius, Lucinius and Eugenius."

The three senators stood – the saintly, white-haired and white-bearded Valerius, the swarthy-looking Lucinius with the tight oily dark curls, and the stocky, bushy-bearded Eugenius, the youngest of the three who was somewhere in his late-thirties. They made their way purposefully but grim-faced onto the dais and, at first, arrayed themselves behind Calidius.

"In summary," Calidius was saying, "*Expurgatio* will be carried out in six distinct phases, which – in most cases – will be preceded by an edict. Valerius, will now talk you through Edict Number 1, Lucinius through Edict Number 2, and so on. Valerius."

"Thank you, Your Imperial Majesty," said the softly spoken Valerius, as Calidius left the dais to his three senators and sat down on the front row of benches facing them. The three senators then arranged themselves triangularly, shoulder to shoulder, so they could each address a third of the *Curia*. Valerius – looking straight ahead at Calidius – then cleared his throat and did his best to project his voice. "Edict Number 1 is to be a purge of all leper colonies."

An immediate buzz of concern went around the two thirds of the *Curia* who had clearly heard the proclamation, shortly followed by a buzz from those behind Valerius – and straight across from Calidius – who hadn't quite caught the elderly senator's words but were now being informed by their neighbours. Once everyone had digested Valerius' words, most were no doubt reflecting that the proclamation was perhaps a touch more chilling, having come from the mouth of one of their gentlest senators. Exactly as Calidius had planned.

Valerius waited for the buzz to die down before continuing. "His Imperial

Majesty's justification is that this hideous disease was brought to us from without – largely from the countries to our east. We shall therefore be dismantling all leper colonies in Liatia and driving the lepers over our eastern borders. This edict will be issued on Day 121. In unity, there is strength."

"Edict Number 2," began Lucinius. He was standing to Valerius' left and side-on to Calidius, but was clearly audible with a voice which projected further than his predecessor. "Edict Number 2, to be carried out on Day 126, will be a closure of all lunatic asylums. Inmates that still retain some of their sanity will be returned to their families. In unity, there is strength."

Another buzz of varying emotions went around the *Curia*. Calidius observed what he had hoped for – that this second proclamation was perhaps more chilling to his senators regarding what it *didn't* say rather than what it did – although he was confident that most of them would be in little doubt as to what would become of those inmates who were *not* deemed to have a vestige of sanity.

"Edict Number 3," piped up Eugenius, side on to Calidius on Valerius' right, "will be a purge of all prisoners of war. All will be executed. We cannot afford to have known enemies of the Empire within our boundaries, nor can we send our known enemies back out beyond our boundaries. In unity, there is strength."

The buzz this time indicated a general approval of this edict. This was a most interesting exercise to observe, decided Calidius.

"Edict Number 4," said Valerius, addressing Calidius and those directly behind him again, "will be announced the day *after* it is executed. This is because the target demographic is large, and comprises known thieves operating in Liatia. Give them a heads-up, and they will melt away. So, our legions will strike against them in the early hours of Day 136. In unity, there is strength."

"Edict Number 5," began Lucinius, "will be a termination of prostitution in Thera."

Calidius kept his eyes drilled on two senators opposite who he knew frequented such establishments. Both went taut with concern.

"We will not have sexually transmitted diseases weakening our people when we need to be strong. In unity, there is strength."

"And finally, Edict Number 6," began Eugenius, "will be another retrospective edict, which will state that overnight, we will have wiped out those trafficking narcotics in Thera. By Day 146, there will be no more drug dealers in our city. Drugs are a scourge on our society. The people who peddle them and consume them, have *nothing* to offer to our empire and we will be better off without either of them. Again, in unity, there is strength."

As the proclamations ended, and the hubbub around the *Curia* began to ramp up, Calidius noticed a middle-aged senator making for the exit. Calidius nodded once at the legionaries guarding the door. Both drew their swords and stood in front of the door.

Realisation of what was happening quickly spread around the room and the hubbub began to die down.

"Where are you going, Publius?" demanded Calidius. His voice rang clear across the *Curia*.

The balding Publius turned to face his emperor. His face was ashen.

"Well?" demanded Calidius. The room was now deathly quiet.

"My father," was all Publius could say.

"Is a leper," responded Calidius. "I know. Where were you going?"

"Your Imperial Majesty," he pleaded. "To drive him east when he is so frail – it is inhuman. He was a legionary of Thera in his youth."

"And now he is a leper. Unclean. Virulent. His life is already over. Would you have him contaminating the healthy and the young when the future of our entire planet is in the balance?"

"He contaminates no one in his colony, Your Imperial Majesty."

"And once his colony has been dismantled?"

"But if we didn't dismantle -."

Publius' chest exploded outwards in a fountain of steel, blood and internal organs. The legionary behind him then snapped his sword-arm backwards to withdraw his weapon, and Publius dropped dead to the floor. There would be further mosaic scrubbing needed later.

Calidius nodded to the three senators on the dais and they returned to their seats, while Calidius himself re-took the stage. He then focused on his wary audience again as the latest shock-induced hubbub died down. Without any hint of mirth, he said: "We appear to have another shelter vacancy. Now," he said, clapping his hands together, once. "Do we have any other objections?"

None were heard.

Calidius began another rotation, wanting to see every face as he summarised. "When we rid ourselves of these six unwanted demographics, we will be stronger than we are today. No one in those six groups can contribute to the strength of Thera, or to any required rebuild. They are all takers, not contributors. I hope that you now understand, that in unity, there is strength. Do I have any questions?"

An hour and forty minutes later, all questions had been answered, and all senators appeared to be satisfied. They really needed one more loyalty reminder though.

"I suspect it is unnecessary for me to reiterate this message. But be assured, that if knowledge of any of these topics gets out of this room, there will be executions. And they will be *hideous* executions. Because the kind of action that I *most despise*," he shouted, pausing for effect and fully aware that he had just ejected a large amount of saliva with his forceful words, "is betrayal."

Calidius looked around the room again. You could hear a pin drop. He was as confident as he could be that he had them all.

"So," he began. "That wraps up proceedings -." He broke off noticing another of the older senators holding up his hand. "Yes, Ostorius?"

"I wondered, Your Imperial Majesty," began doddery old Ostorius, "what is being done about finding the killer of your father, our recently dearly-departed 315th Emperor of Thera."

Calidius just looked at Ostorius, his expression unreadable. *Dearly departed. I shall give you 'dearly departed', Ostorius.* Without a word, Calidius nodded to two of the legionaries standing behind the benches in Ostorius' sector of the *Curia*. Calidius had just had his 'loyalty reminder' presented to him on a plate.

Ostorius began to panic. "I just wondered when the inquest will be opening, that's all."

As the two soldiers seized Ostorius by both arms, Calidius walked smoothly across and drew his dagger. He placed the tip of the dagger underneath Ostorius' chin with his right hand. "There will be no inquest. Old man," he added. And with that, he hammered the heel of his left hand underneath the hilt of his dagger, thrusting it up, through the back of Ostorius' mouth and into the mush of his brain. Calidius then whipped back his dagger with a hideous sucking sound. Ostorius flopped soundlessly to the floor.

Calidius stepped back and calmly addressed the senate, his bloodied and dripping dagger pointed before him, his white robes spattered with Ostorius' blood. "This session is at an end. Please remember your duty and responsibility to the empire. We play by *my* rules, otherwise we descend into chaos and anarchy. Do *not* let me hear any one of you ever mention my father again. We will *not* be investigating the murder of one weak and deviant individual. Not when the very future of our empire," he paused, eyeballing many of his senators, "and indeed the future of our entire planet…hangs in the balance."

Calidius lowered his dagger arm, but continued to sweep his iron gaze across dozens of mute senators. "Just remember, that it is not beyond the bounds of possibility, that in around eighty days' time, we will *all* have ceased to exist. But only if Nessemi lands in western Epanaga. For all other eventualities, we need to action our plan in secret, in unity, and with strength. Now go, all of you. And maintain your silence. You know what will happen if you do not."

Dumbfounded, senators slowly began to rise. A number appeared to be in a kind of horrified stupor, but somehow conveyed themselves towards the exit. All of them had much to think about. The excitement of the pending Games. The brutality of pending *Expurgatio*. But most of all, perhaps pondering on their own and their loved ones' chances of survival. Both short term and medium.

Long term, well…that would have to keep, for now.

CHAPTER 69 — MARTHA

12th Tertiar, 1789   Day 103, 25:55

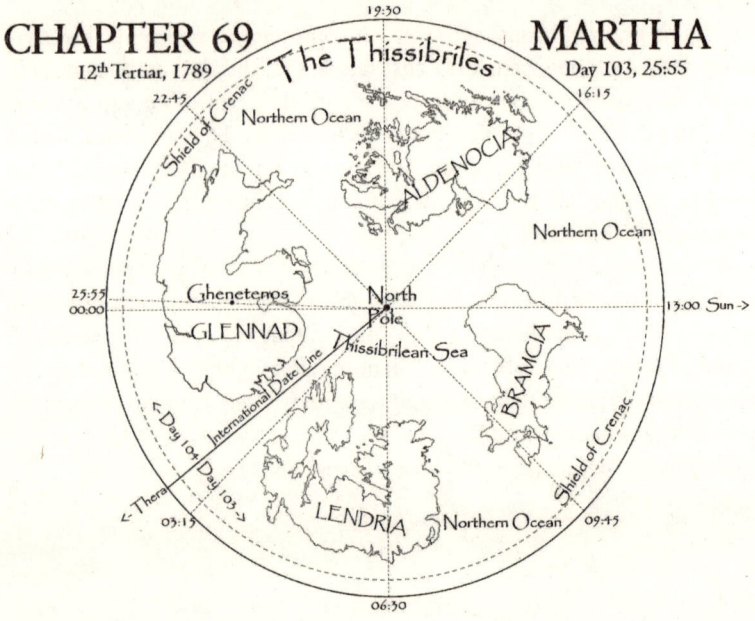

Martha Dolmen was standing stock still in the centre of the circle of stones at Ghenetenos, just as she had twelve days earlier on the eve of the Vernal Equinox at the same time of day. Once again, she was standing in front of the three central monoliths; two upright, the third balanced across the top of the other two. Once again, the stones of the inner circle had torches guttering in their iron sconces, while half way between the outer stones and those inner monoliths was a circle of robed and cowled druids, each of them swaying gently from side to side, hands joined, eyes closed, whilst singing the mournful but beautiful Song of the Stones.

Ernai gaia Theraea, sol estram gaia Theraea, sol extupinian gaia zu destinium Theraea.

Mother be with us, Mother please guide us, Mother please show us our future.

The Vernal Ceremony had been particularly revelatory, this year. The 1st Tertiar was a powerful occasion on any given year, with the length of day and night being exactly the same; a time when everything is in perfect balance. However, the year of 1789 was a significant one for druids, as it had been marked as such by the *Saranti Codex* – a mysterious and ancient druidic text allegedly written on the instruction of Saranti, the ancient druidic god of thunder – but likely written by an ancient High Priest or

High Priestess who was exceptionally well in tune with Mother Thera – perhaps more than any predecessor or successor. Regardless of the author, though, the Codex had marked 1789 as the year of a critical event for Planet Thera, and the Codex was invariably accurate. Hence, for many centuries now, 1789 had been known to Glennadian druids as *Annum Cardo Thera* – the year when everything changes. The Vernal Ceremony of 1789 had not disappointed in providing some of the answers that high priests and priestesses had been striving to uncover for centuries.

Ernai gaia Theraea, sol estram gaia Theraea, sol extupinian gaia zu destinium Theraea. The song continued, hushed and reverent.

Beside her, Emrys Dolman, Martha's son, stood stock still as well, his dreadlocked beard ruffling slightly in the gentle midnight breeze, causing some of the interwoven beads to gently clack against each other. It was a serene, hypnotic sound, blending entrancingly with the druids' song.

In five minutes, they would both step forward to engage with the uprights, she to the left, he to the right. Twelve days should have been enough time for the portal to have re-charged. It was still a calculated gamble, though. Yes, they could have waited longer and maybe learned more – but having had part of the 1789 mystery revealed at the Vernal Ceremony, Martha and her people were desperate to learn the full truth, as soon as possible, to enable optimum preparation. Especially if they really were to be the honoured druids invoking the legendary Ceremony of a Thousand Years on this coming Midsummers Eve. If they were, Martha could only hope that they would be able to complete the sacred ceremony without any external interference.

Ernai gaia Theraea, sol estram gaia Theraea, sol extupinian gaia zu destinium Theraea.

Martha felt her body begin to tingle with the building energy. Keeping calm, she focused her eyes on the outer circle of sinister dark monoliths that reared beyond the inner circle and her fellow druids in between, and remembered her first time here – as a member of the congregation, swaying and singing as her aunt and a cousin had stood where she and Emrys now stood. The year had been 1737 and she had been a child of eight years old, holding her mother's hand to the left and her brother's hand to the right, both of them constantly squeezing her own tiny hands for reassurance. It was still a startlingly vivid memory; that first disconcerting tingle, fifty-two years ago, but just a short breath away in this timeless place.

"*Did you see? Feel?*" her aunt had asked, a short while after the ceremony had finished.

Martha had not replied but had just nodded her head. Her aunt had appeared to look deep into her mind; Martha had felt her presence. "*So you did,*" she had said, eventually; so quietly that only Martha had heard. Martha had known from that day forward that she would take over from her aunt, one day, just as Elyse would eventually take over from Martha.

Brief thoughts of concern for her own daughter were pushed aside as Martha recalled the images conveyed to both herself and Emrys on 1st Tertiar: an object, hurtling towards Thera, on a collision course, having been deflected from its original orbit between Rufus Macula and Tarmia several months ago. An object that would impact with her planet in the early hours of 1st Quinar: Midsummers Day – just as the *Saranti Codex* had forecast, albeit with frustratingly little detail.

And in this year of seventeen hundred and eighty nine, death will come from the sky. Death for hundreds of thousands, but not for all.

There had been many interpretations over the centuries, but most of them had predicted exactly what she and Emrys had been shown during the Vernal Ceremony; an impact of a celestial body upon Thera; more specifically, an impact somewhere in the northern hemisphere. And somewhat disconcertingly, Martha had now made a connection with the approaching object, too. Indeed, Martha knew that if she closed her eyes, right now, and concentrated, she would be able to *feel* its presence and its remorseless advance as it hurtled towards Thera.

Alas, *sensing* its approach was of little help. True, they now knew *when* the impact would occur – as the image of a distant impact had been revealed against the unmistakeable backdrop of their brethren holding a Summer Solstice Ceremony within the stone circle at Ghenetenos; undoubtedly destined to be the Ceremony of a Thousand Years, this year. So, impact *would* occur on the 1st of Quinar, this year – in just eighty days' time. What they hadn't seen, though, was *where* impact would occur and what the ramifications would be – for both the locality of the point of impact and any potential knock-on effects for Ghenetenos.

Most frustratingly, though, the Vernal Ceremony images had not provided any obvious clues about the other great revelation of the *Saranti Codex*: "*…and the Ultimate Doom which shall follow*".

Martha almost snorted out loud. She had never been a great fan of the *Saranti Codex*, firstly because of its ambiguity, but more so because of its over-dramatic wordage and unnecessary usage of capital letters.

And when under the Heel, when Islanders believe that things cannot get any Worse, then shall the Great Revelation be Unveiled. And this Great

Revelation will signal the Nature of our Ultimate Doom, for alas, this Ultimate Doom will Likely bring about the End of our World. Only those of Faith can prevent the Ultimate Doom, but I cannot Reveal how; this, they must work out for Themselves.

Martha's dislike of the *Saranti Codex* didn't mean that she disbelieved it, of course. On the contrary, she very much feared it – partly because many other predicted events could be construed as having come true; but mainly because of her connection with Mother Thera, Theraea, and of the goddess' own fear for the future which Martha could palpably sense. *Theraea, herself, did not know the outcome.* But through their oneness, Martha could sense Theraea's hope; hope that the second disaster, the Ultimate Doom, could be avoided by executing the Ceremony of a Thousand Years. Such was the responsibility upon her own and Emrys' shoulders come the 1st Tertiar.

The pending danger and the Midsummer's Day ceremony were also why, at the right time, Martha would send Edwyn away to safety at Kifsel Place – under the pretext of joining his aunt – while other senior druids would also make similar safety arrangements for their own children and grandchildren. For alas, that particular ceremony would be wholly unsuitable for young and tender eyes -.

With a start, Martha realised that the singing had stopped and the tingling had reached its zenith. It was midnight. Only the sound of Emrys' beads in his beard rustling in the wind remained. Briefly looking to Emrys, she nodded once – and they both stepped forwards. Martha placed her hands flat onto the left-hand upright, and then turned her head to the right as she placed her left cheek onto the stone. Emrys became her mirror image, both hands on the right-hand upright, head turned to the left, looking at Martha with his right cheek on the stone. They then both closed their eyes together and connected…

…with Theraea…

…and Martha was immediately elsewhere, looking down on the west coast of Glennad from above.

What she saw turned her blood cold.

Cold Sanctuary
Book Two of The Nessemiah

"I'm afraid there are good and bad everywhere, Emilya. It's a fact of life that wherever you look, there are strains of malice."

Emilya and Jake have separated to increase their chances of avoiding capture and execution for a crime they have not committed. While Jake and Harry Black lead Prince Magnus a merry dance across Glennad, Emilya and Elyse have perhaps landed in greater peril at Kifsel Place Monastery, where amongst the peace-loving monks, there are a handful with sinister motives.

Meanwhile, unaware that their combined governments are preparing for deadly Nessemi, personal circumstances begin to deteriorate for each of our small cast of northern islanders. And whereas *their* rulers are taking a pragmatic approach to Nessemi, the Theran Empire is rolling out diversions on a massive and brutal scale. As well as the demographic cleansing that is *Expurgatio*, Emperor Calidius is also driving the deaths of thousands in Liatia's fighting pits, where former Demonacian general, Draxaelen, battles to stay alive.

But little does Drax know that time is running out for his revenge; in fact, time is running out for everyone.